M

"Kara...."

She leaned forward, waiting for his next words, hoping he would tell her that he had missed her, that he had spent his every waking moment thinking only of her.

He was watching her closely, his gaze fixed on her face. She could feel the heat of it, the power of it. At that moment, she would have told him anything he wanted to hear, done anything he asked. Though they weren't touching, it was almost as if he were stroking her hair, caressing her cheek.

And then he took a step back, releasing her from his gaze.

"Alexander." Her voice was shaky, uncertain.

"What do you want from me, Kara?"

"Want?"

"I've been much in your mind these past weeks."

Kara stared at him. How had he known that?

"I hear your thoughts. I feel your loneliness, your restlessness." He clenched his hands to keep from reaching for her. "What do you want of me?"

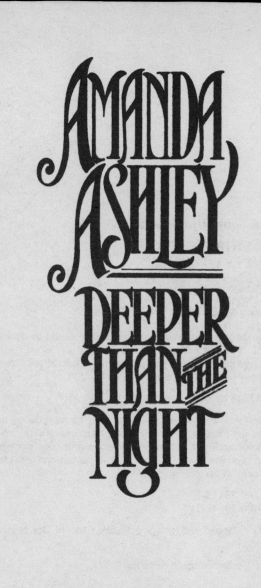

AMANDA ASHLEY

DEEPER THAN THE NIGHT

LOVE SPELL ◆ **NEW YORK CITY**

LOVE SPELL®

July 2007

Published by

Dorchester Publishing Co., Inc.
200 Madison Avenue
New York, NY 10016

ISBN-10: 0-505-52113-X
ISBN-13: 978-0-505-52113-2

The name "Love Spell" and its logo are trademarks of Dorchester Publishing Co., Inc.

Printed in the United States of America.

Visit us on the web at www.dorchesterpub.com.

Deep Persuasion

From whence comes forth the melody
Whispering love to piercing eyes
Dreams sprinkled with stardust
Are hidden in her sighs.

He yearns to hear the winsome song
Amidst the bittersweet refrain
But furrowed scorn upon his brow
Recalls ashes in the rain.

Come closer, bids persuasion
Turn not from tender woes
These anguished depths of yearning
Will move the tempered soul.

Magnificent the union
Of hearts in deep embrace
The bonding of two souls
Which time cannot ease.

—Linda Ware

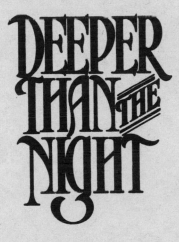

Chapter One

"I'm looking for the vampire."

Alexander Claybourne stared down at the young girl standing on his front porch. She was a cute little thing, maybe nine years old, with curly blonde hair, brown eyes, and a sprinkling of freckles across the bridge of her nose.

"Excuse me," he said, "but did I hear you right?"

"I need to see the vampire," the girl said impatiently. "The one who lives here."

Alexander fought the urge to laugh. "Who told you a vampire lives here?"

The girl looked up at him as if he were slow-witted. "*Everyone* knows a vampire lives here."

"I see. And why do you want him?"

"My sister, Kara, is in the hospital. She was in a car accident." The girl sniffed noisily. "Nana says she's going to die."

Alexander frowned as he tried to follow the child's line of reasoning.

The girl stamped her foot. "Vampires live forever," she said, speaking each word slowly and distinctly, as if he were very young, or very stupid. "If the vampire would come to the hospital and bite my sister, she would live forever, too."

"Ah," Alexander exclaimed, comprehending at last.

"So, is he here?"

"You're quite a brave girl, to come here alone, in the dark of night. Aren't you afraid?"

"N . . . no."

"What's your name, child?"

"Gail Crawford."

"How old are you, Gail?"

"Nine and a half."

"And does your Nana know where you are?"

Gail shook her head. "No. She's at the hospital. They won't let me visit Kara, so Nana made me stay with Mrs. Zimmermann. I snuck out the back door when she wasn't looking."

Gail stared up at the man. Was *he* the vampire? He was very tall, with long black hair. He stood in the deep shadows of the house so that she couldn't see his face clearly, but she thought he had dark eyes. He didn't look like any of the vampires she had seen in the movies. They always wore black suits and frilly white shirts and long capes; this man wore a black sweater and a pair of faded Levi's. Still, everyone in Moulton Bay knew that a vampire lived in the old Kendall house. . . .

Shivering, Gail wrapped her arms around her waist. She had come up here lots of times with her friends, trying to peek in the windows to catch sight of the vampire's coffin. She'd never really been scared in the daylight; after all, everyone knew vampires were harmless during the day. But now it was night.

Leaning to the side a little, she slid a glance past the man. The interior of the house looked dark and gloomy, just the kind of place where a vampire would live.

Feeling suddenly very much alone and more than a little afraid, she took a step backward. The porch creaked under her weight. It was a creepy sound.

Gail summoned her rapidly waning courage. "Will you come and save my sister?"

"I'm sorry, Gail," Alexander said with genuine regret, "but I'm afraid I can't help you."

The girl lifted her shoulders and let them fall in an exaggerated gesture of disappointment.

"I didn't *really* think you were a vampire," she confessed, "but it was worth a try."

Alexander watched the girl as she ran down the stairs, headed for the narrow dirt path that meandered through the woods. The path was a shortcut that led to the main road.

Courageous little thing, he mused, to come out here all alone.

Looking for a vampire.

He watched her until she was out of sight, until even his keen hearing could no longer discern the sound of her flight, and then he closed the door and leaned back against it.

So, everyone knew a vampire lived here.

Perhaps it was time to move on. And yet . . . Pushing away from the door, he walked through the dark house. It was a big place, old and creaky, with vaulted ceilings and wooden floors and leaded windowpanes. The house sat alone on a small rise surrounded by trees and brambles. His nearest neighbor was almost a mile away. It was, he thought, exactly the sort of place a vampire might choose to live. It was exactly the reason he had chosen it. He had been comfortable here, content here, for the past five years.

But perhaps it was time to move on. One thing he didn't want to do was draw attention to himself. Until now, he'd had no idea people speculated on who, or what, lived in this house.

Going into the parlor, he rested one hand on the high mantel and gazed into the hearth. There was something primal about standing in front of a roaring fire. It answered an elemental need deep inside him, though he wasn't sure why. Perhaps it had something to do with the smoky scent of the wood and the hiss of the flames, or maybe it was the surging power held at bay by nothing more than a few bricks.

He stared into the hearth, mesmerized, as always, by the life that pulsed within the flames. All the colors of the rainbow danced within the flickering tongues of fire: red and yellow, blue and green and violet, a deep pure white.

Moving away from the fireplace, he wandered through the house, listening to the rising wind as it howled beneath the eaves. The branches of an old oak tree tapped against one of the upstairs windows, sounding for all the world like skeletal fingers scratching at the glass, as if some long-banished spirit were seeking entrance to the house.

He grinned, surprised by his fanciful thoughts, and by the recurring urge to go to the hospital and have a look at Gail Crawford's older sister.

Hospitals. He had never been inside one. In all the years of his existence, he had never been sick.

Forcing all thoughts of Gail and her sister from his mind, he went into the library, determined to finish the research needed for his latest novel before the night was through.

It was after four when he admitted he was fighting a losing battle. He couldn't concentrate, couldn't think of anything but the brave little girl who had come to him looking for a miracle.

Scowling, he stalked out into the night, drawn by a force he could no longer resist, his footsteps carrying him swiftly down the narrow dirt path that cut through the woods to the thriving seaside town of Moulton Bay.

The hospital was located on a side street near the far end of the town. It was a tall white building. He thought it looked more like an ancient mausoleum than a modern place of healing.

A myriad of scents assaulted his keen sense of smell the moment he opened the front door: blood, death, urine, the cloying scent of flowers, starch and bleach, the pungent smell of antiseptics and drugs.

At this time of the morning, the corridors were virtually deserted. He found the Intensive Care Unit at the end of a long hallway.

A nurse sat at a large desk, thumbing through a stack of papers. Alex watched her for a moment; then, focusing his mind on one of the emergency buzzers located at the opposite end of the corridor, he willed it to ring.

As soon as the nurse left the station, he walked

past the desk and stepped into the Intensive Care Ward.

There was only one patient: Kara Elizabeth Crawford, age twenty-two, blood type A negative. She was swathed in bandages, connected to numerous tubes and monitors.

He quickly perused her chart. She had sustained no broken bones, though she had numerous cuts and contusions; a gash in her right leg had required stitching. She had three bruised ribs, a laceration in her scalp, internal bleeding. Amazingly, her face had escaped injury. She had fine, even features. A wealth of russet-colored hair emphasized her skin's pallor. Indeed, her face was almost as white as the pillowcase beneath her head. She had been in a coma for the last four days. Her prognosis was grim.

"Where are you, Kara Crawford?" he murmured. "Is your spirit still trapped within that feeble tabernacle of flesh, or has your soul found redemption in worlds beyond while you wait for your body to perish?"

He stared at the blood dripping from a plastic bag down a tube and into her arm. The sharp metallic scent of it excited a hunger he had long ago suppressed. Blood. The elixir of life.

He frowned as he glanced down at his arm, at the dark blue vein. He had survived for two hundred years because of the blood in his veins.

"If I gave you my blood, would it bring you back from the edge of eternity," he mused aloud, "or would it release you from your tenuous hold on life and send you to meet whatever waits on the other side?"

He let the tip of one finger slide down the soft,

smooth skin of her cheek and then, driven by an impulse he could neither understand nor deny, he picked up a syringe, removed the protective wrapping, and inserted the needle into the large vein of his left arm, watching with vague interest as the hollow tube filled with dark red blood.

In two hundred years, he had gleaned a great deal of medical knowledge.

Withdrawing the needle, he inserted it into the section of latex tubing that was used to add antibiotics and pushed the plunger, mixing his own blood with the liquid dripping into her vein. He repeated the procedure several times, and all the while he thought of the little girl with curly blond hair who had come to him looking for a miracle.

Alexander smiled grimly as he left the girl's room and headed for the emergency exit located at the end of the hall. He glanced down at his arm. A spot of dried blood marred his skin.

Dark blood.

Inhuman blood.

Mingling with the girl's.

He wondered what madness had possessed him to mingle his blood with the girl's. Would it kill or cure, he mused. Had he been savior or executioner? Unfortunately, or fortunately perhaps, he would never know.

He did not linger over the other very likely consequences that would result from his rash action if she survived.

It was near dawn when he stepped out of the hospital. Drawing in a lungful of cool air, he gazed up at the brightening sky for a long moment. He yearned to stay and watch the sun rise, to feel the blessed heat of a new day, to listen to the world around him come to life, but he dared not linger. He had given Kara Crawford almost a pint of his blood, and it had seriously weakened him. In his present condition, the sunlight could be fatal.

With a strangled cry, he hurried toward home.

Chapter Two

Kara climbed up out of the darkness that engulfed her. Gradually, she became aware of voices: Nana's voice lifted in urgent prayer; Gail's voice, filled with heartache as she begged Kara to come back, please come back.

A man's voice, sounding startled as he exclaimed, "She's coming around!"

A woman's voice, filled with disbelief. "It's a miracle!"

"Miss Crawford? Kara? Can you hear me?" This from the man as he bent over her.

She tried to speak, but no words passed her lips. She tried to nod, but didn't seem able to move. So she blinked up at the white-coated man bending over her.

"Kara?" Gail slid under the doctor's arm and grabbed her sister's hand. "Kara, you're awake!"

19

"G . . . Gail?"

Her sister nodded vigorously. "I knew you wouldn't leave me. I knew it!"

"Stand aside, Gail," the doctor said. Withdrawing a flashlight from his pocket, he checked Kara's eyes, noting their response to the light. "Do you know your name?" he asked.

"Kara Elizabeth Crawford."

"Do you know what year it is?"

"Nineteen ninety-six."

"Do you know where you are?"

"Hospital?"

The doctor nodded. Lifting her right leg, he ran his thumb along the sole of her foot, grunting softly as he watched her toes curl.

"We'll have to do more tests, of course," he said, replacing the covers over Kara's leg, "but I believe she's going to be all right."

"Thank God," Nana murmured. "Thank God."

When Kara woke again, it was dark and she was alone. Four days, Nana had said. She had been in a coma for four days. Where had she been during that time? She had often wondered where a person's spirit went when the body was in a coma. Did it just lie at rest inside the body? Did it roam over the earth like a lost soul? Try as she might, Kara could remember nothing at all, except . . .

She turned toward the window and stared out into the darkness of the night. She seemed to remember a man, a tall, dark man who had seemed more shadow than substance as he hovered near her bedside. But surely he had been just a fever dream, a figment of her imagination. No flesh-and-blood man could possibly have eyes so dark, so ageless. So haunted. No earthly man could move with such soundless grace.

And his voice, deep and resonant and filled with suffering. His voice, speaking her name, communicating with her soul.

If he had been nothing but a dream, it was a dream she would welcome each night of her life.

"Come back to me," she whispered. "Come back to me, my angel of darkness."

Alexander's head snapped up as a faint voice whispered inside his mind. *Her* voice. He knew it was hers though he had never heard it.

"Kara." Her name slid past his lips, unbidden. "What have I done?"

As though he had no will of his own, he found himself rising from his chair, walking out into the night, following the narrow, twisting path that led to town.

Night creatures fell silent at his passing. He was a shadow among shadows. A darkness deeper than the night.

He stood on the sidewalk across the street from the hospital, staring up at the window he knew was hers. She had called him here, the faint lure of her voice more powerful than his will to resist.

He got past the nurse on duty using the same ploy he had used the night before.

Inside Kara's room, he stood beside the narrow bed, watching the steady rise and fall of her chest as she slept. There was a hint of color in her cheeks now. Her lips looked soft and pliable, their color like pale pink roses. Her lashes were thick and dark.

So beautiful, he mused. So fragile. Lightly, he traced the curve of her cheek with his forefinger.

She smiled at his touch, turning her head toward his hand, as though inviting his caress.

With a curse, he drew his hand away.

She came awake between one breath and the next, and he found himself gazing into a pair of dreamy blue eyes. They stared at each other for a long moment.

"How are you feeling, Miss Crawford?" Alexander asked.

"Better." She squinted up at him, trying to see him more clearly in the room's dim light. "Are you one of my doctors?"

He hesitated only a moment before answering, "Yes."

"You saved my life."

"So it would seem."

Kara frowned, wishing she could see his face better. He seemed so familiar.

"You must rest now, Miss Crawford," Alexander said. He took a step backward, hiding in the dark. His blood had saved her. He knew it as surely as he knew the sun would rise in the east.

At his words, she was overcome with a sudden weariness. "Wait. I want to know your name. . . ."

Her eyelids fluttered down as sleep claimed her.

Kara turned her head away while Dr. Petersen examined the stitches in her leg. "Where's the other doctor?"

"The other doctor?"

"The one who came to see me last night."

"What was his name?"

"I don't know. He was tall and broad-shouldered, with long black hair. He . . . he had a deep voice."

"There's no one on the staff who answers that

description." Dr. Petersen smiled indulgently. "No doubt you were dreaming."

"But it wasn't a dream!" Kara glanced at Nana and Gail. "I saw him. I spoke to him."

"There, there," Dr. Petersen said, patting her hand. "No need to be upset."

"I'm not upset. I just . . ." Kara sank back against the pillows. Maybe she *had* dreamed the whole thing.

"I'll stop in to see you tomorrow," the doctor remarked. He paused at the doorway and glanced over his shoulder. "Don't stay too long, Mrs. Corley. She needs her rest."

"I understand," Nana replied.

"I didn't imagine him," Kara insisted after the doctor left the room.

"Now, Kara, if the doctor said there's no one on the staff by that description, I'm sure he's right." Nana glanced around, her keen blue eyes taking in every detail. "It's a nice room," she decided.

"It should be, for what it's costing," Kara grumbled. "Did they say when I can go home?"

"Not for several days."

"But Dr. Petersen said I was making remarkable progress." Indeed, every doctor in the hospital had found an excuse to come by and see the miracle patient whose internal injuries had healed overnight.

"That's true," Nana agreed, "but you've had a bad bump on the head. Dr. Petersen wants to keep an eye on you for another day or two." Nana took Kara's hand in hers and held it tight. "We almost lost you, child."

"I know." It was frightening, to think how close she'd been to death. It was something she didn't like thinking about, and quickly changed the subject. "Gail, how are you doing in school? Did you pass your history test?"

"B-plus," Gail replied smugly. "Cherise got a C-minus, and Stephanie got a D."

"Don't gloat," Kara chided.

"We should go," Nana said, rising. "We don't want to tire you."

"But I feel fine."

"The doctor said you should rest. So rest." Nana kissed Kara's cheek. "It's a miracle," she murmured, blinking back a tear. "A miracle." She patted Kara's shoulder. "Can I bring you anything tomorrow? A book, maybe?"

Kara nodded. "Something to read would be nice. And maybe a strawberry malt from the drugstore?"

Nana smiled. "Now I know you're feeling better. Come along, Gail."

"I'll be there in a minute," Gail said. "I need to tell Kara something."

"All right, but hurry along."

"What is it, Gail?" Kara asked with a smile. "A secret to tell me?"

Gail nodded as she closed the door. "That man who came to see you last night. He sounds like the man I went to see."

"What man?" Kara stared at her sister in alarm.

"You'll laugh."

"Tell me anyway."

"I went out to the old Kendall house."

"The Kendall house! Gail, have you lost your mind? Whatever made you go out there?"

Gail picked up a corner of the cotton bedspread and began to fold and unfold it. "Well, everybody says a vampire lives there, and . . ."

"A vampire! Oh, Gail."

"I thought if a vampire really lived there, and he bit you that you'd get better and live forever."

Kara shook her head. "Gail, there are no such things as vampires. Or werewolves. Or sea monsters, or space aliens, or mermaids."

Gail crossed her arms, her expression mutinous. "There are, too."

Kara sighed. They'd had this same argument numerous times in the last two-and-a-half years. "Are you saying the dark-haired man was a vampire and he came here to bite me?"

Gail nodded.

"Well, he must have changed his mind. I don't have a craving for blood, and I don't have any bites on my neck. And it's daytime and I'm wide awake." Kara took her sister's hand in hers. "It was your prayers that saved me, Gail. Yours and Nana's. You'd better go now. Nana's waiting. I'll see you tomorrow, okay?"

"Okay."

Kara couldn't help grinning as she watched her sister leave the room. Vampires, indeed! Gail's world was peopled with all kinds of monsters—Big Foot and Nessie, aliens from outer space, Dracula and the Wolf Man. Gail loved them all.

With a sigh, Kara closed her eyes. Maybe she had dreamed him, that tall, dark mysterious stranger who had come to her in the quiet of the night.

But she didn't think so.

Alexander paused, his fingers resting lightly on the computer keyboard. She was thinking of him. He could hear her thoughts in his mind, as loud and clear as if she were speaking to him directly.

She was confused, wondering if he had been real or merely a shadow figure conjured from the depths of her subconscious.

As the night grew long, he felt her loneliness, heard the silent call of her tears.

Helpless to resist, he left the house to become one with the night. His black clothing blended in with the darkness as he moved swiftly, silently, down the pathway toward the town.

The hospital loomed before him, the big white building shimmering against the backdrop of the night. For once, the night nurse was absent from her desk. On quiet feet, he made his way down the corridor toward Kara's room. A moment later, he was standing beside her bed.

She looked much improved this evening. Most of the tubes had been removed; her color was better, her breathing less labored. Her hair, freshly washed, was spread across the pillow like a splash of red silk.

She was a part of him now, he thought, and he was a part of her in a way that no other man could ever be. In mingling his blood with hers, he had re-created an ancient, sacred bond, a living link between them that could not be broken. Her thoughts were as clear to him as his own, her need for re-assurance and comfort impossible to ignore.

He stiffened with the realization that she was no longer asleep, but awake and staring up at him through those vivid blue eyes.

"Who are you?" Her voice quivered with fear—fear of the unknown, fear of his answer.

"A blood donor," he replied. "I heard you were recovering, and I wanted to see for myself."

"But . . . I thought . . . last night you said . . ."

"Last night?"

"Weren't you here last night?"

Alexander shook his head, unable to voice the lie aloud.

She frowned. "Maybe it was a dream, then."

"Most assuredly. Good night, Miss Crawford. Sleep well."

"Your name. Tell me your name."

"Alexander Claybourne." He bowed his head. "And now I must go."

"Stay, please. I . . . I'm afraid."

"Afraid?" he asked. "Of what?" It had been centuries since he had feared anything save discovery of what he was.

"Of being alone." She smiled self-consciously. "Of the dark." She'd been afraid of the dark for as long as she could remember, though there was no logical reason for her fear.

"The dark cannot hurt you, Miss Crawford," he said quietly.

"I know." Rationally, she did know, but she feared it just the same. "Please stay. I'm not so afraid with you here."

Ah, foolish girl, he thought, to be afraid of the darkness, but not the stranger hiding in its shadows. "Would you like me to turn on the light?"

"No. The dark doesn't seem so scary with you here." There was a certain excitement in sharing the darkness with this man who was a stranger, an intimacy that would not have been possible with the lights on.

"You're not tired?"

"No. It seems as though all I've done the past two days is sleep."

"Very well." He acquiesced with a slight smile.

"Will you tell me about yourself?"

"There's not much to tell."

"Please." He sat down in the straight-backed chair beside her bed, careful to keep to the shadows.

"What do you want to know?"

"Everything."

Kara laughed. "Well, I was born in Denver. My sister, Gail, was born when I was eleven. A few months later, my folks got a divorce."

She shrugged. Even after all these years, it still hurt. And even though she knew she wasn't to blame, she'd always wondered if the divorce had somehow been her fault.

"I guess they thought another baby would save the marriage," she went on, "but it didn't work. My mom moved us here to live with Nana—my grandmother. When I was fourteen, Mom ran off with a truck driver and we never heard from her again. We hadn't heard anything from my Dad since the divorce, so Nana decided Gail and I should stay with her. My brother, Steve, had just started college when our parents broke up. Nana's been both mother and father to us since my mother left. I went to college for a couple of years, and now I'm a consultant at Arias." She shrugged. "That's it."

"Who, or what, is Arias?"

"Arias Interiors. It's an interior design firm."

"I see."

"What do you do?"

"Do? Ah, my work, you mean? I write."

"You mean books?"

Alexander nodded.

"What do you write?"

"Horror stories, mostly."

"Like Stephen King?"

"More or less."

Kara frowned. "Have you had anything published?"

"A few things. I write under the name of A. Lucard."

A. Lucard! He was the hottest, most prolific writer on the market. His books consistently made the *New York Times* Best Seller List. Personally, Kara didn't care to read horror. Out of curiosity to see what all the fuss was about, she had read one of his books. It had kept her up all night.

"I read one of your books," she remarked candidly. "It gave me the worst nightmares I've ever had."

"My apologies."

"What are you working on now?"

"More of the same, I'm afraid."

"My little sister would love to read your books, but Nana won't let her."

"Indeed? I wouldn't think your sister would be interested in my work."

"Are you kidding? Gail loves monsters."

"And you? How do you feel about . . . monsters?"

"I don't believe in them."

"Then I hope you never meet one." He glanced out the window. He could sense the approaching dawn, feel the promised heat of the sun. "I must go."

"Thank you for staying, Mr. Claybourne."

"Alexander."

"Alexander." She could see him a little more clearly now, a tall, broad-shouldered figure silhouetted against the pale green wall. He wore a black sweater and black jeans. She wished she could see his face, the color of his eyes, the shape of his mouth. He had a most unusual accent, one she couldn't quite place. "Will you come tomorrow?"

"I don't know."

"I wish you would." She pursed her lips, reluctant to ask a favor, yet unable to resist. "Would you bring me one of your books?"

"Of course, but I thought you didn't care for stories about monsters."

"Well, I don't but now that I've met you . . . well, I'd like to give your books another try."

"Then I shall see that you get one. Good night, Kara."

"Good night."

She watched the door close behind him, wishing, inexplicably, that he had kissed her good-bye.

Alexander prowled the dark streets, aware, always aware, of the nearness of dawn, of the necessity of returning home before it was too late. Yet he needed to be outside, to feel the darkness that had become as much a part of him as his arms and legs.

He moved through the city, driven by a horrible sense of loneliness, of separateness. He yearned for a woman to share his life, but dared not take the risk of divulging the truth of what he was. He could only imagine the panic that would result.

He felt the heat of the sun at his back. Soon, the streets would be filled with people, people who lived and worked, loved and laughed, who took their world and everything in it for granted.

With an anguished cry, he sprinted for home, for the safety of shuttered rooms.

He bolted the front door behind him. The house

was cool and dim, a refuge from the burning rays of the sun.

Sheltered by the darkness, he climbed the stairs to his room and closed the door.

His first thought, upon waking, was for Kara. He pushed it aside, determined to forget the young woman with russet-colored hair and dreamy blue eyes. She was an infant compared to him, a child with her whole life ahead of her. A creature of light, she had no need for a man who wore darkness like a shroud, a man who was not like other men.

He wandered restlessly through the empty rooms of his house, unable to concentrate on any one task, his thoughts constantly turning toward Kara.

Leaving the house, he blended into the shadows of the night. Muttering an oath, he began to run, tirelessly, effortlessly. Mile after mile he ran, his feet hardly touching the ground. But no matter how far he ran, he could not outrun the desires of his own heart. He returned home long enough to change clothes and wrap up one of his books. Certain he was making a mistake, but unable to resist the lure of seeing her again, he left the house.

Outside, he closed his eyes and sent his thoughts toward Kara. Her sister and her grandmother had been there earlier, but now they were gone, and she was alone. And lonely.

And thinking of him.

I'm coming, Kara.

He willed his words into her mind. A short time later, he was at the hospital, in her room.

Her smile of welcome, warm and genuine, filled his heart—nay, his very soul—with sunlight.

"Good evening, Kara."

"Hi."

"You look much better."

"I feel much better."

Reaching inside his coat, he withdrew a parcel wrapped in white paper. "I hope it doesn't give you nightmares."

"You remembered! Thank you." She tore off the paper and stared at the cover. It depicted a raven-haired man bending over a woman's slender neck; the light from a full moon glinted off his fangs. *The Hunger*," she said, reading the title aloud. "Sounds a little gruesome."

"Not as bad as some I've written."

"Would you autograph it for me?"

"Of course."

She handed him the book and a pen, then watched as he opened it to the title page.

He wrote for a moment, then closed the book and handed it back to her. "Perhaps you shouldn't read it at night."

"That scary, huh?"

"I've been told my style is dark and heavy-handed."

Kara frowned, remembering the other book she'd read. "Well, your style is definitely dark," she allowed, "but I didn't think it was heavy-handed. Actually, I thought the book I read was really very good. I mean, it was supposed to be scary, and it certainly scared me."

"Which one did you read?"

"The Maiden and the Madman."

"One of my earlier works. I think you'll find *The Hunger* far less grotesque."

"This cover's quite a bit different from your others."

Alexander nodded. "Actually, this is more of a love story than anything else."

"Really?"

He shrugged. "An aberration, I assure you. The plot for my next book is filled with enough murder and mayhem to please the most bloodthirsty of my readers."

"You won't mind if I don't buy it?"

"Not at all."

Kara looked into his eyes, and forgot everything else. She had heard of love at first sight—who hadn't? But she had never believed in such a thing. She had met other handsome men and felt varying degrees of attraction, but nothing to equal what she felt now, an allure that was almost spiritual, as if her soul was reaching out to his. Did he feel it, too? Never before had she understood how a woman could throw away everything for the love of a man, but she had the sudden unshakable feeling that if Alexander asked her to follow him to the other side of the world, she would say yes without a second thought. It was most disconcerting, and a little frightening.

With an effort, she drew her gaze from his. "How long does it take you to write a book?"

"Not long. Three months, sometimes four."

"How long have you been writing?"

"About twelve years." He smiled at her as if he knew she was asking these questions because she feared another lingering silence between them. "Enough about me. Will you be going home soon?"

"Not for another few days. And then I won't be able to go back to work right away."

"How do you feel?"

"Fine."

"I'm glad. I should go now. You need your rest."

"That's what everyone says."

"Then it must be true."

He stood up, knowing he should go, yet reluctant to leave her. She was like a beacon of light, bright and shining, untouched by darkness or evil. He knew the darkness that surrounded him would seem blacker still when he left her. But leave her he must.

"Good night, Kara."

"Good night, Alexander. Thank you for the book."

He smiled at her, then left the room. He would not, could not, see her again.

Kara stared after him a moment, then opened the book to the page he had autographed.

"To Kara—May your faith keep you safe from the monsters of the world." And then his signature, written in a bold scrawl: Alexander J. Claybourne. And beneath that: A. Lucard.

She didn't know what made her read his pseudonym backward, but when she did, a shiver ran down her spine.

D . . . R . . . A . . . C . . . U . . . L . . . A.

"Dracula."

Kara spoke the word aloud, then laughed. A fitting name indeed, for a man who wrote the kind of books penned by Alexander Claybourne.

Chapter Three

He wasn't going to see her again. It was a promise he made to himself upon waking the following evening.

He repeated the words in his mind as he sat at the computer.

He typed them on the screen.

He spoke them aloud.

He wasn't going to see her again.

An hour passed. Two.

Unable to resist the lure of seeing her one more time, he took a quick shower, pulled on a pair of black trousers and a dark gray sweater, and left the house.

He stopped at the florist and bought a huge bouquet of roses—yellow ones because she reminded him of sunlight, pink ones that matched the color of her lips, white ones to match the innocence in her eyes. And a single perfect red rose.

It was just after seven when he entered the hospital. He clenched his jaw as he walked down the corridor toward her room, overwhelmed by the scent of sickness and death. He knew it was only his imagination, yet, as he passed by the intensive care unit, it seemed as if he could see the spirits of those near death hovering above the bodies on the beds, their wraith-like arms reaching for him, silently begging him for what only he could give.

Cursing softly, he turned away, walking blindly down the corridor. He should leave now, he thought. He should never have come here in the first place.

And then he was outside her room, opening the door. And she was smiling at him, her blue eyes clear and bright, her cheeks flushed.

"I was hoping you'd stop by," she said, pleasure evident in the tone of her voice.

Alexander returned her smile as he handed her the bouquet.

"They're beautiful," Kara murmured. "Thank you."

"You put them to shame."

Kara felt herself blushing. "You flatter me, sir."

"Not at all."

"There's a vase in that cupboard," Kara said. "Would you mind putting these in water for me?"

With a nod, he opened the cupboard door, found the vase, and filled it. Taking the flowers, he placed them in the vase, then set it on the table beside the bed.

"So," he said, sitting down in the green plastic chair. "How are you feeling this evening?"

"Much better. Dr. Petersen is quite impressed

with my recovery." She smiled. "He says I can go home tomorrow."

"That is good news, indeed."

Kara nodded. "My brother called today. He's in South America."

"Doing what?"

"Building bridges."

"Has he been there long?"

"About a year. He really likes it, although I'm not sure if it's the country he loves or the beautiful Bolivian girl he's dating. Do you have brothers or sisters?"

"No."

"I have a sister, too. Gail. But then, you met her, didn't you?" Kara laughed softly. "She told me she'd paid you a visit."

"Yes," he replied, smiling. "She came looking for a vampire."

"I'll bet she was disappointed when she didn't find one."

Alexander nodded. "She's quite a brave girl, to go hunting vampires in the middle of the night."

"She's obsessed with all things paranormal," Kara remarked, shaking her head. "When she grows up, she wants to be a vampire hunter."

"An unusual occupation in this day and age."

"In *any* day and age, I should think, since vampires don't exist."

Alexander shrugged. "The inhabitants of some countries would strongly disagree with you."

"You're not serious."

"Indeed. It's only been a century or so since England outlawed the practice of driving stakes through the hearts of suicides to insure that they didn't become vampires."

37

"You sound as though you've made quite a study. But then, I guess that's natural, since you write about them."

"Yes. In ancient times, people were quick to notice that when a wounded man, or beast, lost a great deal of blood, his life force grew weak. They believed that blood was the source of vitality, and so they smeared their bodies with blood, and sometimes they drank it."

He paused, imagining the warm, coppery taste on his tongue. "Vampirism has been documented in Babylon, Rome, Greece, Egypt, China, Hungary. In ancient Greece, the people believed in the *lamia*, who were reported to be demon-women who lured young men to their deaths in order to drink their blood."

Kara shivered. She had never believed in such nonsense, but Alexander spoke with conviction, as though he actually believed such creatures existed. But he would have to believe at least a little, she thought, in order to write such convincing books.

She glanced at the novel he had given her the night before.

Alexander followed her gaze. "Dare I ask if you've read any of it?"

"I've read half of it," Kara replied. She had spent the better part of the day reading. Once she'd started, she had been unable to put it down. It was a dark book, and yet she had been touched by the vampire's love for a mortal woman.

"And?"

"I can see why it made the best-seller lists. I didn't think I'd like it. Not after the other one. But this . . ." She frowned. "The vampire seems so real, so tragic. I can't help feeling sorry for him."

Alexander nodded, pleased that she had seen the humanity in his hero.

"It's quite different from what you usually write, isn't it?"

"Quite."

"Does it have a happy ending?"

"Do you really want me to tell you?"

Kara shook her head. "No, although I must confess, I was tempted to read the end to see how you resolved the conflict."

"How do you think it should end?"

"Happily. There's enough misery in the world."

Alexander nodded. *More than you can imagine.* For a moment, his thoughts turned inward, and then he stood up as he sensed Kara's sister and grandmother approaching.

He turned toward the door as Gail and her grandmother walked into the room. Both came to an abrupt halt when they saw him.

Alexander grinned wryly as Gail stared at him. He didn't need to be clairvoyant to read her thoughts. She was wondering what he was doing there, wondering what her grandmother would say if she found out Gail had gone to see him alone, late at night.

Alexander winked at the girl, hoping to put her at ease, and then realized Kara was making introductions. He shook her grandmother's hand and smiled at Gail, who looked relieved when neither her sister nor Alexander divulged her secret.

He stayed a few more minutes, aware of the older woman's curiosity. Kara's grandmother, Lena, was too polite to stare or ask impertinent questions, but he felt her furtive glances, knew she was wondering where her granddaughter had met him, and why he was visiting her.

As quickly as possible, Alexander bade Kara good night and took his leave.

He was not often trapped in such a small space with mortals. That close, he had been all too aware of them, acutely conscious of the differences between himself and humanity, of their weaknesses and frailties.

Outside, he drew in a deep breath, his nostrils filling with the myriad scents of the night.

He thought of Kara, and cursed the dark loneliness that inhabited his soul.

As soon as he was gone, Nana fixed her attention on Kara. "Who was that man?"

"You mean Mr. Claybourne?"

"Of course I mean Mr. Claybourne," Nana retorted. "What does he do? Where did you meet him? How long have you known him?"

"Really, Nana, you sound just like Sergeant Joe Friday," Kara exclaimed, grinning. "Just the facts, ma'am," she said in a fair imitation of Jack Webb.

"Don't be impudent, Kara Elizabeth Crawford."

Kara sighed. When Nana used that tone, Kara felt like a child again instead of a grown woman.

"I just met him a couple of days ago. He donated some blood, and he came by to see how I was doing." She waved a hand toward the book on her bedside table. "He's an author."

Gail picked up the book and read the title. "A. Lucard! He's A. Lucard?"

Kara nodded.

Gail shook her head. "I don't believe it."

"Well, it's true."

"Are his books as scary as everyone says? Can I read this when you're done?"

"Yes, his books are scary, and no, you can't read it."

"Why not?"

"Because you're too young."

"Am not."

"Are too."

"Girls, that will do. Gail, why don't you go get me a cup of coffee?"

Gail lifted her eyebrows. "Do you really want a cup of coffee, or are you just trying to get rid of me?"

"Just do as you're told, miss."

"Oh, all right," Gail grumbled.

Kara took a deep, fortifying breath as she watched her sister leave the room.

"Now, missy," Nana said, "tell me what's going on between you and Mr. Claybourne."

"Oh, for goodness sakes, Nana, what do you think's going on?"

"If I knew, I wouldn't be asking."

"Nothing's going on. I just met the man!" Kara shook her head in annoyance. She loved her grandmother, but sometimes Nana's old-fashioned ideas of right and wrong made her want to scream. "I'm in the hospital, for heaven's sake. Hardly a fit place for an affair, should I decide to have one."

"Kara!"

"I'm sorry."

"It just seems odd, his coming here."

"What's odd?" Gail asked. She handed a paper cup filled with black coffee to her grandmother.

"Nothing." Nana sat back and sipped her coffee, listening while Gail told Kara about her day at

41

school. A few minutes later, the chimes that signaled the end of visiting hours sounded throughout the hospital.

"Are you still coming home tomorrow?" Gail asked.

"Yes."

Gail turned toward her grandmother. "Can I come with you to get Kara?"

"No, you have school."

"I could miss a day."

"No. Tell Kara good night. We must go."

Gail hugged Kara. "I never get to do anything," she complained.

"When I'm feeling better, we'll go shopping."

"Promise?"

"Promise."

"Good night, Kara," Nana said. "I'll be by tomorrow about ten."

"Good night, Nana."

Kara lay back on the pillows. Now that she thought of it, it was odd that Alexander Claybourne had come to see her. After all, she had donated blood to the Red Cross on several occasions, but she had never known where the blood had gone. And even though she had often wondered who had received it, and if it had perhaps saved a life, she had never gone looking for the recipients.

So, maybe he was just more curious than she was. Or maybe he had some sinister motive. . . .

Kara shook her head. It wasn't like her to be suspicious. Nana often said Kara was too trusting, too gullible, for her own good, and maybe she was. But she preferred to think the best of people instead of the worst. She knew there was evil in the world, but she saw no point in dwelling on it just because the six o'clock news couldn't talk about anything else. After all, there was good in the world, too. And Alexander Claybourne proved it. He had donated blood to a total stranger, and then come by to see how she was doing.

She frowned as she stared at the flowers he had brought her. How had he found out who had received his blood anyway? Wasn't that information confidential?

She plucked the red rose from the vase and sniffed its fragrance. Whatever else he was, he was the most generous man she had ever known. The flowers must have cost him a small fortune, she thought. Roses from a florist were never cheap, and there were at least three dozen buds, all perfectly formed.

They were beautiful, she mused. Then she smiled. He had said she put them to shame. It was one of the nicest compliments she had ever received.

Smiling, she put the rose back in the vase and reached for his book, eager to discover how the romance between the vampire and the mortal woman ended.

Chapter Four

Kara quickly grew bored with staying home. She was used to being on the go. As a consultant, she often traveled to nearby towns to advise large companies on redecorating their offices. She had been returning from just such an assignment when the accident happened. One minute she'd been driving on the highway listening to Billy Ray Cyrus; the next thing she remembered, she was in the hospital swathed in bandages with no memory of how she'd gotten there. She was lucky to be alive.

She flipped through the TV channels. Soap operas and talk shows, talk shows and soap operas. With a grimace, she clicked off the set and picked up Alexander's latest book. She had asked Nana to buy it for her. Unlike *The Hunger*, which had had a strong romance and, much to her delight, a happy ending, this book, titled *Lord of Darkness*, was strictly horror. It was a frightening story, and yet, when she tried to analyze it, she couldn't pinpoint exactly what it was that made it so scary. The horror wasn't lurid. The bloodletting wasn't so gory that it was disgusting. Perhaps it was the fact that it all seemed so plausible, so real.

Alexander had been right about one thing, though. She didn't read his books at night.

She put the book aside when Gail came home from school. "Hi, Pumpkin. Have a good day?"

"It was all right. I got a B on a math test."

"That's great. Nana baked cookies this morning. How about bringing me some, and a glass of milk?"

"Okay." Gail tossed her sweater and books on a chair and went into the kitchen. She returned moments later with two tall glasses of milk and a plate of oatmeal cookies. "Where's Nana?"

"She went over to Mrs. Zimmermann's to play canasta."

"Oh." Gail sat down on the end of the sofa. "How's the book?"

"It's good. He's a very talented writer."

"Why do you think people say a vampire lives in his house?"

"That should be obvious, even to a kid like you," Kara said with a grin. "The man writes about vampires and werewolves."

"I guess. His house was really dark inside when I went there."

"You didn't go inside, did you?"

"No. But I could see inside a little." Gail nibbled on a cookie, her expression thoughtful. "There weren't any lights on."

"Maybe he'd gone to bed."

"It wasn't that late."

"Some people do go to bed early, you know."

"Maybe. It's funny, though."

"What's funny?"

"Well, me and Stephanie and Cherise have gone out there lots of times during the day, and we've never seen anybody around."

"So? Maybe he sleeps late and writes at night."

"Vampires sleep during the day."

"Oh, for goodness sakes, Gail, will you please stop thinking every stranger you meet is a vampire or a werewolf."

"All right, all right. Are you going to eat that last cookie?"

"No, go ahead."

Gail polished off the last of the cookies, finished her milk, then stood up. "I'm going over to Cindy's. Do you want anything before I go?"

"No, I'm fine. Don't be late."

"I won't. See ya later."

"Bye."

Kara looked out the window, wishing she could go outside. It was a beautiful afternoon, bright and clear, a perfect day for a long walk through the park. She couldn't wait until her leg was better. She hated being waited on, hated being house-bound, hated lying on the sofa with her leg propped up on a pillow. And, as much as she loved her grandmother, she couldn't wait to go back to her own apartment. Nana had raised a fuss when Kara decided to move out of the house, but Kara had needed to be independent, to live on her own, even if her apartment was less than a mile away from home.

She wondered what Alexander Claybourne was doing, and if she would ever see him again, and if he thought about her as often as she thought about him.

Alexander prowled the woodland behind his house, battling his desire to see Kara again.

It had been six weeks since he'd last seen her. Six interminable weeks.

His writing had thrived. Tormented by his desire for Kara, he had spent long hours at his computer, pouring his frustration into his writing. Words came easily now. Dark angry words that spewed forth like lava, searing the pages. The anger and the loneliness of two hundred years flowed out of him, unleashed by his longing for a mortal woman with hair like a flame and eyes as blue as a midsummer sky. He could truly sympathize with his vampire now, he thought ruefully.

But he was not thinking of his work in progress tonight. He was one with the darkness as he moved through the woods, his footsteps making hardly a sound. He caught the faint odor of a skunk, the smell of decaying foliage, the stink of a dead animal, the acrid scent of smoke rising from a distant fireplace. He heard the frantic scurrying of the nocturnal creatures who hunted the night, the beating of tiny wings, the death cry of a beast of prey who had not been fast enough to escape the hunter.

He paused when he reached the top of the hill, his gaze sweeping the darkness, searching for Kara. Oh, yes, he knew where her grandmother lived. He had passed by the small red brick residence every night for the past six weeks, tormenting himself with her nearness. Cloaked in the shadows outside Lena Corley's residence, he had listened to Kara's voice, breathed in her scent, read her thoughts.

It would be so easy to take her, to make her his. They were bonded now, eternally linked by the blood they shared. He closed his eyes, imagining the simplicity of it all. He would wait until he had her alone, seduce her with a look, spirit her away to his house. He could spend hours making love to her, and then blot it all from her mind. . . .

A vile oath escaped his lips, and then he was running through the darkness, running away from smooth, suntanned skin and sky-blue eyes, from lips the color of summer roses. Running from the ancient curse that tainted his very soul.

But he could not outrun the memory of her smile, or the soft, sultry sound of her voice.

Back in his own house, he slumped in the chair in front of his computer, wondering why he suddenly felt compelled to write the story of his own life instead of the fiction that came so easily to him.

In all the centuries of his existence, he had refused to dwell on the past. Once he had resigned himself to his fate, he had embraced it. To do otherwise was unthinkable. It was the only way to hang onto his sanity. There was no way back, no point in wallowing in self-pity. No point in lamenting over that which had been forever lost to him.

There had been a short period of time when he had mourned his wife and daughter, when he had mourned his old life, and then he had put the memories behind him, refusing to acknowledge the grief and the pain.

So why, he wondered, why now?

The answer was ridiculously simple, and amazingly complex.

It was because of Kara. Something about her reminded him of AnnaMara, made him yearn for the life he had lost, made him achingly aware of the fact that he was not a mortal man in the true sense of the word.

As always, when he was troubled, he sought escape in whatever book he was working on.

Leaning forward, he switched on the computer. For a moment, he stared at the blank blue screen, and then he pulled up the document he wanted and began to read, starting at page one.

THE DARK GIFT
Chapter 1

I was born in a small village in Rumania, the youngest of seven sons. There was an old legend that decreed that the seventh son of a seventh son was destined to become a vampire. As a child, the thought terrified me. Vampires lived in darkness and drank the blood of the living. The thought of drinking blood sickened me, but it was the thought of dwelling forever in darkness that left me numb with fear, for I had a deep and abiding fear of the night. As far back as I could remember, my dreams had been haunted by nameless terrors. Numerous times I had begged my mother to tell me it wasn't true, that I would not grow up to be a vampire. Numerous times she had held me in her arms and assured me that it was only an old wives' tale. Why did I never see the truth in her eyes?

As I grew older, my dreams grew more intense. The terror that haunted me was no longer nameless, or faceless. It was a woman who embodied the terror that haunted my nights, a woman with olive-hued skin and hair as black as coal. A woman whose amber eyes burned with the fires of the damned.

When I turned two-and-twenty, I fell in love with the blacksmith's daughter. A year later, we were married, and for the next five years I knew only happiness. Our one sadness was that AnnaMara failed to conceive, but I, being somewhat selfish, did not mind. I wanted only AnnaMara. My nightmares had ceased long since. My fear of the dark was swallowed up in AnnaMara's sweet embrace. And then, late one night while we lay entwined in each other's arms, she told me she was carrying my child. Only then did I realize what true joy was. Ah, those blissful days and nights when life was full and perfect, when my love's belly swelled with child, and each day saw our love grow stronger, deeper.

Our daughter was born on a sunlit morning in early spring. She died the following dawn, and her mother with her. Unfortunate, the midwife said. The child had come too soon; AnnaMara died of childbed fever. I buried them on a windswept hill, my wife, my daughter, and my heart.

The nightmares came back that night. . . .

Alexander sat back in his chair and stretched his legs. He had named his heroine after his consort. AnnaMara, with hair like yellow silk and eyes as brown as the soil of earth. He had not willingly thought of her in centuries, yet now, just seeing her name brought it all back—the love they had shared, the happiness they had once known. She had named their daughter AnTares. AnTares, the only child he had ever fathered. The only child that would ever be born to him.

He stared at the computer screen, the words blurring before his eyes. He had not loved a woman since AnnaMara. There had been other women in his life, paid professionals who had eased his lust, but no special woman, none he dared trust with the reality of what he was.

Only now, after more than two hundred years, had he found a woman whose heart he wanted to win, a woman in whom he yearned to confide. But he dared not love her.

For her sake, he dared not love her.

Kara sat on the swing in the backyard, staring at the hills that rose to the east beyond Moulton Bay. As always of late, her thoughts were on Alexander. Where was he tonight? What was he doing? Did he spend his every waking moment thinking of her? Did he find himself suddenly staring into the distance, wondering what she was doing, thinking, wearing?

Seven weeks. Seven weeks since she had seen him last. She'd thought there had been something between them, a mutual attraction, but apparently she'd been wrong. Surely, if he had felt even half of what she still felt, he would have called. After four weeks, she had put her pride and good judgment aside and tried to call him, but the operator had informed her there was no listing for an Alexander Claybourne, or for A. Lucard.

She'd read all his books. Twice. The first time, they had frightened her. The second time, she had detected a common thread running through each story. No matter who the hero might be, he always carried a heavy burden or harbored a dark secret, and he was always a man alone, afraid to love, afraid to trust. A coincidence? A silent plea for help? Or was she just being fanciful?

Where was he? Why didn't he call? Why hadn't he come to see her? Why couldn't she stop thinking of him?

"Kara."

His voice, so soft that she wasn't sure if she'd actually heard it or if her mind was playing tricks on her because she wanted so badly to see him again.

"Kara."

Slowly, hardly daring to hope, she turned toward the sound of his voice. And he was there, a tall, dark figure silhouetted against the blackness of the night.

"Alexander."

Slowly, he moved toward her. A stray moonbeam washed him in silver. And then he was there, standing in front of her, as tall and broad-shouldered as she remembered. His hair, long and black and windblown, framed a strong, angular face.

"How have you been?" he asked.

His voice was as soft as a prayer, as intimate as a lover's caress.

"Fine," she replied. "And you?"

"Fine," he said. "As always."

"How's your new book coming along?"

"Slowly."

"Oh? Why?"

His gaze met hers, his dark eyes intense. "I've had other things on my mind."

"Oh." She felt suddenly breathless, as though someone had sucked all the oxygen from the air. "What things?"

"Kara . . ."

She leaned forward, waiting for his next words, hoping he would tell her that he had missed her, that he had spent his every waking moment thinking only of her.

He was watching her closely, his gaze fixed on her face. She could feel the heat of it, the power of it. At that moment, she would have told him anything he wanted to hear, done anything he asked. Though they weren't touching, it was almost as if he were stroking her hair, caressing her cheek.

And then he took a step back, releasing her from his gaze.

"Alexander." Her voice was shaky, uncertain.

"What do you want from me, Kara?"

"Want?"

"I've been much in your mind these past weeks."

Kara stared at him. How had he known that?

"I hear your thoughts. I feel your loneliness, your restlessness." He clenched his hands to keep from reaching for her. "What do you want of me?"

"I . . . nothing."

"You cannot lie to me, Kara. I know that your nights are long and that sleep brings you no rest. You've wondered why I have not called on you, wondered what I've been doing that would keep me away."

"How do you know these things? You can't read my mind. It's impossible."

"If there's one thing I have learned, Kara, it's that few things in life are impossible."

She looked away, embarrassed to know he had divined her innermost thoughts.

"Do not look away, Kara. I don't have to read your mind to know your thoughts because your thoughts have been mine. My nights, too, are long and lonely. Your image haunts my days. The memory of your smile lingers in my dreams. I want . . ."

"What?" she asked, her voice hoarse. Never had any man said such romantic things to her, or made her feel so desirable. "What do you want?"

"This," he said, and kneeling before her, he cupped her face in his hands and kissed her.

She had been kissed before, and often, but never like this. His touch went through her like satin fire, hot and seductive. His fingers slid to her shoulders, holding her fast, and she felt the latent strength of his hands, sensed the power that radiated from him like heat from the sun.

Kara heard a low groan. Had it come from her, or him? His tongue slid over her lower lip, dipping inside to caress the soft inner flesh. And she felt herself melting, melting from the heat of his touch, the gentle pressure of his fingers kneading her shoulders, gliding down her arms. His hands were cool against her bare skin.

"Kara." His voice was uneven as he drew back.

Drowning in sensation, she looked at him through heavy-lidded eyes. He caressed her cheek, and she turned her face against his palm, wanting more.

He should not have come here. He started to rise, to tell her it had been a mistake, but she grabbed his hand and held it tightly.

"Don't go."

"Kara, listen to me . . ."

"No. I don't think I want to hear what you have to say."

"It's for your own good."

"Now I know I don't want to hear it."

Like a wolf on the scent, Alex turned toward the house. Lena Corley was stirring.

"I've got to go," he said.

"Not until you promise me you'll come back tomorrow."

He could hear Lena Corley calling for Kara. He didn't want the woman to find him here, didn't want to try to explain something that was, at the moment, unexplainable.

"Alexander?"

"Very well. Tomorrow night."

"What time?"

"Is ten too late?"

"No."

"Here, then, at ten." He took a step forward, raised her hand to his lips, and kissed it. "Until tomorrow," he whispered, and stepping into the darkness, he disappeared into the shadows.

"Until tomorrow," Kara repeated, and wondered how she'd ever survive the hours until she saw him again.

He sat in front of the computer, his gaze fixed on the screen, taking up where he had left off.

The nightmares came back that night, more real, more frightening than before. With AnnaMara gone, there was nothing to hold me to my old life, my old home. I bade my parents farewell and left the village without looking back. I was running. Running away from the memory of my wife and child. Running away from the images that again haunted my dreams.

How foolish I was, to think I could outrun

my destiny. I was in France, trying to drown my grief in a tankard of ale, the night she found me.

I don't know how long she stood beside me before she touched me. I only remember looking up into a pair of the most exquisite amber-colored eyes I had ever seen. I knew, at that moment, that I was lost, hopelessly and forever lost, that I would do whatever she asked.

She spoke my name, and I did not question how she knew it.

She took my hand, and I followed her out of the tavern, down a dark street, into a dark house.

I was her prisoner from that night. She did not imprison me with chains, nor did she keep me locked in a dungeon. It was the power of her eyes, the strength of her will, that enslaved me.

I slept by day, and came awake at night. She told me her name was Lilith, and she had been waiting for me since the day of my birth. I thought that an odd statement, as she was a young woman. A beautiful woman, the most beautiful woman I had ever seen. Her hair, as black as the night, fell past her hips like a river of darkness. Her skin was like porcelain, her lips the palest pink imaginable.

She was a wealthy woman. Her house was huge and well-appointed, filled with paintings and tapestries and exotic pottery and figurines. She took me to the opera and the theater, dressed me in fine clothes, taught me to read and to write.

I never saw her during the day. I never saw

her eat. When I dared question her, she said she preferred to stay up late and sleep late, and that she preferred to dine alone.

And I believed her. Only later did I realize that she had clouded my mind so that those facts did not seem unusual or important.

Months passed. I was neither happy nor sad. I did as I was told and gave no thought to the morrow.

Until the night when I woke and Lilith was not there. . . .

Alexander leaned back in his chair, his thoughts turning from Lilith to Kara. She would be waiting for him tomorrow night.

The thought filled him with anticipation. And dread.

Chapter Five

Kara thought the hours would never pass. She fidgeted through dinner, listened impatiently as Gail recited her homework, stared at the TV without seeing a thing.

At eight-thirty, she tucked Gail into bed and said good night to Nana.

At nine o'clock, she took a long, leisurely bubble bath, dressed in a pair of silky black pants and a pale pink sweater, combed her hair, brushed her teeth, applied her lipstick with care.

At ten o'clock, she went out into the backyard and sat on the swing.

And waited.

And waited.

At eleven, she told herself he wasn't coming. And still she waited, wondering what there was about Alexander Claybourne that touched her so deeply.

Perhaps it was the air of supreme loneliness that clung to him. Perhaps it was the feeling that he needed her, although she admitted that was probably just wishful thinking on her part.

"Kara."

His voice. Was it real, or was she still dreaming? "Alexander?"

"I'm here."

She sat up, rubbing her eyes. "I must have fallen asleep."

"You should not be out here. It's cold."

He was wearing a long black coat that reminded her of the dusters old-time cowboys used to wear. Shrugging it off, he draped it over her shoulders.

"You said you'd be here at ten."

"I know."

She looked up at him, waiting for an explanation, an apology, something. But he only stood there, gazing down at her, his dark eyes filled with sadness.

"What is it?" she asked. "What's wrong?"

"I should not have come here."

"Why? Oh, no." She shook her head, certain he was about to tell her he had a wife and the requisite two-point-three children. "You're married, aren't you?"

Alexander laughed softly, wishing it was something as ordinary as a wife that was keeping them apart. "No, Kara, I'm not married."

"What is it then?"

"I'm afraid you have asked the one question I cannot answer."

"Then I won't ask it again."

The simplicity of her reply, the trust shining in

her eyes, was his undoing. Kneeling before her, he took her hand in his.

"Kara, I am not like other men. You must never love me. Or trust me."

"I don't understand."

"Pray you never do."

"But . . ." She bit down on her lower lip, remembering she had promised not to ask why. "Are we never to see each other again?"

"It would be for the best."

"For who?"

"For you."

"Don't I have anything to say about it?"

"No."

"If you don't want to see me anymore, why did you come here tonight?"

"Because I could not stay away."

She smiled triumphantly. "So you do want to continue seeing me!"

"It is my fondest desire."

"Mine, too." She put her hand over his mouth when he started to speak. "No. Don't say another word. I want to be with you. You want to be with me. I don't see the problem."

Gently, he removed her hand from his mouth, then kissed her palm. Warmth feathered up her arm to pool around her heart.

"I hope you never do," Alexander said quietly. Rising, he drew her to her feet. "Your leg—it's better?"

Kara nodded. "The doctor said I can go back to work next week."

"Will you meet me here again tomorrow night?"

She nodded again, happiness welling inside her. "Will you kiss me good night?"

"Will the sun rise in the morning?" he murmured, and then he slanted his mouth over hers, his lips claiming hers in a long, lingering kiss that left her shaken to the soles of her feet.

When he took his mouth from hers, Kara swayed against him, certain she would have fallen but for his arms around her.

"I hope you do not regret this, Kara."

"I won't," she whispered. "I won't."

"Good night, then," he replied, and hoped, for her sake, that she grew tired of him before it was too late.

In the last hours before dawn, Alexander sat in front of his computer, reading what he had written earlier.

THE DARK GIFT
Chapter II

I walked through the house, looking for Lilith. For the first time, I noticed that heavy draperies covered every window, and when I opened one, I saw there were shutters on the outside. I wandered through the downstairs, but she was nowhere to be found. I paused at the bottom of the winding staircase, looking up at the darkness beyond. She had forbidden me to ever go upstairs, but on this night, something drew me. Something stronger than fear of discovery, stronger than mere curiosity.

I knew, with every step that I took, that I was embarking on a journey from which there would be no return, yet something compelled me onward.

I think, even now, that I knew what I would find when I opened her door. Perhaps I had always known. Perhaps it wasn't the power of her mind that had clouded mine all this time, but my own fear.

Mouth dry, heart pounding, I opened the door to Lilith's room, and came face to face with a scene out of one of my childhood nightmares: Lilith, dressed all in black, bending over the body of a young boy.

Though I hadn't made a sound, she looked up, her amber-colored eyes glowing with an otherworldly light. A collage of ghastly images imprinted themselves on my mind: the boy's face, completely drained of color, the crimson stains on the white bedspread that matched the blood dripping from Lilith's lips.

She hissed at me, her eyes blazing. And then, very gently, she lowered the boy's body to the bed and stood up. Slow step by slow step, she walked toward me. Every instinct I possessed screamed at me to run, but I could not move. I could only stand there, horrified, knowing that every nightmare I had ever had was about to come true.

"You should not have come here." Her voice was low and filled with rage.

I tried to speak, to tell her I was sorry, but the words wouldn't come. I could only stare at her face, at the blood that stained her lips.

She put her hand on my shoulder, let it slide down my arm. "You are a beautiful man, Alesandro," she remarked, her voice soft, seductive. "I had hoped to wait another year or two to bring you over, but now . . ." She lifted one slender shoulder. "The Dark Gift should not be bestowed on those who are too young."

I was trembling now, more frightened than I had ever been in my life. She knew it, and it pleased her.

"Please." I forced the word past dry lips. "Please."

"Please what?" she asked, her voice silky, her eyes blazing hotter and hotter.

"Don't."

"Don't what?"

I glanced at the body lying on her bed. "I don't want to be like you."

Slowly, she looked over her shoulder, then back at me. "I see. Would you rather be like him?"

I stared at her, repelled by both choices.

Lilith stroked my cheek. Her hand, usually cool, was warm. Her cheeks were flushed. I flinched as her nails bit into my cheek, breaking the skin. There was blood on her hand when she drew it away, and I watched in horror as she licked my blood from her fingers.

"Sweet," she purred. "I knew you would be sweet."

"No." I took a step backward, turned to run, only to feel her hand on my arm. I was tall and muscular. She was small and slender, yet she held me fast in her grip, and I was powerless against her.

She smiled, exposing her fangs. I knew then what real fear was. Panic-stricken, I lashed out, my fist driving into her face. I had felled grown men with that blow. Lilith didn't flinch. Her hands turned into claws, her fingers digging into my arm, tearing through cloth and flesh. With a groan, I dropped to my knees.

Lilith knelt beside me, eyes burning. "I cannot bear to kill you," she said. "But I fear I cannot let you go. You have seen too much, and you know where I rest. And so . . ."

She drew me into her arms, holding me against her. She smelled of blood and reeked of death.

"Please," I said, hating the weakness in my voice, the trembling I could not control.

"It will be soon over, *mon ange*," she crooned, and she bent over me, blocking everything else from my sight, so that I saw nothing. but her face, and the fires of the damned that burned in the pitiless depths of her eyes.

I felt her teeth at my throat. Fear such as I had never known rose up within me, and then the fear was gone, overshadowed by an ecstasy that was almost sensual. My strength drained away. It grew hard to breathe, to think.

And then I was drifting, floating, lighter than air. Darkness closed in around me, darker than anything I had ever known. I screamed as the blackness surrounded me, but no sound issued from my throat.

I was dying. Alone. In the dark I had feared all my life. I knew it but I was too weak to care. Surely there would be light in heaven, I thought, and prayed to die quickly, that I might find my way out of the darkness and into the light.

And then I felt it. A drop of liquid fire on my tongue. It burned through me, followed by another drop, and then another, until the drops became a river.

I opened my eyes, and knew that I would

never see the world the same way again. That I would never be the same again. . . .

Alexander leaned back in his chair, pleased with what he had written, thinking that, like Alesandro, he would never be the same again.

Chapter Six

She was waiting for him, sitting in the swing as she had the night before. Alexander sensed her presence even before he vaulted over the fence, landing lightly on his feet. Through the darkness, he could see her, a slender form clad in green pants and a white, off-the-shoulder blouse.

As he closed the distance between them, Kara stood up and began walking toward him. They met near a flowering peach tree. For a moment, their gazes met, and then she was in his arms and he was kissing her, holding her, as though he would never again let her go.

"Kara." He held her close, wanting to draw her goodness into him. She smelled of sunlight and flowers. Her skin was soft and warm. Closing his eyes, he let himself bask in her nearness, her warmth. Two hundred years, he thought. It had been two hundred years since he'd last held a woman he cared for; two hundred years since he'd let a woman care for him. He had forgotten how wonderful it was to hold and be held in return.

"I missed you," Kara said. She looked up at him, startled by the intensity of his gaze.

"Did you?" His voice was deep and husky and unsteady.

"Yes. I thought about you all day." She glanced away, then met his gaze again. "Did you think of me?"

"Every waking moment." He slipped his arm around her waist and they walked over to the swing and sat down.

"I had a phone call from the hospital today," Kara said. "They want me to go to the hospital in Grenvale for some tests tomorrow."

"What kind of tests?"

"I'm not sure. Blood tests of some sort."

"Is something wrong?"

"I don't know. When I was in the hospital, all the doctors could talk about was the remarkable recovery I had made, but now they want to do more tests. You don't think the blood they gave me was tainted, do you?" She couldn't bring herself to voice her worst fears, but the threat of AIDS loomed large in her mind.

"I'm sure it wasn't." Alexander stared into the distance. He knew what they had found—a trace of his blood, alien blood.

"Why don't you have a telephone?"

"I find them an intrusion into my life, my privacy."

"But how do you stay in touch with your editor?"

"By mail. I write during the day, and prefer to be

undisturbed by phones ringing. I find it breaks my concentration." He took her hand in his. "Did you try to call me?"

Kara nodded. "A couple of weeks ago," she admitted. "And then today, after I heard from the hospital, I wished I could call you."

"Perhaps I shall have to get a phone then."

She smiled up at him as if she'd just won the lottery. "I'll probably spend the night in Grenvale. Nana's going with me. She has an old friend who lives there. They're going to spend the day together while I'm at the hospital." She stared down at his hand covering hers. "Maybe you could call me tomorrow night?"

"Certainly."

"Here, you can use my cell phone. I'll be staying at the Grenvale Motel."

Alex stared at the compact instrument for a moment, then nodded. "I shall call you there," he said, tucking the phone into his pocket. "And I will see you here Wednesday evening."

"I'll be looking forward to it." She chewed the inside of her lower lip a moment. "Do you think maybe you could come by earlier on Wednesday night so we could spend more time together?"

"If you wish." He watched as her finger traced meaningless patterns on the back of his hand. His life had been like that, he thought, meaningless circles that started nowhere and went nowhere. Until now. "What will your grandmother say?"

"It doesn't matter. I picked up my car from the repair shop today, and I'll be moving back to my own apartment on Thursday. I'll give you my address when I get back."

Alexander nodded, although he already knew where she lived.

"You weren't born in this country, were you?"

"No. Why do you ask?"

"It's the way you talk. I mean, there's nothing wrong with the way you talk. Oh, I don't know how to explain it. It's just the way you turn a phrase sometimes."

Alexander smiled at her. How perceptive she was. English was not his first language, or even his second.

"Would you care to go out Thursday night?" he asked.

"Sure. Where shall we go?"

"Wherever you wish, Kara. A movie, perhaps?"

"I'd like that. I've been dying to see the new Mel Gibson flick."

"What time shall I pick you up?"

"Seven?"

"Seven," he repeated solemnly. "I should go now. It's late."

"So soon?"

"I'm afraid so."

He clenched his fists, afraid to stay longer, afraid the yearning he felt for her would overcome his self-control. The bond they shared called to him, urging him to complete the ritual, to join his body to hers.

Leaning forward, his lips brushed hers in a quick kiss of farewell. "I shall call you at the motel tomorrow night. And don't worry. Everything will be all right."

"I wish . . ."

"What, Kara? What do you wish?"

"I wish you could take me." Except for picking

69

up her car that morning, she hadn't driven since the accident. It was silly to be afraid, but she couldn't help feeling apprehensive.

"I wish I could, too. Unfortunately, I have an appointment tomorrow morning that I cannot break."

"I understand." It was like falling off a horse, she mused, and since Nana didn't drive, there was nothing to do but get back on, only in her case, it wasn't a horse but a dark green Camry.

"Good night, Kara."

"Good night."

He gazed into her eyes and wondered how she had managed to retain such innocence, such trust, in this day and age.

She was a modern woman. She lived alone. She had a job, and yet he sensed a vulnerability about her that set her apart. Perhaps it was that very trait that reminded him of AnnaMara.

Kara stared up at the doctor. His name was Dale Barrett. He was a tall, middle-aged man, with straight brown hair and pale brown eyes that did nothing to invite her trust. "I don't understand."

"I'm afraid we don't, either, Miss Crawford. There's an unusual antibody in your blood that we've never seen before. We want to do some extensive tests."

"More tests?" Kara shook her head. "No."

"Miss Crawford, surely you can see how important it is that we determine the origin of this antibody. At the moment, we don't know what its effects might be. We must determine if it's contagious. I don't want to alarm you, but there's every possibility that this antibody could prove fatal."

"Fatal! But how could that be? I feel fine."

"I understand your concern, Miss Crawford."

"Do you?"

"Of course. I've already made all the arrange-ments. Your room is waiting."

Kara jumped off the table. "Now, wait a minute. I haven't agreed to this."

"I'm afraid I must insist."

"Does Dr. Peterson know about this? Why isn't he here?"

"He'll be coming to see you as soon as you're set-tled." Barrett smiled reassuringly. "Dr. Peterson is a fine doctor, but he's only a general practioner. He wanted to be sure you got the best of care, and that's why he called me in as a consultant. My field of expertise is hematology."

Panic rose up in Kara as two men wearing white lab coats and masks entered the examining room. "I want to talk to my grandmother."

"All in good time." Dr. Barrett pulled a syringe from his coat pocket.

Kara took a step backward. "What's that for?"

"Nothing to be alarmed about."

"What is it?"

"Just something to help you relax."

"I don't want it."

"I'm afraid you're on the verge of hysteria, Miss Crawford. This will calm you." Barrett nodded at the two white-coated men.

"No!" She screamed the word as the two men took hold of her, flinched as she felt the prick of the needle in her arm. "No, please . . ."

She stared up at the doctor, her vision blurring. This couldn't be happening. Alexander! Her mind screamed his name as she tumbled into oblivion.

* * *

Lena Corley shook her head. "I don't understand. What are you saying?"

"I'm afraid we've found an abnormality in your granddaughter's blood, Mrs. Corley. We need to keep her here for further observation until we've determined the cause of the abnormality and determined whether it might be contagious. Or toxic."

"How did such a thing happen?"

"We don't know."

"Was there something wrong with the blood she received?"

The doctor shook his head. "We screen all of our blood donors very carefully. That's why we're so confused. We have the names of the people whose blood was used. They've all been rechecked."

Lena Corley stared at the paper in front of her. They wanted her to admit Kara to the hospital for some extensive tests. The doctor, whose name was Barrett, had informed her that Kara had fainted during an examination and that she was still unconscious. They feared it had something to do with the abnormal red cells in her blood. It was urgent, the doctor said, that they find the cause of her problem as soon as possible. Until then, it was imperative that she be kept in isolation.

"Think of your other granddaughter, Mrs. Corley. You don't want to take a risk of infecting her, now do you?"

"No, no, of course not, but . . ."

"I understand, but you mustn't worry," Barrett said reassuringly. "I promise you that we'll do everything we can for Kara." He handed her a pen. "Just sign your name there, on the first page, and again on page four. I'll take care of everything else."

Lena shook her head as she squinted at the fine

print. "So many big words that I don't understand."

"Of course. All that legal mumbo jumbo. All it says is that we have your permission to keep Kara overnight, and to prescribe treatment for her."

"I don't know . . ."

"Mrs. Corley, time is of the essence in cases like this. Do you really want to put Kara's life at risk by waiting?"

With a sigh of resignation, Lena signed the papers.

Alex called the Grenvale Motel at six o'clock that evening, but the clerk informed him that Kara had not yet checked in. He knew a moment of concern, and then he shrugged it aside. She was a grown woman. Perhaps she had gone out to dinner or shopping. Grenvale was a big city, much larger than Moulton Bay, and it was still early. He would write a chapter, then call again.

THE DARK GIFT
Chapter III

I stared into Lilith's face. "What have you done to me?"

"I have made you immortal."

I stared up at her, knowing what she was, yet refusing to acknowledge it; knowing, in the very depths of my being, that my soul was damned.

"What are you?"

Amusement flared in her eyes. "What do you think I am?"

"I don't know."

73

"You know."

I shook my head. "It's not possible."

"We are known by many names. *Vrykalakes, blutsauger, upiry. Vampyr, Vampyre.*" She smiled. "Vampire, Alesandro, that is what I am. That is what you are."

"No . . ." I stared at her, the embodiment of every nightmare I had ever known, every fear that had tormented me. Vampire. The undead.

"Go outside," she said curtly. "Empty yourself of bodily fluids. Then come back to me."

I did as I was told. Numb to everything around me, I did as I was told. I knew it was winter, that the air was cold, but I felt nothing at all.

She was sitting on the edge of the bed when I returned. "When you wake tomorrow, the transformation will be complete." Rising, she glanced at the window. "It is almost dawn."

I followed her gaze. The window was covered with a heavy green damask drape that would have kept out the light of the brightest day. How, I wondered, how did she know dawn was approaching?

"You may spend the day here, with me," she said. "Tomorrow you must find your own place to rest." She made a sound of disgust when I said nothing, only continued to stand there, staring at her. "Come along," she said, and taking me by the hand, she led me through a narrow door, up a short flight of stairs, into a small windowless room that was empty save for an ornate casket set upon a raised platform.

Dropping my hand, she climbed the stairs of the platform and lifted the lid, revealing a lining of deep green satin.

And then she held out her hand. "Come, Alesandro. The dawn approaches."

I stared at her hand in horror. "No."

"What's the matter?" she asked disdainfully. "Surely you're not afraid of this box?"

I shook my head, too ashamed to tell her it wasn't the coffin I feared, though I must confess I was loathe to climb into it. What I feared was the darkness inside.

"Do as you wish," she said, her voice tinged with disgust.

Turning her back to me, she climbed into the casket, her movements as graceful as a reed bending in the wind.

I stood there for a long while, and then, without knowing how or why, I knew the sun had come up. I felt myself growing heavy, lethargic. The feeling, so unfamiliar, frightened me, and I ran up the stairs and hurled myself into the casket. Lilith was lying on her side to make room for me. She smiled smugly, and then she lowered the lid on the casket, shutting us in darkness.

A hoarse cry of primal fear rose in my throat, and then I was dragged down into a deep black void, all conscious thought swept away.

When I awoke the following night, she was gone. I lay there for a moment, my body wracked with pain such as I had never felt before. And then, realizing where I was, I bolted out of the coffin and ran down the stairs to her bedroom.

She was sitting on a velvet-covered bench, brushing her hair. I realized then that there were no mirrors anywhere in the house.

"Awake at last?" she asked. "I had rather

thought you'd be an early riser, being a farmer and all."

"Lilith, help me."

"What's wrong?"

"I hurt." I wrapped my arms around my stomach, certain I was dying, only then remembering that I could not die.

"It's nothing to be concerned about," she remarked. "It will pass after you've fed."

My gaze darted toward the bed as I remembered the boy she had killed the night before. She had drained his life. That was how she took sustenance. The thought filled me with revulsion, and then, to my horror, I felt my teeth grow long at the thought of the boy's blood on my tongue.

"No." I backed away from her. "I can't. I won't."

"You can," she said coldly. "You will."

"No, never."

"You can come with me now, tonight, and learn to hunt, or you can leave my house and learn to survive on your own."

"And if I don't wish to survive?"

"Then you have only to wait for sunrise. A fledgling such as yourself will burst into flame at the first touch of the sun."

I shuddered at the thought, at the hideous images her words conjured in my mind.

"There is much you need to learn, Alesandro. I can teach you, or I can destroy you. The choice is yours."

I had never thought myself a coward until I faced the very real possibility of dying again. . . .

Chapter Seven

He called the hotel again at eight, and at nine, and again at ten. And always the message was the same: Neither Miss Crawford nor her grandmother had checked in.

Worried now, Alex left the house. Opening the garage door, he pulled his car keys from his pocket and slid behind the wheel of the Porsche. He turned the key in the ignition, listened appreciatively as the engine hummed to life. Backing down the driveway, he headed for Grenvale.

The Porsche flew down the highway. He had grown to love the sense of freedom he experienced behind the wheel. He felt attuned to the car, almost a part of it.

He arrived in Grenvale in record time. Leaving the Porsche in the motel parking lot, he locked the car door, then crossed the blacktop to the motel.

And again the message was the same: Miss Crawford had not checked in.

With a curt nod, Alex left the motel. Standing in the shadows, he let his mind expand. *Kara, where are you?* He waited, listening, and when he sensed no reply, he drove to the hospital. He drove through the parking lot, feeling a ridiculous sense of relief when he saw her car.

He parked the Porsche next to her Camry, then went into the hospital, determined to find out what was going on.

The night nurse listened to him patiently, then shook her head. "I'm sorry, sir," she said, "Miss Crawford is in an isolation unit. She's not allowed any visitors just now."

"I want to see her doctor."

"I'm afraid he's left for the night. He should be back first thing in the morning if you'd like to call then."

"Can you tell me if she's all right?"

"Are you family, sir?"

"No. Dammit, you've got to let me see her."

The nurse glanced up and down the hallway, then leaned forward and lowered her voice. "I shouldn't tell you this, but Miss Crawford's fine. She's just being kept overnight while they wait for the results of her tests. She was a little upset, and her doctor gave her a sedative to help her sleep."

"You're sure she's all right?"

"Yessir. I'm sure you'll be able to see her tomorrow."

"I can't wait until then."

"Well, you could wait here a while, if you like. I could let you know if I hear anything."

"Thank you."

She smiled up at him. "You're welcome, sir."

He sat down in one of the hard plastic chairs, aware that the nurse glanced repeatedly in his direction.

Too restless to sit still for long, he paced the hallway for a time, weighing the wisdom of trying to find Kara on his own.

On the pretext of going to the cafeteria, he walked through the hospital's quiet halls. A sign announced that the Isolation Ward was located on the fourth floor.

Taking the stairs, he walked up to the fourth floor, through the double doors marked ISOLATION UNIT. NO VISITORS BEYOND THIS POINT.

A guard sat at a small desk just inside the doors. He stood up as Alex entered the room. "I'm sorry, sir," he said, "No one's allowed in here without authorization."

Alex nodded. "Sorry, I guess I took a wrong turn." He took a deep breath, felt a surge of relief when he caught Kara's scent. She was here. Deeply asleep. "I'm looking for Intensive Care."

"It's on the fifth floor, sir."

"Thank you." For a moment, he considered trying to overpower the guard. But the man was well over six feet tall, and built like a Minnesota line backer. In the end, it seemed wiser to go home than risk causing a scene, at least for now. If they didn't release Kara in the morning, he'd figure out a way to get her the hell out of there.

Leaving the hospital, Alex drew in a deep breath. A glance at the sky told him dawn was fast approaching.

It was early morning when he reached home. He slammed the car door, then stalked out of the garage and into the house, wishing he'd followed his gut instinct and done whatever he had to do to bring Kara home.

He woke late that afternoon, instantly aware that someone had invaded the house. Rising, he pulled on a pair of jeans and a sweatshirt, then padded, barefoot, down the stairs to the kitchen.

"What are you doing here?"

Gail whirled around, her eyes wide. "I've been waiting for you."

"How did you get in?"

"I . . . the back door was unlocked."

Alexander frowned. In his concern for Kara, and his need to rest and replenish his strength, he had apparently neglected to bolt the door.

Gail cleared her throat nervously. "I need your help."

He lifted one brow. "Indeed?"

"I'm worried about Kara."

"Why? What's wrong?"

"We went to see her this morning, but they said we couldn't, that there's something wrong with her and she has to stay for more tests. Nana said she wanted Kara to come home, but the nurse said the paper Nana signed authorized them to keep Kara as long as necessary. I'm afraid something's happened to her and they don't want to tell us."

Alex slammed his hand against the table. He'd known it all along, he thought angrily, known something wasn't right.

Seeing the dark look in his eyes, Gail squealed and backed away.

Alexander took a deep breath. Damn. He hadn't meant to frighten the girl. "Go on."

"That's all. Nana asked to see Dr. Barrett . . ."

"Who's that?"

"He's the doctor who admitted Kara to the hospital. But they said he couldn't be reached. So Nana came home and called Dr. Peterson."

"And?"

"He said he'd get in touch with Dr. Barrett and find out what was going on, only I don't believe him. I want to see my sister."

Gail tried to blink back her tears. She didn't want to cry in front of this man, didn't want him to think she was just some whiny kid. "What do you think's wrong with her?"

Alexander swore a very old, very vile oath. "I don't know, Gail, but I'll find out. I promise you that. Here," he said, offering her a paper towel, "dry your tears. Does your grandmother know you're here?"

"No. She's so upset, she's taken to her bed. Mrs. Zimmermann is staying with her." Gail blew her nose and wiped her eyes. "Do you really think you'll be able to find out what's wrong with Kara? I know it's something awful, or they'd tell us."

"I'll find out what's going on," Alexander said. "Don't doubt it for a minute."

Gail sniffed, then smiled. "I believe you."

"Good. You'd better run on home now. You don't want to upset your grandmother. She has enough to worry about."

"All right. You'll call as soon as you find out what's wrong with Kara?"

"I will."

Impulsively, Gail wrapped her arms around his waist and gave him a hug.

Startled, Alexander could only stare at her. In

two hundred years, no child had ever embraced him. It stirred old feelings, familiar feelings that belonged to another life, another time. He felt oddly bereft when she let him go.

Flashing him a shy smile, Gail ran out of the house.

Alexander stared out the window. Kara was being kept in isolation. He digested that fact, and knew he was to blame.

He had given Kara his blood without considering the consequences. Mixing his blood with hers must have caused some sort of chemical imbalance. No doubt the doctors in charge of her case had been told of the abnormality, and when they couldn't pinpoint it, they had decided to do some experimenting. And what better way to do research than with the source close at hand?

The thought of Kara being kept in isolation while doctors examined her filled him with fury.

And a rising sense of dread as he considered the consequences if Kara's doctors somehow discovered the true cause of the abnormality in her blood.

He could not leave her there. The risk of discovery was too great. He hadn't survived for two hundred years by taking unnecessary chances. For her sake, and for his own, he had to get her out of there.

She woke to darkness. There was a foul taste in her mouth; her stomach felt queasy. For a moment, she lay still, wondering where she was, and then, in a rush, it all came back to her: the examination, Dr. Barrett telling her they wanted to do further tests, her refusal, the prick of the needle in her arm.

She slid her legs over the edge of the bed and

stood up. Groping in the dark, she found a light switch and turned it on.

She was in a small, square room furnished with nothing save the bed and a small table. A door led to a tiny bathroom that had a small sink and a toilet. No shower; no tub. There was a plastic glass on the sink, a thin white washcloth, and a bar of soap.

She washed her hands and face, then filled the glass with lukewarm water and rinsed her mouth. Where was she?

Returning to the other room, she looked around again. There was a window above the bed. Climbing on the mattress, she pulled back the shade. The window was barred.

She whirled around as the door opened.

"You can't get out that way," Dale Barrett said.

"Where am I?"

Barrett closed the door, then leaned against it. "In isolation." He reached into his pocket and withdrew a nasty-looking syringe. "I need to take some blood."

"No."

"We can do this easy or hard, Miss Crawford, it's up to you." His eyes narrowed ominously. "But mark me well, we will do it."

"I want to go home."

"All in good time."

Kara glanced at the syringe, then at the door.

Barrett smiled and shook his head. "The hard way, then." He opened the door, and two men dressed in white lab coats and masks entered the room.

Kara backed away, but there was no place to go, nothing to use for a weapon, no one to hear her if she screamed. She screamed anyway.

Screamed in anger when the two men grabbed her arms, screamed with frustration when they forced her down on the bed.

Screamed in panic when they uncovered the restraints on the bed and strapped her arms and legs to the solid steel frame.

Barrett stood over her, shaking his head. "This would be so much easier for all of us if you would just cooperate."

"Why are you doing this?"

"I told you before. We found an unknown antibody in your blood. We haven't been able to identify it as yet, but it might be toxic. Until we know for sure, we need to keep you isolated, not only for your own protection, but for that of your family and anyone else you might come in contact with."

"An unknown antibody," Kara remarked. "But that's impossible."

"I wish it were. We need to make sure your life isn't in danger." Barrett smiled inwardly, pleased with how readily she had accepted the lie. The unknown antibody in her blood seemed to possess remarkable healing powers. If what he suspected was true, if he was able to reproduce that antibody in quantity, he would be able to save countless lives. It was something he had dreamed of all his life. "Henry, roll up her sleeve."

Barrett pulled a vial of alcohol and a cotton swab from his pocket, then prepared her arm.

Kara flinched as Barrett inserted the needle into her vein. Watched, in morbid fascination, as the syringe filled with blood. "I don't understand. I've had blood tests before, and they've never found anything unusual," she said, her voice betraying her panic. "Maybe one of the donors is the one with the unusual blood type. Why don't you examine them?"

"We have. Nothing irregular about any of them."

"But there has to be!" She stared at the blood. Her blood. Would they take more and more until there was nothing left?

The room began to spin. Barrett's face began to blur. "Alexander." His name was a moan on her lips, a plea, a prayer. "Alexander, help me."

She was afraid, so afraid. "No, don't," she begged, but it was too late. Barrett had pulled another syringe from his pocket. The needle pricked her arm, and the world spun faster.

"Alexander!" She tried to scream his name, but no sound emerged from her lips. . . .

Alex paused as he entered the hospital, all his senses suddenly alert.

And then he heard Kara's voice, screaming in his mind, calling his name.

The lobby was crowded with people. Stifling the urge to run, he made his way down the hallway to the staircase, then took the stairs two at a time until he reached the Isolation Unit.

He peered through the glass on one of the doors. There was no one in sight.

Thanking Fate for his good fortune, he stepped through the door. Kara's scent was stronger now, tinged with fear. He followed it to a green door located at the end of the hall.

He listened a moment to ascertain that she was alone; then he opened the door and stepped inside. The room was dark, but he saw her clearly. She was lying on a narrow bed, breathing deeply.

Silently, he crossed the floor and drew back the

covers. He noted absently that she was wearing a pale green hospital gown, but it was the heavy straps confining her arms and legs that held his attention. He swore under his breath as he unfastened the cruel restraints. She stirred slightly, but didn't awaken.

The sound of footsteps alerted him that someone was coming. A moment later, the door opened and a slender man in a white lab coat stepped inside and flicked on the light switch.

"Damn, you gave me a start!" the man exclaimed. "Who are you, anyway?"

Alexander stared at the tray in the man's hands, at the number of syringes it held. A line from a movie sprang quickly to mind. He uttered it with a wry smile. "Your worst nightmare."

"Yeah, well get the hell out of here. I've got work to do."

"Indeed?"

For the first time, the man seemed to realize he was in danger. "I . . . uh, I can come back later."

"I don't think so. What kind of tests are you doing on the girl?"

"Just blood tests," the man said, taking a wary step backward. "One of the doctors seems to think her blood has some sort of unusual healing agent."

"Indeed? Tell me more."

"I can't. I'm not a doctor or a scientist. I just take samples of blood and urine, that's all."

"You're lying."

The man swallowed noisily. "I . . . uh, overheard them saying they'd injected a diseased rabbit with a little of her blood and the animal recovered completely in a matter of hours."

Alexander swore softly. He knew his blood had

saved Kara's life; it had not occurred to him that her blood might now have the same ability to heal. He glanced past the man, closing the door with the power of his mind.

The man glanced over his shoulder, his expression one of panic as he watched his only means of escape slam shut. Before he could scream, Alexander choked him into unconsciousness.

With a sardonic grin, Alexander filled the empty vials with the man's blood, then carefully replaced the glass tubes in the tray. He stared at the vials for several moments, feeling his mouth water with the ancient urge to drink his enemy's blood. He was reaching for one of the vials when Kara moaned. Muttering an oath, Alex slipped an empty syringe into his pocket, then turned away from the tray.

Lifting Kara, he held her against him with one arm while he picked the man up and put him on the bed in her place.

Cradling Kara against him, he carried her out of the room and shut the door behind him. Moving quietly, he made his way down the corridor to the stairway.

He paused when he reached the ground floor and peered around the corner. A security guard stood at the back entrance, a cigarette in one hand, a Styrofoam cup in the other.

Alexander held Kara close, debating whether he should look for another exit, or knock the guard out. He was still debating what to do when the telephone rang. Grimacing, the guard snubbed out his cigarette and went to answer the phone. With a sigh of relief, Alex hurried down the corridor and out the back door.

Kara stirred in his arms. She moaned softly, then

snuggled against him. He tried to tell himself she didn't know it was him, that she was only seeking the comfort of another body, but the urge to shelter her, to protect her, swelled within him. He had gotten her into this predicament, and he would get her out.

He walked swiftly down the street to where he'd left the Porsche. After settling Kara on the passenger seat, he sat behind the wheel, pondering his next move.

It was late. He would take her to his place for the night, he thought. Tomorrow . . . Alexander frowned. He couldn't let her go home. Not now. He had a terrible feeling that he knew what the doctors had discovered in her blood. If he was right, they wouldn't stop until they had her in their clutches again.

It was near dawn when he reached home. He parked the car in the garage behind the house, then lifted Kara into his arms and carried her inside, up the stairs to the master bedroom. It was the only room he had furnished on the second story. He put her to bed, an odd feeling welling within him as he tucked his blankets around her. He had often imagined her in his bed, but not like this.

For a moment, Alex stood at the foot of the bed, gazing down at her. He would kill anyone who tried to harm her. He did not vocalize the thought, was hardly aware that it had crossed his mind. It was simply a fact, irrefutable, inevitable.

"Rest, Kara," he said quietly. "You're safe now."

"Alexander?"

"I'm here."

Her eyelids fluttered open. "Alexander?"

"I'm here, Kara." He moved to the side of the bed and took her hand in his.

She stared up at him, her eyes unfocused, her expression muddled. "Where am I?"

"Safe now. How are you feeling?"

"Kind of woozy."

He brushed a lock of hair from her brow. "It will pass."

"I'm so thirsty."

"I'll get you a drink." He left the room, returning in moments with a cup of cool water.

Sitting on the edge of the bed, he drew her into his lap and held the cup to her lips. "Slowly," he said.

He could feel her body trembling as she drank the water. When she was finished, he set the cup aside, then wrapped his arms around her.

"Sleep now," he whispered.

Like an obedient child safe in her father's arms, Kara closed her eyes, trusting that he would make her bad dreams go away.

Alex held her until he was certain she was sleeping soundly, then settled her under the covers and left the room.

Outside, he stared, unseeing, into the darkness. An unusual healing agent in her blood, the man had said.

Lost in thought, he moved through the woods, his ears attuned to the sounds of the night. A faint rustling sound caught his attention. Glancing over his shoulder, he saw a large rat regarding him from a pile of leaves. Holding the rodent's gaze, Alex quickly caught the creature.

Returning to the house, he fed the rat a small

amount of poison, then watched impassively as the rodent collapsed.

Taking a knife from one of the kitchen drawers, Alex went upstairs and pricked Kara's finger. She stirred, but didn't awaken as he drew a small amount of her blood into the syringe he'd taken from the clinic. Her blood was unusually dark, he mused, almost as dark as his own.

Returning to the kitchen, he injected her blood into the rat. Within minutes, the rat's strength returned.

"Amazing," Alex muttered as he scooped the creature off the table, careful to avoid its bared teeth.

He frowned as he stared at the empty syringe. His blood had saved Kara's life and, in the process, had wrought a mysterious change in hers. No wonder the doctors were so curious about the unusual antibody in Kara's blood, so eager to test it. No doubt they would be even more interested to discover the true source of that healing power.

He stared at the syringe for a long moment, wondering if mingling his blood with that of another human would produce the same healing agent.

Feeling morbidly curious to see the effect of his own blood in action, he gave the rat a second dose of poison; then, when the rodent was on the brink of death, he injected the rat with his own blood. In less than twenty seconds, the rodent recovered completely.

Alex swore softly as he turned the rat loose outside, then went into his study to work, and to ponder the events of the last few minutes.

The study was his favorite room in the house, the only one that held anything remotely personal, and those items were few: a lock of AnnaMara's hair, kept in a lacquered box; a piece of jade he had picked up in China more than a century ago; an ivory elephant he'd bought in Ceylon; a tapestry that had been woven for him by a woman he barely remembered; several pieces of Navajo pottery; a statue he had found in a small shop in Venice.

There were several paintings on the walls: a peaceful landscape done in muted shades of green and gold, a picture of a young woman who looked remarkably like AnnaMara, a turbulent seascape that was painted in shades of dark blue and gray.

The largest painting hung over the fireplace. It was a brooding piece of work by an unknown artist. The scene depicted a man clad in a long black cloak, looking small and alone as he stood on a mountaintop, his head tilted back as he gazed at a magnificent sunrise.

Not much to show for two hundred and thirty-five years, Alexander mused, and yet he had never been one to pick up souvenirs, to keep mementos of his past. Perhaps because he had such a long past. Or perhaps it was because there had been few occurrences, or people, he wished to remember.

But he would remember Kara. If he lived another two hundred years, he would never forget her. Though he had known her but a short time, she had become a part of him. Knowing it was wrong, knowing that his interference in her life had already cost her dearly, he was nevertheless determined to stay with her as long as possible.

To protect her, if necessary.

To love her, if she would let him.

For as long as she would let him.

Chapter Eight

Kara woke late that afternoon, feeling as though she were awaking from a bad dream. Scattered images lingered in her mind: waking up in a sterile room, being strapped to a bed, Dale Barrett draining her of blood, a nightmare image of Alexander, his mouth stained with crimson.

Fever dreams, she thought, looking around. But this was no dream. She was in a strange bed, in a strange room, clad in a hospital gown.

She sat up, realizing that, in her drugged state, she had confused dreams with reality. But that still didn't tell her where she was.

Slipping out of bed, she drew on the robe hanging on the back of the door, then padded out of the room and down the stairs. The house was empty, silent. She peeked into the parlor, admiring the oak floor, the paneled walls. The furniture was sparse:

a curved sofa with a high back, a single chair covered in a dark green print. An enormous bookcase took up one entire wall. An entertainment center stood opposite the sofa, complete with a TV and a stereo.

There was a small bedroom furnished with a bed and nothing more, a small old-fashioned bathroom with a claw-footed bathtub, and a large kitchen. There was a coffee maker on the counter, along with an unopened can of coffee, a box of filters, and a small box of sugar.

Her stomach growled as she plugged in the coffee pot and filled the container with water. The refrigerator, which was the oldest one she had ever seen, was empty save for a carton of milk, a package of bacon, a dozen eggs, a jar of blackberry jelly, and a carton of butter. There was a loaf of whole wheat bread on the counter. Uncertain of where she was, she hesitated to make herself something to eat. And then she saw the note, propped against a vase that held a single red rose.

Kara, it said, *I know you have many questions, and I regret that I cannot be there to answer them. However, a business appointment calls me away. I'll be gone until late this afternoon. You must not go home under any circumstance, or let your family know where you are. Please make yourself at home and I will explain everything when I return.* It was signed, Alexander.

Kara read the note twice, her confusion mounting. Why shouldn't she go home? Nana must be worried sick. She glanced around, only then remembering that Alexander had no phone. Well, she could walk. It wasn't that far. Of course, she wasn't exactly dressed for a stroll.

First things first, she mused. She was starving. She smiled as she saw that Alexander had set the table for her. There was a frying pan on the stove, and she fixed a quick breakfast of bacon, eggs and toast, and washed it down with a glass of low-fat milk.

She would have washed the dishes, but there was no soap. Frowning, she went through the cupboards, surprised to find they were all empty. No dishes other than those on the table. No packages of cereal or rice. No canned vegetables or fruit. No snacks of any kind. No condiments other than the salt and pepper on the table. Nothing.

She stared at countertop where she had left the dishes to dry. One plate, one knife, one fork, one spoon, one spatula, one frying pan, one cup, one glass. None of the items in the fridge, and those had been few, had been opened. Not the milk, not the butter, nothing. It was as if all the food in the house had been bought for her use. Did he never eat at home?

Still frowning, she went into the den and knew immediately that this was where he spent the majority of his time. He had told her to make herself at home, and so she wandered around the room, admiring a delicate sculpture, a Greek urn that was obviously an antique, the smooth symmetry of a piece of jade, the intricate pattern on a piece of Indian pottery, the muted colors in an exquisite tapestry that also appeared to be very old.

She perused the books in the bookshelf. There were numerous volumes on history, both ancient and modern, several dictionaries, a thesaurus, and a variety of books that dealt with paranormal themes, everything from time travel and reincarnation to werewolves and vampires. One shelf held the complete works of A. Lucard.

Turning away from the bookcase, she paused to study the painting over the fireplace. It was one of the most beautiful things she had ever seen. The man, who stood with his back to her, seemed small and sad as he stood atop a lonely mountain. It was a remarkable painting, the sunrise vibrant with color, so alive she could almost feel the heat of the sun's rays. She would not have been surprised to see the man move.

"Amazing," she murmured.

Alexander's desk was located beside the fireplace. She hesitated a moment, her conscience battling her curiosity, and then she sat down in his chair.

She didn't know what secrets she hoped to find in the desk, but the drawers revealed nothing unusual, only the items one would expect to find in a writer's desk: paper clips, pencils, stamps, envelopes, extra computer disks, a letter from his editor informing him that *The Hunger* had been sold to China, Russia, England, Australia, and Poland.

With a sigh, Kara sat back in the chair. The arms seemed to wrap around her, and for a moment she imagined that it was Alexander holding her.

Abruptly, she leaned forward and switched on the computer. It took only a few moments to find his files, to locate the book he was currently working on.

Feeling as though she were eavesdropping, yet unable to turn away, she read quickly through the first few chapters. It was an interesting story, told in the first person, totally unlike anything else he had written. By the time she reached Chapter IV, she was totally engrossed in the story.

THE DARK GIFT
Chapter IV

She taught me to kill that night. I had seen death before. From plagues. From old age. From injuries that refused to heal. But I had never seen anyone deliberately take a life until that night.

Lilith hunted with the stealth of a cat. She took me into the city and we walked the streets until she found her prey: a fair-haired young man with ruddy cheeks. I watched, chilled to the bone, as she stalked him, following him until he was alone. She took him swiftly, burying her fangs in his throat, her expression one of ecstasy as she drank his blood, his life.

He was not quite dead when she drew away. "Come," she said. "You must drink."

"No." I couldn't. I wouldn't.

"Hurry, *mon ange*," she said. "He will be dead soon, and you must never drink from the dead."

I shook my head, the need inside me struggling with the horror of what she wanted me to do. With what *I* wanted to do. The smell of blood was all around me. I should have been sickened, repelled, disgusted, and I was all of those things. And yet, overriding every other sensation was a horrible hunger that would not rest. It rode me with whip and spurs, goading me, calling to me, urging me to drink, until, with a sob of despair, I fell on the young man, my hands drawing him toward me. I felt a stabbing pain as my teeth transformed into fangs, and then, hating myself, I drank. And drank. Until Lilith pulled me away.

I turned on her, snarling with rage.

"Enough, *mon ange*," she admonished sharply.

We hunted the next night, and the next. Sometimes she stalked her prey, sometimes she flirted with the young men she chose, teasing them, taunting them, leading them on, until she tired of the game and closed in for the kill. It excited her, the power she had. Sometimes she let them struggle, laughing at their puny mortal efforts to overpower her when she had the strength of ten.

I craved the blood, the hunt excited me, but I loathed the killing. And I hated her when, years later, she told me the killing was unnecessary.

"You can spare their lives, if you wish," she remarked one evening. "You can even dine on the blood of beasts, should the need arise."

"I don't have to kill?" I stared at her, thinking of the lives I had taken. "Why didn't you tell me this sooner?"

"I did not think of it," she replied with a shrug, as though the taking of a human life was of no more importance than swatting an insect.

I felt a sickness deep in my soul. I had lost count of the number of people I had killed. I had tried in vain to appease my conscience by telling myself it was necessary, that it was the only way to ease the hunger—that awful, unbearable hunger that would not be refused or denied. Many times I had wished for the courage to end my life, to put an end to the killing, the insatiable hunger, the guilt. And now, as calmly as if she had told me she was going shopping for a new hat, Lilith had informed me that I could have spared all those lives.

Had I been able, I think I would have killed her.

Instead, I resolved to leave her. I was no longer a fledgling, in need of her instruction or her protection. . . .

"What do you think of it?"

Kara gasped, one hand going to her heart, at the sound of his voice. "Oh, Alexander, you startled me. It's very good. One would almost think you write from personal experience."

"Indeed?"

"I . . . I hope you don't mind. My reading it, I mean."

He lifted one thick black brow. "Rather late to be asking my permission, don't you think?"

"I'm sorry. Please don't be angry with me."

"I'm not angry, Kara. How are you feeling?"

"Better, thank you. How did I get here?"

"You don't remember?"

Kara shook her head. "Everything's sort of fuzzy."

Alex slipped his hands into his pockets. Last night, needing to put some space between them, afraid she would ask questions he couldn't answer, he had taken his rest in the attic. Now, looking at her, he wondered how much to tell her.

"I remember Dr. Barrett . . ."

"He was keeping you in isolation. Gail said he wouldn't let your grandmother see you, and she was afraid."

Kara nodded.

"I decided to get you out of there."

A faint smile tugged at her lips. "Like the Seventh Cavalry."

Alex shrugged. "Perhaps you'd like to take a bath, wash your hair," he suggested, abruptly changing the subject.

"Very much. And then I've got to go home. My grandmother must be frantic by now."

"You'll find clean towels and a change of clothing in the bathroom."

Rising, Kara crossed the room and kissed his cheek. "Thank you."

Alexander stared after her, wondering what she would say when he told her she couldn't go home. Not now; perhaps not ever.

Chapter Nine

"What do you mean, I can't go home?" Kara stared at Alexander, her brow furrowed.

"Just what I said," Alexander replied calmly. "You must realize it isn't safe."

"Not safe?" Kara shook her head, completely bewildered.

"Barrett's up to something, Kara. I don't know what, but I don't trust him, and you shouldn't either. Barrett was holding you against your will. They refused to let your grandmother see you."

Kara shook her head, refusing to believe a reputable doctor would be up to something sinister.

"I want to take you away from here."

"Away?" Kara stopped pacing. Standing by the window, she turned to face Alexander. "No, I can't leave Nana, or Gail."

"I don't think you have any choice."

"Dammit, Alexander, you're scaring me!"

"You should be scared. There's something not right here, and until I know what it is, I don't want you going home."

Maybe he was right. Maybe she shouldn't go home right away. She slid a furtive glance in his direction. She couldn't deny the attraction she felt for Alex, couldn't refute the feelings of her own heart, but what did she know about him, really? Nothing. Not one darn thing. And he expected her to go away with him. The thought held a certain appeal, and yet, for all she knew, he could be working with Barrett.

"You can trust me, Kara."

Kara took a step backward. Was he reading her mind? But no, such a thing was impossible. Wasn't it?

"How do you know what I was thinking?" she demanded.

Alexander shrugged. It took less than no effort at all to read her mind, but he couldn't tell her that.

"It's a logical assumption. You have no reason to trust me. In your place, I would feel the same."

She looked skeptical, and more than a little fearful.

"I won't hurt you, Kara. You must believe that."

Alexander ran a hand through his hair. He had to take her away from here. No doubt Barrett was searching for her even now. If what Alex suspected was true, an unscrupulous man could make millions by selling vials of Kara's blood to the sick, the dying. And if they should discover who he was, what he was . . . Alex didn't even want to think of the consequences. He would be questioned, examined, kept in a cage while they harvested his blood.

All these years, Alexander mused. He had lived here two hundred years and never known about the miraculous change that had been wrought in his blood. His inherent powers had multiplied, but he had never suspected that the healing power in his blood could be transferred to another, or that he had the ability to heal the sick as he was able to heal himself. Even when he had given Kara his blood, he hadn't been certain of the outcome.

He felt Kara staring at him. With an effort, he wiped his face clean of expression.

"I've got to go home, Alexander. I can't just disappear without letting Nana and Gail know where I am."

"Right now, I think they're better off not knowing."

"Where do you want to go?"

"I have a place up in Eagle Flats. You'll be safe there."

"Are you sure you want to do this? I mean, won't your life be in danger, too, if you're with me?"

"I don't think your life is in danger, Kara. Only your freedom."

"I wish I knew what this was all about."

"They didn't tell you anything?"

"Not really. Only that there was some abnormality in my blood, and they were afraid it might be contagious, or toxic. They said they'd have to keep me in isolation until they discovered what the problem was." She let out a long sigh of exasperation. "They said they had checked all the blood donors, and all of them were normal."

Alexander grunted softly, waiting for her to make the connection, to ask the questions he couldn't answer.

Kara stared at Alex for a long moment, her mind racing. And then she knew, knew without a doubt.

"It's your blood," she said flatly. "It's your blood that's caused all this trouble, isn't it? That's why you were so interested in my recovery, why you kept coming to see me. You wanted to make sure I was all right."

"Kara . . ."

"It's true, isn't it? Your blood is tainted, or . . . or something."

"I assure you, my blood is quite normal." It wasn't a lie, he thought ruefully. His blood was normal. For him.

"I don't believe you. You're hiding something. I know you are."

She stood frozen in place, her eyes blinking rapidly, her heart pounding even as her mind refused to accept what she was thinking. Good Lord, Gail was right! The thought that Alexander was a vampire was inconceivable, and yet it was the only thing that made sense. She had never seen him during the day. She had never seen him eat . . .

A faint smile curved Alexander's lips as he perceived her thoughts. He wasn't a vampire. Not in the true sense of the word, but he decided that was information best kept to himself. At least for the time being.

"Kara . . ." Alexander held out his hands in a gesture of appeal. "Kara, I assure you, I'm not a vampire."

"You're doing it again!" she exclaimed.

"Doing what?"

"Reading my mind. How do you do that?"

Alex shook his head in denial. He would have to be more careful. "We talked about this once before,

I think. After all, Gail came here looking for a vampire. It's only natural that the thought should linger in your mind. I've had the feeling ever since then that you thought she might be right. Come, I want to show you something."

She hesitated a moment, then followed him out of the den and into the kitchen, wondering what he wanted to show her.

"Look, Kara." He pointed at the window opposite him. "Look."

Confused, she glanced at their reflections in the window.

"Vampires cast no reflection, no shadow." He crossed the floor to the counter, picked up a banana. Peeled it. And took a bite. "They don't eat."

"But your cupboards are empty; you don't have any soap to wash dishes . . ."

"I don't cook." He tossed what was left of the banana into the trash. "I don't like to eat alone. When I get hungry, I go out." He shook his head at the doubtful expression on her face. "Will you feel better if I take you out to dinner on our way to Eagle Flats?"

"Maybe."

"You don't have to be afraid of me, Kara," he said quietly. "I won't hurt you."

She felt suddenly foolish. "Okay, so it was stupid of me to think you were a vampire. It's just that I've been so worried, so . . . so upset by everything that's happened."

"I know." He moved slowly toward her and held out his arms in silent invitation.

She hesitated for the space of a heartbeat, and then she stepped into his embrace, sighing as his arms closed around her.

He stroked her hair. "You'll come away with me, then?"

"Do I have a choice?"

"Not really."

"Why do I have the feeling that you'll truss me up and toss me in the trunk of your car if I say no?"

"Probably because that's just what I'll do."

She wasn't altogether sure he was kidding.

"I think we should leave tonight."

She didn't want to go; she was afraid to stay. In the end, it was easier to give in. "Tonight!" She glanced at the jeans and sweatshirt Alexander had given her earlier. "I can't leave tonight. I need to go home and pack . . ." The words died in her throat. She couldn't go home.

"We'll buy whatever you need on the way."

"Where's my cell phone? I want to call Nana."

Alex shook his head. "Not now."

She stared at him in mutinous silence, but didn't argue. Calls could be traced.

He was relieved that she had decided to see things his way. "Just let me get a few of my things together, and we'll go."

Kara wandered through the house, trying to make some sense of what had happened, while Alexander packed. If none of the blood donors were at fault, maybe the problem was hers, and hers alone. Maybe her blood had always been abnormal and no one had ever detected it before. And maybe it *was* Alexander's blood that was at the root of whatever the problem was, and he was just afraid to tell her.

Going into the den, she sat down in his chair and closed her eyes. Maybe it hadn't been a blood donor at fault at all. Maybe Dr. Peterson had given her the wrong blood. Maybe the hospital had made some kind of mistake, and Barrett had kept her in isolation in hopes of correcting the problem before anyone else found out about it.

Kara smiled grimly. That made far more sense than anything else.

"How long will it take to get to your place?"

"We should be there by tomorrow night."

"I've never been up to Eagle Flats. I hear it's pretty."

"Yes."

Kara stared out the restaurant window. They had left Moulton Bay three hours ago, and her apprehension about running away had increased with every mile that passed. Gail and Nana must be worried sick. She had to call home, had to tell them she was all right.

When the waitress arrived, Kara ordered a Caesar salad and a glass of 7-Up, then excused herself to go to the rest room.

Heart pounding, she stepped into the phone booth near the rest rooms and dialed the operator. Moments later, Gail answered the phone. Kara's fingers tapped nervously on the wall as she waited for Gail to say she would accept the charges.

"Gail, I don't have time to talk or explain. I just want you to know I'm okay. Tell Nana not to worry."

"Kara, where are you? Two men from the hospital came here looking for you. They said you've got some contagious disease."

"It isn't true, honey, don't worry. Listen, I've got to go. I'll call you again as soon as I get a chance."

"Kara . . ."

"I love you, Gail. Bye."

Kara hung up the phone, then pressed her forehead against the wall. Men were looking for her. Maybe she really was sick. Maybe just being out in public was putting innocent lives in danger. . . .

"Kara."

Startled by his voice, she turned around.

"You called home, didn't you?"

She felt a shiver of trepidation at the accusation in his eyes. "I had to."

"It was a stupid thing to do."

She started to argue, then changed her mind. He was right. It had been stupid. Whoever was looking for her might have managed to bug Nana's phone. Perhaps, even now, Dale Barrett or someone like him was speeding down the highway toward the restaurant.

"You're right, it was stupid. I'm sorry."

"We'd better go."

"But . . . what about our food?"

"We'll get something on the road."

Alexander left some money on the table and they left the restaurant.

Kara sat huddled in her seat as Alex turned the key in the ignition. The engine hummed to life and Alex pulled out of the parking lot. Kara glanced over her shoulder, her gaze sweeping the parking lot and the road behind them. Were they being followed, even now? Why hadn't she listened to Alex? Why was she with Alex? Maybe he was in on it. Maybe she'd jumped out of the frying pan and into the fire. . . .

She slid a glance in his direction. He was staring straight ahead, watching the road, but she had the distinct impression that he knew her every thought.

How could she keep him from reading her mind? If she wanted to get away from him, how could she do it if he knew what she was thinking, feeling?

Forty-five minutes later, he pulled into a McDonald's drive-through and ordered burgers and fries and two large cups of coffee.

She couldn't stifle a feeling of relief when she saw Alex bite into the hamburger. After all, one bite of a banana didn't really prove anything, and no matter what she'd said to the contrary, she hadn't been able to shake the feeling that there was something inhuman about Alexander Claybourne. Now, watching him eat something as mundane as a Big Mac and fries made her realize how ludicrous such thoughts had been.

The darkness and the motion of the car made her sleepy. Leaning her head back against the seat, she closed her eyes.

Kara came awake slowly. Keeping her eyes closed, she turned over, thinking she'd just sleep for another ten minutes, and then she'd get up and go to work. . . .

And then she remembered. She wasn't going to work today, perhaps not for a long time. With a start, her eyelids flew open and she found herself staring into Alexander's face, which was only inches from her own.

He was lying on his side, asleep. In her bed. She glanced around the room. A motel, obviously, judging from the ugly picture bolted to the wall and the pay TV. She peeked under the covers, felt her cheeks grow hot when she saw that she wore only her bra and underpants. He'd undressed her while she slept.

Her gaze flew back to Alex's face. He was still sleeping. It wasn't right for a man to be so beautiful, she thought. His lips were full and perfect. His nose was straight. His lashes were thick and dark. His skin was an even brown, as though he spent a great deal of time in the sun, yet she had never seen him in daylight. . . .

He couldn't be a vampire! It was ludicrous to even think such a thing. He was, however, very much a man. A very attractive and desirable man. The thought of being in bed with him when he woke up was something she didn't even want to consider.

Moving as carefully as possible, she eased over to her side of the mattress and sat up. Looking at her watch, she saw that it was almost four. She'd never slept so late in her life.

Grabbing her clothes from the chair, she went into the bathroom to take a shower.

Alex groaned softly as the bathroom door closed behind Kara. He had slept at her side through what had been left of the night and all day long, aware of every move she made. Several times, she had brushed against him; once, she had cuddled up to him. Not even the fact that he had slept in his jeans had kept his body from reacting to her nearness, to the brush of her thigh against his leg, the touch of her hand on his bare chest.

He had not been with a woman he cared for in more years than he cared to recall, and the need that had surged through him had been excruciating. It was not common for those of his kind to go so long without sexual gratification. Kara's nearness, added to the fact that he was becoming increasingly fond of her, had fueled his desire. The fact that she was beautiful, inside and out, and less than a breath away, had been sheer torture. A torment he could have easily escaped by sleeping on the chair, or on the floor, yet he had been powerless to resist the opportunity to be near her.

He felt his desire spring to life anew when he heard the shower. The thoughts and images running rampant through his mind shamed him, yet he could not help but imagine how she looked standing under the water. . . .

With an oath, he threw the covers aside and got out of bed. There was a carafe of hot water and some packets of instant coffee on the table in front of the window and he quickly made a cup, then drank it down, cursing softly as the hot liquid burned his tongue. Served him right, he thought irritably.

Pulling back the heavy curtains, he glanced outside. The sky was heavily overcast and promised rain before the day was out. He was standing at the window, staring out into the parking lot, when he heard the bathroom door open. Taking a deep breath, he counted to ten, then turned around.

"I'm sorry," Kara said, "I didn't mean to wake you."

"You didn't. There's coffee on the table."

Kara nodded, wondering why he seemed so tense.

"I'm going to take a shower, then we'll go. We'll get something to eat on the road."

"All right." She went to fix herself a cup of coffee, acutely conscious of Alex moving about behind her as he pulled clean clothes from the duffel bag he had packed the night before.

She heard the bathroom door shut, and she let

out the breath she'd been holding.

It was close to six that evening when they left the motel. The tension between them seemed to grow as the night went on. After they left the motel, they had stopped at a roadside restaurant for dinner, and again at a strip mall so she could buy some clothes.

Since she had no money with her and didn't want to be indebted to Alex for more than was absolutely necessary, Kara had selected only a few essential items, but Alex had insisted she buy several dresses, as well as slacks and sweaters, shoes, socks, a nightgown, robe and slippers, as well as toiletries. She had promised to pay him back, but he had dismissed her offer with a wave of his hand.

"I don't need your money, Kara," he had said quietly.

The words *What do you need?* had risen in her throat, but she had choked them back, afraid of what his answer might be.

Chapter Ten

Kara stared out the window, watching the lights of the city grow faint as Alex drove the Porsche up the narrow mountain road.

"When do you think I can go back home?" she asked after a lengthy silence.

"When I think it's safe."

"When will that be?"

"I don't know, Kara. I'm sorry."

Kara chewed on her lower lip, wondering how he'd know when it was "safe." Tall pines lined the winding road as they climbed upward. They had been traveling all night, stopping only to buy gas or to get something to eat, although Alex ate very little. Their last stop had been at a grocery store, where Alexander had bought several blocks of ice and an ice chest, along with enough food to supply a small army. Soon, they would arrive at his place. And then what?

She was all too conscious of the physical attraction that hummed between them, vital, irrefutable, almost tangible. How could they live in the same house day after day without . . . A wave of heat flooded her cheeks at the thought of being in his arms, in his bed. How could she feel this way about a man she hardly knew?

She didn't remember falling asleep, but she woke with a start when the car came to a stop. Disoriented, she sat up and looked around.

"It's all right, Kara," Alexander said. "We're here."

Here proved to be on top of a mountain. "But . . ." Kara frowned at Alexander. "Where's the house?"

"It isn't a house, exactly."

"What is it then, exactly? A cave?"

A faint smile curved his lips. "In a manner of speaking."

Without further explanation, he got out of the car and removed two of the cardboard boxes from the trunk.

With a sigh, Kara reached into the back seat. Grabbing the packages that contained her new clothes, she slid out of the car and followed Alexander along a short dirt path that led to what looked like a dead end. Her heart seemed to jump into her throat as she peered over the narrow ledge. One misstep would send her plummeting a thousand feet into the valley below.

She moved closer to Alexander, watching in silent fascination as he placed his hand over an oddly shaped striation in the rock face. There was a low rumble, and then, to Kara's astonishment, a portion of the rock slid back, revealing a large cavern hewn out of the mountain.

Shades of *Star Trek* and *Indiana Jones*, Kara thought. She stood at the entrance for a moment, then followed Alexander into the dark maw.

She saw the movement of his hand. The mountain closed behind them. Light flooded the antechamber.

Kara blinked as she glanced around. The walls of the cavern were fashioned of smooth white stone. She looked up at the ceiling, but could not detect the source of the light.

"Coming?"

Kara glanced at Alexander, who was watching her carefully. "You are going to explain all this, aren't you?"

"Later."

"Later? I don't think so." She dropped her packages on the floor—on the ground, actually—and stared at him, her arms crossed over her chest.

Alexander moved down the narrow passageway. "I'm going to put this stuff away, then go back and get the rest," he said. "Your room is the first door on the left at the end of this passage."

"Infernal man," Kara muttered.

Retrieving her packages, she made her way down the corridor. She passed a dark room on her right—the living room, perhaps? Another few steps took her to the first door on the left. There was no knob, no lock. With a grimace, she stared at the blank wooden door; then, remembering how Alex had opened the portal to the cavern, she placed her hand against the wood. The entrance slid open, and after a moment's hesitation, she stepped inside.

It was a small, oval-shaped room. There was a

double bed topped with a dark blue quilt, an elegant three-drawer dresser made of antique oak, an oil lamp fashioned of brass with a delicate glass chimney, and a beautiful Navajo rug woven in muted shades of blue and green. Nothing else. A small round window made of thick glass overlooked the valley below.

She crossed the floor and touched the window, wondering how he had managed to put a window in the side of a mountain. The glass felt odd, hard and soft at the same time.

Frowning, she turned to regard the room again. It was spartan, she thought, but what furnishings the room contained were exquisite.

It took only a few minutes to unpack, and then she went to look for Alexander, determined to find the answers to the questions tumbling through her mind.

The room across from hers appeared to be the kitchen. It held a small, square table, a single chair, a Coleman stove, several ice chests, and a small sink. Where, she wondered, did the water come from, and where did it go?

She tapped her finger on the counter. The water probably came from a spring. As for where it went . . . she stooped and opened the door under the sink. A pipe ran from the sink into a hole cut in the floor. Rising, she grunted softly. No doubt the water drained directly into the mountain. There were several shelves cut into the rock wall, which held a few cups and plates and some pots and pans.

Two steps carved from stone led down into a large sunken room. There was a fireplace in one corner. The vent went through the rock ceiling. Clever, she mused. No doubt it reappeared on top of the mountain where any telltale smoke would be diffused by the trees. A large oil lamp sat on a smooth-topped tree stump beside an oversized black leather sofa. Soft yellow light from the lamp filled the room.

There was a large oak bookcase along one wall. Every shelf was filled with books. What looked to be a bearskin was spread in front of the fireplace. A small round window offered a view similar to that in the bedroom.

Kara shook her head. Mountains that moved. Windows cut into solid rock. Glass that felt hard and soft at the same time. What next?

"Alexander?"

She stepped into the corridor and headed toward what she hoped was the entrance, only to meet Alexander coming toward her, the last of the groceries cradled in his arms.

"Here," she said, reaching for one of the cartons. "Let me help."

Her fingers brushed his as he handed her one of the boxes, and she felt a frisson of heat shoot up her arm. He felt it, too—she knew it by the sudden awareness that flickered in his eyes. Face to face, neither speaking, they regarded each other for a long moment before Alexander stepped past her, headed for the kitchen.

They spent the next twenty minutes putting the groceries away. When the last can had been put on the shelf, Kara turned to face Alexander.

"It's later," she said.

Alexander sighed. "It's quite simple, really," he said. "I own the mountain. I built this place as a sort of retreat."

"Retreat? From what? World War Three?"

116

"Why not?"

Kara shook her head. "I don't buy it, Alex. Not for a minute."

"Believe me or not, Kara, it's your choice. But the truth is, I do own this mountain, and I did build this place."

Incredibly, she did believe him. She also knew he wasn't telling her the whole truth. "How does one install windows in a mountain? And what about that glass?"

"What about it?"

"I don't know, it feels . . . funny. And the light in the entrance to this place. Where does it come from?"

Alexander ran a hand through his hair. She was too smart, too curious, for her own good. And his.

Kara tapped her foot on the floor. "I'm still waiting for those answers."

"Modern technology, Kara. It's as simple as that. The glass is made to withstand stress. The light is recessed."

She stared at him for a long moment, and he knew she was considering his answers. "So, what do we do now?"

"Stay put, for a while at least. We've got enough food to last several weeks. There's plenty of water. Wood for a fire."

"Heat, food, and shelter," Kara said with a faint grin. "All that primal man needed to survive."

"It has served me well in the past."

She lifted one finely arched brow. "Is there a . . . a rest room?"

"A small one. It's the last door at the end of the passage. There's no bathtub or shower, I'm afraid. When you wish to wash, you can do so in the sink, or you can bathe in the hot spring located a short distance from here."

Kara sighed. She had never liked camping, and even though this wasn't a tent outdoors, it was still far too rustic for her taste.

"I'm sorry," Alexander said, observing her obvious dismay. "Hopefully, we won't have to stay here too long."

"Hopefully."

"It's late," he said. "You must be tired."

"Yes." She folded her arms, suddenly very much aware that she was alone in a cave with a man she hardly knew, a man whose dark eyes smoldered with desire. A man who was far too tempting for her peace of mind.

Drawing her gaze from his, she wished him a good night and went to her room. Inside, she took several deep breaths. She had to accept the fact that she might be here for several days; weeks, perhaps. She couldn't contact Gail or Nana. She'd surely lose her job.

Standing there, it was hard to believe anyone wanted to do her harm. Easier to believe that Alexander had kidnapped her and brought her to this strange place for his own ends. She waited for some sense of fear, of terror, but none came. Instead, a creeping warmth spread through her as she thought of spending her days and nights here, alone, with Alexander Claybourne.

She remembered the nights he had met her in her grandmother's backyard. His kisses had been more potent than her grandfather's Irish whiskey, his voice husky with suppressed longing. The attraction that had sizzled between them had been dampened by Dale Barrett's attempt to hospitalize her, but it hadn't dissipated, not completely. It was still there, simmering beneath the surface.

Her stomach fluttered as she undressed, then slipped into the floor-length baby-blue nightgown Alexander had bought her. She smoothed her hands over the silky material, wondering what he would think if she went to his room and slid under the covers beside him.

It was a pleasant fantasy and she dwelled on it for several minutes before extinguishing the lamp and crawling into bed. The blanket smelled faintly of Alexander. She ran her hand over the pillow, imagining him lying there beside her, his big body sheltering hers.

Sleep was a long time coming.

Alexander paced the floor, his muscles taut as he pictured Kara in his room, lying in his bed, her head on his pillow. He had not stayed here for any length of time in years. Long ago, it had been his haven, a place of refuge, of safety. Now he came here only on rare occasions.

He prowled the room for several minutes, then wandered down the corridor. Pausing at Kara's room, he pressed his ear to the door, comforted by the soft, steady sound of her breathing.

Whirling away from the door, he went outside and stood on the ledge that overlooked the fertile valley below. Lifting his arms overhead, his face turned up to the night sky, he absorbed the moon's pale silver light as another might bask in the golden glow of the sun.

Seconds lengthened into minutes. Eyes closed, he drew the moon's energy deep within the core of his being. The coolness of the light rejuvenated him; the faint whisper of the wind as it blew over the mountaintop filled him with a sense of peace. Of home . . .

Alexander swore softly. Why had he thought that? He had not thought of home in years. Now, a flood of memories spilled into his mind—recollections best forgotten, remembrances that could, after all these years, still cause him pain.

AnnaMara . . . AnTares . . .

Their names whispered through the corridors of his mind like the breeze filtering through the leaves of the trees. His arms felt suddenly heavy and he lowered them to his sides.

So many years had passed since he had last seen his home. So many years since he had last seen the dark mountains that surrounded the city where he had been born, their jagged peaks like the teeth of a sloe-eyed boar. He could almost hear the distant rumble of thunder as one of ErAdona's many dry storms passed overhead. And, if he closed his eyes, he could almost hear AnnaMara humming softly as she worked in the garden. Sweet, gentle Anna-Mara . . .

"Alexander?"

With a start, he whirled around to find Kara standing in the moonlight. Clad in a long blue gown, she looked like a goddess bathed in quicksilver and shadow.

"Did you need something?" he asked.

"I had a bad dream and I . . . When I looked for you, you were gone."

"I was just getting some fresh air." He saw the curiosity in her eyes and wondered if she would put her question into words.

She hesitated for the space of a heartbeat. "Why

were you standing in the moonlight like that?" For a moment, it had looked as though he had been absorbing the essence of the moonlight into his body, but that was ridiculous.

"Like what?"

"I don't know. Almost like you were . . ." She shrugged. "I don't know. It looked pagan, somehow."

"Indeed? Are you afraid I might be planning to sacrifice you to some heathen god?"

"Of course not." In spite of her bold words, she took a step backward, folding her arms over her breasts in a protective gesture that was as old as time.

"You're quite safe, I assure you."

"When I couldn't find you, I went looking for another bedroom, but there isn't one. I didn't mean to put you out of your bed."

We could share it, you and I. The words, though unspoken, hovered between them.

Kara's gaze locked with Alexander's. Heat radiated from the depths of his black eyes, warming her as effectively as a furnace. She felt her limbs grow heavy, her knees weak. Her heart seemed to slow to a stop, and then it began to beat rapidly, as though she'd been running for miles in the hot sun.

"Kara . . ." His voice was low and rough, almost raw.

She tried to look away, but at that moment, no power on earth could have drawn her gaze from his. Desire blazed in his eyes, awakening an answering hunger deep within her being, making her yearn to be in his arms.

Alexander swore under his breath. It was wrong, and he knew it. But he reached for her anyway. And she stepped into his embrace willingly, a sigh of contentment escaping her lips as his arms closed around her.

"Alex?"

She tilted her head back, and he gazed into her eyes, beautiful blue eyes that were smoky with desire. Her lips parted invitingly; a faint flush pinked her cheeks.

With a groan, he slanted his mouth over hers and kissed her. A distant rumble of thunder echoed the hammering of his heart as he drew her closer, felt her body fit itself to his.

He drank from her lips, savoring her sweetness. She was warm in his arms, warm and willing. It would be so easy to take her, to sweep her into his arms and carry her to bed, to bury himself deep within her. So easy . . . and afterward, she would hate him for it, hate him for what he was, for not telling her the truth.

With an effort, he wrenched his mouth from hers and drew back. "Kara . . ."

"Don't talk. Just hold me."

And because he couldn't bear to let her go, he closed his eyes, his chin resting lightly on the top of her head. He would hold her as often, and as long, as she would let him. And how long would that be, he wondered, when she knew what he was?

He didn't know how long they had been standing there when he felt her shiver against him.

"You're cold," he said, and lifting her into his arms, he carried her into the cavern.

He held her easily in one arm as he closed the door, and then he carried her into the main room and sat down on the sofa.

Kara closed her eyes, her head nestled against

Alexander's shoulder. She felt a sudden warmth, and when she opened her eyes again, there was a fire in the hearth.

Kara lifted her head and stared at Alexander. "How did you do that?"

"Do what?"

"Light the fire."

"It was already lit."

"No, it wasn't."

Alex went suddenly still and, for a moment, Kara thought he had stopped breathing. A deep sigh escaped his lips as he settled her on the sofa and stood up.

"What's wrong, Alex?"

He looked into her eyes, those dreamy blue eyes that had captivated him from the beginning, and knew he couldn't deceive her any longer.

"There's something you need to know," he said heavily. "Something I should have told you a long time ago."

Kara's hand flew to her throat as an icy coldness spread over her. He *had* been hiding something from her. She had known it all along. Something about her condition, whatever it was. And from the look on his face, it wasn't good news. Dear Lord, had he brought her up here to tell her she was going to die?

She stared up at him, her heart pounding heavily. "What is it, Alex?"

Alexander swore a vile oath. Where to start?

"Alex, tell me!"

"Kara, do you remember I told you once that you must never love me, or trust me?"

"Yes." She frowned, wondering what that had to

do with whatever it was that was wrong with her blood.

"Kara, I'm not from here."

She frowned. Not from Eagle Flats? What did that have to do with anything?

Alex shook his head. "I mean I'm not from Earth."

She stared at him blankly. She heard the words, but they made no sense. Not from Earth? What was he talking about?

"I came here more than two hundred years ago from a distant planet."

"Alex, this is no time for jokes."

"Believe me, I am not joking."

Kara grimaced. "Alex, please . . ."

"It's the truth."

Speechless, she continued to stare at him. It would have been easier to believe he was a vampire. At least vampires were, or had been, human. . . .

"You were right, Kara," he said quietly. "There's nothing wrong with your blood. Nor is there anything wrong with my blood."

He paused, and Kara stared at him, her breath trapped in her throat.

"There's nothing wrong with my blood," he repeated, and his voice was infinitely sad, "except that it's alien blood."

Alex ran a hand through his hair, determined to tell her the truth, or at least as much of it as he thought she could handle at the moment.

"Did you know Gail came to me when you were in the hospital? She thought I could help you. I don't know what drew me to your side that night, but I felt compelled to give you some of my blood. Even now, I'm not sure why."

He paused, his hands clenched into fists. "The same compulsion drew me back the next night. Then, when you were in the hospital in Grenvale, I learned there'd been some sort of drastic change in your blood, and I knew it had to be the result of mingling my blood with yours. The night I took you to my house, I caught a rat and fed it poison. When it was near death, I injected the rat with some of my blood. It recovered in less than a minute."

He paced the length of the floor, then stopped and stared into the fire. "Something in the air of your earth, the water, I don't know what, must have caused some kind of chemical mutation in my blood. I don't know what. I don't know why."

Kara couldn't speak. She could only stare at him. The rational part of her mind insisted that his story was simply too bizarre to be believed while another part, some tiny totally illogical part, had to smile. If Alex was to be believed, then Gail had been right all along. There were aliens. Perhaps there were vampires as well. Maybe Nessie did exist. And Bigfoot.

Slowly, she shook her head. "I don't believe you. It's impossible."

"Maybe you'll believe this," he said, and turning away from her, he removed his shirt and trousers.

Kara stared at Alexander's back. Part of her mind registered the fact that he didn't wear anything underneath his clothes, that he was tall and broad-shouldered and perfectly formed, but even as she found herself admiring his well-muscled physique, she felt herself recoiling from the visible proof staring her in the face. A dark, diamond-shaped pattern ran down the length of his spine, feathered across

125

his buttocks, and continued down the backs of his legs.

It reminded her of the kind of skin peculiar to the alien invaders she'd seen on an old TV series.

He glanced at her over his shoulder. "Convinced?" His voice was hard and cold and flat.

"What . . . is that?"

"It's perfectly normal."

"Normal?"

"Indeed."

Hardly aware that she was moving, Kara stood up and approached him. Hesitantly, she ran one fingertip over his spine, exploring the raised ridge of flesh that ran the length of his back. It felt coarser, thicker, than the rest of his skin, almost like soft leather. The dark stripe grew lighter in both color and texture as it continued below his waist and down the backs of his legs.

Repelled, yet curious, she touched him again, felt him shudder as her fingers brushed against his spine. Thinking she had hurt him in some way, she withdrew her hand.

But she couldn't tear her gaze away from his broad back, from that peculiar ridge of inhuman flesh. It was unlike anything she had ever seen. Alien. And even as she stared at his back, at the strangely compelling pattern on his spine, she found herself wondering if he was different from earthly men in other ways.

Riveted to the spot, she watched the play of muscles in his back as he slipped on his shirt and trousers.

Unable to help herself, she backed away from him when he turned around to face her.

"You're afraid of me now," he said, and there was

a wealth of sadness in his voice.

Incapable of speech, Kara shook her head. *Alien. Alien.* The words repeated themselves in her mind.

The fear in her eyes pained Alex far more than he had anticipated.

"I won't hurt you, Kara," he said quietly. "I'd swear it on everything I once held dear if I thought you would believe me."

She swallowed hard, wishing she could think of something witty or brilliant to say. Instead, she felt her throat grow thick, felt the sharp sting of tears behind her eyes.

"Kara, say something."

She lifted her shoulders and let them fall. "Gail will be thrilled to know she was right," she murmured, and burst into tears.

He took a step toward her, wanting, needing, to comfort her, but her outthrust hand held him at bay.

"Don't touch me!" On the verge of hysteria, Kara turned and ran out of the room, sobbing.

Chapter Eleven

He stared after her while shards of pain splintered through him. The sound of her voice seemed to reverberate off the walls: *Don't touch me! Don't touch me . . . Don't . . .*

A coarse oath escaped his lips. He hadn't let himself care for anyone in two hundred years. Not that he had lived like a monk. Though he wasn't human, he was still a man, with a man's hungers, a man's needs. Needs that, since coming to earth, had been gratified only after a cash transaction. The women who had satisfied his lust had been willing to do whatever he asked. A few had thought it odd that he insisted the room they met in be kept completely dark; most had thought it strange that he refused to let them see him naked, but he hadn't cared. He had never spent more than fifteen minutes with any of them. He had satisfied his lust and left their beds, ashamed of the need that had driven him to seek them out in the first place. Never, in two hundred years, had he trusted another living soul with the knowledge of who and what he was. He had lived on the edge of humanity, alone but never really lonely, until he gazed into Kara Crawford's dreamy blue eyes.

Now, for the first time, he had found a woman whose touch he craved. He had risked letting her know who he was, had shown her what he was, and she had looked at him with horror and revulsion. It shouldn't have hurt. It was exactly the reaction he had expected, but that didn't lessen the pain.

His steps were heavy as he left the cavern. He stood in the yard, hardly aware of the rain as he pondered what to do next. He couldn't take her home. She wouldn't want to stay here, not with him, not now.

How could he let her go?

How could he make her stay?

He couldn't. Tomorrow he would give her the keys to his car. If she was smart, she would find a place to hide, someplace where no one knew who she was.

No doubt she would feel safer with Barrett than with him.

Weary to the depths of his soul, he stared up at the night sky. His world was out there, millions of miles away in another galaxy, and everyone he had ever known, everyone he had ever loved, was long dead. As he should have been.

He felt suddenly tired—tired of being alone, tired of living in the shadows. Tired of living, period.

Crossing the yard, he activated the opening in the rock face, then stepped out onto the narrow ledge.

He stared dispassionately into the blackness that yawned below, and for the first time since he'd arrived on earth, he contemplated ending his life. It would be so easy. One step over the edge into nothingness and all his troubles would be over. . . .

"Alex? Alex, where are you?"

He whirled around at the sound of her voice.

"What are you doing out here?" Kara asked, glancing around.

"Nothing."

She stared past him, her eyes widening with the realization of what he meant to do.

Taking hold of his arm, she gave a slight tug. "Come inside," she urged. "We need to talk."

He shook off her hand; then, as though he had no mind or will of his own, he followed her through the opening, touched the lever to close the portal, then followed her into the cavern.

Kara sat down on the sofa. Alex stood at the opposite end of the room, his hands shoved deep into the pockets of his Levi's.

"What do you want to talk about?" His voice was flat, emotionless.

Kara's raised her eyebrows. "What do you think?"

"I would think you'd be anxious to get away from here." He withdrew his right hand from his pocket and tossed his car keys at her. "You can leave any time you wish."

"Just like that?"

"Just like that."

Kara looked at the keys in her hand, then dropped them on the low table beside the sofa. "I thought you were going to protect me."

"Indeed? And who's going to protect you from me?"

"Do I need protecting from you?"

"What do you think?"

"Alexander, I'm sorry for what happened before. But you've got to understand. I mean . . ." She held out her hands, palms up. "You can't blame me for being a little shocked."

"And you're not shocked anymore?"

"I don't know. It's . . . it's just so hard to believe. Even after . . . after what you showed me."

He didn't say anything, just looked at her, his gaze shuttered and cold. She could feel the tension radiating from him, see it in the rigid set of his shoulders.

"Tonight . . . the fire in the hearth. It wasn't already lit, was it? You did it."

"Yes."

"How?"

"I don't know how to explain it to you, Kara. I think it, and it's done."

"Is that how you cut windows in the mountain?"

"No. I have some . . . some tools from home."

"Did you make the glass in the windows?"

"Yes."

"What other tricks can you do?"

"More than you want to know."

"I never saw you during the day. Why?"

"Earth's sun is much stronger than that of Er-Adona. Even a little is like poison to me."

"So you sleep during the day and go out at night."

"Yes." He smiled enigmatically. "Just like Dracula."

"You said you came here over two hundred years ago."

"Yes."

He didn't look a day over thirty-five. Perhaps two

131

hundred was considered middle-aged where he came from. "Do all your . . . Is it normal for your . . . your people to live so long?"

"No."

"Talk to me, Alexander, please. I want to understand."

She lookcd so earnest, Alex felt himself relenting in spite of his determination to keep her at arm's length.

"I don't know why I've lived so long. At home, a normal life span is a hundred and twenty-five years."

"Are you immortal, then?"

Alex shook his head. "I don't think so, but I must have undergone some sort of mutation. I don't know. I only know that my body's aging process has slowed. As near as I can tell, I've only aged about ten years since I came here."

Ten years in two centuries, Kara mused. It was incredible. Beyond comprehension. Imagine living for centuries instead of decades. Never being sick. It was the fabled Fountain of Youth, only there were no magical waters. The magic was in Alex's blood. And yet, for Alex, it hadn't been a miracle, but a curse. Two hundred years of loneliness, of avoiding the sun, of living in the shadows, on the edge of humanity. No wonder he wrote about vampires!

"Alexander? Why did you come here?"

His gaze slid away from hers. He was reluctant to tell her the truth, certain it would only make her more afraid of him than she already was. And yet, she had a right to know.

"Alex?"

"There is no war where I come from," he said,

speaking slowly. "No crime as you know it. We have no need for locks or jails. Our society is one of total peace and tranquility. Before I was . . . before I left, there had been no crime for over three hundred years."

"That's amazing!"

"Not really. Punishment on ErAdona is swift and final. There are no second chances." His gaze met hers. "My distant ancestors were an uncivilized and warlike people. After centuries of bloodshed and violence, the women of my planet decided it was time for peace. They gathered their children around them and barricaded themselves in the cathedrals, refusing to come out until the men destroyed their weapons of hand-to-hand combat and swore to live in peace.

"In time, we invented sophisticated weapons of war to repel invaders, but there are no confrontations among our own people. It is not tolerated."

Alex inhaled deeply, then blew out a long, slow breath. "But even in the most placid of societies, there are occasionally those who refuse to conform . . ."

He paused and Kara saw his hands ball into fists. Was he speaking of himself? "Go on."

"His name was Rell and he was the son of one of ErAdona's ruling families. He . . . he wanted a woman who belonged to another, and when she refused him, he took her by force. And then, when he realized what he had done, he . . . he killed her. He buried her body in a dry lake where he hoped it would never be found. . . ."

Alex's voice trailed off. He was staring at his hands, clenching and unclenching them, and Kara knew he was caught up in the past, that he had forgotten she was there.

"Alexander?"

He blinked several times. "I found her three weeks later." He would never forget the horror of it, the dark black blood encrusted in her hair and clotted over the hideous gash at her throat, the awful smell of her decomposing body.

"AnnaMara . . ." Unbidden, her name whispered past his lips.

"Alex, it's all right. You don't have to tell me any more."

"I found the man who killed her, and I choked the life out of him with my bare hands. And then . . ."

He looked at Kara, at the compassion shining in her eyes, and knew he could not tell her the rest, could not tell her that he had hacked Rell's body to pieces.

He paced the floor, suddenly restless. "When the council learned what had happened, I was arrested and confined to my dwelling. Some of the council members argued that I should be executed, since, like Rell, I had also taken a life. But my father intervened in my behalf, reminding the council that, anciently, it would have been my right to avenge my wife's honor. And so the council decided to be lenient." He spat the last word from his mouth as if it tasted bad. "Instead of having me executed, I was exiled. My parents were entrusted with the care of my daughter, and I was banished from our galaxy to this small, warlike planet."

"I'm sorry, Alex, truly I am."

He stopped pacing and stared into the hearth. "They refused to let me see my daughter before I was sent away," he said, his voice dull with grief. "And now she's dead."

Kara bit down on her lower lip, wishing she could erase the hurt from his past. Wanting to comfort him, she went to stand behind him, hoping her presence would ease his pain. She stared at his rigid back, compelled to reach out, to offer the solace of her touch.

"Don't," he said. "Don't touch me. There's blood on my hands, in my soul."

"Alex, please let me help."

"Nothing can help. Go away, Kara. Now, while you can."

She stared at his back for a long moment, then turned and left the room.

In bed, huddled under the blankets, Kara stared at the ceiling, her heart breaking for the pain Alex had suffered. He had avenged his wife's death, and lost everything. It wasn't fair. She tried to imagine a world without war, without crime, without poverty. Without Alex.

Turning on her side, she closed her eyes, her own troubles seeming minor compared to those of the man in the other room.

There was a terrible awkwardness between them the next day. Kara had prepared a late breakfast, always conscious of the man in the next room. Alex hadn't eaten anything, only drunk a cup of hot black coffee.

He had stood in the living room, staring out the small round window, his hands shoved into his pants pockets, while she ate her solitary meal, then washed the dishes in water warmed by a solar heater. And all the while she had tried to think of some way to ease the strained silence between them.

She had yearned to go to him, to run her fingers through his hair, to press her cheek against his broad back and tell him she was sorry, but she was afraid—afraid of what he was, afraid of being re-buffed, and even more afraid of what might happen between them if she stayed. And so she had eaten her solitary breakfast and then washed and dried the dishes.

And now she stood in the opening between the living room and the kitchen, staring at his back and wondering what to do.

"It's stopped raining." His voice was low and soft, yet she had no trouble hearing him. "You should go now."

"Go?"

He nodded. "Take my car and whatever else you need."

For a moment, the thought held a certain appeal. She could leave this place, this strange, troubled man, and go home. Only she couldn't go home. Bar-rett might be waiting for her.

Kara shuddered, remembering the deranged look in the doctor's eyes when he spoke of testing her blood. She knew now what he was looking for. He had discovered the healing agent in Alex's blood . . . She caught her breath with the realization that freedom lay within her reach. All she had to do was get to a phone, call Barrett, and tell him that it was Alex's blood that held the strange antibody.

The thought had barely crossed her mind when Alex turned away from the window, his deep black gaze locking on hers.

"Go on," he said, his voice bitter. "Do it."

"Do what?"

He jerked his head toward the end table. "My keys are there. You can find a phone on your way home."

She stared at him. "You *can* read my mind, can't you?"

"When I want to."

"I asked you about that once before, and you lied to me."

He didn't deny it.

"Why did you lie to me?"

"How could I explain it?"

"I don't know. It must be handy, being able to read minds."

"I can only read yours."

"Really?"

"It's a link, forged by the blood I gave you. During the ErAdonian mating ceremony, it's customary for the man and woman to exchange a small amount of blood. Not only does it forge a strong bond between them, but it enables them to share their innermost thoughts, to communicate telepathically over long distances."

He shook his head, wishing he could think of a way to make her realize the danger she was in. "You can tell Barrett whatever you like, but he won't believe you."

"I think he will. It might take him a few minutes to accept, but once he thinks about it, he'll realize it's the only explanation that makes sense."

"And you expect me to sit here and wait for him?"

"Of course not. I just want him to leave me alone. I just want to be able to go home again."

He could hardly blame her for that. He closed his eyes for a moment, remembering the stark beauty of ErAdona and all he had lost.

"Do what you have to, Kara." He looked at her for a long moment, then left the cavern.

For a time, Kara stared after him, her mind reeling as she tried to sort out her feelings, tried to decide what to do, who to trust, where to turn.

Suddenly, she had to get away, had to be alone to try and sort out her jumbled emotions. With a wordless cry, she picked up his keys, ran into the bedroom, threw her clothing and toiletries into a couple of shopping bags and ran out of the cavern.

A cold wind buffeted her as she tossed the bags onto the seat, then slid behind the wheel of the Porsche.

Standing outside in the shadows, Alex watched her drive away. He could have made her stay. He could have kept her imprisoned in the cavern. He could have overpowered her free will and forced her to do as he wished. But he didn't want a mindless robot. He wanted her love, and her trust, freely given.

Standing on the ledge, he watched the headlights pierce the darkness as she drove down the mountain.

She was going.

It was for the best.

As the distance between them grew, the emptiness inside him expanded, and with it an all-consuming rage that would not be ignored.

His hands curled into tight fists as bitterness roiled up inside him. She was gone.

He felt hollow inside, lifeless, and utterly alone.

He swore under his breath, a cold fury building within him as his gaze swept over the room. She had walked on the floor, sat on the sofa, warmed herself by his fire.

Not since he had first come here two hundred years ago had he given in to the terrible urge to destroy, but he surrendered to it now.

Like a wild thing, he stalked through the cavern. He shattered the lamp, grabbed the books from the shelf and hurled them into the fire, toppled the bookcase to the floor, ripped the sofa to shreds.

Going into the kitchen, he threw the dishes against the walls, smashed the kitchen table, broke the chairs apart as if they were made of kindling rather than solid wood.

Breathing hard, he moved down the hallway to the bedroom and flung open the door. He would destroy the bed and everything else she had touched, and her memory with it.

A long wail of pain rose in his throat as her scent filled his nostrils. Flinging himself down on the bed, he closed his eyes, and the fragrance that was Kara rose all around him, feminine, clean, provocative.

She was gone, and he would never see her again.

With a choked cry, he wrapped himself in the blanket she had used, his rage swallowed up by an overwhelming sense of grief and loss.

"Kara," he murmured brokenly. "Be well."

Chapter Twelve

Kara drove down the mountain like a maniac, her anxiety to get away from him, from what he was, making her reckless.

Alex. He wasn't a man at all, but a creature from a distant planet.

He had lived on earth for two hundred years. Shades of *Highlander*, she mused ruefully. Alexander was a real-life immortal, and she had fallen in love with him.

For the first time in her life, she had fallen head over heels in love with a man who wasn't a man at all. It would have been funny if it wasn't so tragic.

She hit the brake when she reached the bottom of the mountain, shrieked as the car fish-tailed, then shuddered to a stop. Her hand was shaking as she turned off the ignition.

She was away from him, she thought bleakly.

Now what? When she'd left him, she had every intention of getting in touch with Dale Barrett and telling him everything. Even if he didn't believe her immediately, she was certain he was the type of man who would check it out anyway. All she had to do was find a phone, put Barrett on another trail, and maybe her own life would return to normal.

All she had to do was find a telephone.

There was a gas station about ten miles down the road. No doubt she'd find a phone booth there.

With a sigh, she folded her arms over the steering wheel, rested her forehead on her arms, and cried. In spite of what she'd said to Alex, she knew she wouldn't betray him to Barrett. In every movie she had ever seen—*Starman* and *E.T* quickly came to mind—aliens had been badly treated by their human captors. She had no doubt that Alex would find himself locked in a laboratory somewhere, the victim of numerous experiments. He would not go peacefully, of that she was certain. What if he killed someone when they tried to capture him? What if someone killed him?

She couldn't turn him in, and she couldn't go home, not until she knew it was safe. So, she thought again, what was she going to do?

Lifting her head, she stared into the darkness. It was raining again, as if the heavens and all the angels shared her sorrow.

Resolutely, she turned the key in the ignition. She couldn't just sit here all night. She had to do something. Find a motel. Get some rest. That was what she needed, she thought, a good night's sleep. Maybe then she'd be able to think more clearly.

She checked into the first motel she came to, carefully signing a phony name.

In her room, she locked the door, then dragged a chair in front of it as an added safety precaution.

She washed her face, undressed, and slipped into bed.

The sheets were cold, as cold as the ache in her heart.

She wouldn't think of him. She didn't want to think of him.

She could think of nothing else. Only Alex. The sound of his voice. The touch of his hand in her hair, his lips on hers. The way he looked at her, as if she were the finest, most precious thing he had ever seen.

It wasn't fair! She wanted a home and a family. She didn't even know if it was possible for a human and an alien to conceive a child . . . A harsh laugh escaped her lips. What was she thinking? There was no way for them to have a life together, no way at all.

Pulling the covers over her head, she cried herself to sleep.

It was late afternoon when she woke. For a time, she stared up at the ceiling, wondering what she should do.

Forcing herself to get up, she fished through one of the shopping bags, then went into the bathroom and brushed her teeth. She flipped on the TV while she combed her hair, then gasped as she saw her face on the screen.

". . . Crawford, who left a medical facility in Grenvale several days ago. Crawford has been infected with a rare blood disease that is virulent and highly contagious. Anyone with information on Crawford's whereabouts should contact . . ."

Kara switched off the TV. She needed to call home, to assure Nana and Gail that she was all right. She reached for the phone, her finger poised over the keypad. What if Barrett was behind this? What if he had found a way to tap the phone . . .

Think, Kara. She had to get in touch with Nana. With a smile of satisfaction, she dialed Mrs. Zimmermann's number. Elsie Zimmermann had been their neighbor for the last ten years. She was a feisty elderly woman who was renowned for her oatmeal cookies and minding her own business.

"Hello?"

"Mrs. Zimmermann, this is Kara."

"Kara! Where are you, child? Your grandmother is frantic with worry."

"I know. Would you do something for me? Would you go get Gail for me? Don't tell her why, just get her over to your house. And don't say anything to Nana."

"But she'll want to know—"

"I'll tell her everything as soon as I can. Please, Mrs. Zimmermann, this is urgent."

"All right, Kara. Hang on."

A few minutes later, Gail's voice came over the wire.

"Kara? Kara, where are you? A doctor was here looking for you. He said you ran away from the hospital, and your life is in danger. I don't remember his name."

"Dale Barrett?"

"Yeah, that was it."

"Don't trust him, Gail, and don't believe anything he says. I'm fine. How are you? How's Nana?"

"We're okay. Don't worry. We saw your picture on TV."

143

"Yeah, me, too. When was Barrett there?"

"He comes by every day, asking questions. Where are you, Kara? When are you coming home?"

"I don't know." She couldn't go home, not now, not if Barrett was sniffing around. "Listen, Gail, don't tell anyone I called."

"But—"

"Promise me, Gail. You can't tell anyone. Not even Nana."

"She's worried, Kara."

"I know. I'll call you again when I get a chance."

"Okay."

"I love you, sis."

"I love you, too."

"Let me talk to Mrs. Zimmermann. And remember, you can't tell anyone I called."

"All right. Bye."

Moments later, Mrs. Zimmermann was on the phone again. "Kara?"

"Yes. I know this must seem strange, but you can't tell anyone I called. Not even Nana."

"I don't like the sound of this, Kara."

"I don't like it, either, but you've got to believe me when I say this is a matter of life and death. I don't want Nana or Gail to be in danger because of me."

"Are you in some kind of trouble, Kara?"

"Not the way you mean. I've got to go now, Mrs. Zimmermann. Please keep an eye on Gail and Nana for me."

"I will, child. God bless you."

"Thank you."

Kara stared at the phone after she replaced the receiver in the cradle. She had hoped Barrett would give up, but he seemed to have the tenacity of a bulldog. So, where did that leave her? She hated to

think what would happen if Barrett got hold of her
again. No doubt he would lock her away where
she'd never be found, and then he would start selling her blood to the highest bidder. And people
with terminal diseases would pay for it, she
thought. Oh, yes, they would pay any amount the
good doctor asked if they thought it would cure
them. And maybe it would. Did she have the right
to refuse to help the sick, the dying, if it was within
her power to do so? But what about her rights? She
would never have a life of her own again.

A life of her own . . . She stared into the mirror
over the dresser. Alex had given her his blood. It
had saved her life. Would it also extend her life?
Would she become sensitive to the sun? She tried
to imagine what it would be like to live for two hundred years, to have to spend the rest of her life
avoiding the sun, but it was beyond her comprehension.

She pressed her hands to her temples. Her head
was throbbing, her eyes felt red and raw, and there
was a terrible pain in the region of her heart.

She missed Alex. Just thinking of him stilled the
throbbing in her head. She remembered asking
him how he'd lit the fire, asking him what other
tricks he could do. And his cryptic response, *More
than you want to know.*

In the space between one heartbeat and another,
she knew she had to go back. She would be safe
with Alex. But it was more than that. Her life
seemed empty without him, dull and meaningless,
as though someone had leeched all the joy, all the
zest, out of living.

Moving quickly, she took a shower, put on a pair
of clean slacks and a sweater, then went to the res-

taurant across the street, where she ordered a turkey sandwich and a malt to go. She had found a pair of sunglasses in her purse, and she kept them on, hoping no one would recognize her.

Minutes later, she was back in the car. She drove to a shady place to eat, hardly tasting a bite. All she could think of was seeing Alex again. The fact that he was an alien no longer seemed as important, or as frightening, as it had the night before. And yet . . .

She stared out the window. Except for that peculiar ridge of flesh on his back, Alex looked like any other man, but what if they were incompatible sexually? Maybe the people of his planet didn't procreate in the same manner as those of earth.

She frowned, then shook the thought from her mind. She would worry about that later. For now, she wanted, needed, to see him.

She brushed the crumbs from her lap, wiped her mouth, then drove to the gas station to fill the tank. And then, her heart pounding with anticipation at seeing Alex again, she turned the car toward Eagle Flats.

He rose at dusk to prowl through the wreckage of the cavern. He hoped Kara had the good sense not to go home. He knew she would be unable to resist calling her grandmother, but a phone call should be harmless enough, if she kept it short and made it from a pay phone.

He swore an ancient oath. It was no longer any of his concern what she did or where she went. Tomorrow he would leave here. He would return to Moulton Bay and collect his things, and then he'd leave town. Leave the country. Perhaps he'd go back to Australia. He'd always planned to go back some day. Now seemed like the perfect time. He had no ties here, nothing to keep him. He could write anywhere.

He kicked aside the wreckage that had once been the kitchen table, overcome by the ancient urge to hunt in the old way, to kill his prey with his bare hands, to taste its sweet, warm blood on his tongue.

The men of ErAdona had overcome their blood-thirsty nature centuries ago, but he was a throwback to an older, more violent time. It was a part of him he loathed, a part of him that lay dormant, all but forgotten, until rage unleashed the beast within him, and it woke, ravenous and all but uncontrollable. It was the reason he felt such an affinity for the vampires he wrote about. He knew what blood lust was, what it was like to be caught in the clutches of a hunger that was both repugnant and pleasurable.

Feeling confined by the cavern's walls, he went out into the night. Stripping off his clothing, he lifted his face to the moon, absorbing the pale light into himself, hoping it would calm him, but the beast within would not be pacified.

With a growl, he started to run up the mountainside, surrendering to the anger and the frustration surging through him.

Soundlessly, effortlessly, he ran through the darkness, blending with the shadows, his heart and soul at one with the other predators of the night.

Kara switched off the ignition, ran a hand over her hair, and took a deep breath, wishing she knew what she was going to say to Alexander when she saw him again.

Gathering her packages and her purse, she slid out of the car, locked the door, and made her way to the cavern's entrance.

She placed her hand over the odd-shaped striation in the rock face, felt her heart beat with excitement as, with a dull rumble, the portal slid open.

"Alex?" Calling his name, she stepped inside. The rock slid back into place automatically; a light came on as soon as the door closed behind her.

"Alex?" Dropping her packages inside the doorway, she walked down the narrow corridor, gasping when she came to the living room. Furniture, tables, bookcases, all had been destroyed. The kitchen was also a shambles.

She made her way down the corridor to the bedroom. Relief whooshed out of her lungs in a sigh. This room, at least, had not been demolished.

She stepped into the room and looked around, wondering what had caused the destruction in the other rooms. Where was Alex? Had Barrett found him after all?

A noise from the other room made the hair rise along the back of her neck. And then she heard footsteps walking down the corridor.

Mouth dry, palms damp with fear, she turned toward the door.

Chapter Thirteen

Alex came to an abrupt halt when he saw Kara standing in the bedroom. He had caught her scent as soon as he entered the cavern but, trapped in his own misery, he had ignored it, thinking it to be nothing more than a cruel reminder that she had been there and gone.

"Kara!"

"Hello, Alex."

Hands clenched, he stared at the woman he had never thought to see again. Hope smothered his anger; her presence calmed the beast that had been clawing at his insides.

He took a deep breath before asking, "Did you call Barrett?"

"No."

He arched one black brow, his gaze intent upon her face. "Why not?"

Kara shook her head. "I thought about it, but I just couldn't."

"So, why are you here?"

Feeling suddenly nervous, Kara licked her lips. What should she say? Neither of them had ever mentioned love, or spoken of commitment. What if he'd been glad to be rid of her? What if he didn't want her back?

"I want you," Alex said quietly, and it took all his willpower to withstand the urge to drag her into his arms and never let her go. "Never doubt that."

For once, Kara was glad he could read her mind. It would be so much easier if he would just read her thoughts, her feelings, than to have to try to express them in words.

But he was in no mood to make things easy for her. "Why are you here?" he asked again. "What do you want?"

Kara looked deep into his eyes. *I love you*, she thought. *I want you to love me. Hold me. Kiss me* . . . She swallowed, trying to form the words, to push them past a throat gone suddenly dry.

"Alex, I'm . . . I'm so sorry for the way I acted before. Don't hate me for it, please. I didn't mean to hurt you."

"It's all right, Kara." There was forgiveness in his words, but his voice remained cold.

Hold me, she thought, *I need you to hold me.*

Alex folded his arms over his chest. "We need to talk."

She didn't like the sound of that, didn't like the tension that was evident in his voice, in every taut line of his body.

"Let's go outside." He stood aside so she could precede him out the door.

Her steps felt heavy as she walked outside, acutely aware of Alex's presence behind her. The silence between them seemed ominous, like the stillness before a storm.

Once outside, she sat down on a flat rock, feeling the damp chill of the stone penetrate the material of her slacks. She gestured toward the cavern. "What happened in there?"

"That's one of the things I want to talk to you about."

Hands clasped tightly in her lap, Kara looked up at him. The moon was full and bright and she could see him clearly. He was barefooted and shirtless, his body damp with perspiration, his hair tousled.

He closed his eyes for a moment, his face lifted to the moonlight, and she thought how beautiful he was, tall and dark, like a pagan prince worshipping the night. She let her gaze run over him, felt her admiration turn to revulsion when she saw the blood on his hands. She hadn't noticed it before; now, she couldn't seem to see anything else.

Aware of her scrutiny, Alex wiped his bloody hands on the jeans he had pulled on when he first entered the cavern. "You accused me of being a vampire before, and I denied it."

Kara nodded. She had a terrible feeling she knew where all this was headed.

Unable to help herself, she placed her hand over her throat, felt the wild throbbing of her pulse. She stared at the blood on his hands again. Was he going to attack her? Rip her throat out?

She stood abruptly, her courage deserting her. "I'm tired. Maybe we could discuss this tomorrow?"

"No."

Kara sat down again, her hands clenching and

unclenching in her lap. "Go on."

"You accused me of being a vampire," Alex repeated quietly, "and in a manner of speaking, it's true. My ancestors were a wild, untamed race of people. The men were warriors, predators who drank the blood of their enemies in the belief that the life force of those they had killed would then be theirs. During times of intense stress, our men were occasionally subject to uncontrollable rages that bordered on madness. As my people became more civilized, the drinking of blood was forbidden. War among our own was outlawed. Such behavior was gradually bred out of our people and peace prevailed. Inevitably, there were throwbacks. When you left . . ."

He took a deep breath, ashamed to admit his weakness. "I was angry when you left me." He lifted one hand and slowly made a fist. "I felt the madness come on me, and I set out to destroy everything that reminded me of you."

Kara nodded, her heartbeat accelerating as she waited for him to go on. She couldn't take her gaze from his face, couldn't help wondering if he would have destroyed her, too, if she had come upon him then.

He knew her thoughts, but could not condemn them. Even if he frightened her away forever, she had to know the truth. All of it. "With the madness came the ancient urge to hunt, to kill, to glut myself with blood."

He blew out a long sigh. "In ancient times, those who could not control the lust for blood were banished from our planet and transported to earth. I've often wondered if perhaps it was some distant ancestors of mine who formed the basis of earth's vampire legends."

"There was blood. On your hands." He saw the revulsion in her eyes and knew she was wondering who, or what, he had killed.

"A mountain lion," Alex said flatly.

"Did you . . . did you drink its blood?"

"No."

"Why not?"

"Because of you." He had been bending over the animal's neck, his mouth watering as the scent of warm fresh blood filled his nostrils, when suddenly an image of Kara had filled his mind. He had seen himself through her eyes, seen her horror, her revulsion, and he had been ashamed.

"Is that why you write about vampires, because you share their . . . their lust for blood?"

"You're very perceptive, Kara Crawford. My people share many of the characteristics attributed to your fictional vampires."

She was staring at him, her eyes wide, as she waited for him to go on.

"I can manipulate inanimate objects with the power of my thoughts. I seem to be immune to the diseases of your planet. My metabolism is much slower than yours. I can't abide your sun, and so I usually stay up late at night and sleep during the day. Not the sleep of the undead," he added, hoping to reassure her.

"Can you also turn into a bat or a wolf, and dissolve into a mist?"

A faint smile tugged at his lips. "Handy tricks, to be sure, but beyond even my powers. Is there anything else you want to know?"

"Are you . . ." She looked away, biting down on

her lip, wishing she could think of a delicate way to ask an indelicate question. The fact that she was curious at all made her cheeks burn.

"You're wondering if I'm like the men of earth," Alex said. "Wondering if the sexual habits and mores of my people are different from yours."

Kara nodded.

"The answer is yes, and no. Anything else?"

"Just one thing. Do you love me, Alex?"

"Yes." In a swift movement, he knelt before her and took her hands in his. "I've loved you since the first time I saw you, lying there in the hospital. Nothing will ever change that, Kara."

With a hand that trembled, Kara caressed his cheek. He had said he loved her; she knew she loved him. But was that enough for two people from different worlds?

"Kara, tell me what you want me to do."

"I don't know. I thought if I knew you loved me, it would make everything all right, but it only makes things more complicated."

"What do you mean?"

"Where do we go from here?"

"Wherever you want."

She shook her head. "I don't know what I want. Everything is so . . . confused. Did you know they're showing my picture on TV? Telling people I have a virus that is highly contagious and might be fatal? Barrett's not going to give up. I called Gail, and she said he'd been at the house asking for me. I told her not to tell anyone I called, not even Nana. My grandmother must be worried sick. . . ."

"I'm sorry, Kara. I've brought you nothing but trouble."

"You saved my life!"

154

"You might have recovered without my help." He shook his head, remembering the night he had given her his blood, the gamble he had taken with a life not his own. "You could have died."

"But I didn't."

"Kara . . ." His hands spanned her waist, and then he drew her down onto his lap and kissed her.

Warmth spread through her, chasing away the cold and the fear and the indecision. She slid her arms around him, her hands roaming over his broad back.

"Alex!" She lifted her hand and stared at the dark stain on her palm. "You're hurt!"

"The cougar scratched me."

"It feels deep. Let me see." She stood up and moved around behind him. His blood glistened blackly in the light of the moon. "That needs to be sewn up."

"I'll be all right."

"But it could get infected."

"I can't go to a hospital, Kara," he remarked with a rueful grin. "Anyway, it isn't necessary."

"What do you mean?"

"Kara, I've been here two hundred years. In all that time, I've never been sick. Any injuries I've received have healed in a day or two."

"At least let me wash the blood away."

"If it will make you feel better."

He stood up and followed her into the kitchen. While Kara looked for a clean rag, he went to the sink and washed his hands; then he sat on the floor while she rinsed the blood from the scratches on his back.

He glanced over his shoulder. "You're no longer repulsed by my appearance?"

Kara studied the dark strip of skin that ran down his spine. "No." She washed away the last of the blood, then dried his back with a towel. "I wish you had some bandages."

Alex stood up and took her in his arms. "Stop worrying."

Kara nodded, suddenly too aware of his nearness to speak. His eyes were dark, smoldering with suppressed desire. She could feel the heat radiating from him, feel the evidence of his desire.

"I want you, Kara," he said, his voice rough with need.

"I know."

He kissed her again, gently, as if he were afraid she might shatter in his arms. His tenderness tugged at her heart, and she had a sudden urge to hold him, to comfort him.

"Kara?"

"Yes, Alexander?"

"I don't want to hurt you."

"What do you mean?"

"You're so fragile. I'm afraid I might crush you."

"I'm not made of glass, Alex."

He lifted her into his arms and carried her into the bedroom, lowered her to the bed, then stretched out beside her and drew her close. At last, she was in his arms again. He closed his eyes, absorbing her nearness, her very essence, as he absorbed the light of the moon. She was like sunshine and satin in his arms, warm and soft. Her fragrance filled his senses, her skin was supple and smooth beneath his hands. He buried his face in the wealth of her hair.

"Alex . . ." Desire unfolded within her like a flower opening to the sun. Her hands moved restlessly over his arms, his chest, his shoulders and back, delighting in the sensations that came from touching him—the powerful muscles in his arms, the sleek warmth of his skin, the rough silk of his hair.

Her hand stilled as it brushed against the peculiar, rough-smooth feel of the ridged flesh along his spine. Alien flesh . . . the thought crept, unbidden, into her mind.

She felt his body stiffen beneath her palm, felt the tension that pulsed through him as he drew back.

"Alex . . ."

The pain in his eyes stabbed her to the heart. Wordlessly, he sat up and turned his back to her, as though to say, *Take a good look.*

She felt his withdrawal in the deepest part of her soul. "Alex, please . . ."

Please what, she thought, hating the gulf that stretched ever deeper between them, hating herself.

"It's all right, Kara," he said, and his voice was flat, empty of emotion.

She stared at his back. The narrow strip of flesh that loomed before her eyes seemed to grow wider, darker, until it filled her line of vision.

He stood up, and she knew he was going to leave her, and that if she let him walk away, she would never see him again.

"Alex! Don't go! Please come back to bed."

He whirled around to confront her, the skin across his cheekbones taut, his dark eyes filled with torment. His hands were tightly clenched at his sides, and she shrank back against the headboard as she remembered the destruction those hands had wrought.

The movement was not lost on Alex. Eyes narrowed, he took a step toward her, an angry growl rising in his throat as she raised her arms to fend him off.

"I thought you weren't afraid of me," he said, sneering.

"I'm . . . I'm not."

"No?"

He could feel the anger, the frustration, swirling through him as he took another step forward. "You should run away, Kara. Run from the monster as fast as you can, and maybe I'll let you go."

"Alex, don't." She stared up at him, her heart racing. For a moment, she was sorely tempted to run away, and then, with a defiant toss of her head, she squared her shoulders and met his gaze. "I'm not afraid of you, Alexander Claybourne."

With a strangled cry, he dropped to his knees and buried his face in his hands. She stared at him for a moment, the sound of his anguished cry tearing at her soul.

"Oh, Alex," she murmured, and slipping out of bed, she went to him without a qualm. Pressing his head to her belly, she stroked his hair. "I'm sorry, Alex. I'll never be afraid of you again."

For a moment, he let himself bask in her touch, pretending she was his, would always be his. He had been alone so long. The people of ErAdona were known throughout the galaxy for being a warm, affectionate people. Living alone, unloved and untouched, had been the hardest part of his exile.

He savored the touch of Kara's hand in his hair a moment more, and then he stood up.

"It won't work, Kara," he said, his voice as cold

as stone. "I was a fool to think otherwise. The differences between us are too vast."

"No!"

He turned away from her then, his steps heavy as he walked toward the door. "Good-bye, Kara."

"I love you, Alex. Please don't leave me."

Her words stopped him, but he didn't turn around, only stood there with his head bowed, his back toward her.

Crossing the floor, she went to stand behind him. Slowly, gently, she brushed her lips over the raised ridge of flesh along his spine, felt him tremble at her touch.

"I love you," she said again. "I didn't mean to hurt you. Say you forgive me."

"I forgive you," he said quietly. But he still didn't turn around.

"Alex, please . . ."

"Please what? I can't change what I am."

"I don't want you to change. I'm not asking you to change. Only to love me, as I love you."

Slowly, he turned to face her. "Tell me what you want, Kara. But know this—if I stay, it's for always. Not just until it's safe for you to go home. My people are not like yours. We mate for life, not for the moment or until we find someone new, but for always."

"For always," Kara murmured.

"Then I pledge you my love, my life, for as long as I live. From this night forward, you will be my woman. I will defend you to the death, and love you until my last breath."

They were the most beautiful words she had ever heard.

"Will you be my woman, Kara Elizabeth Crawford?"

"Yes, Alexander. And I promise to love you, and only you, for as long as I live. I'll stay by your side in good times and bad. I'll share your laughter, and your tears, and I'll love you until my last breath."

"Kara . . ." He whispered her name as he slanted his mouth over hers. She was his now, always and forever his. Where he came from, marriage was an exchange of vows between a man and a woman. No license was required. No minister or magistrate was needed, though some preferred to be married within one of ErAdona's magnificent cathedrals, to have friends and family in attendance. But the marriage itself took place in the hearts of the man and the woman. Kara was his now, always and forever his, bound to him by the words she had spoken, as he was bound to her.

Sweeping her into his arms, he carried her back to bed. "You must tell me if I hurt you."

"You won't."

He placed her on the mattress and sank down beside her. "It's been a long time since I've been with a woman."

"That's all right," she murmured, winding her arms around his neck. "It's been a long time since I've been with a man."

"How long?" Jealousy rose up within him, hotter than the boiling waters of the ErAdonian Sea. "How many?"

"None."

His eyes widened with disbelief. "You've never been with a man before?"

"No."

Alex frowned. If she'd never been with a man, she

probably wasn't using any method of birth control. On ErAdona, a woman took a capsule which prevented conception for a year; if she decided she wished to become pregnant before the year was over, she took a second capsule to reverse the effects of the first. A similar capsule was used by the men. But here on Earth, methods of birth control were less sophisticated.

"What's wrong?" she asked.

"I don't want you to get pregnant."

"Pregnant!" She'd been so caught up in the first blush of love, so eager for his touch, she hadn't given a thought to getting pregnant. Unwanted pregnancies were something that happened to other people.

Alex nodded. "It could happen, although I'm not sure it's possible."

"Why not?"

"We're from different worlds, Kara. It might not be possible for us to create a new life." He tucked his finger beneath her chin, forcing her to meet his gaze. "Does it make a difference? If it does, tell me now." Before it's too late, he thought, knowing that once he possessed her, he would never let her go.

"I don't know." She'd never really given it a great deal of thought. She'd always assumed that someday she'd get married, but she'd never given much thought to having children. She'd just presumed they'd come along in their own good time—a handsome little boy and a pretty little girl.

She looked at Alex and imagined having his child. A little boy, with Alex's black hair and dark eyes. And a tiny stripe down its back . . .

"Kara?"

"It doesn't matter," she said, pushing her fears

161

aside. "I love you, Alex. I'll love your children if God grants them to me. And if not . . ." She shrugged. "If not, then I'll be content to be your wife."

His arm tightened around her, drawing her closer, as he uttered a silent prayer that she would never regret her decision.

Kara felt his lips move in her hair, felt the warmth of his breath against her neck. In that instant, she wished they could make love, but Alex was right. It was better to wait until there was no danger of her becoming pregnant. "I wish . . ."

"I know." A sigh of frustrated longing swept through him. "For tonight, just let me hold you."

Kara nodded as she settled into his embrace. "Yes," she whispered. "Hold me and never let me go."

Chapter Fourteen

They slept late. It was early afternoon when Kara woke to find herself pressed against Alex, her legs entwined with his, her head on his shoulder. She studied his face for a long while. He was so beautiful. It was hard to believe that he was over two hundred years old. Hard to believe he was from another planet. In a small way, she could sympathize with his plight. He had been sent away from his home, forbidden to return. She was in exile, too, she mused, but at least she had hope of returning home, of seeing her loved ones again.

Strange as it seemed, she thought she might be content to stay in his mountain retreat, in his arms, for the rest of her life.

She closed her eyes for a moment, wondering what it was going to be like to spend her life with this man. She was his now, and he was hers, as surely as if they had been married in front of an ordained priest. She thought about what'd he'd said the night before, about not having children. How would she feel in ten years, twenty, watching herself age while he stayed young?

With a sigh, she pushed her troublesome thoughts away. She was bound to Alex now, bound by vows of love and commitment. Whatever problems they might encounter in the future paled beside the more important problems of the present—like Dale Barrett wanting her blood.

When she opened her eyes again, it was to find Alex watching her, his dark eyes filled with tenderness.

"Kara." He whispered her name as his fingers trailed over her cheek. "Do you know how empty my life was until I met you?"

She nodded, lost in the yearning she could see swirling in the depths of his eyes. Black eyes that seemed to see into the furthest reaches of her heart and soul.

"It was the same for me," she murmured. "I think I've been waiting for you my whole life. Maybe, deep inside, I knew you would come." She laughed softly. "But that's impossible, isn't it?"

"Is it?"

Looking at him, feeling his nearness, it didn't seem impossible at all. "What are we going to do now?"

"Whatever you want, Kara."

Her gaze slid away from his. "I want to go to the store."

Alex arched one brow. "The store?" he asked, pretending he didn't know what she was talking about. "Why do you need to go to the store? We have enough supplies to last a week or so."

She punched him in the arm. "We don't have *everything* we need."

He watched a tide of color wash into her cheeks, and he grinned. "Ah," he said. "There's an all-night drug store not far from here. I'll go as soon as it's dark."

"I could go now," Kara remarked, wondering if he thought it brazen of her to suggest such a thing.

Alex shook his head. "Tempting as the thought is, I don't want you going anywhere alone." He grinned down at her. "But I'm glad you don't want to wait."

After a late lunch, they set about cleaning up the mess in the cavern's main room. Kara glanced at Alex, awed by the strength the man possessed. The table and chair had been smashed beyond repair; the sofa had been ripped apart as if it had been made of toothpicks instead of solid wood and leather. The only item not completely destroyed was the bookcase. She shuddered to think of his rage turned against a living creature.

She saw Alex go suddenly still and knew that he had divined her thoughts.

"You needn't be afraid of me, Kara," he said quietly. "I would never harm you. You must believe that if you believe nothing else."

"I'm not afraid of you, Alex. *You* must believe that." She smiled at him. "I've rarely seen you during the day time."

Alex grunted softly. "Unlike your vampires, I am not compelled to sleep during the day. I need only stay out of your sun."

Their gazes held for several seconds, both thinking of the night to come, and then they turned back to the task at hand.

When they finished cleaning up the debris, there was nothing left in the cavern's main room save for the bookcase and the bear rug.

Kara glanced at the empty bookcase, at the pile of ashes in the hearth. "I'm sorry about your books."

"It doesn't matter."

Kara felt the pull of his gaze, felt her heart begin to beat faster as he moved slowly toward her. Energy pulsed between them, throbbing in time to the beat of her heart. Warmth engulfed her; she felt herself drowning in the fathomless depths of his ebony-hued gaze.

A low groan escaped his lips as he drew her into his arms. "I've been fighting the urge to hold you all day," he said, his voice low and sandpaper rough. He rained kisses over her cheeks, her eyelids, the delicate curve of her throat. "Tell me to stop, Kara. Tell me how dangerous it is for us to be together."

"We've got to stop," she said agreeably, but her arms wrapped around his neck and her body molded itself to his until she could feel his heartbeat pounding in rhythm with hers.

"Yes," he said, his voice like a hot wind against her throat. "We've got to stop."

Lifting her into his arms, he carried her to the hearth and placed her on the rug, then followed her down to the floor. "Kara, *natayah* . . . do you know how desperately I need you?"

"I know." She brushed a lock of hair from his face, traced the shape of his mouth with her fingertips.

"Make me stop, Kara. I can't do it on my own. I've wanted you too long, waited too long . . ."

His gaze burned into hers, hotter than the sun at noonday, brighter than the tail of a comet.

"Push me away," he said, "now, before it's too late. I don't want to hurt you."

"You won't."

"You don't know that. You don't know what I'm capable of."

"I'm not afraid." Kara pressed herself closer, felt the very real evidence of his desire. His need inflamed her own and she moaned softly as she writhed beneath him, silently begging him to satisfy the sweet desire he had stirred within her.

Alex stared deep into her eyes, the hunger for her flesh pulsing through him. She was his woman now, and he burned with the knowledge that she was his, that he could hold her and touch her. And with that knowledge came the fear that he might do her harm, that he would take and take until he had drained her of energy, of life itself. Not that he would deliberately harm her, but sometimes, caught up in the heat of passion, he forgot how fragile these earth creatures were, how weak their hold on life, how easily they broke in his hands.

"Alex . . ."

With a muttered curse, he looked away, breaking eye contact. As much as he wanted her, needed her, he would not take her, not without the means to prevent conception. To his knowledge, none of his race had ever mated with an earthling. In his brief encounters with other women, he had always used a contraceptive to ensure that no pregnancy would result. He had no idea if he could father a child with an earth woman, or what the consequences to Kara might be should his seed take root within her womb.

The thought of hurting her cooled his ardor and gave him the strength to draw away. Her cry of protest rang in his ears as he stood up and left the cavern.

He watched the last rays of the setting sun vanish beneath a cloak of twilight. Head tilted back, he stared into the heavens, overcome by a yearning for home, for that which was familiar and forever lost. Two hundred years he had lived on this planet, and he was still a stranger. Two hundred years since he had allowed a woman to hold him, to love him.

He felt her presence behind him, caught her scent on the wind stirring through the pines.

"Alex?"

"Go back into the cavern, Kara. You're not safe with me."

"I'm not afraid."

"I am. I can't be near you and not touch you. I can't touch you and not want to make you mine."

"It'll be dark soon," she reminded him. "And then . . ."

Slowly, he turned to face her. "Kara, you know what I am. How can you want me to touch you?"

"I love you." She shook her head. "I love you. Nothing else matters." She grinned up at him, hoping to erase his sour expression. "I've been your wife since yesterday, and I'm still a virgin. Don't you think it's time we remedied that?"

"Past time," he agreed.

It seemed he was gone for days, but in truth it was less than an hour. Surely the fastest anyone had ever traveled down the narrow mountain road and back again.

Kara felt suddenly shy as Alex swung her into his arms and carried her into the bedroom. The heat of his gaze lit the candles on the wall, and then he was lowering her to the bed, stretching out beside her.

"Don't be afraid," he whispered.

"I'm not," she replied, but it was a lie and they both knew it.

"Kara, we don't have to do this."

"No, I want to, really . . ."

Alex took a deep breath. Perhaps he was rushing her. He couldn't blame her for being anxious and uncertain. With a sigh, he slipped his arm around her and drew her close. He felt the tension thrumming through her, could almost hear the fierce pounding of her heart.

"Relax, Kara. I'm just going to hold you, nothing more." Gently, he rubbed his knuckles over her cheek, his movements slow and soothing.

"I'm sorry."

"It's all right, Kara. It's better this way. When this mess with Barrett is over, I'll take you home."

"What do you mean?"

"This isn't going to work."

"Alex . . ." She started to rise, but he held her in place.

"It won't work between us," he said quietly. "I was a fool to think otherwise." He stilled her protest by placing his hand over her mouth. "No matter how much alike we are, Kara, I'm afraid it will never be enough to overcome our differences. I think you'll always be a little afraid of me, and I can't live with you, knowing that. I don't blame you for the way you feel. It's natural to be afraid of what we don't understand."

Kara took his hand from her mouth, pushed his other arm away, and sat up.

"You idiot! I'm not afraid of you. Don't you think I know you won't hurt me? Honestly, Alexander Claybourne, sometimes you make me want to scream!"

He stared up at her, his brow furrowed. "I don't understand."

Kara let out a huff of exasperation. "Men! The only thing I'm nervous about is . . . is that I've never . . ." She shook her head, wondering why it was so hard to say what was on her mind. "I've never gone all the way before, you jerk, and I feel stupid because I'm so nervous, and I don't know why. I know what's involved, I know how it's done, I've just never done it! And I'm afraid you'll be disappointed. . . ."

Her voice trailed off and she looked away, feeling incredibly stupid.

"That's what this is all about? You're afraid you'll disappoint me?"

She nodded, too embarrassed to meet his gaze. She was supposed to be a grown woman, but she suddenly felt as if she was fifteen years old and out on her first date.

"Kara . . ."

"I love you, Alex," she whispered.

Wrapping his arms around her, he pulled her onto his chest. "And I love you. Never forget it. Never doubt it for a minute. I love you. . . ."

Cupping her face in his hands, he kissed her gently. And that kiss burned away all of Kara's doubts and fears. She loved him. She wanted him. And he was there.

His kisses, the touch of his hands, were like magic. Eager, unashamed, she explored the man who held her heart and soul. She rained kisses over his broad shoulders, across his chest, down his belly. She ran her hands over the muscles in his arms and legs. She made him turn over so she could press kisses to his back; she ran her tongue over his spine, intrigued by the rough texture of ridged flesh, the contrast between that and the smooth skin on his shoulders.

Vulnerable and acquiescent, Alex let her get acquainted with his body, let her touch and caress him until she had satisfied her curiosity, until he was certain she knew every inch of his body as well as she knew her own. It was the most exquisite torture he had ever endured, lying there while her warm hands and soft lips moved over him, arousing him until he ached with need.

She trailed her fingertips over the ridged flesh of his spine, and he groaned with pleasure so deep it was almost pain, a pleasure he had thought never to feel again. On ErAdona, when a woman stroked a man's spine in such an intimate fashion, it meant she had agreed to be his life mate. Once she touched him there, they were considered mated even though no words had been spoken. It was also a source of great sexual pleasure.

"What is it?" Kara asked. "What's wrong?"

"Nothing."

"I thought I'd hurt you."

"No, Kara, quite the opposite."

"What do you mean?"

"Touch me again, Kara. Run your hands over my back."

"Like this?"

Alex closed his eyes, drowning in sensation, as she massaged his back, pausing now and then to run her tongue along his spine.

Kara laughed softly as the evidence of his desire grew unmistakable. "I seem to have touched on an ErAdonian erogenous zone," she mused.

His purr of contentment was loud and rough, like the muted roar of a lion.

She reveled in the knowledge that she had brought him pleasure, and then she heard him groan again, saw the fire blazing in his eyes, and the laughter died in her throat. How cruel she was to tease and torment, she thought, and how patient he was to let her do it.

But he wasn't the only one in distress. You couldn't play with fire without getting burned, and she yearned for him, ached for him, in the deepest core of her being.

"Now, Alex," she murmured, and waited impatiently as he sheathed himself in protection before tucking her beneath him.

And then he was a part of her, his body a warm, sweet invasion of her flesh, and she knew that she had been born for this moment, this man, and that nothing in her life would ever be the same again.

Later, while she lay in a near-drugged state of completion, he fetched a bowl of warm water and bathed her from head to foot, washing away the stain of her maidenhead, the perspiration that had dried on her skin. He bathed her gently, almost reverently, and she thought she had never felt so pampered, so cherished, in all her life.

"I love you, Alex."

"And I you, *natayah*."

"You called me that once before. What does it mean?"

"Beloved one."

"Na-tay-ah." She tried the word on her tongue, liking the sound of it, the way he had looked at her when he said it.

Alex quickly washed himself, then slid into bed and drew Kara into his arms again. "Are you all right?"

"Of course. Why wouldn't I be?"

"I was afraid I might have hurt you."

"No. It was wonderful." She grinned. "Was it good for you?"

Alex chuckled. "Indeed."

"As good as . . ."

"As?"

"I don't suppose you've lived like a monk for the last two hundred years."

"No." He lifted one brow in disbelief. "Don't tell me you're jealous of those women?"

"Of course not."

"Kara." He drew her closer, holding her body tightly to his. "I paid them for the use of their bodies. There was never any more to it than that. Never."

She nodded. He had answered her question, and she believed him, but he had been in love before, been married before, and she couldn't help wondering how it had been with his wife.

Caught up in the aftermath of their lovemaking, trying not to be jealous of a woman who had been dead for over a hundred years, she forgot that, when he chose, he could read her mind.

"Kara." Lifting himself on one elbow, Alex gazed down into her eyes. "I love you beyond words. You've given me new hope for the future, restored my passion for life, for living. I've never felt this way about another woman. Never."

He took a deep breath, unable to ignore the guilt that rose in his heart as he realized that what he had felt for AnnaMara paled beside the love he felt for Kara. He had never loved any woman the way he loved this gentle earth woman; should he live another two hundred years, he knew he would never love like this again.

"I'm sorry, Alex. I know I have no right to be jealous. I know you loved her."

He nodded. "But it was never like this, Kara. I loved her. I would have died for her, but she never filled my heart, my thoughts, my very soul, the way you do."

"Oh, Alex . . ."

Touched to the depths of her being, Kara slipped her arms around his neck. "I love you, Alex. Maybe I am jealous, but I can't help it. I . . . I wish I could have been the first woman in your life."

"Ah, Kara," he murmured helplessly.

Blinking back her tears, she smiled up at him. "I'm going to make you forget those other women, Alexander Claybourne. If it takes the rest of my life, I'm going to make you forget there was ever anyone else."

"I'm at your mercy, *natayah*," he replied, grinning. "Do to me whatever you wish. . . ."

"I'm serious." She dragged her hands down his chest, raked her nails along the insides of his thighs, then ran her palms along the sensitive flesh of his spine. "I'm going to burn those women out of your mind and heart."

"I'm already burning," he said, his voice silky with desire. "Can't you feel the flame?"

"Oh, yes," Kara said, laughing softly as the evidence of his desire swelled against her belly. "Oh, yes."

And then she was on fire, too, writhing in the inferno of desire that burned between them, and for Kara there was only Alex, and for him there was only Kara, always and forever Kara, burning away the memories of the past, and he knew his life hadn't truly begun until he met the woman he held in his arms, and in his heart.

Chapter Fifteen

Kara woke slowly, unwilling to surrender the beautiful dream she'd been having. And then she felt Alexander's breath caress her neck, felt the welcome weight of his leg lying across hers, the heat of his palm curved over her breast, and she knew it hadn't been a dream at all.

Turning her head, she saw Alex sleeping beside her. Thick black lashes lay upon his cheeks. His lips, full and sensuous, were slightly parted. She watched the steady rise and fall of his chest, marveling anew at the width of his shoulders. Just looking at him was enough to make her heart beat fast, make her yearn to touch him, to run her fingers over his chest and feel the smooth warmth of his skin. How strong and handsome he was! And how much she loved him, this man from a distant planet.

Two hundred years, she thought. He had been on earth for two hundred years. The things he must have seen, the changes, the wars, the advancements in science and medicine, and yet how infantile it all must seem to him. His people had achieved space travel in a time when her ancestors were still commuting by horse and buggy.

Two hundred years, and in all that time, he had been alone. She ached for him, ached in the deepest reaches of her heart and soul, as she tried to imagine what it had been like for him, a stranger in a strange world, afraid to reveal the truth of who he was, afraid to trust those around him, forced to live forever in the shadows.

The curve of his jaw tempted her touch and she traced the outline with her fingertip.

"I'll make it up to you," she whispered. "I don't know how, but I will. I promise."

"Make what up to me?"

His voice, low and husky with sleep, startled her. "You're awake," she exclaimed softly.

He made a soft sound of assent as he opened his eyes. Placing one hand behind her head, he drew her closer, claiming her lips with his. "What are you going to make up to me, Kara?"

She shook her head as she felt a faint blush creep into her cheeks. "Nothing."

His lips nibbled at her ear. "Tell me."

"I was thinking how awful it must have been for you these past two hundred years, living alone, needing . . . someone to love. . . ." She took a deep breath, embarrassed that he had overheard her words. "I . . . I want to make you forget all those lonely years and . . ." Her gaze slid away from his. It sounded so silly when spoken aloud.

"Go on," he coaxed softly.

"I want to make you happy, Alex."

"You already make me happy."

"Do I?"

Nodding, he trailed his fingertips down her cheek. "More happy than I've ever been in my life."

"I'm glad."

Needing to touch him, she ran her hands over his shoulders, then slid her arms around his waist and hugged him close. Restless with wanting him, she caressed his back, her fingertips exploring the ridge of flesh along his spine. It didn't repel her now. It was a part of him, a part of who and what he was.

And it was all so incredible.

She knew so little about him, about his past, she was suddenly filled with questions. "Is Alexander the name you were born with?"

He shook his head. "I was named HeshLon, after my paternal grandfather."

"HeshLon." She repeated the name, liking the sound of it. "Where did the name Alexander Claybourne come from?"

"The phone book," he said with a wry grin.

"I like HeshLon," she said. "It suits you. Tell me, what are houses like where you come from? Do your people sleep in beds and cook on stoves?"

Alex grinned, surprised it had taken her curiosity so long to emerge. "Yes, *natayah*, we sleep in beds and cook on stoves, although our stoves are powered by our sun rather than electricity. Our houses are very similar to yours in design and function, although they're built of different materials."

"Like what?"

"They're made of a kind of, I don't know, plastic brick, I guess you'd call it. It warms our houses in the winter, and cools them in the summer."

"Really? That's amazing." She sat up, her curiosity building. "Is your food the same as ours?"

"In a way." Sitting up, he put his arm around her shoulders and drew her up against him. "We have fruits and vegetables and a kind of bread. Our animals are also much the same as yours," he went on, anticipating her next question. "We have four-legged beasts and birds and insects, and animals that produce milk. Some are used for food, although meat is eaten sparingly on ErAdona."

"What did you do before you came to earth? Did you have a job?"

"I was what you would call a mining engineer."

"Really? What did you mine?"

"An ore similar to uranium. It's very rare, and very valuable."

"Are there others of your kind here?" she asked, wondering why the thought hadn't occurred to her before.

"Not to my knowledge."

"Is there any way you can contact your people?"

"No."

A sigh rose from deep within him; for a moment, she saw a lingering trace of sadness in his eyes.

"I'm sorry, Alex."

His arm tightened around her shoulder. "It doesn't matter anymore," he said quietly.

The words, the unspoken implication that she was enough for him, filled Kara's heart with warmth. "I love you, Alex."

"I know."

"Reading my mind again?"

"No. I can see it in your eyes, hear it in your voice, feel it in your touch."

He smiled at her, a wave of tenderness sweeping through him. The two hundred years of loneliness and exile had been worth it, he thought, worth every second for this time in Kara's arms. Gladly would he have waited two hundred more to find the love and acceptance he had found in her arms. Her love humbled him, made him weak with gratitude.

He laughed softly as he heard her stomach rumble. "You're hungry," he remarked.

"Yes."

"Let's get you something to eat then."

"Will you eat with me?"

"If you like."

Thirty minutes later, Kara stood at the stove preparing ham and scrambled eggs. Alex sat on the floor. She could feel his gaze on her back. She had heard that phrase a thousand times, and it had been nothing more than words. But she really could feel his gaze moving over her, soft, warm, as tangible as a caress.

"Would you tell me something?" she asked, glancing over her shoulder.

"If I can."

"Is this where you landed when you were sent here?"

"No. They set me down high in the Black Hills."

"What did you do? How did you survive?"

Alexander frowned, remembering. "The team that brought me here left me enough supplies to last a season, as well as a weapon to defend myself and tools with which to build a shelter. I hid my supplies, and explored my new world. The touch of the sun was a torment beyond belief, and I soon learned to avoid it. There were no white people to speak of on the land back then, just Indians.

"I watched them from a distance, fascinated by their primitive lifestyle. In many ways, they reminded me of my ancient ancestors.

"I'd been here less than a week when I got deathly ill. I thought I was going to die. I know now that it was my body's reaction to a new environment. I was adjusting to the violent change in the atmosphere, the food, the water.

"The Indians found me and took care of me. I was sick for several days."

"What did they think about the flesh on your back?"

"They thought it a strange sort of tattoo. When I recovered, they indicated I was welcome to stay, and I agreed. I had no wish to be alone in this strange place. I quickly learned their language, their ways."

He paused while she filled two plates and handed him one. She offered him a cup of coffee, as well, then sat down beside him, her back to the wall.

"Go on."

Alex stared at the food on his plate. He had no appetite, no need for food at this time. Still, he took a bite because she had cooked it for him, because he didn't want to hurt her feelings.

"Time passed quickly. Everything was new to me and I had much to learn. I stayed with the Indians for almost fifteen years, a part of their village, yet never really a part of them. They thought it strange that I left my lodge only at night, that I refused to take a wife. The shaman explained that my idiosyncrasies were to be accepted, that I had been touched by the Great Spirit. In truth, I stayed inside during the day because I could not tolerate the sun. I didn't take a wife because I was afraid of contaminating her, afraid of what might happen if an earth woman became pregnant with my child."

Alex stared at the eggs congealing on his plate. There had been a woman he cared for, a woman he might have loved had he let himself. But he had turned away from her, and she had married another.

"Gradually, it became evident to the others, and to me, that I wasn't aging. I was never sick. Wounds healed quickly and left no scar. Once, I was captured by the Crow, along with several other warriors. They threw us in a hole, covered it with a bearskin, and left us there for three weeks without food or water. The other men weakened and died. When it became evident that I wasn't going to die, the Crow medicine man declared that I was *wakan*—holy—and they took me back to the Lakota. The people I had lived with shunned me after that. They thought I was an evil spirit, and so I was banished once again. . . ."

It was a story that had replayed itself over and over again. He had found a place he liked, settled down for a short time, then left before people began to wonder why he didn't grow older. At first, he had sought the company of others until he realized it was practically impossible to be sociable without becoming involved. In the end, he had cut himself off from any close association with others.

For a time, he had traveled. It was during that time that he had gained an appreciation for the people of Earth. In spite of their inability to live together in peace, they had erected some marvelous monuments, created some of the most beautiful paintings and sculptures he had ever seen, built breathtaking cathedrals. And the earth itself was a beautiful place, more verdant than his home world.

But always, no matter how far he traveled, he returned to the place where his people had left him, hoping, perhaps, that someday someone would come back for him. And when even that hope died, he had turned to writing, living and loving vicariously through the fictional characters he created.

Kara put her plate aside, her appetite forgotten, saddened by the loneliness that had crept into his voice as he recounted the long, lonely years of his life.

"Are you truly immortal then?" she asked, and realized that she had asked that question once before.

"Everything dies, sooner or later." He smiled at her as he placed his plate on top of hers. In the beginning, the changes in his body had been terrifying; his increased sense of smell and sight and hearing had confused him. His physical strength and stamina were far greater than they had been on ErAdona.

"When I left the Indians, I came here, to this mountain. I built this place using the tools I had buried earlier. I've lived all over the world since then, but I always come back here, to this place." It was home, he thought, or as close to a home as he'd had since he'd been banished from ErAdona. "I've upgraded the furnishings from time to time." He grinned at her as he glanced around. "I guess it's time to refurbish again."

She smiled back at him, but it was a sad kind of smile.

"Kara, you needn't pity me."

"I don't, really. I admire you. I mean, at first it must have taken a great deal of courage, of fortitude, just to survive. And later, as time passed . . ." She shrugged. "I remember watching a vampire movie where one of the vampires said it took a special kind of person to be one of the undead, to stay the same while everything else changed."

Alex nodded. It was true. It had been hard, watching the world change, watching people die, while he went on, and on. But none of that mattered any more.

Kara had brought new meaning to his life, given him a reason to live, hope for the future.

Rising, she refilled her coffee cup, then sat down beside Alex again. "When did you start to write?"

"I'm not sure. Seventy, eighty years ago. Of course, I've had to change publishers and pseudonyms from time to time," he added with a wry grin.

"Yes," Kara said, grinning back at him, "I would think so. Was being a writer something you always wanted to do?"

"No. It was just a way to pass the time. Writing's a solitary profession, something I could do without any interference from anyone else. I've never met any of my agents, or my editors. All my business dealings have been done by mail and an occasional phone call." He laughed softly. "The fact that I don't do book signings, and that I refuse to have my picture taken has added to the mystique of A. Lucard."

"I guess I've been quite a hindrance to your writing, haven't I? I'm probably keeping you from a deadline."

"It doesn't matter."

"You don't have to entertain me, you know. You could spend your days writing if you want." She smiled shyly. "As long as you save your nights for me."

Alex laughed softly. "My nights will be yours, *natayah,* and my days, for as long as you want them."

His words brought a blush to her cheeks, and he thought how beautiful she was.

"Have you always written about vampires and werewolves and the like?"

"No. Originally, I wrote science fiction. You know, space ships and alien invaders." He grinned, remembering. "And then I saw Bela Lugosi in *Dracula* and realized for the first time how similar my lifestyle was to that of your vampires."

"I can't wait to tell Gail that you're from another planet. She'll be thrilled."

"You can't tell her, Kara. You can't tell anyone."

"But she'd be thrilled to death. She's always been so certain that flying saucers were for real. She wouldn't tell anyone."

Alex shook his head. "It's a risk I can't take."

"I understand." Leaning over, she kissed his cheek, then gathered up the dishes and carried them into the kitchen.

Alex watched her wash and dry the dishes, hoping she really did understand. One word, the slightest suspicion that he was from another planet, and they would never know another peaceful moment. They would be hounded, hunted, until he was captured. He'd had two hundred years to witness man's inhumanity to man, two centuries of watching whole cultures destroyed because they were different, because they had stood in the way of wealth or progress. During that time, he had seen countless men like Dale Barrett, men who were willing to sacrifice their honor, their integrity, for the promise of fame and fortune.

He had no desire to be a stepping stone for Barrett's rise to celebrity and glory.

That evening, they went for a walk. Alex carried a long, narrow implement that he explained was like a chain saw, only more refined. They were going to cut down a tree, he said, and the tool in his hand would not only fell the tree, but cut the lumber to the length and thickness he required.

"Do you have any more gadgets like that?"

"A few."

He didn't elaborate, and she didn't ask, but she knew it was with the use of other tools from home that he had cut the windows into the mountain and fashioned the glass. No doubt other alien technology lit the entrance to the cavern.

The woods were beautiful at night. Hand in hand, they walked through the moon-dappled night until Alex found a tree he considered suitable. Kara watched in awe as he attached the object in his hand to the base of the tree.

Thirty minutes later, the tree was at their feet, cut into a dozen workable pieces. He shouldered the wood with ease and carried it up the hill, dumping it in the yard alongside the cavern.

Kara shook her head, amazed by his strength. He'd carried the load up the hill as though it weighed nothing at all, and he wasn't even breathing hard.

Alex turned to find her staring at him. "What's the matter?"

"Nothing." She grinned. "I was just thinking that I used to dream of Prince Charming carrying me away on a horse. Instead, my true love is a combination of the Highlander and Superman."

Alex grinned back at her. "Are you complaining?"

"Oh, no. I think it's wonderful. I mean, talk about a girl's fantasies coming to life."

He grunted in wry amusement. "Is that what I am? A fantasy?"

"No. You're the best reality I've ever known."

He pulled her into his arms and nuzzled her shoulder, and then, laughing softly, he raked his teeth along the side of her neck. If he was really a vampire, now would be the perfect time for a midnight snack.

"What's so funny?" Kara asked.

"Nothing. How about a bath?"

Kara drew back and frowned up at him. "Is that your subtle way of telling me I stink?"

Alex shook his head. "Maybe it's my not-so-subtle way of trying to get you out of your clothes."

"Oh." She slid her gaze from his, grateful for the darkness that hid the flush she felt climbing into her cheeks.

"That hot spring I mentioned isn't far from here." He reached into his pocket, withdrawing a bar of soap he'd picked up on their way out of the cavern. "Shall we?"

The spring was located within a copse of ancient pine trees and lacy ferns. It was like a fairy place, Kara mused. The water glistened like a pool of molten silver in the full light of the moon; the grass was soft beneath her feet.

For all that they had spent the previous night making love, she couldn't help feeling a little shy as they sat down at the edge of the pool.

Her heart began to pound erratically as Alex removed his shirt and reached for his belt buckle.

"Kara?"

Amanda Ashley

"Hmmm?"

He gestured down the mountain. "Would you rather I waited for you down there?"

"No, it's just . . . no."

Sensing her uneasiness, he turned his back, peeled off his Levi's, and slid soundlessly into the pool.

"Why don't you wear underwear?" She clapped a hand over her mouth, but it was too late to call back the words.

Alex turned in the water, head cocked to one side as he regarded her.

"I didn't mean to ask that," she said, wishing she could disappear under a rock.

"You can ask me anything you wish. The people of ErAdona wear very little in the way of clothing. Our men usually wear loose shirts and trousers made of finely woven cloth. The women wear long gowns of a material similar to your silk. No one wears anything underneath." He made a vague gesture. "Even after two hundred years, it's a habit I find hard to break."

Kara nodded, mesmerized by the sight of him. The water caressed his broad shoulders. The moonlight shimmered in his hair. She could feel the heat of his gaze as he waited for her to join him.

She took a deep breath. "Don't watch me."

With a nod, Alex turned his back, but he didn't have to see her to know how she looked, what she was doing. He could hear the muted brush of cloth over her skin as she removed her sweater, her shoes and socks, her jeans. There was a faint whisper of nylon and lace as she slipped off her panties and bra, followed by a faint splash as she stepped into the water. A change in the wind carried her scent to his nostrils and he took a deep breath, inhaling her fragrance.

He moved to deeper water, then turned to face her, his breath catching in his throat as he saw her standing before him, clad in water and moonlight.

"You are so beautiful, *natayah*," he murmured.

"Am I?"

Alex nodded. She looked like the ErAdonian goddess of fertility. He watched the color rise in her cheeks, felt his blood thicken as his body grew heavy with desire.

"Kara . . ."

She couldn't speak, could hardly breathe, as he moved toward her. Unable to draw her gaze from his, she waited, her heart pounding wildly in her breast. Tall and broad-shouldered, roguishly handsome, he cut smoothly through the water, the heat glowing in the depths of his eyes hotter than the bubbling spring.

And then his hands were on her shoulders, and he was bending toward her, until she saw nothing but his face, felt nothing but his hands sliding slowly, sensuously, down her back, locking around her waist, drawing her body against his.

With a low groan, he slanted his mouth over hers, his tongue skimming across her lower lip like a silken flame.

Her skin was on fire and her bones were melting, she thought, dazed. Her legs felt like straw; every nerve ending tingled with awareness. Her head fell back, giving him access to the hollow of her throat.

His lips trailed down the exposed curve of her neck as his hands slid sensuously upward until they cupped her breasts.

"Alex," she moaned softly. "Alex, please . . ."

"What, Kara?" He drew back, his gaze burning into hers. "Tell me what you want."

She couldn't put it into words; instead, she pressed brazenly against him. "Alex . . ."

With a muffled cry, he swung her into his arms and carried her to the edge of the spring, and there, partially submerged in the warm swirling water, he joined his flesh and his spirit to hers.

She writhed beneath him, her nails clawing at the ridged flesh of his back, exciting him still further. Her legs locked around his waist to hold him close as she whispered his name over and over again, begging him to end the sweet torment. And then she was soaring, flying, reaching for that one moment of fulfillment and perfection.

His own release followed immediately. She felt the warmth and heat of him as his life poured into her, filling her, making her complete.

For endless moments, there was only the muted sound of the water lapping against their bodies and the harsh rasp of his breath in her ear. Never, she thought, never had she dreamed such ecstacy, such unity, existed.

She hugged him closer, wishing they could stay entwined in each other's arms forever.

She frowned as he began to draw away. "What is it?" she asked, her gaze searching his. "Alex?" A cold, nameless fear ensnared her heart when she saw his face. "Alex, what's wrong? You're scaring me."

He shook his head. "Kara, I'm sorry."

"Sorry?" Feeling suddenly vulnerable, she sat up and crossed her arms over her breasts. "Why?"

"We never should have made love."

"Oh?" Her voice sounded small and incredibly

young. "I'm sorry you feel that way."

"Kara." He drew her into his arms, holding her in his lap as if she were a child. "I didn't mean it like that. It's just that we didn't use any protection."

"Oh," she murmured, relieved. "Is that all?" In spite of the fact that she had agreed with him that now was not the time to think about having a baby, she couldn't help but think how wonderful it would be to have Alex's baby. A boy, with his father's black hair and dark eyes.

"Kara."

"What?"

"I told you before that I didn't know if I could father a child with an earth woman."

Kara nodded. "I remember."

He took a deep breath. "I don't know what would happen to you if you did get pregnant."

"What do you mean?"

"That should be obvious. We're from different planets. My blood is different from yours, different than it was when I first came here. I don't know what effect these changes might have on a child, or . . . or on you. A pregnancy might be dangerous, even fatal, to you both."

Kara shivered. The water lapping at her feet felt suddenly cold. *Dangerous. Fatal.* His words echoed in her mind.

"Kara, I'm sorry."

"It's not your fault. I wanted it as badly as you did. Maybe more."

"But I knew better."

"Alex, it's done. There's no sense tearing yourself up inside. Anyway, there are always risks when a woman gets pregnant," she added, hoping to allay not only his fears, but her own. "It's part of life."

But she couldn't help wondering what would happen if she did get pregnant. What had she done? What kind of child would result from their union?

Alex stood up, carrying her with him. "You're cold," he said.

She nodded, though it wasn't the cool air that was making her shiver. *Dangerous. Fatal.* The words repeated themselves in her mind, frightening her in spite of her bold words.

As if she were a helpless child, she let him dry her off and dress her. She watched while he pulled on his pants, her gaze drawn to the dark stripe down his back. He slipped his shirt over his head, and then he lifted her into his arms and carried her up the mountain, into the cavern.

Inside, Alex removed her clothing and tucked her into bed. Undressing, he slid in beside her and gathered her into his arms.

Please, please, please . . . Just the single word, playing over and over in his mind.

Please let her be all right.

Please don't let my seed take root within her womb.

I've been alone so long. Please don't take her from me. . . .

He held her all through the night, praying to the gods of his home world, to the Great Spirit of the Lakota, begging for mercy.

Forgive me, he pleaded. *Punish me, but please don't let anything happen to the woman asleep in my arms.* . . .

Chapter Sixteen

When Kara woke the next morning, it was late and she was alone. She felt a rush of panic, and then, hearing the sound of hammering, she relaxed. He was here.

She stared up at the smooth stone ceiling, remembering the night past, the self-recrimination in Alexander's eyes, the fear. It had been for her, that fear.

She placed a hand over her stomach. What if she was pregnant? Would that really be so terrible? Except for that peculiar strip of ridged flesh on his spine, Alex looked exactly like any other man. She grinned wryly. It wasn't as if he was Jabba from *Star Wars*, or the gill-man from the Black Lagoon.

She grunted softly as a new thought occurred to her. Alex had mentioned the fact that his blood was different from hers and might cause her harm, but he had already given her some of his blood, and nothing had happened. Had he forgotten that?

Throwing off the covers, she scrambled out of bed, dressed in jeans and a sweatshirt, and went into the main room.

She paused in the doorway, her gaze moving over Alex. He was building a table from the tree he had felled the night before. For a moment, she admired the play of muscles in his broad back and shoulders. He glanced over his shoulder to smile at her, and happiness bubbled up within her, as effervescent as sparkling champagne.

"Good morning," she said, stepping into the room.

"Good morning." He finished hammering one of the table's legs in place, then brushed a lock of hair from his face. "Did you sleep well?"

Kara nodded. "Did you?"

He shook his head. "No."

"You were worrying about me, weren't you?"

He nodded, his gaze moving over her face.

"I'm fine, honest." She sat down on the floor, legs bent, her arms resting on her knees. "Don't you think maybe you're worrying for nothing? I mean, you gave me your blood and nothing bad happened."

He frowned, and Kara knew she'd been right. He had forgotten.

"So," she said brightly. "Maybe there's nothing to worry about. Anyway, I'm probably not pregnant. I am hungry, though. Are you? Oh, sorry." She grinned self-consciously. She'd forgotten he didn't need to eat every day.

"Go make yourself some breakfast," Alex said. "The table should be done when you're ready."

Rising to her feet, Kara crossed the floor toward the kitchen, thinking she would rather eat sitting on the floor than standing at the table, and then she saw the chairs, two of them. Stout, serviceable, the backs intricately carved, one slightly larger than the other. An image of the three bears rose in her mind and made her smile. One for papa bear, and one for mama bear . . .

"You do nice work, Alex," she called over her shoulder.

"Thanks."

He watched her move around the kitchen, thinking how different the cavern felt with Kara to share it. Thinking how different he felt. Maybe she was right. Maybe he was worrying for nothing. He had given her his blood, and she hadn't suffered any ill effects. He stared at the hammer in his hand, trying to stifle the rush of hope that flooded through him as he imagined what it would be like to share his life with Kara. And then, unable to help himself, he pictured Kara holding his child. Ah, to give her a son, he thought, to hold a child of his own in his arms again . . .

AnTares . . . His grip tightened on the hammer until his knuckles went white. After his arrest, the council had refused to let him spend any time with his daughter. He had begged them to reconsider, to let him tell her good-bye, but to no avail. The counsel's only concession had been to allow his parents to bring AnTares to the docking bay the morning his ship was to depart.

He closed his eyes, remembering the day he had seen his daughter last, her clear gray eyes awash with tears. She had reached out to him, begging him not to leave her. The sound of her cries had followed him as he was led to the ship. He had yearned to go to her, to try to explain why he was being sent away, why he would never see her again. In desperation, he had turned to the head of the counsel, pleading for DaTra's understanding, begging to be allowed to hold his daughter one last time, to tell her he loved her, but DaTra had adamantly refused. On board the spacecraft, Alex had stared out the ship's view port, his gaze fixed on his daughter's face, until all ports had been sealed and she had been lost to his sight forever.

Alex hammered the last nail in place and righted the table. After all these years, the thought of her still had the power to cause him pain. *AnTares, forgive me . . .*

"Alex?"

He looked up to find Kara watching him. "I'm sorry, did you say something?"

"I asked if you wanted a cup of coffee, or maybe a glass of water."

"No, thank you."

"Is everything all right?"

"Fine."

She tilted her head to one side, her expression doubtful. "You don't have to tell me if you don't want to," she said quietly. "But you don't have to lie, either."

"I'm sorry, Kara. I was thinking about my daughter."

She nodded, not knowing what to say.

He carried the table into the kitchen and put the chairs in place, one on each side.

"Will you sit with me while I eat?" Kara asked. She placed her plate and a cup of coffee on the table and sat down.

With a nod, Alex sat across from her.

"What shall we do today?" she asked.

"I don't know. I'm afraid there isn't much to do up here." He glanced at the empty bookcase. Even reading was no longer an option.

Kara regarded him over the edge of her coffee cup. "I have an idea."

He looked at her expectantly, and then, watching her cheeks bloom with color, he knew what she had in mind.

"Kara . . ."

She looked at him through wide, innocent eyes. "We can't go out while the sun's up," she said, smiling seductively. "So we can't go for a swim, or a walk." She shrugged. "We can't sit and read because you burned up all the books. So, can you think of a better way to pass the day?"

"No."

"Good." Pushing away from the table, Kara stood up and took his hand.

Heart pounding, his body humming with awareness and desire, Alex let her lead him into the bedroom. He stood passively, the blood rushing through his veins, thrumming in his ears, as she began to undress him.

When he reached for her, she swatted his hands away. "Not yet," she murmured, and so he stood there, his body trembling with longing, while she ran her hands over his flesh, pressed her lips to his chest, bent to explore his navel with her tongue.

He groaned as the ache to hold her grew painful. "My turn," he said with a growl, and with slow deliberation, he began to undress her, his hands sliding seductively over her flesh until she, too, was quivering with need.

Swinging her into his arms, he carried her to bed. He felt her gaze on his back as he took the necessary precautions, and then she was in his arms, whispering his name, urging him to hold her, to love her, and never let her go.

And he was more than willing to oblige.

They spent the afternoon in bed, making love, sleeping, making love again, until darkness settled over the mountain.

Later, after a leisurely bath at the hot spring, they went for a long walk through the woods.

"Alex, do you think Barrett's given up yet?"

"I doubt it."

"I need to call home."

"I know, but it's too soon. Maybe in a couple of weeks."

Kara nodded. As eager as she was to call home, to let Nana and Gail know where she was, to make sure all was well at home, she knew Alex was right.

They drove to town the following night and put a deposit on a new black leather sofa and a matching chair for the main room. Tomorrow, Kara would rent a truck to carry them up the mountain.

After leaving the furniture store, they wandered through a bookstore, buying whatever piqued their interest, until they had almost enough books to restock the bookshelf. They bought a portable stereo and spent an hour choosing cassettes.

Their last stop was at the grocery store where they bought bread and milk, a variety of canned goods, and some fresh fruits and vegetables. Alex lifted an eyebrow in amusement as Kara dropped a dozen candy bars into the shopping cart.

"Sweets for the sweet?" he murmured.

"Just give me my chocolate and no one gets hurt," she retorted with a saucy grin.

Time passed quickly, the days turning into weeks, the weeks into a month.

In spite of everything, Kara had never been happier. She put her fears for the future behind her, determined to enjoy this time with Alex. She quickly adjusted her lifestyle to his. They stayed up late at night and slept late in the morning. Sometimes they spent the afternoon reading. Alex was a voracious reader with a wide range of interests. He might read Shakespeare one day, and Tom Clancy's latest novel the next. He also enjoyed medieval history and philosophy. Some days they played cards; poker, canasta, pinochle, gin rummy, he was adept at them all. He taught her to play chess.

At other times, when he was feeling melancholy, he told her of his life on ErAdona, of his parents and his daughter. He rarely mentioned his wife. Life on ErAdona sounded very much like life on Earth, only much more peaceful. Kara tried to imagine cities without crime or pollution, tried to imagine being able to walk down the streets of New York or Los Angeles late at night, alone and unafraid.

In the evening, they often went for long walks. Now was one of those times. Kara had grown to love the night. She found beauty in the darkness that she had never seen in the daylight, heard things she had never noticed before. She listened to the wind whisper love songs to the pines, heard the soft scurrying sounds of the small night creatures that came out only after sundown. She saw an owl questing for prey, a doe tiptoeing through the forest. She felt a shiver run down her spine the first time she heard the melancholy cry of a coyote.

Sometimes it surprised her, how happy she was, living in a cavern on the top of a mountain, far from the world she had known.

She glanced at Alex, walking beside her, and knew she would be content to spend the rest of her life here, in this place, with this man.

She wasn't surprised when their journey ended at the hot spring. It had become their special place, a magical place.

Heat rose within her, warm, alive, exciting, as Alex reached for her. She craved his touch, burned for his kisses. No longer shy, she let her hands drift over his hard-muscled body, a body she now knew as intimately as she knew her own. She began to undress him with infinite care, wanting to prolong the pleasure. She loved to touch him, to watch his eyes grow hot with desire as she removed his shirt and ran her fingernails over his chest and back, letting her palms slide slowly, seductively, over the unique ridge of flesh on his spine.

His groan of pleasure filled her with joy. Never, she thought, never had she dreamed that love could be so wonderful, so beautiful.

Locked in each other's arms, they sank to the ground. Heart pounding, Kara lay back while Alex undressed her with gentle hands, his dark eyes aglow with love and desire. And then he was kissing her again, his tongue moving over her like a flame of fire.

She drew him deep inside her, wanting to shelter him, to shield him, to absorb him into herself.

"Alex!" She cried his name aloud as his body merged with hers. Her nails raked his back, fueling his desire, until she writhed beneath him. "I love you," she gasped. "Love you!"

The words rose in her throat, repeating themselves over and over again as he carried her higher, higher, until they soared above the earth, bodies and souls melded into one.

Natayah . . .

She heard his voice in her mind, an exultant cry as she shuddered to completion beneath him.

Kara, ah, Kara . . .

She felt his warmth spill into her, filling her, and then he buried his face against her shoulder, his body trembling convulsively.

"I love you, Alex." She whispered the words as she stroked his hair. "I love you so."

Much later, after a leisurely soak in the hot spring, they lay side by side in the moonlight. Kara gazed up at the stars, wondering again which one was his. There was so much about him she didn't know.

"You're very quiet," Alex remarked. "Is anything wrong?"

"No. I was just wondering . . . do your people believe in God?"

"Of course."

Turning on her side, she raised herself on her elbow so she could see his face. "Tell me what you believe."

"Our beliefs are much like yours. We believe in one God, a superior Being who created the universe. It is against our laws to steal, to kill, to lie."

"Do you have churches?"

"Yes."

"Do you have more than one religion?"

"No. In that, my people are different from yours.

201

Every race of people I've ever encountered believes in a Supreme Being, but it is the same God, Kara. It doesn't matter whether you call him *Wakan Tanka*, Elohim, or Allah. He is the same. Omnipotent. Eternal. Without beginning of days or end of years."

Kara nodded. What he said was what she had always believed. She remembered a scripture she had read once that had stuck in her mind: "Worlds without number have I created; and I also created them for mine own purpose . . . For behold, there are many worlds that have passed away . . . And there are many that now stand, and innumerable are they unto man; but all things are numbered unto me, for they are mine and I know them. . . ."

"Were you . . . *are* you a religious man?"

Alex nodded, the burden of killing Rell pricking his conscience. But he did not regret killing the man; he would do it again even though he knew it was wrong.

"Have you been to other planets?"

Alex turned on his side to face her. "Some. People are the same wherever you find them, Kara. They're all humanoid. One head, two arms, two legs. There might be minor differences in skin or hair texture, but none of them look like the ridiculous creatures depicted in your books or movies. They don't fly around the galaxy abducting people and subjecting them to bizarre experiments. Most are too busy living their own lives to worry overmuch about life in another part of the galaxy."

"I always thought that if we found people on other planets, they'd be just like us," Kara remarked. "I mean, my Bible tells me that God created man in His own image." She shrugged. "I always thought if that was true, then people would be the same all over. It's kind of nice to know I was right. Do they—I mean, have any of the people from other planets . . . You know what I mean. Have any of the people from your planet had children with other races?"

"Not to my knowledge."

"Never?"

"I don't know, Kara. I only know that, among my people, it's forbidden to mate with those from other worlds. I can't help but think there must be a good reason behind such a strict directive."

Knowing he was probably right made her feel suddenly alone. She didn't want to think about it anymore. He'd told her that people were alike all over, and yet it seemed they weren't exactly alike, after all.

She stretched out on the ground again, her arms folded behind her head as she stared up at the stars. Thoughts of Gail and Nana crowded her mind.

"I wonder how things are going at home," she remarked, anxious to change the subject. "I've got to call Gail."

He nodded slowly. He understood what she was feeling, knew she needed to assure herself that she wasn't cut off from everyone and everything she loved. It was a feeling he knew well.

"Who did you call last time?"

"Mrs. Zimmermann next door."

"All right. Tomorrow night, we'll call Mrs. Zimmermann."

Chapter Seventeen

They drove down the mountain at dusk. Kara could hardly sit still, so anxious was she at the prospect of calling home.

They pulled into the first gas station they saw to make the call. Kara fidgeted nervously while she dialed the number. The phone seemed to ring forever.

"She doesn't answer," Kara said, hanging up the receiver.

"We'll try again tomorrow night."

"No. I want to call home. I have to get in touch with Gail."

"Kara, we talked about that before. It might not be safe."

"I don't care! I have to call home, Alex. I have a feeling something's wrong."

He studied her face for a moment, then sighed in

resignation. "I'll make the call. No one will recognize my voice."

Kara nodded in agreement. Dialing quickly, she thrust the receiver into his hand.

The phone rang three times, then a female voice Alex didn't recognize answered the phone. "Hello?"

"Hello. May I speak to Kara, please?"

"I'm sorry, she's not here. May I take a message?"

"Is Gail there?"

"Yes. May I ask who's calling?"

"I'm a friend of Kara's."

"Oh?" There was a world of curiosity in the word.

"May I speak to Gail, please?"

"Who should I say is calling?"

Alex grimaced. "Who am I speaking to?"

"This is Mrs. Zimmermann."

Alex held the receiver out to Kara. "The neighbor lady's on the phone."

Kara's hand was shaking as she lifted the receiver to her ear. Something *was* wrong. She knew it. "Mrs. Zimmermann?"

"Kara, is that you?"

"Yes. Is everything all right?"

"I'm afraid I have some bad news, dear. Your . . . your grandmother . . . she's, I mean, ah, she's in the hospital."

"The hospital! What happened?"

"She collapsed at the grocery store."

"Collapsed! Is she all right? When did it happen?"

"It happened day before yesterday," Mrs. Zimmermann said, sounding flustered. "At first they thought it was a heart attack, but they've ruled that out."

"Where's Gail?"

"She's here. Hold on, I'll get her."

Moments later, Gail's voice came over the phone. "Kara, Kara, where are you? When are you coming home?"

"As soon as I can, sweetie. How's Nana?"

"I don't know. Dr. Petersen said it was caused by stress. They're giving her some kind of medicine. I don't know what it is." Gail sniffed loudly. "He said she'll probably be all right. But what if she isn't?"

"Gail, has Barrett been around?"

"Every day. And he's not alone. There's two guys with him. They look like—like crooks."

"What hospital is Nana in?"

"The one here in town. Dr. Barrett suggested moving her to Grenvale for some kind of test. He says they have better facilities there."

"Tell Nana to stay where she is, Gail. Tell her to insist she wants Dr. Petersen to look after her. Is Mrs. Zimmermann staying with you?"

"Yes. I'm scared, Kara. Please come home."

"I will. Have you called Steve?"

"I tried, but he's out in the jungle somewhere and they can't get hold of him."

"All right. Don't tell anyone I called. I've got to go now, Gail. Try not to worry. I'll be home as soon as I can."

"All right. Bye."

Kara hung up the receiver and turned away from the phone. "Oh, Alex, Nana's . . ."

"I know," he said, drawing her into his arms. "I heard."

"I've got to go home."

"I can't let you do that. You heard what Gail said. Barrett's been there every day."

"I don't care. I've got to see Nana." She looked up at Alex, hope shining through her tears. "You can

206

help her, can't you, the way you helped me? She'll get better if you give her some of your blood. I know she will. Please, Alex, I can't let her die."

"Kara . . ." His hands knotted into fists. What she was asking was impossible. He hadn't managed to survive here for two hundred years by taking chances. His life span might have increased drastically, but he wasn't truly immortal. He was subject to pain and death just like any other living creature. "As much as I'd like to, I can't do what you want."

"Why not?"

"I can't."

"Very well, then, I'll go alone."

"Dammit, Kara, I understand how you feel, but I can't let you go home. I won't let you put your life in jeopardy."

"If you won't go with me, then I'll go alone. But I am going! Nana's taken care of me since I was fourteen. I can't desert her now, when she needs me most. I can't, and I won't."

She stared at Alex through her tears, feeling as though he had betrayed her. She had counted on him to help her, and he'd let her down.

"If you won't give her any of your blood, then I'll give her some of mine. Maybe it will work just as well as yours, but even if it doesn't, I've got to go. I've got to try."

Alex stared at the tears shining in her eyes, at the stubborn tilt of her head, and knew he couldn't let her face Barrett alone.

"Your blood would work just fine, Kara."

"What do you mean?"

"Just what I said." Alex took a deep breath. It was time she knew the truth. In a voice devoid of emotion, he told her the whole truth about the rat and how he had tested her blood, as well as his own. Both had restored the rodent's health, though his own blood, unmixed and undiluted, had worked more quickly.

"Why didn't you tell me this before?"

"I don't know."

Kara shook her head. "It's not possible."

"It's very possible. It appears your blood now contains the same healing agent as mine, whatever that might be. That's why Barrett needs you. I think he wants to try and isolate whatever it is that generates the healing. Don't you see? If he can mass produce it, he'll be a millionaire many times over. And if he can't . . ."

"And if he can't, he'll just take my blood a little at a time and sell it to the highest bidder."

Alex nodded.

Kara shuddered. It was a frightening thought. For a moment, she imagined herself kept in a cage, well-fed and well-cared for, but a prisoner nonetheless, kept in isolation while Barrett siphoned off her blood, selling it a little at a time while he tried to find a way to reproduce it.

"It's a frightening thing to consider, isn't it?" Alex asked quietly.

"Yes." She understood now why he had kept to himself, why he had never let anyone know what he was.

"Now do you understand why I can't let you go home?"

"I have to go, Alex. I have to help Nana if I can. Please try to understand."

Short of locking her up inside the mountain, there was no way to stop her. "All right, Kara," Alex said heavily, "I'll take you home."

She collapsed against him, her shoulders heaving as sobs wracked her body.

"Don't cry, *natayah*," he murmured. "Please don't cry. You shall go home."

"Thank you, Alex."

He nodded. "We'll leave tomorrow as soon as it's dark." Holding her away from him, he wiped away her tears with his fingertips; then, taking her hand in his, they walked back to the car.

Gail's footsteps were heavy as she walked home from school. She had called the hospital last night after she'd talked to Kara. The nurse had assured her that Nana was resting comfortably.

Turning down the street toward her house, she wondered when Kara would get home, and where she'd been for the last five weeks.

She frowned when she saw the dark blue car parked in the driveway. Barrett again. He came by every day to ask if Kara had called. She wasn't sure, but she thought she'd seen that same car following her to and from school.

Gail muttered a nasty word. She didn't like Barrett, even though he'd never said or done anything to earn her dislike. She didn't like him and she didn't trust him any more than she trusted those two men who were always with him. Their names were Kelsey and Handeland. Barrett said they were his associates. She wasn't sure what that meant, but she didn't like the sound of it at all. The two men were always wandering through the house, looking in the closets, poking into drawers, rummaging through Nana's desk. Several times a day, they walked through the neighborhood. She knew they were looking for Kara.

Barrett was sitting on the sofa, talking to Mrs. Zimmermann, when Gail entered the house. She didn't see his associates, so she assumed they were outside, prowling around the neighborhood.

"Ah, Gail," he said. "There you are."

"Hello."

He smiled at her, ignoring her sullen expression. "Still no word from Kara?"

"No."

He nodded slowly. "I hope she calls soon. Every day without treatment only decreases your sister's chances of a full recovery."

"What does she need to recover from?"

"As I told you before, we found a gross abnormality in her red blood cells. I'm afraid it may prove fatal." He shook his head. "Her condition could also prove to be contagious." He smiled his oily smile. "If you come into contact with her, you might also be at risk." His gaze bored into hers. "Are you sure she hasn't called home?"

"I'm sure." Gail held his gaze as long as she could, wondering if he knew she was lying. Suddenly nervous, she glanced at Mrs. Zimmermann, at the floor, out the window. "I've got to go now. I've got homework."

"You're lying, aren't you, Gail? She called last night, didn't she?"

Gail shook her head. "No."

Barrett slammed his fist on the coffee table. He had spent the last week finding a suitable place for a lab, had spent a good portion of his life savings setting it up. He swore under his breath. He had waited years for a break like this, had devoted countless hours to research, hoping to find a way to extend the human life span, and now, when he finally had what might be the answer to years of research, they couldn't find the damn woman. Every day wasted meant lives lost that might have been saved.

"I'm tired of this!" he exclaimed. "Tired of waiting!" Rising, he crossed the room and grabbed Gail by the arm. "Tell me the truth, dammit!"

"I am! Honest!" She stared up at him, frightened by the fury in his eyes. "You're hurting me."

"Stop that," Mrs. Zimmermann cried. Jumping to her feet, she took hold of Barrett's hand and tried to pull him away from Gail. "Leave her alone!"

Barrett shook Mrs. Zimmermann off. "Talk to me, Gail. I don't want to hurt you, but I've been patient long enough. Where is she?"

"I don't know." She was crying now.

"I'm going to call the police," Mrs. Zimmermann said.

"I don't think so." Barrett's voice, cold as ice, stopped her in her tracks. "Pick up that phone, and I'll break the kid's arm."

"You wouldn't!" Mrs. Zimmermann stared at Barrett, her face pale, her expression one of stunned horror. "You . . . you're a doctor."

"That's right." A cruel smile twisted Barrett's lips. "After I break her arm, I can set it. Now tell me what I want to know!"

"Don't tell him anything," Gail said, sobbing. "I'm . . . I'm not afraid."

She cried out as Barrett twisted her arm behind her back. "Aren't you?" he asked.

Elsie Zimmermann's face paled as Barrett's gaze pierced hers. "Kara . . . she . . . she called last night."

"Mrs. Zimmermann, don't!"

"Shut up, kid." Barrett gave Gail's arm a sharp twist. "Go on, Elsie, what'd she say?"

"Not much. She just called to see how everyone was." Mrs. Zimmermann clasped her hands to her breasts. "I told her Lena was in the hospital."

"Did she say she was coming home?"

"No." Elsie Zimmermann shook her head. "I told you what you wanted to know. Now, unhand Gail."

Barrett grunted softly. "You must have talked to her, too, kid. What'd she say?"

"Nothing. She just said I shouldn't worry."

"But she's coming home, right?"

"No. She knows you're here. I told her you came by every day." Gail smiled smugly. "Kara's too smart to come home."

"Yeah? Well, we'll see about that." He gave Gail a shove toward the sofa. "Sit down, kid. You, too, Elsie." He patted his coat pocket. "I've got to make a couple of phone calls, and I want you two to sit there and be quiet. Understand?"

Mrs. Zimmermann nodded. "I'm sorry, dear," she whispered, wrapping her arms protectively around the girl. "So sorry."

Gail nodded, praying that Kara really was too smart to come home.

Alex drove past Kara's house twice, all his senses alert, every nerve in his body warning him of danger. They had gone to the hospital first only to discover that Kara's grandmother had been transferred to another hospital at her doctor's request.

"Transferred?" Kara asked.

"Yes," the nurse had said, checking Lena Corley's

file. "Dr. Barrett from Grenvale General is now in charge of your grandmother's care."

A sudden coldness settled in the pit of Kara's stomach. "Do you have a number where I can reach him?"

"Yes, right here," the nurse said. "I'll write it down for you."

Kara stared at the paper the nurse handed her. The phone number was her own.

"He's got her," Kara said as they left the hospital. "Barrett's got my grandmother."

"So it would seem." Alex drove by the house a third time, then parked the car at the end of the block and turned to face Kara. "Something's not right in there. You stay here while I go check it out."

"What if Barrett's there?"

"I'm sure he is. But he doesn't know me."

"You'll be careful?"

Alex nodded. "If I'm gone more than ten minutes, you go back up the mountain and wait for me. If I'm not there by tomorrow night, try to get in touch with your brother."

"I'm not leaving you."

"Dammit, Kara, don't be a fool. You won't do your grandmother or Gail any good if you're locked up in some lab. Even if it takes a year for Barrett to give up, at least you'll still have your freedom."

"We're wasting time."

"Promise me you'll leave if I'm not back in ten minutes," Alex said. "Promise me, or we're going back, now, even if I have to tie you up and carry you."

"Oh, all right, I promise."

"I expect you to keep it."

"Be careful."

"I will." He gazed at her for a long moment; then, grasping her by the shoulders, he drew her close and kissed her, hard. "Remember your promise," he said, and slid out of the car.

His sense of danger grew stronger as he approached the house. Standing on the porch, he let his senses expand. There were a number of people inside. He recognized Gail's scent among them.

Taking a deep breath, he knocked on the door.

Chapter Eighteen

Gail blinked up at the tall man standing on the porch. "Mr. Claybourne," she murmured. "What are you doing here?"

"I came to see you, of course."

"Me?" Gail felt a twinge of apprehension as she stared at Alex. He loomed tall and menacing in the pale yellow glow of the porch light. Dressed all in black, with long black hair and penetrating black eyes, he was the perfect image of what she'd always imagined a vampire would look like.

"I thought I'd take you out for ice cream."

"Oh, I . . ." Gail licked her lips nervously, then glanced over her shoulder. Barrett was standing behind her, out of Claybourne's sight. "I can't. Nana needs me here."

"How is your grandmother?"

"Not very well."

"I'm sorry to hear that. Tell her I hope she feels better soon."

"I will."

"Good-bye."

"Bye."

Gail watched him walk down the steps, her mind churning with questions. Where was Kara? Why had Alexander Claybourne really stopped by? She wanted to call him back, wanted to run after him, but she felt Barrett's hand on her arm.

"Shut the door," Barrett ordered curtly.

Gail hesitated a moment, felt Barrett's fingers dig into her arm. Reluctantly, she closed the door.

"Who was that?"

"Just a friend of mine."

Barrett looked at her, his expression skeptical. "A little old for you, isn't he?"

"He's not a boyfriend," Gail said sarcastically. "Just a friend. He's a writer."

"Claybourne?" Barrett frowned.

"He writes horror stories," Gail said. "I used to think he was a vampire."

Barrett laughed as he pushed her toward the living room. "A vampire, huh? Very funny. Sit down."

Gail sat on the sofa and picked up the book she had been reading. It was one of Alexander's vampire books. She knew she wasn't supposed to be reading it, but there was no one there to stop her. Mrs. Zimmermann didn't know she wasn't supposed to read Claybourne's books, and Nana was too sick to care. Gail concentrated on the story. There was a lot of it that she didn't understand, but it kept her mind off Barrett and the other three men who had taken over the house.

She stared at the pages, silently praying that Kara

wouldn't come home and that Barrett would get tired of waiting and go away.

Alex walked away from the house, aware that he was being watched. He had sensed someone standing behind Gail. Barrett, perhaps? There had been others in the house, as well. He had recognized Nana's scent among them. The others had been strangers.

He paused in the shadows beyond the house, wondering what their next move should be, wondering if there were more of Barrett's men keeping watch outside. He considered having Kara call the police, but they had no evidence that Barrett was doing anything illegal. And if Kara confronted Barrett in the presence of the authorities, Barrett would most likely inform the police that he suspected Kara was infected with a deadly virus and insist that she be quarantined in his care.

Alex grunted softly, thoughtfully. Barrett was a respected member of the medical community. Alex had no doubt that the police would accept the doctor's word over his, especially when a police medical examiner studied Kara's blood work.

Alex muttered an oath as he walked down the street toward his car. They'd have to handle this on their own, and in such a way that neither Gail nor her grandmother, nor Mrs. Zimmermann, was put at risk.

He had considered and rejected several plans of action by the time he reached the Porsche. For a moment, he stared at the broken window, refusing to accept the fact that she was gone.

Rage swelled within him, growing stronger with each passing moment. He took a deep breath, and the scent of her fear stung his nostrils.

Unable to contain his fury, he struck the fender of the Porsche with his fist. The metal crumpled as if it were made of tissue paper.

"Damn you, Barrett," he hissed. "If you harm a hair of her head, you'll regret this night as long as you live."

Kara hovered on the edge of awareness. Voices penetrated the darkness—voices that sounded loud, then faded away. She felt the sharp prick of a needle in her arm as someone drew blood. Her head hurt. Nausea roiled in her stomach. There was a bad taste in her mouth.

She swam through layers of darkness, but, try as she might, she couldn't open her eyes. She cried Alexander's name, but no sound emerged from her lips. And then she felt the sting of another needle and she was falling, falling into a deep black void. . . .

She felt better when she woke the second time. She took several deep breaths to clear her head, opened her eyes, and wished she hadn't.

She was in a stark white room. White walls. White floor. White sheets on the hard, narrow bed.

She tried to sit up, and realized her arms and legs were strapped to the bed.

"No. No!" She tried to fight the terror that rose up within her as she saw a rack of glass vials on the table near the door.

Vials filled with blood.

Her blood.

Kara closed her eyes and took a deep breath, trying to control the fear surging through her. Barrett had found her again. It all came rushing back. She'd been sitting in the car, waiting for Alex, when two men had appeared at the window. She had locked the doors, but to no avail. One of the men had calmly broken the window of the Porsche and unlocked the door, then held her immobile while the second man held a rag over her nose and mouth. She hadn't even had time to scream.

"Alex will find me. Alex will find me."

She murmured the words over and over again in an effort to shore up her flagging spirits. He loved her. He would find her.

Her hands clenched into fists as she heard footsteps outside the door, and then Barrett was striding into the room, his face a mask of annoyance as he pulled a syringe from his pocket.

Kara glanced at the numerous vials on the table. "Haven't you already taken enough blood?" she asked caustically.

Barrett glared at her. "What have you done?"

"Done? What do you mean?"

"Your blood's not the same as it was."

"I don't understand."

"That makes two of us, I'm afraid." He jabbed the needle into her arm, frowning irritably. "The last time I injected a little of your blood into a diseased lab rat, it recovered in a matter of minutes. This time there was almost no change."

"I should think the answer would be obvious," she retorted with more courage than she was feeling. "Apparently the magic's worn off." Hope flooded her as she realized what that meant. If her blood had returned to normal, Barrett wouldn't need her anymore.

"Have you been sick? Had a high fever? Anything?"

"No." She met Barrett's gaze. "Can I go home now?"

"Not until I get some answers." Barrett withdrew the needle, then stood beside the bed, staring at Kara thoughtfully. "You said you'd given blood before and it was always normal, so whatever induced the aberration must have been caused by the blood you received while you were in the hospital."

He ran a hand through his hair, then began to pace the narrow confines of the room. "The blood you received in the hospital came from your grandmother and the neighbor woman," he said, thinking out loud. "I gave you a transfusion of their blood today while you were unconscious, but neither effected any change."

He stood beside the table, staring at the blood samples. "Did anyone else give you blood while you were in the hospital?"

"No, of course not. How could they?"

"Yes, how could they?" Barrett turned to face her. "You called for someone while you were unconscious," he remarked thoughtfully, and then he swore. "Alex. Alexander." He nodded, obviously pleased. "It was Claybourne, wasn't it?"

"Why would he give me blood? I hardly know the man."

"Your sister said she once thought he was a vampire," Barrett remarked, thinking aloud. "I wonder why."

"That's ridiculous."

Barrett shrugged. "Maybe. And, the lab technician. He said the man who knocked him out had superhuman strength, that he closed the door without touching it."

"You're a doctor. Surely you don't believe such nonsense."

"You'd be surprised at what I believe in," Barrett retorted. "That was Claybourne's car you were in when Kelsey found you, wasn't it?"

"No." Kara shook her head. "No."

"He's the key, isn't he? The missing part to the puzzle."

"No!" She pulled against the thick leather straps. "Please, let me go!"

"I think not." Barrett grinned at her. "We have ways of making you talk," he said, and then he laughed. "I've always wanted to say that."

Going to the door, he hollered for someone named Kelsey. Moments later, the man who had broken the window of the Porsche appeared.

"Prepare an injection of sodium pentobarbital."

With a nod, Kelsey went to do as bidden.

Kara stared at Barrett, hating him. Fearing him because he would soon have the power to make her betray Alex. She tried to erase his name, his memory, from her mind, but she knew it was impossible.

And then Kelsey was back, handing a needle to Barrett, and Barrett was inserting the needle in her vein, telling her to count backward from a hundred.

Knowing it was useless to resist, she did as she was told, and all the while, she prayed that Alex would understand and forgive her.

Mind reeling from what he'd heard, Dale Barrett leaned back against the wall, his arms dangling at his sides, as he stared at Kara Crawford.

Alexander Claybourne was from outer space.

It was incredible, preposterous, totally impossible.

And yet it had to be the truth. He had questioned Kara for over an hour, and always her answers had been the same. Claybourne was an alien. He had given Kara his blood, and it had wrought some sort of mysterious change that had, temporarily at least, endowed her blood with miraculous curative powers. She had claimed that he was sensitive to sunlight, that he drew strength from the moon.

It was inconceivable, and yet he knew it was true. It was the only answer that made sense.

Barrett wiped the perspiration from his brow, his mind whirling with unanswered questions.

Would the alien's blood effect the same change when mixed with other human blood types, or did the blood have to be A positive, like Crawford's, or did it have to be mixed with Crawford's specifically?

Was it necessary to mix human blood with the alien blood to achieve the desired result, or did the alien blood alone possess the same healing power?

And what about longevity? Crawford had said the alien was over two hundred years old. Would a transfusion of alien blood increase a mortal life span, as well?

Questions, so many questions, and the alien held all the answers.

Barrett smiled as he pushed away from the wall. Finding Claybourne shouldn't be too hard, not when he had the perfect bait for the trap.

He had always dreamed of saving lives, but this . . .

He closed his eyes, his mind reeling with possibilities. And every one of them was wreathed in dollar signs.

Chapter Nineteen

Alexander prowled the city, searching for Kara. He looked up Barrett's home address and went there, but the house was dark, and he sensed no human presence inside.

He went to the hospital in Grenvale, but they had no record of her there, and he had no sense of her presence in the building.

Where was she?

Knowing it was dangerous, he drove up and down the city streets, his eyes burning from the light of the rising sun until, with a cry of rage and frustration, he headed for home.

He was trembling with pain and an over-powering sense of weakness by the time he reached the shelter of the house.

Locking the door behind him, he staggered into the den and sank down on the floor. Eyes closed, he took several deep breaths, wondering if he would ever overcome the ill effects of the earth's sun, if he would ever be able to walk in the light of day without experiencing pain and weakness.

Gradually, the pain lost its intensity and he opened his eyes, staring at the painting over the fireplace. He had often imagined that he was the man in the painting, that, just once, he could stand atop a mountain and bask in the warmth of the rising sun.

With an effort, he gained his feet, then climbed the stairs to the bedroom. He needed sleep, needed to replenish his energy, his strength, before nightfall.

Stretching out on the bed, he opened his mind, searching for Kara. *Call me,* he begged. *Whisper my name, tell me where you are, and I'll come for you.*

But no answer came to him.

Feeling helpless and alone, he closed his eyes and willed himself to sleep, knowing that, for the moment, there was nothing else he could do.

Barrett stood at Kara's bedside, his hands fisted on his hips. "I want you to call him. Now."

"I can't. He doesn't have a phone."

Barrett laughed humorlessly. "Call him with your mind!"

Kara shook her head. "I can't."

"You can, and we both know it. Don't make me angry, Kara. You won't like what happens if you do."

"Threaten me all you want. I won't call him."

Barrett swore under his breath. The girl had been defying him for two days. At his wit's end, he had gone back to her house, intent on bringing her sister back to the lab with him, certain Crawford would relent if he threatened her sister's life, only to find the man he left to watch three seemingly helpless females locked in a closet and the girl, her grandmother, and the nosy neighbor all gone without a trace.

He shook his head. He should have known better than to leave Mitch Hamblin behind. The kid was eager and willing, but he was young. Fortunately, youth was something he'd outgrow, if he lived long enough.

Barrett grinned humorlessly. Hamblin had looked as sheepish as hell when he emerged from that closet. When asked for an explanation, Hamblin had replied that the girl had asked him to get something off the shelf in the closet and then had slammed the door and locked him in.

Barrett turned away from the bed and stared at the vials of blood on the metal table beside the door. He had performed every test he could devise, but to no avail. Whatever healing properties the girl's blood had once possessed had disappeared completely.

His only hope was to find the alien.

"I can make her do whatever you want."

Barrett grimaced at Handeland's quiet words. Joe Handeland was a brute of a man. Barrett had no doubt he could do exactly what he said.

Barrett sighed heavily. He didn't approve of violence, but the girl was stubborn, and he was desperate. "All right," he said, "just don't kill her."

Handeland nodded. "Maybe you'd better leave the room."

Fear turned Kara's blood to ice as the man called

Handeland loomed over her. She cried Barrett's name, her voice shrill.

"What do you want?"

"You can't mean to leave me alone with this . . . this man."

"That's up to you," Barrett replied. He stood on the other side of the bed, staring down at her. "Will you call Claybourne?"

"I can't," Kara sobbed. "You know I can't."

Barrett shrugged. "Remember what I said, Handeland. No permanent damage."

"Yeah, yeah," the big man muttered impatiently. "Go on, get out of here."

Kara stared at Handeland. Strapped to the bed, she was as helpless as a butterfly pinned to a board. Her blood thundered in her ears as she watched Handeland roll up his shirt sleeves. He had arms as big as tree trunks and the biggest hands she had ever seen. She remembered those hands grabbing her, holding a rag over her nose and mouth.

"Last chance, girl," he said.

Kara stared up at him. For all his bulk, he was a soft-spoken man, with mild gray eyes and wheat-colored hair.

"Please," she whispered. "Please don't hurt me."

"That's up to you. You do what the doc wants, and I'll leave you be."

"What are you going to do to me?"

Handeland picked up a scalpel. It looked no bigger than a toothpick in his hand. "Guess."

Kara watched in morbid fascination as he turned the surgical instrument this way and that. Lamplight reflected off the shiny metal blade. She cried out as he dragged the flat part of the knife over her cheek, down her throat, over her breast.

"I spent a year studying to be a doctor," Handeland mused. "I always wanted to perform an operation. Ever had your appendix removed?"

Kara shook her head. In spite of her resolve to suffer in silence, a scream rose in her throat as Handeland lifted her hospital gown and made a small incision over the site of her appendix, just deep enough to draw blood.

Plucking a white towel from the table, Handeland wiped up the blood. "A little deeper, I think."

"Stop, please!"

"Sure thing. All you've got to do is call him."

"Why are you doing this?"

"The oldest reason of all," Handeland replied. "Money. Barrett promised to make me a rich man." He ran the edge of the blade over Kara's cheek.

The metal felt like ice as it cut her skin. She gasped as a thin trickle of blood slid down the side of her face.

"I could peel your skin off an inch at a time."

"Do it then!" she screamed. "Do it!"

With an oath, Handeland placed the knife under her left breast. With deliberate slowness, he pressed the point of the blade against her skin.

"Call him," Handeland said, "or he won't want what's left."

Kara's scream rang in Alex's mind. Anguish and fear clawed at him, as real as if he were experiencing them himself. And then, into his mind flashed an image of Kara writhing in pain, her body streaked with blood.

Crying her name, he sprang out of bed, his mind opening, expanding, searching for her.

"Kara!" Her name was a sob on his lips. "Kara, where are you?"

Alexander . . .

His own name resounded in his mind, followed by a low moan, and then there was nothing.

But it was enough.

Moments later, he was in his car, Kara's anguished cries burning like a beacon in his heart and soul, leading him out of the city.

He drove steadily through the darkness, his every thought focused on Kara. He knew he was probably walking into a trap, but it couldn't be helped. He couldn't risk going to the police, didn't want Kara to be subjected to their questions. Even if they believed Barrett had kidnapped her, they would want to know why. If Barrett revealed what he knew about Kara's blood, there would be other doctors eager to take up where Barrett had left off. He couldn't subject her to that, couldn't take a chance that his own identity might be discovered. And yet, what if he couldn't save her? What if going to the police was the only way to save her?

He lifted his foot from the accelerator as doubts crowded his mind. And then her voice sounded in his mind again, erasing every other thought but the need to find her, to destroy the man who was causing her pain.

"Is everything ready?"

Kelsey nodded. "Stop worrying, Barrett, he won't get away."

"We've got to take him alive. He'll be no good to us dead."

Kelsey let out a sigh of exasperation. "You've told

me that about ten times. I think I've got the message."

"Sorry," Barrett muttered. "It's just that I've never been this close to being rich before."

"You really think this guy's blood is going to pave our way to fame and fortune?"

"I'm counting on it."

Kelsey shook his head skeptically. "Aliens from outer space. I can't believe you fell for that crap."

"I believe her."

"Whatever." Kelsey went suddenly still, his head cocked to one side. "He's here."

"You know what to do. I'll be waiting."

With a curt nod, Kelsey drew his revolver as he hurried down the darkened hallway. He heard a faint clanking sound as the heavy iron outer door swung open, followed by the sound of footsteps as Claybourne entered the passageway.

The trap was set. Kelsey grunted softly as he heard the outer door slam shut behind the alien.

A dozen high-powered spotlights flooded the corridor with light.

Kelsey grinned as a net woven of thick nylon cord dropped over the alien. Handeland ran forward and grabbed the rope, securing the ends.

A roar of outrage rose in Alexander's throat. Blinded by the lights, he struggled to free himself from the net, but the harder he struggled, the more entangled he became.

And then he felt a sharp prick in his arm and the world went black.

Chapter Twenty

The sound of voices roused Kara from a drugged sleep. Her eyelids felt as if they were weighted with lead; her stomach roiled with a nausea that was becoming all too familiar.

With an effort, she opened her eyes, felt her last hope for rescue dwindle and die when she saw Alex lying on a narrow metal table beside her bed. In addition to the thick leather straps that bound his arms and legs to the table, there were iron bands strapped across his chest and waist so that he was virtually immobile.

She stared at his chest, but he didn't seem to be breathing. His skin looked pale; there were dark shadows under his eyes. Had they killed him?

Yearning to touch him, she tugged against the leather straps that bound her arms to the cot's frame, but the restraints held fast.

"Barrett!" She screamed the doctor's name. "I know you're here somewhere. Answer me!"

She heard the sound of footsteps in the corridor, and then Barrett filled her line of vision. "What do you want?" he asked irritably.

"Is he dead?"

He looked at her as if she were none too bright. "Of course not, only heavily sedated."

"What are you going to do with us?"

"I'm going to give you a transfusion of his blood, of course."

Kara closed her eyes, wondering if she would ever be free again. The last two days had been like a living nightmare from which she couldn't awaken. And now Alexander was part of it.

She heard Barrett leave the room, and she opened her eyes again, her gaze resting on Alexander's face. How did Barrett know how much of a sedative to administer to Alex without killing him? What if Alex was allergic to the tranquilizer? What if a second transfusion of his blood didn't produce the desired results? What if it did? Would the two of them spend the rest of their lives locked in this room while Barrett grew rich off their blood?

She felt a hysterical urge to laugh. Talk about vampires!

"Alex? Alex, can you hear me?"

Restless and afraid, she glanced around the room. They'd moved the two of them while she was unconscious, she noticed absently.

She frowned as the room began to grow brighter. And then she felt her breath catch in her throat as she spied the long, narrow skylight directly above Alex.

The sun was rising.

Morbid images filled her mind, images of Dracula slowly aging and disintegrating when exposed to the sun. But surely things like that didn't happen in real life.

"Barrett! Barrett!" She screamed his name again and again, her voice echoing off the walls, ringing in her ears, but no one came to answer her cries.

She stared at Alex, saw his hands clench as a narrow ray of golden sunlight streamed through the skylight to rest on his face. He groaned softly, his head turning from side to side in an effort to avoid the light.

"Alex? Alex, can you hear me?"

He turned his head toward her, regarding her through eyes clouded with pain. *I . . . hear . . . you . . .*

"The sun, what will it do to you?"

It . . . weakens me . . . negates . . . my powers . . . He drew a deep breath in an effort to fight off the darkness that hovered around him.

"It won't . . . It isn't . . . ?" Unable to voice the thought aloud, Kara licked lips gone suddenly dry. What if it killed him?

Not fatal, Alex said, perceiving her thoughts. *Only painful . . . like fire . . .* Unless he was weakened by an excessive loss of blood. Then the sunlight could be lethal. But he couldn't tell her that, not now, when her eyes were filled with fear.

Kara gazed deep into Alexander's eyes, and suddenly she felt his pain as if it were her own, felt the sun burning his skin, felt it draining his energy, his will to live.

"This is all my fault," she whispered brokenly. "If I'd been stronger . . ."

No . . . my fault . . . should have expected . . . He closed his eyes as a violent tremor wracked his body. He could feel the sunlight warming his blood, making it flow hot and heavy through his veins. His skin felt tight and dry, like charred paper.

"Alex? Alex, answer me!"

The sound of her voice speaking his name soothed his torment, but he lacked the strength to form a reply. As from far away, he heard the sound of footsteps. Barrett's voice giving orders. The sting of a needle pricking a vein in his arm, the sensation of blood being drawn from his body.

Summoning what little energy he had left, he turned his head to the side, saw his blood flowing through a long narrow tube into a vein in Kara's arm.

The sight, its significance, sickened him. Filled with regret for the misery he had caused the woman he loved, he closed his eyes again and plunged into the waiting darkness.

He regained consciousness slowly, and with the return of awareness came the knowledge that Kara had betrayed him. No one else knew the devastating effect the sun had on him. No one else knew that he was inhuman, or that his blood was different from that of anyone else on the planet.

Too weary to open his eyes, he let his senses probe the room. Even in his weakened state, he knew that he was alone, and that it was night. The metal table beneath him was cold; his skin felt blessedly cool.

Time passed. After a while, he opened his eyes and glanced around the room. It was stark and white, bare of furniture or decoration save for the table on which he lay and a metal cart that held a number of needles, swabs, a scalpel, and several other instruments. The room had a single door, no windows save for the skylight over his head.

A sigh of resignation escaped his lips as he gazed at the skylight. Now, at night, it was covered, no doubt to prevent him from absorbing the light of the moon. She had been thorough in her betrayal, he mused bleakly. Dawn was only hours away, not enough time for his strength to return. He shuddered at the thought of spending another day at the sun's mercy.

Closing his eyes again, he summoned what strength he had and let his mind search for Kara. Some instinct, some deep well of trust, told him she would not have willingly betrayed him. Perhaps, if she was near, he would be able to sense her presence, hear her thoughts.

At first he sensed nothing, and then images flickered in his mind: A small green room. An iron-barred window covered with a board. A utilitarian wooden chair, a small table, a lamp with a bare bulb. Kara, kneeling beside a narrow bed, her head bowed, her hands clasped. She was praying. Praying for him.

Kara . . .

Alex?

He clenched his hands into fists as he fought to focus on her voice. *Are you . . . all right?*

Yes, she replied tremulously. *Are you?*

Where . . . where are you?

I don't know.

Tell me . . . what's happened?

Barrett gave me some of your blood, and then he drew some of mine. Shortly after that, they locked me in this room. I haven't seen Barrett since.

He clung to the sound of her voice, to the knowledge that she was still alive and apparently unhurt. *Has he said anything?*

No. They must be testing my blood to see if there's been any change since the transfusion. Alex, I'm afraid.

She wasn't afraid for her own life, he knew, but for his. Her concern wrapped around his heart, warm and soft, like layers of cotton.

Alex? How long can you endure the sunlight?

As long as I must.

But you've always avoided it!

It's only painful, Kara. He hesitated, wondering if he should tell her the truth.

Alex? What aren't you telling me?

There's no danger, he replied slowly, *unless Barrett bleeds me excessively.*

I'm sorry I got you into this.

Not your fault . . . Indeed, he mused ruefully, he had no one to blame but himself. If he had stayed out of her life, none of this would have happened. And yet, he couldn't be sorry he had saved Kara's life, only that he had caused her pain.

It's not your fault, either. And I'm glad we met, glad for the time we had together.

Alex stared at the skylight, stunned by the knowledge that she had read his thoughts.

Why are you so surprised? she asked. *We've been communicating this way for quite a while.*

But I was sending you my thoughts . . . planting them in your mind . . . and reading yours in return.

So?

I did not send the thoughts you just received.

So now I can read your mind? He heard the wonder in her voice.

So it would seem.

Alex, it's almost morning.

I know . . . He stared at the skylight. He could sense dawn approaching, knew the sun was climbing over the horizon. Soon, the cover would lift, leaving him exposed to the burning rays of the sun. And even as the thought crossed his mind, the cover began to roll back.

He closed his eyes against the brightness, groaned softly as he felt the first faint rays of the sun touch his skin. Soon the pain would be excruciating. How long could he endure the light of the sun before it killed him? He had always been careful to avoid the sunlight, but had no idea what effect two days of constant exposure would have.

Alex? Alex, are you all right?

He heard her voice but lacked the strength, the concentration, to answer.

Kara called Alex's name again, but he didn't answer. She tried to probe his mind, but to no avail, and then she heard the sound of footsteps in the corridor outside her room, the rattle of a key in the lock. A moment later, Barrett entered her room.

"So, how are you feeling?" he asked.

"You mustn't leave Alex in the sun."

"Oh?"

"He'll die. You don't want him dead, do you?"

"It didn't seem to do him any harm yesterday other than causing some discomfort."

"I know, but too much will kill him."

"You wouldn't lie to me, would you?"

"Yes, but not about this."

"So, that's the way it is." Barrett rubbed a hand over his jaw.

"Please don't make him suffer."

"I'll take care of it. You're quite right. I don't want him dead. You, on the other hand, seem to have outlived your usefulness."

Kara went suddenly cold all over. "What do you mean?"

"We've conducted several preliminary tests. It seems that it's the alien's blood that holds the key. His blood is incredibly powerful. When mixed with human blood, it produces the necessary curative powers in varying degrees of potency. Unfortunately, the results don't last." Barrett shook his head. "We've established the fact that, to secure permanent results, the alien's blood must be pure, so, as you can see, we have no further need of you."

"Then I can go home?" Even as she voiced the question, she knew what Barrett's answer would be.

The doctor shook his head. "I'm afraid not."

"Please."

"I'm sorry, but you must know I can't allow you to leave here."

"I won't say anything to anyone, I swear."

"I'd like to believe you, but I'm afraid I can't. There's too much at stake here. Surely you can see what a marvelous find this is! His blood restores life! Think of what we might accomplish. At this time, it doesn't seem to be effective in healing broken bones, but it cures disease. It restores life!" Barrett shook his head. "With sufficient research, we might discover that the alien's blood holds the key to curing cancer, AIDS, heart and kidney disease. The possibilities are endless."

Barrett began to pace the floor. "And the possibility of extending our life span. Think of it! He's lived for two hundred years. Of course, there's no way to know if an injection of his blood will lengthen a normal life span, or if there might be more involved than that, but think of the possibilities!"

He rubbed his hands together, the gesture reminding Kara of a miser contemplating an increase in his wealth. "We've already started testing on lab rats. In time, we'll need human subjects, but they shouldn't be hard to find."

"No doubt you're doing all this out of the generosity of your heart," Kara remarked sarcastically, "and this boon to mankind will be available to rich and poor alike."

Barrett stopped pacing. "The first, experimental doses will, of course, be offered free. After that, I'm afraid we'll have to be more circumspect." He shrugged. "After all, the alien has only so much blood. Unless we can find a way to reproduce it synthetically, I'm afraid the price will be dear."

Kara stared at Barrett, horrified by his constant use of the term "alien." To Barrett, Alex was no longer a man, but an inhuman species. As such, he didn't merit consideration or mercy. Barrett could experiment on Alex, abuse him, confine him, with a clear conscience.

"You can't keep Alex locked up for the rest of his life!" Kara exclaimed in horror. Alex might live another two hundred years. She tried to imagine what it would be like for him, to spend the rest of his days locked up, being poked and prodded, while vials of his blood were sold to the highest bidder.

"The rest of his life," Barrett repeated. "Who

knows how long that might be?" He chuckled softly. "Don't waste your time worrying about him. He's not human, after all." Barrett frowned thoughtfully. "Think of it! I hold the living proof that there are life forms on distant planets. Who knows, once I've found a way to reproduce his blood synthetically, I might turn him over to the government."

Barrett nodded slowly, as if a new thought had just occurred to him. "Think of what he might be able to tell them, the advances we could make in space travel. This could be a boon to the space industry! Well, no point in thinking of that now," he said briskly. "I've got too much to do."

With a curt nod, Barrett headed for the door.

"Wait!" Kara grabbed the doctor's arm. "What are you going to do with me?"

"I'm afraid you've become a liability, Miss Crawford. But don't worry. I am a doctor, after all. Your demise will be quick and painless, I promise."

"No! Please let me go home."

"I'm sorry." He stared at her, a flicker of genuine regret in his pale blue eyes. "Sorry," he said again, and left the room.

The sound of the key turning in the lock sounded like a death knell.

Kara stared at the door. Quick and painless. Somehow, the words weren't very comforting.

Chapter Twenty-one

Pain. It was all he knew. He closed his eyes against the harsh glare of the sun, but there was no way to avoid its light, or its heat upon his naked flesh.

Weak, so weak he couldn't concentrate, couldn't control his thoughts. Couldn't resist the memories . . .

Of AnnaMara . . . smiling at him across a dinner table when he came courting . . . letting him steal a kiss . . . promising to love him for as long as she lived . . .

AnnaMara . . . lying beside him, holding him in her arms.

AnnaMara . . . giving birth to their daughter . . .

Anguish, stronger and deeper than the pain of the flesh, rose up within him.

AnnaMara . . . holding AnTares in her arms . . . how many mornings had he sat beside her while she

*nursed their daughter . . . how many nights had he
listened to her sing the soft lullabys of ErAdona?*

*AnnaMara . . . lying in a pool of her own blood . . .
the life forever gone from her eyes . . .*

"No!" He opened his eyes and the images dissolved in the brilliant light of the sun.

In an effort to avoid the light, Alex turned his head to the side, and saw Barrett staring down at him.

"I'm told sunlight bothers you," the doctor remarked. "Is that correct?"

Alex hesitated, wondering whether to tell the truth, or if a lie would serve him better.

"Well?"

"It bothers me," Alex said, thinking that "bothered" was an understatement at best.

"I'll arrange to have the skylight covered during the afternoon. Will that help?"

Alex nodded, disgusted with himself for feeling grateful to the man.

"She told me you've been here for two hundred years," Barrett remarked. "I want to know everything. Every detail of how you got here, where you came from, how you survived."

Filled with nervous energy, the doctor paced the floor. "Your race has mastered space travel. Have you explored other planets? Found life there? Are there others of your kind here?"

He looked at Alex, waiting for answers that did not come.

Barrett's eyes narrowed. "You would be wise to tell me everything I want to know."

"And if I refuse?"

"You won't," Barrett replied, his expression smug. "The woman seems to care for you, and I'm guessing you also care for her. Unfortunately, she has become something of a liability, one I can't afford to keep around, if you know what I mean?"

"You can't just . . . just exterminate her!" Alex exclaimed, horrified by the casual way the doctor spoke of killing.

"I can. But don't worry, I promised her it would be quick. However, if you refuse to cooperate with me, I'll have to renege on that promise."

"Let her go, and I'll tell you whatever you what to know."

"I can't do that. You know as well as I do that she'll go running to the police the minute she's free. I can't allow that."

"Bring her to me. I have the power to make her forget everything."

Interest sparked in the doctor's eyes. "What power?" Barrett paused to check the IV dripping into the alien's vein. "What do you mean?"

"She carries my blood. We're connected. I can control her mind. I can make her forget everything. You, me, everything."

Barrett shook his head. "I don't believe you."

"I can prove it. Tell me something she can't possibly know, and I'll plant it in her mind." He shuddered convulsively as the sun's heat scorched his flesh. "But . . . not . . . now."

"Why not now?"

Alex closed his eyes. "Can't think. The sun . . ."

Barrett rubbed his jaw, his brow furrowed in thought. If what the alien said was true, there was more at stake here than money or fame. Much more.

Going to the door, Barrett called for Kelsey.

"Yeah, Doc?"

"From now on, I don't want the alien exposed to the sun for more than a couple of hours in the morning and late afternoon."

"Why? I thought you said the sun kept him weak."

Barrett nodded. "It does, but there's a chance too much might prove fatal. Let's cover it from twelve to four and see what happens."

"Right. You still want it covered at night?"

"Definitely. Tomorrow, I want the cover in place by, oh, say eleven. I want to try an experiment tomorrow night, so I'll need you and Handeland to be here at seven."

Kelsey glanced at Alex. "Right. Anything else?"

"No. I'll be in the lab if anyone needs me."

The tension drained out of Alex as the door closed behind the two men. As near as he could figure, it was a little after ten. That meant another two hours before they covered the skylight.

A long, shuddering sigh rippled through his body. Another two hours of feeling the sunlight on his skin, burning his eyes, leeching his strength, until it became an effort to breathe, to think. He comforted himself with the fact that it was only another two hours. He could endure it for that long. He had to endure it, for Kara's sake.

He tried to focus his thoughts on a way to escape. He needed to think, to plan. He had to find a way to get Kara away from this place before it was too late.

But try as he might, he couldn't concentrate, couldn't think. His skin felt tight, his blood ran hot—hot with pain and rage. Hot with the ancient need to hunt, to destroy his enemies. To taste their blood upon his tongue.

Vampire . . .

He turned his face toward the wall, troubled by the images the word conjured in his mind. He had written about vampires for years. Perhaps, in some vicarious way, he had been living out his own suppressed desires through the lives of his characters. Perhaps the men of ErAdona would never be free of the innate urge to drink the blood of their enemies.

Hands clenched, he stared into the sunlight, hoping its heat would burn the hate and the anger from the depths of his soul.

But the pain only fueled his rage. Barrett would pay, he vowed. Pay for the fear and pain he had caused Kara. Pay for the pain that he himself was suffering, for the indignity of being strapped to this metal table. Oh, yes, Barrett would pay!

Alex? Alex, can you hear me?

Kara's voice, soft and sweet, filled with concern. It washed over him like cool water, easing his pain, smothering his anger.

Alex? Please answer me if you can.

I hear you, Kara.

Are you all right?

He took a deep breath. *Yes.*

I told Barrett the sun was dangerous for you. Has he done anything to protect you from it?

Not yet. Tomorrow . . . tomorrow he wants to do . . . to do some sort of test.

A test? What kind of test?

Can't explain now . . . He took a deep breath, his hands clenching and unclenching as he struggled against the thick leather straps that bound his wrists to the table. But he was weak, so damn weak.

Alex?

So . . . tired . . . try not to worry . . . will get you . . . out of this . . . promise . . .

Alex, I love you.

Love you . . . Love you, love you. He repeated the words over and over again. It was his last thought before he surrendered to the darkness of oblivion.

Shortly before eleven o'clock the next morning, the heavy cover rolled into place, shutting out the sun's blinding light.

Alex sighed with relief, feeling the tension drain out of him as the room grew blessedly dark. The pain in his flesh receded almost immediately. Never before had he been exposed to the direct rays of the sun for such a long period of time. It might take days, perhaps weeks, for his body to regain its full strength.

Closing his eyes, he took a deep breath. Perhaps now he would be able to formulate a plan of escape.

He was aware of Barrett beside him, fiddling with the IV bottle, and he wondered what drugs the doctor was giving him along with the glucose and saline.

He'd been here for three days, Alex thought wearily. Surely the longest three days of his life. In that time, Barrett had drawn copious amounts of blood, taken urine samples, examined Alex from head to foot. This morning, the doctor had cut a small sliver of tissue from the ridged flesh on his back. The pain of the scalpel on the sensitive skin over his spine had been excruciating, and the only thing that had kept him from screaming had been the thought of the revenge that would be his once he'd attained his freedom.

"Remarkable," Barrett said. "Simply remarkable."

"What's remarkable?" Kelsey asked.

"The similarities between humans and this alien." Barrett laughed with real amusement. "All these years, Hollywood and the tabloids have imagined aliens as intellectually superior to us, but physically inferior. They've always been depicted as diminutive creatures with scrawny arms and legs and huge soulful eyes, when, in reality, their appearance is almost exactly like ours."

"Yeah, except for that funny looking leathery strip on his back."

"Hmmm, yes, that is odd. But that seems to be the only aberration. Two arms, two legs, with the requisite number of fingers and toes. Very humanoid."

"Oh, I almost forgot. Phillips says he needs more blood."

"So soon? What's he doing with the stuff, drinking it?" Barrett laughed, amused at his own humor.

"He said ten cc's would be enough. He's got two dozen vials ready to go. How much you figure to sell them for?"

"I haven't decided." Barrett readied a syringe, found a vein in the alien's arm, then watched the syringe fill with blood, noticing again that it was darker and thicker than human blood. "Each case will be different, depending on income and need." He handed the vial to Kelsey. "Take that to Phillips. And remind Handeland that I want him here at seven tonight."

"Right."

"Has Mitch had any luck finding the old ladies and the girl?"

"Not yet, but he's still looking. I'll drop this off at the lab, and then I'm going to lunch."

"Seven," Barrett reminded him. "Don't be late."

"Yeah, yeah," Kelsey muttered.

Barrett grunted as Kelsey left the room. The man was an irritant, but he was loyal, and, like Handeland, he was capable of doing whatever needed to be done.

His gaze ran over the alien. He was a remarkable specimen, apparently in his prime, long and lean, with well-muscled arms and legs. A creature from outer space. It was still hard to believe. He shook his head. By this time next year, he'd be a wealthy man. His name would be known throughout the civilized world. His life story would be related in newspapers, magazines, medical journals.

He smiled as he imagined himself restoring health and vitality to those who could afford the price of a vial of blood. People would pay whatever he asked to save the life of a loved one stricken with a fatal disease or on the brink of death. But that was only the tip of the iceberg. How much more would people be willing to pay for the promise of immortality? There would have to be tests, of course. Once he had proved that the alien's blood increased the life span of lab rats, he would have to conduct tests on human subjects. That was the least of his worries. He had no doubt that he would find volunteers by the hundreds, the thousands. People who were sick, dying, would be only too happy to volunteer simply for the chance of being cured of their disease. Testing might take years, but he was a patient man. As soon as he sold the first vials of blood, he would have enough money to do all the research required.

He glanced at the alien. They couldn't keep him strapped to that table forever. They'd have to find a place to house him, some place close at hand so his blood would be readily available, some way to regulate the amount of sunlight he received, a way to keep him docile without inflicting any permanent physical damage.

The alien's eyes opened, and Barrett wondered what the creature was thinking. It was an intelligent species. He would be wise to remember that at all times.

Barrett took a deep breath, feeling a surge of power flow through him. Soon, he would have everything he had ever dreamed of: wealth, fame, power, his name in the record books alongside Curie and Salk.

Soon, he would have answers to the questions that had plagued scientists for centuries.

Soon, he would hold the power of life and death in his hands.

Alex waited until Barrett left the room and then, knowing it was futile, he tugged against the straps that imprisoned him. He had to get out of here, had to get Kara out of here before it was too late.

He glared at the heavy straps that bound his wrists, at the iron bands that crossed his chest, remembering how Barrett and Kelsey had talked over him as if he were a piece of furniture, as if he couldn't speak or think. It was humiliating, degrading, to know that Barrett considered him less than human simply because he came from another planet.

Insufferable creature! If only he weren't so weak,

he'd rip the leather straps apart, and then he'd rip Barrett and Kelsey to shreds. If only . . .

Muttering an oath, he closed his eyes. There was no time for anger or thoughts of revenge, not now. It was time to rest, to gather his strength for the battle to come.

Chapter Twenty-two

Barrett was prompt. He showed up in Alexander's room with his two accomplices at seven sharp. It didn't escape Alex's notice that Kelsey and Handeland were both carrying weapons. Kelsey favored a .357 Magnum, while Handeland carried a Luger.

"So," Barrett said, getting right to the point. "Let's get to it, shall we?"

"I'm ready when you are."

"The way I understand it, I'm to tell you something the woman can't possibly know, and you're going to send it to her telepathically. Is that right?"

Alex nodded.

Barrett grunted softly. "Something she couldn't possibly know." He stroked his jaw thoughtfully. "My mother's maiden name is Dagdiggian. My favorite color is yellow. And I have eighty-five dollars in my wallet. Three twenties, two tens, and five ones. Tell her that." Barrett opened the door. "I'll be waiting in her room. Kelsey, Handeland, keep an eye on him."

"Right, doc."

Kara?

Alex? What's wrong?

Nothing. I don't have time to explain. Barrett's coming to your room. Be careful while he's there. I don't want him to know that you can communicate with me. I've told him I can control your mind, that I can make you forget everything that's happened.

Can you?

Yes. Listen to me. He should be there any time.

He just came in.

All right.

He's asking me questions. What should I do?

Answer him. His mother's maiden name is Dag-diggian. His favorite color is yellow, and he's carrying eighty-five dollars in his wallet. Three twenties, two tens, and five ones.

A few minutes later, the doctor returned to Alex's room.

"Impressive," Barrett remarked. "Very impressive."

"Now will you let her go?"

"It doesn't prove anything except that you can plant thoughts in her mind. How will I know you've erased everything from her memory?"

"You'll know. She won't know who you are. She won't remember anything that happened after the accident."

"I don't know."

"Don't listen to him," Handeland said. "There's too much at stake here. If you don't have the balls to take care of the girl, I'll do it."

251

"Shut up," Barrett snapped. "I'm making the decisions here, and don't you forget it."

"He's right," Kelsey said. "All the alien has to do is tell the girl to pretend she doesn't remember anything. There's no way to prove he's done it."

"Of course there is, you idiot! Another dose of pentobarbital will tell me what I need to know." Barrett jerked a thumb toward the door. "Go on, you two, get out of here."

Kelsey and Handeland exchanged glances.

"Here, you might need this," Handeland said. He handed his Luger to Barrett. "Let's go, Nate."

"I'm comin'," Kelsey replied. "Holler if you need us."

"I didn't think you could do it," Barrett remarked. "I want to know more about this mind link. If I gave your blood to Kelsey, would you be able to communicate with him in the same way?"

"I don't know. I've never given my blood to anyone but Kara." The lie rolled easily off his tongue.

"I see." Barrett drummed his fingers on the cart beside the table as he pondered the possibilities of mind control. "What other tricks have you got up your sleeve?"

"A few."

"Tell me."

"Not until you let her go."

"Are you in love with her?"

"What if I am?"

Barrett shrugged. "It poses some interesting questions. Is it possible for you to mate with our species?"

"Let her go."

Barrett swore. "I can make you talk, you know.

A dose of sodium pentobarbital can be very persuasive."

"And I can be very stubborn."

"You mean the drug won't work?"

"I don't know what the effect would be. Could be fatal. Could alter my blood chemistry in some way. Who knows?"

"There are tests . . ."

"Tests take time. Let her go, and I'll tell you whatever you want to know. I give you my word."

"Your word?" Barrett sneered. "What makes you think I'd take your word?"

"My people have mastered space travel. We've banished war from our planet. There's very little sickness. The average life span of my people is a hundred and twenty-five years. We're not savages, doctor. We're not sub-human. We're not animals. My word is as good as yours." He grinned wryly. "Better, no doubt. Were you on my planet, you would be considered vastly inferior."

"But I'm not on your world. You're on mine. And I mean to take advantage of everything you know."

Alex took a deep breath, held it for stretched seconds before he released it. "Then let her go."

"Answer me one thing. Is it possible for you to procreate with our people?"

"No."

Barrett grinned. "You're lying. I think, before I turn her loose, we'll find out."

"No! It could be dangerous to Kara. I won't put her life in danger."

But Barrett wasn't listening. "Consider the possibilities," he said, pacing the floor. "A half-alien baby. Think of the research, the chance to study an alien life form from infancy, to raise it as my own."

"Your own guinea pig, you mean. Dammit, Barrett, we had a deal!"

"We had nothing."

Anger surged through Alex as he envisioned the kind of life his child would have. Years of testing, of never having a normal life, never knowing who its real parents were. Barrett would either keep the child locked away, a secret from the rest of the world, or he would exploit the child like some kind of freak.

Rage added strength to his limbs. With a feral cry, Alex yanked against the straps that held him. The one on his right wrist broke with a loud snap.

Barrett whirled around, the gun at the ready. "Kelsey! Handeland! Get in here!"

With a cry of triumph, Alex jerked his left hand free. Taking a double-handed grip on the iron band across his chest, he gave a mighty heave, but the strap held.

A roar of frustration rose in his throat as Kelsey and Handeland burst into the room.

"Hold him!" Barrett shouted.

Setting the gun aside, Barrett grabbed a syringe from the cart and plunged the needle into a vein in the alien's left arm.

With a strangled cry of rage, the alien went suddenly limp.

"Damn, that was close." Barrett sagged against the wall, amazed by the creature's strength. "Kelsey, he's getting too strong. See that he gets more sun." he said. "Joe, replace those straps with thicker ones."

"What set him off?" Kelsey asked.

Barrett shook his head. "I told him I was going to conduct a new experiment."

"Yeah? What kind of experiment?"

"I want to find out if it's possible for his species to impregnate ours. I thought he'd be pleased at the prospect of a little extracurricular activity."

Joe snorted. "He's a fool if he's not. She's quite a looker."

"Forget it, Handeland. She's not for you."

"Can't blame a guy for dreamin'. I'm gonna get some coffee. You want some?"

Barrett nodded absently. An alien baby. A new source of blood. Perhaps a way to improve the human race. The possibilities were endless and fascinating.

An hour later, the leather straps on the alien's wrists and ankles had been replaced with bands of tempered steel. As an additional precaution, Barrett secured a thick leather strap over the alien's neck so he couldn't lift his head.

"That should hold him," he said. "I want you to make some modifications in here."

"What kind of modifications?"

"We can't expect the alien to mate while he's strapped to a table. I want you to make me a good strong collar for his neck and a chain that would hold an elephant, and another collar and chain for his ankle. And something solid to bolt them to. And I want a bed. Something comfortable. And I want it all stat."

"Right, doc. Anything else?"

"No, I think that's all for tonight."

"Sure you don't want candles and champagne, too?" Kelsey asked with a smirk.

"Just do as your told."

"Right. Joe, give me a hand."

With a last glance at the alien, Barrett turned out the light and left the room.

Tomorrow should prove to be a most interesting day.

Alex shook his head. "It won't work."

"Why not?"

"The sun."

Barrett shook his head. "I think you're lying."

"You've seen how it weakens me. I can't . . . perform during the day."

Barrett frowned. Did he dare let the alien mate at night?

Alex closed his eyes against the sun's heat, wondering if he would ever be free again. He tried to conjure up an image of the cavern in Eagle Flats, the blessed coolness to be found within the thick rock walls, the ageless serenity of the mountains. And, in a moment of utter depression, he wished for death, an end to captivity, to pain.

"I'm going to give you one chance," Barrett remarked. "I've ascertained that the woman is at peak fertility. You will mate with her tonight. If you refuse, if you try to escape, she'll be dead tomorrow. Do we understand each other? Look at me!"

Alex opened his eyes and met Barrett's cold brown gaze. "I understand."

"I'll bring her to you at dusk."

"You gonna watch?"

A faint flush crept up the doctor's neck. "No. I'll examine her in the morning. If you've failed to do your duty, I'll give her to Handeland."

"You're a miserable excuse for a human being."

"Perhaps. But I shall soon be a very wealthy man."

"Yes, but will you be able to sleep at night?"

"Quite well, I assure you. You had better get

some rest now. You'll need your strength."

As soon as Barrett left the room, Alex opened his mind. He heard Kara's thoughts almost immediately.

Alex. I've been so worried. What's going on?

Barrett wants a child.

What?

He wants us to mate so he can have the child.

No, I won't do it.

I'm afraid you don't have any choice in the matter.

What do you mean? You're not going to . . . to . . .

Rape you? No. But if I don't do what he wants, he's threatened to kill you tomorrow morning.

He couldn't see her face, but he could almost feel the blood drain from her face. *He means it, Kara.*

She heard his voice, but couldn't focus. A baby. If she got pregnant, she'd have to stay here for nine months, and then Barrett would take the child. It was a reprieve of sorts, but at what cost? The thought of going through childbirth, then having her child taken away from her by a monster like Barrett, made death at the doctor's hands seem almost welcome.

Kara?

I'm scared, Alex.

I know. Is there anything in your room that could be used as a weapon?

No. Not even a butter knife.

It was what he had expected, but he was disappointed just the same. *It's okay. Try not to worry. . . .*

You should try to get some rest, Alex. You sound awful.

Kara . . . I love you.

I love you. . . .

He broke the connection, and she felt its loss

keenly. It had been days since she had seen him. No matter what happened tomorrow, at least they would be together again tonight.

She clung to that thought as the hours passed. Tonight she would see Alex.

Kara's heart was pounding like a jackhammer as Handeland led her down a narrow hallway, up a short flight of stairs, and into the room with the skylight.

Her gaze darted around the room. The metal table was gone and a double bed stood in its place. Alex sat on the edge of the mattress, a sheet drawn over his lap. She stared at the heavy iron collar around his neck, at the thick chain fastened to the bed's iron frame. A similar collar and chain, fastened to an enormous bolt in the concrete floor next to the bed, circled his left ankle.

He looked up when she stepped into the room. The look in his eyes, the guilt, stabbed her to the heart.

I'm sorry, natayah, he said, speaking to her mind. *Forgive me.*

"Sorry there's no champagne and soft music," Barrett said. He took Kara by the arm and pulled her toward the bed. "But this is the best I could do on such short notice."

Kara jerked her arm from Barrett's grasp. "You're despicable. I can't believe you're a doctor." She shook her head. "Have you no conscience? You're supposed to help people, ease their suffering."

"My dear, if I can isolate the healing agent in this creature's blood, mankind will owe me a debt it can never repay."

"And you think the end"—Kara gestured at Alex, at the chains that bound him—"justifies the means?"

"Sometimes, in order to make advancements, people get hurt. History is filled with stories of people who sacrificed their lives for the good of others."

"The good of the many outweighing the needs of the few," Kara muttered, remembering a line from an old *Star Trek* movie.

"Exactly. And now I will bid you good night." Barrett fixed the alien with a sharp stare. "Don't fail me," he warned, and left the room.

There was the sound of a key turning in the lock. The lights in the room dimmed.

Kara went to kneel in front of Alexander. "Are you all right?" She touched the heavy collar at his throat as if it were a live snake. "How can you breathe with that thing on?"

"Breathing is the least of my worries," Alex replied wryly. Bending over, he lifted Kara onto his lap, his arms wrapping around her, holding her close until their hearts beat as one.

"Alex, what are we going to do?"

"Get the hell out of here."

"How?"

"I'm going to try to spring the lock on these chains. And if that doesn't work, I'm going to kill Barrett when he comes back."

Kara blinked at him. "Spring the lock? Can you do that?"

"I hope so. It was cloudy today, not much sun. I slept all afternoon. With any luck, by midnight my strength will have returned enough so I can spring the locks telepathically."

"I love you, Alex. Whatever happens, I love you. You won't forget that, will you?"

He cupped her face in his hands. "I won't forget." He caressed her cheek with his knuckles, traced the curves of her face with his fingertips. Soft, so soft. She wore a plain white hospital gown; her hair fell over her shoulders, shimmering like a living flame in the faint light. She had never looked more beautiful.

Leaning forward, he covered her mouth with his and kissed her gently. He wanted nothing more than to lay her down on the bed and show her how much he loved her, but now was not the time. He needed to save his strength, and so he stretched out on the bed, drawing her down beside him, wrapping his body protectively around hers.

"I need to sleep, Kara. Wake me if you hear anyone coming."

She nodded. Needing to touch him, she brushed his hair back from his face, then stroked his shoulder, hoping to soothe him, to help him relax.

He watched her for a long while, his eyes heavy-lidded, and then, holding her hand in his, he closed his eyes and slept.

Kara lay there in the semi-darkness, watching him sleep, her heart hurting for the pain he had suffered. He was such a brave man. He had said he would kill Barrett if they couldn't escape. He had said it so casually, his voice indifferent, as if killing was of no import at all. As repulsive as the thought was, it was far more acceptable than the alternative of bearing a child and having Barrett take it from her, of being disposed of when she was no longer needed. More acceptable than never seeing Alex again.

She gazed up at the narrow patch of sky visible through the skylight, watching the stars as they followed their inevitable course. Which star was Alexander's? She tried to imagine what it had been like for him, being banished to an alien planet, being sent away from everything he knew and loved. It pleased her to think that he had been fated to be hers, that some higher power out in the cosmos had sent Alex to earth because he had been meant to be hers, as she was meant to be his.

"You're quite a romantic, Miss Crawford."

"Are you reading my mind again, Mr. Claybourne?"

"Guilty as charged." Alex opened his eyes and smiled at Kara. "Is that what you really think? That I was sent here because we were fated to be together?"

"It sounds kind of silly when you say it out loud."

"I don't think it sounds silly at all."

His hand cupped the back of her head and he drew her gently toward him. His kiss was featherlight, yet it singed every fiber of her being.

"How do you feel?" she asked.

"Pretty good." He glanced up at the sky. "It's a little after midnight." He smiled at her. "Give me a kiss for luck?"

"Two kisses," she said, and pressed her lips to his—a long, lingering kiss that spoke of passion; a short, quick kiss that promised more to come.

Sitting up, Alex swung his legs over the edge of the bed.

Kara sat beside him, her heartbeat quickening. "What should I do?"

"Nothing. Try to keep your mind blank while I concentrate."

261

"Maybe I could help?"

He shook his head. "I'm afraid the energy from your mind would be too distracting."

"All right."

He took a deep breath, let it out in a long, slow sigh.

Kara watched his face, knew that he had shut her out of his thoughts, out of his mind. She could almost see the power gathering around him, coalescing, vibrating, as he focused every ounce of his energy on the heavy padlock that held the iron cuff in place on his left ankle.

Kara shook her head, a little frightened by the intense expression on his face. The veins in his neck bulged, the muscles in his jaw tensed, the knuckles on his fists were white and strained.

What kind of man was he? The thought skittered through her mind before she could call it back, but he seemed unaware. His expression never changed. And then, after what seemed like hours, his eyes narrowed. There was the sound of metal turning against metal. Alex bent down and opened the padlock, then removed the shackle and chain from around his ankle.

She stared at him in awe, wondering how he could remove the collar from his neck when he couldn't focus his eyes on the lock.

But, of course, he focused on the padlock that fastened the end of the chain to the bed. Moments later, he was free.

Rising, he coiled the length of chain dangling from the collar around his left hand. "Let's go."

Stark naked, with a thick collar at his throat, his long black hair framing his face, he looked like a pagan god of war.

He stared at the door; a moment later, it swung open. Alex peered up and down the hallway, then stepped into the corridor.

Kara followed him, watched as he closed and locked the door. "Stay close behind me," he warned softly.

He didn't have to tell her twice. She planned to stick closer than his shadow.

Their footsteps seemed as loud as thunder to her ears as they tiptoed down the hallway. They passed three rooms with the doors ajar, small cubicles similar to the one that had imprisoned Alex. A fourth room contained numerous cages filled with rats and mice. She wrinkled her nose at the strong smell of ammonia and disinfectant.

Two corridors opened at the end of the one they had taken. Alex glanced left, then right, then turned left, his steps sure as he glided soundlessly over the black-and-white tiled floor.

Needing the assurance of his touch, Kara reached for his hand. He glanced at her briefly, his teeth gleaming whitely in the dim light of the hallway.

Kara froze at the sound of voices. Familiar voices. Kelsey and Handcland.

"Full house," she heard Handeland say. "Three pretty ladies and a pair of fours."

Kelsey swore. "That's four hands in a row," he complained.

"What can I say? I've always been lucky."

There was the sound of cards being shuffled.

Kara looked up at Alex. *What now?*

Wait here. He smiled reassuringly, then moved down the hallway. He paused outside an open door and peered cautiously inside. Kelsey had his back to the door; Handeland was studying his cards. Their weapons lay on the table. There was no sign of Barrett.

There was no way to sneak past them without being seen. For a moment, he considered back-tracking in search of another exit, but there was not time for that. There was always a chance that Barrett would go to the room to check on them. Or he could show up here at any moment.

Hoping the element of surprise would give him the edge he needed, Alex burst into the room.

"What the . . . ?" Handeland dropped his cards, reached for his gun, and fired.

The bullet struck Alex in the arm.

Kelsey swung around in his chair, his eyes widening as Alex struck him across the jaw. The chain wrapped around Alex's fist made an ugly squishing sound as it tore into flesh. With a strangled cry, Kelsey slipped to the floor, blood gushing from his face and mouth.

Still moving, Alex flung Kelsey's chair aside and reached for Handeland. There was an explosion as Handeland pulled the trigger. Alex staggered back, then lurched forward, one hand locking around Handeland's throat, squeezing, squeezing, until the man's eyes rolled back in his head and he went limp.

Moving quickly, Alex went through Handeland's pockets until he found the key to the collar. Clutching it in one hand, he grabbed Handeland's gun, then hurried out to Kara.

Her eyes widened and all the color drained from her face when she saw the blood dripping down his arm, flowing from his shoulder.

"Come on," Alex said urgently. "We don't have much time."

Kara stared at him, unable to move, unable to speak.

"Don't faint on me, Kara," Alex said. "We've got to go. Now. And I don't think I can carry you."

She nodded. Forcing one foot in front of the other, she followed him down the dimly lit hallway. A door loomed in front of them. She was surprised to find it unlocked.

She glanced at her hospital gown, at Alex's nakedness, at the chain dangling from the collar around his neck, at the blood oozing from the wounds in his arm and shoulder, and none of it seemed real.

Outside, the street was dark and quiet. A full moon hung low in the sky. For the first time, she got a glimpse of the building that had imprisoned them. It was a small square structure built of faded red brick. All the windows were barred; two were boarded up. From the outside, it looked like an abandoned store of some kind.

Like a robot, she followed Alex down the street. They passed a vacant lot, a couple of ramshackle houses, a grocery store that had bars on the door and the windows.

She stood to one side while Alex tried to unlock the door of a battered Chevy pickup. She heard him swear softly as his power failed him. A moment later, there was the tell-tale tinkle of breaking glass; then he reached through the window and unlocked the door. She slid across the seat to the passenger side. The cracked leather was cold and rough against the back of her legs.

"Here, hold this," Alex said. He thrust a large

brass key into her hand, tossed the gun on the seat.

She heard him groan softly, heard the rattle of the chain, as he reached under the dash to hot wire the car. Moments later, the engine coughed to life. He didn't turn the lights on until they were well away from the lab.

In a haze, she watched the faint white line in the center of the road. This was a nightmare. That was the only explanation. In a few minutes, she'd wake to the sound of Nana's voice scolding her for sleeping so late, then Gail would come running in, begging to go to a movie with Cherise, or to McDonald's for dinner when Kara got home from work. Ordinary things. Everyday things . . .

They passed a small wooden sign.

LEAVING SILVERDALE, it read. DRIVE SAFELY.

Silverdale. She had no idea where it was.

After a time, she became aware that the truck was slowing down. She glanced at Alex, felt the pain of his wounds as if they were her own, and knew he was on the verge of losing consciousness.

A moment later, she grabbed the wheel as he slumped toward her.

Chapter Twenty-three

Kara pulled the truck off the road. Putting the gear shift in park, she slipped out of her gown, wondering how she'd turn the engine off without the key. Tearing the flimsy garment into strips, she bandaged Alex's arm, then made a thick pad and pressed it over the wound in his shoulder, tying it in place with another strip of cloth. That done, she removed the heavy collar and chain from his neck and tossed them out the window.

She felt Alex's forehead, wondering if it felt hotter than usual. Fumbling on the dash, she turned on the heater, then put the truck in gear and pulled onto the narrow two-lane road once more. She drove with no destination in mind. She didn't know where they were, didn't know where to go for help. She couldn't go home, even if she knew which direction to go, couldn't check Alex into a hospital even if she could find one. The road was deserted. Not so much as a gas station or a telephone.

She imagined pulling into a gas station and asking for help, grimacing as she pictured the reception they'd get.

She considered turning around. Maybe there was a town behind her. Maybe she should try and find a cop. Too bad she didn't know where to find a donut shop, or a police station. She felt a bubble of hysterical laughter rise in her throat as she pictured herself walking into some small-town precinct, stark naked, and telling them that she had escaped from a mad doctor who wanted to get rich selling alien blood to wealthy sick people.

She tried to rouse Alex, but he was unconscious. Or dead.

No! She put her hand over his heart, relieved by the faint but steady rise and fall of his chest. He was alive, thank God. Not knowing where else to turn, she murmured a prayer, begging for help, for a place to hide until Alex was better. She was hungry and tired and afraid, so afraid.

And then, as if in answer to her prayer, she saw a rustic cabin off the side of the road. In the moonlight, it looked like a fairy-tale cottage. Snow White's house, she thought, or maybe Piglet's. It was a pretty little place, located on the edge of a small lake.

"Thank you, Lord." She whispered the words over and over again as she pulled off the road, put the truck in park, and set the brake.

Opening the door, she slipped out of the truck and went to look in one of the windows. Shivering with the cold, she walked around the cabin. She found a note on the front door. Ripping it free, she carried it back to the truck, squinting to read it in the headlights.

Lucy, Tried to get hold of you, but you'd already left. Something came up at work and I had to go back to the city. Stay if you want. Will call you next weekend. Randy.

Below that, was another scrawl.

Randy, Sorry we missed each other. Call me at work next Friday. Phil's getting suspicious. Will call you before then if I can. Love, Lucy.

Crumpling the note in her hand, Kara tried the door. It was locked. She frowned for a moment, then ran her hand over the ledge above the door. Nothing. She glanced at the flower pot sitting on the porch, then grinned as she lifted it and found a key.

"Thank you, Randy," she murmured. Unlocking the door, she stepped inside.

It was a quaint little one-room cabin, the perfect place for a rendezvous. There was no phone, no electricity, a single window that overlooked the lake. A Coleman stove stood on a small square table; there was a box of groceries on the sink top. She poked inside, finding a loaf of French bread, mayonnaise and mustard, apples, oranges, bananas, paper plates and cups, a bottle of rum. An ice chest revealed a carton of milk, a couple of steaks, some lunch meat and a variety of cheeses. There was also a six-pack of beer, and a two-liter bottle of 7-Up.

A pair of sleeping bags were spread in front of

the fireplace; there was a good-sized pile of wood on the hearth, a box of matches on the mantel, and a Coleman lantern.

Pleased that Lucy had decided not to stay at the cabin without Randy, and grateful that she hadn't gone inside and seen the groceries, Kara murmured another prayer of thanks, then hurried outside.

Alex lay across the seat, his eyes closed, his breathing rapid and shallow. He'd told her once that he'd never been sick, that he had always recovered quickly when he was hurt. She wondered if his body's ability to heal itself included gunshot wounds.

"Alex? Alex, wake up!"

His eyelids fluttered open and he stared at her, his gaze unfocused.

"You've got to get up. I've found a place to stay."

He nodded, groaning softly as he sat up.

"The engine," she said. "Can you turn it off?"

Grunting softly, Alex reached under the dash and disconnected the wires. The sudden silence seemed deafening.

"Put your arm around my shoulder," Kara said. "It's not far."

He didn't argue. Kara groaned as she shouldered some of his weight. Mercy, but he was heavy! One step at a time, they made it into the cabin.

Kara helped Alex get settled on one of the sleeping bags. then went to close and lock the door.

She was surprised and relieved to find the cabin had running water and clean towels.

She felt the bile rise in her throat as she began to wash the blood from Alex's shoulder. The bullet hole was small and ugly, and it didn't go all the way through.

"Alex? Alex, what should I do?"

He glanced at the bloody hole in his shoulder. "Now might be a good time for one of us to faint."

"Very funny."

"Yeah. Mind if I go first?"

"Don't you dare faint on me!" The wound continued to ooze blood and she pressed the cloth against it in an effort to stop the bleeding. "I don't think the wound in your arm is too serious, but your shoulder . . . I think the bullet's still in there."

"I'm afraid you're right." He dragged a knuckle over her cheek. "Think you can get it out?"

"I don't know."

"I can do it if you're not up to it."

"You!"

"It wouldn't be the first time."

"You've been shot before?"

"Once, a long time ago."

"When? Where?"

"In the Dakotas." Alex frowned, remembering. "You've heard of Custer?"

"Of course."

"I was fighting with the Cheyenne. Beautiful people, the Cheyenne."

"The Cheyenne? You were fighting on the side of the Cheyenne at the Little Big Horn?"

"Hell of a fight. Custer was an idiot to divide his troops the way he did." He grimaced as pain surged through him.

"Are you all right?" Kara asked anxiously.

He nodded. "I missed the main battle, of course, but there was still some fighting going on after dark. I was prowling around the hill where Reno and some of his men were holed up when I took a bullet in my leg. I dug it out myself. I don't recommend it."

"Thanks," Kara muttered dryly.

He mentioned the battle so casually, a battle that had taken place a hundred and twenty years ago. She looked into his eyes, trying to imagine the life he'd led. America was an infant when compared to most of the countries of the world, and Alex had been here almost from the beginning. Sometimes she forgot how old he was.

"Kara?"

"I'll do it." She spent the next few minutes looking for something to use as a probe, finally settling on a thin-bladed knife she found in a drawer. She heated it over the Coleman stove, then rinsed it with rum. "Maybe you'd like a drink of this?" she suggested, offering him the bottle.

"Why not?" Alex lifted the bottle and took a long swallow. "Not bad." He looked at the knife, at the way it shook in her hand, and grinned. "Maybe *you* should have a drink. Might steady your nerves."

Kara took the bottle and stared at it. She'd never been much of a drinker, but she took several long swallows, felt the expensive liquor slide smoothly down her throat.

"Ready, doc?"

Kara nodded, and Alex lay back on the sleeping bag, his hands clenched. "Go on," he said. "Get it over with."

One more drink. A deep breath, and she was ready. She'd seen it done in living color in movies, read about it, and still she wasn't prepared for the blood, the feel of the knife slipping into flesh. Once, Alex took hold of her hand, steadying her.

She gave a triumphant gasp when the tip of the knife hit the bullet. Moments later, the slug lay in her palm.

She looked at Alex, looked at the bloody chunk of lead in her hand, and knew she was going to faint.

Alex caught her before she hit the floor. Feeling a little light-headed himself, he covered Kara with the sleeping bag, then rose, unsteadily, to his feet.

Picking up a clean washrag, he doused it with rum, swore a violent oath as he pressed the cloth over the wound in his shoulder. He rigged a bandage by tearing a white cotton dish towel into strips.

Aware of the approaching dawn, he stretched out beside Kara and closed his eyes.

He woke abruptly, his gaze drawn to the bright light filtering through the thin curtain. He couldn't endure the sun, not now, not after all the blood he'd lost.

"Kara." He shook her shoulder. "Kara, wake up!"

"What's wrong?"

"The window. Cover it."

"What?" She blinked at him for a moment; then, as comprehension dawned, she scrambled out of the sleeping bag, picked it up, and draped it over the curtain rod. "Is that better?"

Alex nodded. "Thanks."

Crossing the room, she knelt beside him. The bandage on his shoulder was stained with blood. The material looked very white against his bronzed skin. "How do you feel?"

"I'll be all right."

"I know, but how do you feel?"

273

"Weak."

"You should eat something. And drink plenty of water."

"Yes, ma'am."

"I'm serious. You need to rebuild your strength. You rest, and I'll fix breakfast. French toast okay with you?"

"Fine."

"You saved my life again," she said softly.

"My pleasure."

She basked in the love shining in his eyes, wishing he wasn't hurt, that they could spend the day making love.

"Maybe tomorrow," Alex said, his voice low and husky, his eyes dark with promise.

Kara felt her cheeks grow hot. "You're reading my mind again."

His smile was slow and lazy and not the least bit guilty.

Kara's cheeks grew hotter. "I'd better fix breakfast."

He slept all that day, leaving Kara to wander around the small cabin. She found a blue-and-yellow sundress in a box next to the stove and put it on. It was a trifle large, but it beat running around naked.

Late in the afternoon, she went outside and sat in the sun. Head back, she gazed out at the lake, her mind wandering. Her first thoughts were for Gail and Nana. What had Barrett done with them? Were they home, waiting for her, or—good Lord, what if they were locked up in the same building where she and Alex had been held? And what about Barrett? Was he looking for her even now? Had

Alex killed Handeland? Was she ever going to have a normal life again? If she left the state and changed her name, would she be able to get on with her life?

She watched the sun set in a splash of orange and ocher. It was so peaceful here, she mused, so quiet, while her whole life was in constant turmoil. Once, after watching a James Bond movie, she had wished for a little excitement in her life. Well, she'd found it. In spades. She pressed a hand to her head, feeling a headache coming on.

And then she felt Alex's hand on her shoulder. He knelt behind her, his fingers massaging away the pain, his presence driving away her doubts. With a soft sigh, she closed her eyes and gave herself over to the wonder of his touch.

"Better?" he asked.

"Hmmm, yes. Alex, I've got to go home. I've got to find out what happened to Nana and Gail."

"They aren't there."

He came around to sit beside her and she studied his face. He looked better. The dark smudges were gone from his eyes, the lines of strain and weariness had almost disappeared.

"Do you know where they are?"

"I overheard Barrett ask Kelsey if they'd been found yet. I think they managed to get away. I'm sure they're safe."

Kara relaxed, her worries for her sister and grandmother somewhat alleviated by Alex's assurance that they had escaped.

Alex caressed her back and shoulders. Her skin was smooth and soft and warm beneath his fingers. Her hair smelled of sunshine. Bending forward, he pressed his lips to her shoulder. Clad in the colorful sundress, with her hair tumbling down her back, she looked young and innocent and as vulnerable as a newborn kitten.

Alex swore under his breath. She should have been home with her family, looking after her sister and her grandmother, dating a man who could give her children. Instead, she was here, with a man who had brought her nothing but trouble. She'd probably lost her job. Her life was in danger. She had no idea where her family was, or when she'd ever be able to go home. And it was all his fault. His hand stilled, his fingers resting lightly on her shoulder.

Kara turned her head so she could see Alex's face, the smile dying on her lips when she saw his expression. "What is it? What's wrong?"

"Nothing."

"You're lying." She met his gaze, her eyes narrowing as she tried to read his mind. After a moment, she frowned. Why couldn't she read his thoughts as she usually did? And then she realized that he had erected a barrier of some kind.

"That's not fair," she said, her voice thick with accusation. "You read my thoughts whenever you wish. I should be able to do the same."

"Life is unfair, Kara." He lifted his hand from her shoulder and stood up.

Kara stared at him. He was naked save for a towel wrapped around his waist. A faint breeze blew over the lake, ruffling his hair. The setting sun left its signature across the sky in bold strokes of crimson and ocher, casting his figure in shades of gold and bronze. He looked like the Greek god Apollo, she thought, strong and handsome and possessed of remarkable powers. She tried again to read his thoughts, and again she couldn't penetrate the wall he had erected between them.

Slowly, she stood up. She willed him to turn around, to acknowledge her, to confide in her. She ached to go to him, to take him in her arms and tell him she loved him. Instead, she crossed her arms over her breasts and attempted to shield her own thoughts.

Minutes passed, and still he stood there with his back toward her. Her patience at an end, Kara turned on her heel and walked back to the cabin.

She made dinner because she needed something to do. They had been so close only a short time ago. High on a mountaintop, they had exchanged vows to love and cherish each other. They had made love, their joining more than just physical intercourse. And now it felt as though they were hundreds of miles apart.

When dinner was ready, she started for the door to call him, only to find him standing there, his dark eyes filled with unbearable sorrow. She wondered how long he had been there, and what he was thinking to make him look so sad.

"Sit down," she said. "Supper's ready."

With a nod, he took a place at the table. She'd fixed steak and eggs. His steak was rare, just the way he liked it.

They ate in silence. Kara refused to meet his gaze, and he ached for the pain he had caused her, was causing her even now, and yet he said nothing. He'd known all along it had been wrong for him to interfere in her life. For two hundred years, he had carefully avoided attachments to humans. It was time to end his relationship with Kara before it was too late, before he ruined her life completely, or got her killed. He could not endure the guilt of knowing his mere presence put her life in jeopardy, could not have her death on his hands. Somehow, he would get her safely home, reunite her with her family. And if he had to kill Barrett to accomplish it, then he would do so without a qualm.

Rising from the table, he thanked her for the meal, then crawled into the sleeping bag and closed his eyes. Leaving her would not be easy for either of them. She might miss him for a time. She might even hate him. But someday, when she had a husband and children and a normal life, she would thank him.

Chapter Twenty-four

He had shut her out, and she didn't know why. Lying in her sleeping bag that night, Kara ran over the events of the day in her mind, wondering what she had said, what she had done, to make him angry. She had tried several times to make him talk to her, to tell her what was wrong, but he had replied, politely, that nothing was wrong, he was only tired.

He was lying.

She had checked his injuries, amazed to see that the wounds, so bloody and ugly the night before, had nearly healed.

She wanted him to take her in his arms, needed him to hold her, to assure her that everything would turn out for the best.

She hesitated a few moments more, and then she slid out of the sleeping bag and went to gaze out the window at the man who was causing her heart such pain.

He was standing near the lake's edge, his head thrown back, his arms spread wide, as he gazed up at the night sky. The moon's pale light danced across the face of the still water and bathed Alex in a shimmering silver haze.

He looked so beautiful, and so alone, it made her heart ache. Why wouldn't he confide in her? Didn't he know how deeply his silence was hurting her?

An owl hooted softly in the distance. Alex had told her that some tribes of Indians believed that the call of an owl near a lodge meant impending death. The sound drew his attention and as he turned toward it; Kara saw his face, saw the pain and loneliness in his expression.

Needing to touch him, to comfort him, needing his comfort in return, she ran out of the cabin, heedless of the fact that she wasn't dressed.

"Alex, I'm sorry." She threw her arms around him, burying her face in his shoulder. "Please forgive me."

Instinctively, his arms closed around her. "Forgive you?" Alex asked, startled by her apology. "What have you done?"

"I don't know." Her words were muffled against his shoulder. "Why have you shut me out? I feel so alone."

"Kara . . . *natayah* . . ." He stroked her back, his hands restless, his desire stirring at her nearness, at the silkiness of her flesh pressing so intimately against his. "Kara . . ."

"Don't send me away," she begged. "Don't shut me out."

Rising on tiptoe, she pressed her body against

his. "I love you, Alex." She tilted her head back so she could see his face, and then she kissed him deeply, fervently.

And he was lost. Lost in the magic of her touch, the soul-deep love he had seen in her eyes.

With a helpless cry of surrender, he cradled her in his arms, carrying her gently to the ground, covering her face, her neck, her breasts, with hungry kisses. His hands slid over her slender frame. Her skin was smooth, silky, vibrant beneath his fingertips. She arched against him, low moans of pleasure rising in her throat, encouraging him, inflaming him, until he had no thought save to possess her, to show her with his hands and his lips that he loved her, only her, now and forever.

Her thighs parted eagerly to receive him, and then he was a part of her—heart and soul and mind and body. Every thought, every breath, was hers.

Kara held him close, closer, until even the moonlight couldn't slip between them. Her fingers stroked the ridged flesh of his back, her fingernails following the faint pattern along his spine. She stroked him, she scratched him, and stroked him again. She cradled him within the deepest part of her, her heart pounding to the same frantic rhythm as his. She watched his face, entranced by the sheer beauty of him, by the passion blazing in his eyes.

She sobbed his name as waves of ecstacy shuddered through her, heard his answering cry as his life force filled her with warm liquid heat.

Locked together, they tumbled slowly back to earth.

Alex loosed a deep sigh. Never had he experienced anything so wonderful, not even with AnnaMara. Though he had loved his wife, he had not needed her as desperately as he needed Kara. And yet, mixed with the sense of wonder was a horrible sense of guilt.

What if Kara got pregnant? Barrett had told him this was the perfect time to impregnate her. The thought was staggering. As much as he yearned for a child born of their love, he was afraid to face the possibility, didn't want to consider the consequences that might result from the mating of ErAdonian and earthling.

Kara made a soft sound in her throat, and he realized he was probably suffocating her with his weight. Rolling to the side, he carried her with him, holding her in his arms. He felt a sudden need to put distance between them, to be alone with his thoughts, but he knew she would not understand. She would be hurt, thinking that he was shutting her out again. He couldn't bear the thought of causing her more pain, and so he held her close, one hand stroking her hair, until her breathing grew even and shallow and he knew she was asleep.

"Forgive me, *natayah*," he murmured.

He stared up at the sky, torn by conflicting emotions. He should never have gotten involved in her life . . . he should never have touched her . . . she was the best thing that had happened to him in two hundred years . . . she might be pregnant even now . . . he had ruined her life . . . he wanted her . . . he needed her.

He loved her.

He didn't want to love her, or need her, or want her.

He never should have touched her.

He wanted her again. Even now his blood was warming, thickening with desire . . . She stirred in his arms, murmured his name, and he held her tighter, knowing he would never be happy without her at his side, knowing that, sooner or later, he would have to let her go. No matter how earth-like he appeared, he was ErAdonian. A dog and a cat might fall in love, he mused bleakly, but they were two different creatures, never meant to share more than friendship.

They stayed at the cabin until the food ran out. During those three days, Alex closed his mind to everything but making Kara happy. They walked along the lake at night, took long moonlight swims, slept late in the morning. He had vowed not to make love to her again, but each night she teased him with her kisses and her touch, tempting him beyond his ability to resist. Daily, he prayed for forgiveness, prayed she would not get pregnant, prayed for the strength to leave her when the time came.

He memorized every line of her face, every curve of her slender body, the sound of her laughter, the husky timbre of her voice when she was in the throes of passion, the color of her eyes, the texture of her hair, the taste of her skin against his tongue. He told her he loved her in every way he could, and hoped she would still believe it was true when he had to let her go.

Kara stared around the small cabin. She hated to leave the place. Even though it was small and cramped and equipped with only the barest of necessities, it had been a perfect place for a honeymoon.

She glanced at Alex. He stood near the door, a

towel wrapped around his waist.

"You didn't have to get all dressed up on my account," Kara remarked with a grin.

"Very amusing. Let's go."

Still grinning, she followed him outside, waited while he performed a little male magic under the dash to start the engine.

"You want to drive?" she asked.

"No, you go ahead." He slid into the passenger seat and sat back, his arms folded over his chest.

Settling herself behind the wheel, Kara switched on the headlights. "Which way?"

"Turn left when you reach the road."

"You know where we are?"

"More or less." Last night, he had determined their location by the position of the stars. If his calculations were correct, they were about seventy miles from Moulton Bay.

Kara glanced at him as she drove. His wounds had healed, leaving no trace. She had seen it, yet it was still hard to believe that Alex had been shot, twice, and healed completely in three days. For the first time, she could understand Barrett's motives, even if she found them reprehensible. And yet, she couldn't help thinking of all the good Alex could do, the people he could help, the lives he could save.

He was reading her mind again. She knew it the moment he spoke.

"How would I decide which lives to save, Kara?" he asked quietly. "I can only give so much blood. Do I sell it to the rich? Give it to the poor? How do I decide which life has more worth? A mother of three? A father of four? A child? A grandmother? There are millions of people, Kara, and I'm only one man. I'm not the Almighty. I don't want to hold the power of life and death in my hands. I don't want to make those kinds of decisions."

He hadn't mentioned his own life, his own needs, but she knew he would never have any kind of private life if people knew the miraculous power of his blood. Everyone would want a piece of him—the public, the press, scientists, doctors, preachers and talk shows. He'd never be able to go back to Moulton Bay, never have the time or the privacy to write another book. Some might think it selfish, his refusal to help, and if he was a mere human, she might think so, too. But he was an alien, and she knew that he would be hounded the rest of his life if people found out who he was, what he was. And that, she thought ruefully, could be a long, long time. Not only that, but his freedom would be forever lost. He would spend the rest of his life in a cage, being examined, questioned, analyzed.

Selfishly, she realized that they would never have a life together if the world discovered his identity. And she wanted a future with Alex more than anything she had ever wanted in her life.

Right or wrong, selfish or not, she intended to have it.

They were driving on fumes and luck by the time they reached Moulton Bay. The clock on the dash put the time at nine-thirty.

She'd no sooner parked the truck in the garage than the engine sputtered and died. Opening the door, she slid from behind the wheel and followed Alex into the house.

Alex moved unerringly through the darkness until he heard her stumble. Cursing his thoughtlessness, he switched on a light.

"Are you all right?" he asked.

"Fine." Lips compressed, she rubbed her knee where she'd hit it against a table. "Want to kiss it and make it better?"

Her words were light, teasing, but he saw the hope in her eyes, heard the yearning in her voice.

With an effort, he hardened his heart against her. "I need a shower," he said. "I'll wait if you want to go first."

"No, you go ahead."

With a curt nod, he went up the stairs. Moments later, she heard the sound of water running.

For a moment, she thought of joining him, and then, with a sigh, she went into the kitchen. In his present mood, he had probably locked the door.

She fixed herself a cup of strong black coffee, sipped it slowly as she wondered how they'd locate Gail and Nana. Maybe one of the neighbors would know where they'd gone. And what about Barrett? Just thinking of him caused her to shiver with revulsion.

After rinsing the cup and putting it in the sink, she went through the house, making sure all the doors and windows were locked, wondering if it had been smart to come back here. It wouldn't take much effort for Barrett to find out where Alex lived.

She was wandering through the den when she felt Alexander's presence behind her. Slowly, she turned to face him. He was wearing a pair of faded Levi's and a black sweater. His feet were bare, his hair was still damp. He looked beautiful and sexy. And distant.

"Your turn," he said tonelessly. "I'll see you in the morning."

With a nod, she left the room and went upstairs.

She didn't know what was bothering him, but she intended to find out. Soon.

Alex watched Kara leave the room; then he sat down at his desk and stared at the computer. After a moment, he switched it on.

Calling up the file that contained his latest manuscript, he scanned the material from page one. The manuscript was far from finished, but he felt driven to work on the conclusion to the story, despite the fact that it was out of sequence.

He thought a moment, and then began to write.

I gazed at Melynda, knowing the time had come when there could be no more lies between us. I had courted her for over a year, never letting her know what I was, certain that the love in her eyes would turn to fear, or worse, to revulsion, when she knew I was not the man she thought I was, but I could wait no longer. Melynda had declared her love for me, and I, foolishly perhaps, had admitted I felt the same. Our kisses, innocently chaste at the beginning of our courtship, had grown more passionate, more intense, once our feelings were spoken aloud. The desire between us blossomed into a flower of rare beauty, but I could not take her virginity, could not forge that bond of intimacy between us.

"What is it?" she asked. "What did you want to tell me?"

Filled with self-loathing for what I was about to do, I gazed into her eyes and prayed that she would be able to forgive me for my deception . . .

Alex sat back in his chair, his palms resting on either side of the keyboard.

He doubted there would be a happy ending for himself and Kara, but he could grant one to his vampire.

With a sigh, he began to write once again.

Hesitantly, I told her the truth, then waited for her to spurn me, to flee in terror from the monster who had dared to love her.

"Vampire?" she exclaimed softly. Her eyes narrowed as she looked at me. "Vampire?" she said again, and began to laugh.

At first, I thought her hysterical with fear. Tears rolled down her cheeks; she held her sides as laughter continued to bubble from her lips.

"Vampire! Oh, Alesandro, is that all?"

"Is that *all?*" I asked, shocked by her reaction. "All? Isn't that enough?"

"I've known about that for months," she said, wiping the tears from her eyes.

"Known? How could you have known?"

"I'm not blind, or stupid," she replied with a toss of her head. "You never eat, you cast no shadow, I never saw you during the day." She shrugged. "I saw how you looked at me that night I pricked my finger on a thorn. I saw the hunger in your eyes before you turned away. I saw, and I knew."

"And you don't care?"

"Of course I care, but . . ." She smiled up at me. "I thought you were going to tell me you were married."

"No," I said, my mind still reeling with her

ready acceptance of what I was. "I'm not married."

"But you will be soon," she predicted.

"Will I?"

"I'm sure of it," she said, and rising on her tiptoes, she pressed her lips to mine, and in that kiss was the promise of forever . . .

Forever, Alexander mused as he saved the file and exited the program. He had stayed in Moulton Bay too long. It was time to move on. Time to find a new place to live, a new name, a new identity. For him, it wouldn't be hard. He had no family to leave behind, no ties to bind him to one place. He could abandon civilization, hide out in a jungle in the Amazon until Barrett was dead . . .

"Alexander?"

He whirled around, startled to see Kara standing in the doorway. It was the first time she had taken him unawares. "I thought you had turned in for the night."

Kara shrugged. "I'm not tired."

"I am." He stood up, his chair between them. "I'm going to bed."

"No, you're not."

He arched one thick black brow. "No?"

"Not until we get this straightened out."

"Get what straightened out?"

"I want to know where you think you're going without me, and why."

Too late, he realized that while he was writing he had neglected to maintain the barrier between his mind and hers.

She crossed her arms over her breasts and regarded him solemnly. "I'm waiting."

Alex stared at her. She was wearing one of his T-shirts and a pair of his socks, and nothing else. She should have looked ridiculous; instead, she looked young and innocent and vastly appealing. Her legs were long and slender. A wave of heat suffused him as he imagined them wrapped around his waist.

"I'm going to bed," he said firmly, and brushed past her before she could stop him.

In his room, he shut the door, stripped off his sweater, then went to the window and stared into the darkness. He had to get her out of here. She'd never be safe with him, not until Barrett was no longer a threat. Until then, he had to find her a refuge of some kind. But where?

He went suddenly still as the door opened.

"I'm still waiting."

Her scent, soap mingled with toothpaste and strawberry shampoo, was intoxicating. Hands clenched at his sides, he glanced over his shoulder. "Go to bed, Kara."

"All right."

Too late, he remembered there was only one bed in the house—his—and she was walking toward it.

"Kara . . ." He raked his hands through his hair, then shoved them into his pockets to keep from sweeping her into his arms.

She sat on the edge of the mattress looking up at him. "I'm listening."

"Have you always been this stubborn?"

"Pretty much."

"Kara, I don't want to cause you any more trouble."

"Then don't." She patted the mattress invitingly.

Alex shook his head. "Kara, please . . ." The words, meant to be a firm denial, fell from his lips like a prayer. "I'm only thinking of you."

"I know, but I'm a big girl, Alex. I can make my own decisions. You promised to love me and defend me," she reminded him quietly. "You promised me your life, Alexander Claybourne, promised you would be mine for as long as you lived. Have you forgotten?"

"No."

"Have you stopped loving me?"

"No."

"I promised to stay by your side in good times and bad. Would you send me away and make me break that promise?"

He groaned low in his throat, as if her words had pierced his heart.

"Would you?"

"To save your life, I would do anything. Anything. Even send you away."

"You've never done me any harm. Giving me your blood saved my life."

"Getting you pregnant could be fatal."

"I'm willing to take that chance."

"I'm not."

"Isn't it a little late to worry about that now?"

Her words cut through him like a knife through water. What if she was already pregnant?

"I didn't mean it like that," Kara said quickly. "I only meant we've already made love numerous times and nothing bad has happened. Maybe you're worrying for nothing. Maybe you were right, and it isn't possible for us to have a child."

"And maybe it is." He looked at her, sitting on the bed, her beautiful blue eyes warm with love, and wondered what kind of monster he was that he wanted nothing more than to go to her, to wrap her in his arms and bury himself deep within her.

"You're not a monster, Alex." She smiled as a low groan rumbled in his throat. "Now you know how I felt when you were reading my mind."

"Kara, what am I going to do with you?"

"Love me, Alex. Just love me as I love you."

"With my dying breath, *natayah*."

"Prove it."

He shook his head. "Since I can't make you listen to reason, I'll make a bargain with you."

She tilted her head to one side. "A bargain?"

"No more lovemaking between us until we're sure you're not already pregnant."

"And then?"

A muscle twitched in his cheek. "One of us will be neutered."

"Neutered!" she exclaimed, horrified by the idea. "What's wrong with just using a contraceptive?"

"None of them are foolproof."

"Neutered." She said the word as if it tasted bad. "Which one of us?" Kara shook her head as his gaze slid away from hers. "No, Alex, I can't . . ."

"I can't go to a hospital, or a doctor's office, Kara. I can't take a chance like that."

"But . . ." She bit down on her lower lip. She wanted to shout at him, to scream that she wanted children, his children if she could have them.

"Perhaps it's time for you to re-think our relationship, Kara, to make sure you understand what you're giving up."

Kara stared up at him, mute. She didn't want to re-think anything. She didn't want to live without Alex, and yet the thought of permanently putting an end to any hope of having children silenced the denial that rose to her lips.

"I'll sleep on the sofa," Alex said, and left the room, quietly closing the door behind him.

Kara stared at the door. To be sterile. Never to have children. Even adoption might be out of the question. She didn't know what legalities were involved in adopting a child. She was certain that Alex must have a phony birth certificate. He drove a car, so he probably had a driver's license. He earned money, so he probably had a social security number. A harsh laugh escaped her lips. In two hundred years, he had probably accumulated numerous forms of identification.

Alien.

Two hundred years.

It hit her then, really hit her for the first time. Alex was an alien. He had told her that people were the same all over, and yet he was still from another planet, another race of people. What if she did get pregnant? What might the result be? Images of newborn babies flashed through her mind—babies with four arms and two heads, babies with skin like leather, babies with three eyes . . .

She was letting her imagination run wild and she knew it. Alex was perfectly healthy and so was she. If they were able to conceive a child, there was no reason why they couldn't have a perfectly formed baby. It was far more likely that she would be unable to conceive at all, and that brought her back to her original quandary. Did she love Alex enough to give up all hope of ever being a mother? But even as she asked herself that question, she knew there was more involved, much more. What would happen to their relationship when she aged and he did not? How would they ever be free of Barrett? Did she want to spend her whole life looking over her shoulder? Even if they changed their names and left the country, she'd always be waiting, wondering if Barrett was still looking for them. And what about Nana and Gail? Barrett had used her sister and grandmother to get to her in the past; she knew he wouldn't hesitate to do it again.

And then she thought of a life without Alex, and knew she would make any sacrifice necessary to be with him.

Rising, she went to stand at the window. It was raining. She stared at the downpour through eyes blurred by tears and knew the cloudburst outside was nothing compared to the storm raging in her heart.

Alex wandered through the house, acutely aware of Kara's turbulent emotions. No doubt she would leave him now. It would be for the best. She deserved a normal life, with a man who could share the daylight with her, give her children, grow old at her side. She deserved to be happy, secure. Living with him would always carry an element of danger. If she wanted to go to the zoo, to the beach, on a picnic, for a walk in the park on a summer day, she would have to go alone.

Feeling as if the walls were closing in on him, he went out into the backyard and let the rain wash over him.

How would he go on without her? If his life had seemed empty before, how much more desolate would it be now, when he had known Kara's love, heard her laughter, felt the touch of her hand? And yet, no matter how much he loved her, he could not give her the kind of life she deserved.

He wanted her to be happy.

He wanted to carry her back to his mountain lair and never let her go.

He wanted a home and a family, the love and companionship of a woman with dreamy blue eyes, the sound of a child's laughter.

He wanted Kara.

And yet he knew the best thing he could do for her was get out of her life.

And he knew, with a certainty that was too awful to be borne, that he didn't have the strength to do what was right; he knew that, if his weakness was the cause of her death, he would have nothing left to live for. If that day came, he would walk out into the sun and let it destroy him.

Burdened with a weight of sorrow too heavy to bear, he sank to his knees, his tears mingling with the rain.

Kara stared at the lone figure standing in the yard. Rain pelted his head and chest, soaking his trousers. She didn't have to probe his mind to know what he was thinking, what he was feeling. His pain was hers. His thoughts were her thoughts. She felt his loneliness, his yearning for a home and a family, his fear for her life should she become pregnant, the strong sense of guilt that everything that had happened to her was his fault. He wanted her, but he was afraid, afraid for her life, her future, afraid of causing her pain.

She pressed her hand to her heart as he dropped to his knees, his head bowed, as if in surrender.

She was the cause of his anguish. The knowledge that he was hurting because of her cut her to the quick.

A heavy sigh shuddered through her as she realized what she had to do. For his sake, she would leave him, now, tonight. In time, he would forget her. He might even find someone else to love. In time.

She laughed softly as she wrapped a blanket around her shoulders and crept down the stairs and out the front door. If there was one thing Alex had plenty of, it was time.

Chapter Twenty-five

She was soaked to the skin, chilled to the marrow of her bones, by the time she reached Nana's. The house was dark, the front door locked. Her Camry was parked in the driveway. Nana must have had it towed home from the hospital in Grenvale.

Making her way toward the rear of the house, Kara took the key from its hiding place underneath a flowerpot and let herself in the back door.

Not wanting to alert anyone who might be watching the house for her return, she made her way through the dark house toward her bedroom. Shedding the wet blanket, Alex's t-shirt and socks, she pulled on a black sweatshirt and a pair of fleece-lined sweats, thick cotton socks, and a pair of running shoes.

She was feeling her way along the top of her dresser, looking for her comb, when she discovered her handbag. Inside, she found her wallet and car keys, which she shoved into the pocket of her jeans.

She towel-dried her hair, ran a comb through it, then went into the kitchen and made herself a cup of strong black coffee.

Where would Gail and Nana go?

She pondered the question as she finished her coffee; then, setting the cup aside, she went into the bathroom she had shared with Gail and closed the door before flipping on the night light.

Ever since Gail had learned to read and write, she had loved to leave notes for her sister. Usually, the notes had been silly jokes, sometimes they were hurriedly scrawled apologies for using Kara's make-up. Gail had always left the notes in a blue and white tin container that had once held perfumed bath salts. Kara had kept the canister because she liked the design, and it had become their private mailbox.

Hardly daring to hope, Kara picked up the canister and removed the lid. Murmuring a silent prayer, she withdrew a rolled-up piece of paper.

"Kara, I locked Barrett's watchdog in the hall closet. Nana, Mrs. Zimmermann, and me are running away. I don't know where we'll go. We're taking Mrs. Zimmermann's car. I'll call Cherise every day at four and every night at seven. Her number's in the book. Don't worry about us. Nana is feeling much better. I love you. Gail."

Switching off the light, Kara left the bathroom and went into the kitchen. According to the clock on the microwave, it was just after midnight.

She poured herself another cup of coffee, then sat at the kitchen table, wondering if it was safe to spend the night in her own bed, or if she should go to a motel.

Lost in thought, she listened to the rain beat against the aluminum patio cover. No doubt Alex would think she had left him because she didn't love him enough to accept the sacrifices she would have to make to stay with him, when nothing could be further from the truth. She had left him because she did love him, because she couldn't bear to see the pain in his eyes and know she was the cause. She knew in her heart that if anything happened to her, Alex would never forgive himself.

But, oh, how she yearned for the comfort of his arms around her! She wasn't afraid of anything when she was with him. He made her feel strong, invincible. With Alex at her side, she could face anything. Anything, except knowing she was the cause of his sorrow.

Feeling heavy-hearted and more alone than she'd ever felt in her life, she went into her room and gathered up a blanket and her pillow and climbed up into the attic.

She would sleep here tonight. Tomorrow, she would go to Cherise's house and wait for Gail to call.

Dale Barrett paced the floor of the lab, his fists jammed into his pants pockets. He cursed softly, unable to believe his bad luck as he glared at the two men sitting hunched over the table.

Mitch Hamblin looked sullen; Kelsey's expression was impossible to read. Most of his face was covered with a thick bandage. The chain wrapped around the alien's fist had done a remarkable bit of damage.

"She'll go home," Barrett said. "Sooner or later, she'll go home."

"I'll find her," Hamblin said.

"No, I'll find her." Kelsey stood up, his eyes narrowed. "I want him, and he'll be with her."

"I want him alive!" Barrett's gaze bored into Kelsey's. "You can dispose of the girl if she gets in the way. Do it in front of the alien," Barrett said, exposing a sadistic streak few knew he possessed. "That should be vengeance enough for what he did to your face. But I want him alive. I need him alive."

"And I want him dead!" Kelsey's hand strayed to the bandage on his face. His nose had been broken; it had taken thirty stitches to sew up the gash that ran up his left cheek to his hairline.

"He's no good to us dead," Barrett reminded him. "Once we have him again, you can do anything you want to him, except kill him."

"Anything?"

Barrett nodded. "Within reason. But I need him alive, at least until I've obtained a sufficient quantity of his sperm and I can reproduce the healing agent in his blood. And then . . ." He shrugged. "And then he's yours."

Kelsey nodded. "I'll go with the kid to make sure nothing goes wrong."

"I don't need a nursemaid," Hamblin said, bristling.

"Take Kelsey with you," Barrett said. "He can make sure you don't get yourself locked in another closet, and you can make sure he brings the alien back alive."

Mitch and Kelsey glared at each other a moment, then left the room.

Barrett stared after them. This time, he thought, this time he would have it all.

Alexander woke to an intense sense of loss and knew immediately that Kara had left the house. And in that same instant, he knew why.

Sitting up, he buried his face in his hands. She had touched his mind last night, felt his fear, his pain, and she had run away to spare him further anguish.

Cursing himself, cursing the weakness that had overwhelmed him the night before, he rose from the sofa and ran up the stairs to the bedroom. Opening the door, he stepped inside, and her scent embraced him, wrapping around him like an invisible web fashioned of her very essence.

"Kara . . ."

Crossing the floor, he sank down beside the bed and ran his hand over the sheet.

"Kara, what have I done?"

He pressed his face to the mattress, inhaling her scent. He'd been a fool to run away from the lab, a fool to be afraid, when the answer was so simple. Kill Barrett. Destroy his notes. Dispose of the blood samples and anything else Barrett had that related to Alex's existence.

So simple. And yet the thought of killing Barrett sickened him. He had been banished from Er-Adona because he had shed a man's blood. And yet, what other choice did he have? So long as Barrett lived, Kara's life, and his own, would be in danger.

Rocking back on his heels, Alex stared at his hands. Strong hands with long capable fingers.

Hands that had killed before. Hands that could kill again.

He stared at the window. It was mid-afternoon. The storm had passed and the sun was shining brightly.

"Kara," he murmured. "Forgive me."

Restless with the need to see her, to hold her, he wandered through the house. Never before had it seemed so empty. Never before had he felt so alone. Having known her, having tasted her love, how had he ever thought he could live without her? She had offered him her love. Even after she knew what he was, she had given him her love, taken him into the deepest part of herself. She had saved his life, restored his hope, his reason for living. And what had he done? He had offered to let her stay with him if she would give up all hope of having children, if she would submit to an operation she found repulsive.

She had loved him with all her heart, asking nothing in return. She still loved him, loved him enough to leave him because she thought she was causing him pain.

"Oh, Kara, *natayah . . .*" How would he ever make it up to her? Would she even let him try?

"Kara . . ."

Alex. Alex . . .

Her voice, calling his name over and over again.

He stared at the window, at the lethal sunlight kept at bay by a layer of heavy draperies. And in his mind, he heard her voice again, low and tinged with desperation.

Alex!

* * *

Kara cowered in the attic, listening to the voices below. The inertia that had held her in its grasp the night before fled as adrenaline pumped through her veins. How could she have been so stupid as to stay here? Why hadn't she taken her car and gone to a motel last night? She recognized Kelsey's voice, but not that of the man Kelsey called Mitch. They were here, in the house, looking for her. She could hear them wandering from room to room, opening doors, looking inside closets.

Fragments of their conversation drifted upward.

". . . not here."

"Have to wait . . ."

"Barrett could be wrong . . ."

Kara pressed her ear to the floor, straining to hear more. And then the voices were directly below her, and she could hear everything they said.

"Barrett said to wait, so we'll wait. Might as well make ourselves at home." Kelsey's voice. "You hungry?"

"Yeah, I could eat something."

"Why don't you go order us a pizza? I'll call Barrett on my cell phone and tell him we're here."

The sound of their footsteps moving away.

Kara released the breath she'd been holding, only vaguely aware that she'd been repeating Alex's name in her mind over and over again, clinging to it, finding hope and strength in the name of the man she loved.

She sat up, her back to the wall, and drew in several deep breaths. She had to get out of here, tonight, before they discovered the attic.

She closed her eyes, felt the sting of tears behind her lids. She had to get to Cherise's house, had to talk to Gail, to assure herself that Nana and her

sister were well. They'd arrange to meet somewhere
. . . and then what? Spend the rest of their lives hiding, running?

"Oh, Alex," she whispered. "What am I going to do?"

Kara was in trouble. The thought clawed at his mind, relentlessly, without pity. She was in trouble, and it was all his fault.

He prowled the house, as restless as a caged lion, as he waited for the sun to go down. Imprisoned by his body's weakness. Tormented by visions of Kara being captured, tortured. Because of him.

And then he heard her scream, and all rational thought fled his mind.

They'd found her! Kara held her breath as the trapdoor swung open.

"I'm sure I heard something up here," Kelsey said. He struck a match and held it over his head, peering into the darkness.

Not daring to breathe, Kara pressed herself against the wall, hoping Kelsey wouldn't see her in the shadows.

"See anything?" Mitch asked.

"No. I'm going in."

Panic surged through Kara as she glanced around the attic, her gaze searching for something, anything, that she could use as a weapon.

Kelsey's footsteps were very loud in the small space. He swore as the match burned his fingers, then quickly lit another.

And then he was there, staring at her, his eyes wide with surprise and satisfaction.

Kara hesitated a moment, startled as a face as

white as a sheet appeared before her. With a cry, Kara grabbed a heavy brass candlestick and swung it at his head.

Kelsey jerked his head out of the way, and the candlestick landed with a dull thud against his shoulder.

"Why you . . ." With his free hand, Kelsey struck her across the face. Hard. Twice.

Kara reeled back, her ears ringing, her cheek throbbing.

Kelsey snatched the candlestick from her hand and tossed it into a corner. Grabbing her by the arm, he shoved her toward the attic entrance.

"Mitch!"

"Yeah?"

"Come and get her."

Moments later, she was sitting on the sofa, her hands securely bound, while Kelsey called Barrett.

"We've got her." Kelsey said. He nodded. "Right. Uh-huh." He glanced out the window. "I don't think that's a good idea. There's a bunch of kids playing outside, a couple of women gossiping. Yeah. Okay. We'll wait for you here."

Kelsey hung up the phone.

"What'd he have to say?" Mitch asked.

"He said to sit tight. He's on his way."

Mitch nodded.

"You order us something to eat?"

"Yeah. You like anchovies?"

"Right now I could eat 'em alive," Kelsey muttered. He crossed the floor to stand in front of Kara. "See this?" he said, lifting a hand to the heavy bandage on his face. "He did it. And I aim to make him pay. And you, too."

Kara swallowed the lump of fear rising in her

throat as Kelsey lifted his hand to strike her again. She cast a frantic glance at the window, dismayed to see the sun was still shining.

She choked back a cry as Kelsey slapped her again, and then again. She tasted blood in her mouth and knew he'd cut her lip.

"Hey, man, ease up."

"Shut up, Mitch! This doesn't concern you."

Kelsey was drawing his arm back, ready to hit her again, when the doorbell rang.

"Pizza's here," Mitch said.

"Not a word," Kelsey said, his voice thick with menace. "You understand?"

Kara nodded.

Kelsey's gaze bored into hers for a moment, then he looked over at his partner. "I'll cover her from the kitchen."

Kara blinked back tears as she watched Mitch walk toward the front door.

When he was out of sight, she collapsed against the couch, her eyes closed. She heard the door open, the muffled sound of voices, a long silence, and then the sound of footsteps.

Unable to believe her senses, she opened her eyes to find Alexander staring down at her, a pizza box balanced in one hand, his eyes filled with concern as he studied the red welt on her cheek, the blood oozing from her lip.

Are you all right?

She nodded. *Kelsey's in the kitchen.*

The warning came too late. Kelsey stepped through the doorway, grinning as he aimed his gun at Alexander's chest.

"Nice of you to bring lunch," Kelsey remarked. "What'd you do with Mitch?"

Alex didn't say anything, just stared at Kelsey. And then he lifted his other hand, revealing Hamblin's weapon. "Drop your gun."

Kelsey reacted in the blink of an eye, the gun in his hand swinging from Alex to Kara as he thumbed back the hammer. "You drop *your* gun, or she's dead."

"You'll die first."

"I'm willing to take that chance," Kelsey said, his eyes cold. "Are you?"

"No."

"Then drop the gun."

Slowly, Alex did as he was told.

"Put the box down."

Again, Alex did as he was told. Conscious of Kelsey following his every move, he placed the pizza box on the coffee table, his gaze never leaving the man's face.

Kara.

I hear you.

Can you distract him?

Yes.

Now.

Groaning softly, Kara lifted her bound hands to her cheek, and then she began to cry, softly at first, and then louder.

"Shut up," Kelsey growled. "Mitch? Can you hear me?"

Kara began to sob. "Please let me go," she cried. She tugged at Kelsey's coat, forcing him to turn toward her. "Please let me go!"

"Get your hands off me!"

Kelsey batted Kara's hands away, but she hung on tightly. "Please let me go!" She pulled on his coat again.

In that instant, Alex dropped to the floor, grabbed Mitch's gun, and fired. The bullet struck Kelsey in the chest and he stumbled backward, crashing down onto the sofa beside Kara. The gun fell from his hand and skittered across the floor.

Alex grabbed Kara, staggered, then pulled her to her feet and started toward the kitchen.

"Don't move."

Alex glanced over his shoulder to see Kelsey's partner standing in the doorway. Blood trickled from the cut in the young man's temple. Kelsey's .357 was steady in his hand.

"Don't move," Hamblin repeated.

Alex swore softly. "Let us go."

Hamblin shook his head.

"I'll make it worth your while," Alex said. He felt Kara stir beside him and he squeezed her hand, willing her to be silent. "I'm a wealthy man. Just name your price, and it's yours if you let us go. Barrett doesn't have to know. You can tell him we escaped."

"I don't believe you."

"A hundred thousand dollars," Alex said, his voice caressing the words. "All you have to do is let us go."

"How will I get the money?"

"Come with us. I'll write you a check."

Hamblin licked his lips. A hundred thousand dollars was a pile of money, more than he'd ever dreamed of. It made the few hundred dollars Barrett paid him each week seem like chicken feed.

Kara's gaze moved from Alex to Hamblin and back again. She could feel Alex swaying beside her. Tightening her grip on his hand, she let her mind merge with his, felt the pain that engulfed him.

Comprehension dawned as she glanced at the window. The sun was still up. He had come after her during the day, exposing himself to the sun's deadly light.

Hamblin shook his head again. "No. I'd be a fool to trust you, and a bigger fool to go anywhere with the two of you."

"Then let Kara go. She's no use to Barrett any longer. It's my blood he wants. My blood he needs."

Again, Hamblin shook his head.

"He's going to kill her," Alex said, his voice edged with panic. "Do you want her blood on your conscience?"

For the first time, Hamblin looked uncertain.

"My checkbook is in my desk at home. Once Barrett's taken me back to his lab, you can go to my house and get it. Fill out a check. Bring it to me. I'll sign it."

Kara looked up at Alex, worried by the sudden choppiness of his words. She could feel the weakness growing within him, knew he remained on his feet by sheer force of will. Remorse filled her heart. She never should have come home, should have known Barrett would look for her here, that Alex would come after her.

"A hundred thousand dollars," Alex said again. "No one will know."

Hamblin licked his lips. It sounded so easy.

"Make up your mind," Alex said. He clung to Kara's hand, drawing on her strength. The trip across town to her house had been excruciating. Even inside the truck, the sun had found him, burning his eyes, draining his strength. But he'd known he couldn't wait for nightfall, known Kara was in danger. Had it been dark, had his strength been undiminished, he would have lunged at Hamblin and wrested the gun from his grasp. But not now. Not when it took all his energy just to remain on his feet.

"Okay," Hamblin said. "She can go."

Kara shook her head. "No, Alex, I'm not leaving you."

"Go on, Kara." *I'll find you.*

How?

Trust me, Kara. You've got to go now, before he changes his mind.

I don't want to leave you! Not here. Not like this.

Kara, get out of here! I'm in no danger. Barrett needs me alive.

Leaving him was the last thing she wanted, but she knew it was the right thing to do. At least, if she was free, she might be able to help. If Barrett caught her again, the best she could hope for was to be imprisoned while he experimented on her. The worst-case scenario was one she couldn't bring herself to contemplate.

Rising on tiptoe, she wrapped her arms around Alex. "I love you," she whispered, and then she kissed him. And for a moment, nothing else existed in all the world but this man and the love that enveloped them.

And then Alex was putting her away from him, urging her to go.

And because she knew it was the only way to help him, she went. Tears blurred her vision as she unlocked the door to her Camry and slid behind the wheel. She started the engine, then sat there for a moment, staring at the house, afraid she'd never see Alex again. Blinking back her tears, she backed out of the driveway and drove down the street.

She saw Barrett's car pull up in front of the house as she turned the corner.

Alex sank down onto the sofa as soon as he knew Kara was safe. The drive across town had been torture; now he closed his eyes and surrendered to the pain.

He heard footsteps and knew that Barrett had arrived. And still he sat there, his eyes closed, conserving what little strength he had left while he listened to the two men.

"Where's the girl?" Barrett asked, his voice sharp.

"She got away."

"Got away? How?"

"The alien tried to fight. He killed Kelsey, and then turned on me. We struggled, and the girl escaped."

"Secure his hands," Barrett said curtly. "Use these."

Alex opened his eyes as Hamblin cuffed his hands together. They weren't ordinary shackles. A few inches of heavy chain ran from one thick iron cuff to the other.

Alex smiled faintly. Barrett was taking no chances this time. But it didn't matter. Kara was safe.

"Let's go," Barrett said.

Alex shook his head. "The sun . . ."

"We're going," Barrett said firmly. "Now."

It was useless to argue. Barrett wanted to move him now, while he was too weak to cause any trouble.

"Keep him between us," Barrett said.

Alex blinked against the sunlight as they left the house. The street, filled with kids an hour ago, was deserted. A nondescript dark brown van stood at the curb. Barrett backed it up the driveway, opened the door, and motioned Alex inside. Hamblin climbed in beside him, and Barrett closed the door.

Hamblin leaned closer to Alex. "That checkbook better be there," he whispered.

"It's there."

Moments later, Barrett opened the back door of the van and dumped Kelsey's body inside. "I went through the house and wiped everything off," he informed Hamblin.

"What are you gonna do with Kelsey?"

"We'll dump him in an alley somewhere. There's nothing to connect him with us."

A few minutes later, they were headed out of the city.

Back to Silverdale, Alex surmised. With a sigh, he closed his eyes and willed himself to sleep. He would need all his strength for what was to come.

Chapter Twenty-six

Sarah Waite answered the door, her face registering surprise and alarm when she saw Kara.

"Hello, Mrs. Waite," Kara said, combing her fingers through her hair. "Is Cherise home?"

"Yes, she is." Mrs. Waite narrowed the opening in the doorway. "Is anything wrong?"

"I need to talk to Cherise. Please, it's important."

Mrs. Waite hesitated a moment, then took a step backward. "Come in. Cherise is in the front room watching TV."

"Thank you."

Cherise Waite was a pretty girl, with a slender figure, brown eyes, and straight brown hair. She glanced up as Kara entered the room, her eyes growing wide.

"Kara!"

"Hello, Cherise. Has Gail called today?"

"Not yet. It's only three-thirty. She always calls at four."

Kara glanced at Mrs. Waite. "Is it okay if I wait here?"

"Of course. Would you like a cup of coffee?"

"Yes, please."

"Make yourself at home."

Kara sat in the easy chair next to the sofa. "Has Gail said anything to you?"

"No. She just calls twice a day and asks if I've heard from you. What's wrong?"

"It's better if you don't know."

Cherise blinked at her several time. "You're in some kind of trouble, aren't you?"

"Yes, but please don't ask me any questions, Cherise. I can't tell you anything. Believe me, you don't want to know."

"What kind of trouble?" Mrs. Waite asked. She handed Kara a cup of coffee, then sat down on the sofa. "Is there anything we can do?"

"No. I'm afraid no one can help."

Kara sipped the coffee. On the drive to the Waites' house, she had contemplated going to the police. She'd imagined the conversation in her mind.

"I want you to arrest Dr. Dale Barrett."

"On what charge?"

"Kidnapping."

"He kidnapped you?"

"Yes. And the author, Alexander Claybourne."

"Am I to understand the doctor was holding you for ransom?"

"No. You see, Alex is an alien whose blood has the power to heal . . ."

She knew, logically, the conversation wouldn't go

like that. She wouldn't have to mention anything about Alex being an alien. But she had no proof that she had been kidnapped and held against her will, and even if the police arrested Barrett, the doctor would deny everything. And even if she could convince the police to search the lab where she'd been held, it wouldn't prove anything. Having a laboratory was no crime. Barrett was a doctor. The hospital in Grenvale knew he had been her doctor, so even if the police found samples of her blood, Barrett would have a valid alibi.

For a moment, she considered going to the government, but then she remembered bits and pieces of stories she had heard about other alien landings, like the one in New Mexico that the government had supposedly kept from the American people in order to prevent a panic.

Perhaps she could call one of those groups that was always claiming to have seen flying saucers. No doubt they would believe her, but what would they want in return? Exclusive rights to tell the story? Worldwide vindication? Pictures, movie deals. And, inevitably, the government would get involved, spouting rhetoric about national security while they dragged Alex off to be examined by a team of doctors and scientists.

She practically jumped out of the chair when the phone rang.

"Yes," Cherise said, "she's here."

Cherise handed the receiver to Kara, and then she and her mother left the room.

Kara's hand was trembling when she took the phone. "Gail?"

"Kara! Oh, Kara. Are you all right?"

"I'm fine. How are you? How's Nana? Where are you?"

"We're fine. Nana's much better. She's worried about you, though. Where've you been?"

"Is Mrs. Zimmermann with you?"

"Yeah. We're staying at her daughter's house. Her name is Nancy Ralston."

"Where does she live?"

"In Darnell."

Darnell? Why did that sound so familiar? "Let me talk to Nana."

Moments later, Lena was on the phone. Kara couldn't contain her tears as she heard her grandmother's voice assuring her that she was well.

"How are you, child?" Nana asked, worry evident in her tone.

"I'm fine, just fine. Nana, where's Darnell?"

"It's east of Moulton Bay, about five miles from Eagle Flats."

During the next half hour, she answered her grandmother's questions, telling her everything except the truth about Alex.

"Stay there, Nana. I should be there late tomorrow."

"All right, Kara. Be careful."

"I will. Tell Gail I'll see her later."

Kara felt much better when she hung up the receiver. Nana and Gail were all right.

"Will you stay for dinner?" Sarah Waite stood in the doorway, a kitchen towel over her shoulder.

Kara shook her head, the thought of food making her feel nauseated. "I don't want to be a bother."

"It's no bother."

"Thank you," she said, "I'd like that."

"You look tired. Would you like to lie down for a while?"

Kara nodded.

"Cherise will show you the spare room. I'll call you for dinner. About seven?"

"Thank you again."

"Is Gail all right?" Cherise asked.

"She's fine. She's on vacation with Nana."

"Here's the guest room," Cherise said, opening a door at the end of a long hall. "I'll come for you when dinner's ready."

"Thanks, Cherise."

Closing the door, Kara stood there for a moment, then sat down on the bed and removed her shoes. Lying back, she stared up at the ceiling and took a deep breath. She was safe. Tomorrow she'd see Gail and Nana. She tried to take comfort in that fact, tried to tell herself that everything would be all right, but all she could think of was Alex, at Barrett's mercy again.

She closed her eyes, and her mind filled with images of Alex surrounded by vampires with Barrett's face—human vampires draining Alex of blood, of life, selling little vials of Alex's blood, getting rich, while Alex was confined to a cage, his freedom forever lost while he was fed and groomed like a prize bull. She imagined Barrett collecting Alex's sperm, testing it, artificially inseminating some unsuspecting woman . . .

"Oh, Alex, no . . . no." Sitting up, she wiped the tears from her eyes, wondering if Barrett would return to the lab in Silverdale. But surely he wouldn't be that foolish, that arrogant.

And yet, maybe he would. He'd never expect her to walk into the lion's den looking for Alex. Not when she'd been lucky to escape with her life.

She worried her lower lip with her teeth. Maybe Barrett would have someone there, waiting for her, just in case.

I'm afraid you've become a liability, Miss Crawford, he'd said not long ago. *But don't worry, I am a doctor, after all. Your passing will be quick and painless . . .*

The calmness with which he had spoken those words still had the power to chill the blood in her veins. But she couldn't abandon Alex, couldn't leave him at Barrett's mercy, not when he had sacrificed his freedom for hers. Not when she loved him more than life itself.

Somehow, she would find him again.

He struggled through layers of darkness, groaned low in his throat as he opened his eyes and saw the skylight overhead. He blinked against the glare of the sun. Sometime during the drive back to the lab, Barrett had drugged him. It had left a bad taste in his mouth, made it hard to think coherently. He sat up, realizing, as he did so, that his hands were still shackled. A short chain had been attached to one of the cuffs, tethering him to the iron bed frame.

A noise behind him drew his attention, and he turned around to see Barrett hunched over a tray that contained a dozen glass vials filled with blood.

"How much?" Alex asked, his voice as dry as sandpaper. "How much are you selling my blood for?"

Barrett glanced up and smiled. "It varies," Barrett replied. "The president of a bank paid me thirty thousand dollars to see if I could cure his little girl of leukemia. I received a check from a prominent

Hollywood director offering me fifty thousand to treat his wife. One of the country's leading attorneys wrote me a check for a hundred grand. He's suffering from heart trouble. And that was just this morning."

Alex swallowed in an effort to clear the dryness from his throat. "Have you tried it? Does it work?"

Barrett nodded. "I gave the bank president's daughter an injection of your blood this morning. She's already showing signs of improvement. The Hollywood case is being flown in next week. The attorney arrives next Friday."

"What if they couldn't pay?" Alex glanced at the tray again. "Would that little girl still have received my blood?"

"Not at this time," Barrett said. "New vaccines are always expensive. Overhead, tests, new equipment . . ." He waved his hand in the air. "Once we've perfected the vaccine, the price may come down."

"No doubt you'll be a very rich man by then," Alex remarked sarcastically.

"I'm not doing this for the money!" Barrett shouted, his face livid. His gaze slid away from Alex's and he took several deep, calming breaths.

Alex closed his eyes. His blood had saved a child's life. He tried to take satisfaction in the thought, but it was hard to get past the bitterness that threatened to choke him as he imagined spending the rest of his life in a cage while Barrett sold his blood to the highest bidder.

"Well," Barrett said, "I think that's all you can spare for a while. Hamblin will be in with your dinner shortly."

Barrett left the room, and Alex stared after him,

the thought of food making him sick to his stomach.

A short time later, the door opened again and Mitch Hamblin entered the room. He was a good-looking kid, with slicked-back dark brown hair, and eyes older than his years.

Hamblin placed a covered tray on the bedside table, then reached into his pocket and pulled out a slip of paper. "You gonna keep your word, Claybourne?"

A wry grin tugged at the corner of Alexander's mouth. It was the first time anyone here had called him by name. He was the creature, the alien, the monster. "You got a pen?"

Hamblin tossed a ballpoint pen onto the tray, then stood watching, eyes wide, as Alex filled out the check and signed it.

Alex picked up the check and waved it slowly back and forth. "How much do you want to let me go?"

The kid's pale green eyes lit up with interest. And greed. "You've got more?"

Alex nodded.

Hamblin rubbed his jaw, his expression thoughtful. "How much are you offerin'?"

"Another hundred thousand."

Mitch whistled under his breath, his gaze fixed on the piece of paper waving before his eyes. Another hundred thousand dollars. He'd be a rich man, able to buy silk suits, go to Vegas, rub elbows with the high rollers . . .

"Hamblin?"

Mitch settled his back against the wall, his arms crossed over his chest. "I've been drivin' your Porsche. Nice car."

"It's yours, too. If you'll let me go."

"It's mine now."

"Yeah, I guess it is. How much?" Alex asked, trying to keep the anxiety out of his voice. "How much to let me go?"

"I'll think about it," Mitch said. He plucked the check from Alex's hand and slipped it into his pocket. "First I wanna see if this one clears."

"How about bringing me a glass of water?"

"I'll ask the doc."

Alex stared at the door after Hamblin had left the room, sickened by the thought of Barrett getting rich off his blood, and yet he couldn't help feeling a sense of satisfaction that his blood was saving lives. He couldn't help wondering if the same link that existed between himself and Kara now existed between himself and the little girl. It seemed unlikely. He had given Kara a considerable amount of blood, far more than was contained in the vials Barrett was selling.

Rising, he stretched his back and legs, then tugged against the chain. Damn! He had to get out of here. The sun beat down on his head and shoulders, draining him of strength, of energy.

He licked his lips, wishing the kid would bring him something to drink.

With a sigh, he sank down on the cot and closed his eyes.

He woke with a start as the door burst open and Barrett entered the room, his face flushed with anger.

"Damn fools," Barrett muttered.

Alex lifted one brow. "Something wrong, doc?"

"The last batch of blood we took was contaminated. We'll have to draw more."

Alex swore under his breath. "So soon?" he sat up, his back to the wall.

"You know what they say, time is money."

Alex grunted, his stomach clenching as Barrett pulled a handful of vials from his coat pocket and spread them out on the table.

Muttering under his breath, Barrett pulled a tourniquet from his other pocket. "Make a fist."

"No."

"Do as I say, dammit, or I'll strap you to a table again."

Alex glanced past Barrett. A new man, Kent Jarvis, stood in the hallway, idly paring his fingernails with a knife.

Knowing it was useless to resist, Alex watched as Barrett tied the strip of rubber around his arm, then located a vein. He was about to draw blood when Hamblin entered the room.

"They need ya in the lab, Doc. One of the machines is malfunctioning."

Barrett swore under his breath. Turning on his heel, he left the room. Jarvis trailed after him. Hamblin followed. He paused in the doorway, gave Alex an enigmatic look, then closed and locked the door.

Too agitated to sit still, Alex stood up and paced back and forth beside the bed, though the chain prevented him from taking more than a few steps in any direction.

He tugged against the chain that shackled him to the bed; then, taking a deep, calming breath, he sat down and tried to focus his energy on the lock. But the sun was still his enemy, draining his strength, his power to concentrate. Sweat dripped down his back, beaded across his brow, as he tried to focus his thoughts on the lock.

Come on, he thought desperately. *Come on!*

Kara checked the address her grandmother had given her, then pulled up to the curb and turned off the ignition. Stepping from the car, she hurried up the flower-lined path to the front door.

Minutes later, she was being hugged by Nana and Gail while Mrs. Zimmermann and her daughter stood by, smiling. Later, Mrs. Zimmermann introduced Kara to her daughter. Nancy Ralston was an attractive, middle-aged woman with curly brown hair and gray eyes. Kara learned that Nancy was married to an accountant and that she had three children, all of whom were away at summer camp.

Nancy produced a pot of coffee and some donuts, and Kara spent the next half hour answering what questions she could and avoiding the others.

Gail looked at her strangely a few times, and Kara knew that her sister suspected she was hiding more than she was telling.

Late that night, after everyone else had gone to bed, Gail and Kara sat in the kitchen, drinking hot chocolate.

"How long will we have to stay here?" Gail asked.

"I'm not sure." Kara shook her head. Maybe they'd never be able to go home again.

"Where's Alexander Claybourne?"

"I don't know."

"Did you ever find out what was wrong with your blood?"

"Not exactly, but I'm fine now."

"Is Barrett still looking for you?"

"I don't know."

"You don't know much of anything, do you?" Gail remarked candidly.

Kara let out a sigh. "At this point, I'm afraid I don't. Listen, Gail, I'm leaving in the morning."

"I'm going with you."

"No."

"Why not? You're going to look for Mr. Claybourne, aren't you?"

"Yes."

"Maybe I can help."

"It's too dangerous."

"Kara, why won't you tell me what's going on?"

"Because you're better off not knowing."

"It's because he's a vampire, isn't it?"

Kara hesitated. "Don't be silly."

"Am I? There's something different about him. I know there is."

"What do you mean?"

"I don't know how to explain it, I just know. I knew it that first night when I went to his house."

"You never said anything."

"I didn't think you'd believe me. I didn't want you to say I was being silly."

"I never said you were silly."

"Not in words, maybe, but I know you think it's dumb for me to believe in vampires and aliens and stuff like that. And maybe it is. But I believe it anyway."

"Gail, if I tell you something, will you promise never to tell anyone else?"

"I promise."

"You can't tell Cherise or Stephanie. Not even Nana."

"I promise."

"Alex isn't a vampire."

Gail made a face.

"He's an alien."

Gail blinked at Kara several times. "An alien? You mean, like from outer space?"

Kara nodded.

"I was right!" Gail exclaimed. "I knew it!"

"Gail, listen, Alex is in danger, and I've got to find him."

"I'll help you."

"No."

"Please?" Gail leaned across the table, her expression earnest. "If it wasn't for me, you might be dead now. You owe me a favor."

"Blackmail?" Kara exclaimed. "You're trying to blackmail me? Your own sister?"

"Yes. Is it working?"

"Oh, Gail, what am I going to do with you?"

"Take me with you."

"I'll think about it."

"Promise?"

"I promise." Kara picked up the cups, carried them to the sink, and rinsed them out. "It's late. Let's go to bed."

"Okay."

Later, lying in the twin bed next to Gail's, Kara stared into the darkness, wondering where Alex was, if he was well. She closed her eyes, concentrating on Alex, trying to send her thoughts to him, to read his in return, but to no avail. She refused to think of what the silence might mean, telling herself that distance alone accounted for the fact that she couldn't reach him; she refused to consider any other possibility.

Chapter Twenty-seven

Kara rose with the dawn, wanting to get an early start, even though she wasn't sure where to look first.

Swinging her legs over the edge of the bed, she closed her eyes as a wave of dizziness assaulted her. Stomach churning, she ran into the bathroom, dropped to her knees in front of the toilet, and retched.

"Kara? Are you all right?"

"Fine," she mumbled. Tearing off several sheets of toilet paper, she wiped her mouth, then stood up. Surprisingly, she felt much better.

"Are you sick?" Gail stood in the doorway, looking worried.

"I don't think so." She wiped the perspiration from her forehead, remembering, as she did so, that she'd felt sick to her stomach yesterday morning, too.

"Kara?"

"I think I'm pregnant."

Gail's eyes widened. "Pregnant!"

Kara nodded, wondering why it hadn't occurred to her before. She was pregnant.

"Who's the father?"

"Alex."

Gail's mouth fell open, her expression one of utter astonishment. "But he's . . . Does he know?"

"No." And he probably wouldn't be too happy with the news when she told him. Unbidden came the memory of Alexander's voice, warning her that a pregnancy could be dangerous, even fatal, for her and the child.

"Are you scared?"

Kara nodded. "Gail, what am I going to do?"

Gail shrugged. "I don't know." And suddenly, it was as if Gail were the older sister, and Kara the younger. "I guess you'll either have the baby, or not."

Kara met her sister's gaze. "An abortion?" She shook her head. "I couldn't." Not Alex's baby. She remembered telling him that she would love any child God might grant her. She had been so sure of those words when she had said them, but now . . .

She couldn't kill it, couldn't murder her own unborn child. Even if it was half-alien, even if it was a monster, she couldn't commit murder. And it was murder. No matter what the pro-choice people said to the contrary, once conceived, the fetus was a human being with a God-given right to life. She believed, with all her heart, that if it was wrong to kill a child once it was born, it was also wrong to kill it in the womb. She had seen pictures of babies who had been aborted—tiny human beings who had been vacuumed out of their mother's wombs, arms and legs torn off. Who knew what horrible pains those unborn children had suffered? How could anyone ever say such a thing was right?

"Gail, I have to find Alex." Just saying his name gave her strength.

"But how? Where will we look?"

"We'll start in Moulton Bay."

An hour later, Gail had a bag packed and they were ready to go. Kara and Gail thanked Nancy and her husband for their hospitality, then bid Nana a tearful good-bye.

"You'll be careful?" Lena said. "Promise me you'll be careful."

"I will," Kara said. She hugged her grandmother close, relieved that she seemed fully recovered from her earlier illness. "Try not to worry, Nana. I'll call as soon as I can."

Lena Crawford nodded. She hugged Kara once more, kissed Gail on the cheek, then stood in the driveway, blinking back her tears, while Kara drove down the street.

Gail glanced out the back window and waved. "She'll be okay, won't she?"

Kara nodded. "Of course. Nancy will take good care of her."

"Where are we going to go first?"

"Alex's house."

"You think he's there?"

"No, but I've got to look. If he hasn't been there,

I'll know. And if he has been, well, I'll know that, too."

Gail frowned. "How will you know?"

"I just will."

"If you say so." Gail turned on the radio. Locating KROQ, she sat back, her foot tapping in time to Meat Loaf's latest hit.

They spent the night in a motel. In the morning, they drove to a small restaurant for breakfast. Gail ordered pancakes, Kara settled for dry toast and coffee. After breakfast, they stopped at one of the mall shops so Kara could buy a change of clothes, underwear, and a nightgown. From there they went into a drug store where she bought a comb, a hairbrush, a toothbrush, and a lipstick, and a small overnight bag to carry everything in. As she paid the bill, it occurred to her that she'd been doing a lot of buying on the run since she met Alexander Claybourne.

They were on the road again by eleven-thirty.

"Where will we look if Alex isn't home?" Gail asked.

"In Silverdale."

"Silverdale? Why? What's there?"

"Barrett has a lab there."

"I never even heard of Silverdale. Do you know how to get there?"

"No, but I'll find it if I have to."

It was almost three o'clock when they reached Moulton Bay. Kara's heart was pounding as she drove down the street to Alexander's house and pulled into the driveway.

Kara's steps were slow as she walked around the back of the house and opened the back door. She knew immediately that Alex hadn't been there recently. The house was dark and cold, empty of all trace of life.

Her footsteps echoed off the walls as she walked down the hallway toward the den. She was hardly aware of Gail behind her as she stood in the doorway, her gaze drawn toward the painting over the fireplace. She stared at the man in the picture, at the long black hair ruffled by the wind, at the broad shoulders that seemed slightly bent, as if he carried the weight of the world on his back. She knew it wasn't Alex, knew she was being fanciful to even think so, and yet it could have been Alex.

"He's not here," Gail said. She pointed at the painting. "Kind of looks like Alex, doesn't it?"

Kara nodded, wondering if she'd ever see Alex again.

"This place gives me the creeps," Gail remarked. "Are you sure he isn't a vampire?"

"Quite sure. Stay here. I'll be right back."

"Where are you going?"

"Upstairs for a minute."

"I don't want to stay down here alone."

"I'll just be a minute."

Gail looked at her sister oddly, but didn't argue further.

Drawn by a power she couldn't explain, Kara climbed the steps to Alex's bedroom. She stood inside the door for a moment, her eyes closed. Was it her imagination, or could she feel his essence lingering in the room?

She opened the closet door and ran her hand over his clothing. Pressing her face against one of his coats, she took a deep breath, filling her nostrils with his scent.

"I'll find you," she whispered. "Somehow I'll find you."

Alex woke with a start, Kara's name on his lips. It must have been a dream, he thought, and yet . . . He sat up and summoned her image to mind. Kara. Rich russet-colored hair. Dreamy blue eyes. Skin as soft as a sigh. Kara . . .

He closed his eyes and knew, knew, she was in his house, thinking of him.

He tried to reach out to her, to warn her away, but the distance between them was too great. Perhaps, if the sun hadn't been directly overhead, if he'd been able to concentrate, he would have been able to reach her. But not now, not with the sun blinding him, burning him.

It was dusk when he woke again.

Hearing Barrett's footsteps outside the door, he sat up, his body tensing.

Barrett entered, followed by Hamblin and Jarvis. He pulled a syringe from his lab coat. "We'll need some blood," he said.

"No."

"No? No? It would be to your advantage to do as you're told."

"Really? Why? What are you going to do to me if I refuse?"

A cold smile twisted Barrett's lips. "Jarvis was a friend of Kelsey's. He'd love to have a crack at you."

"Let him take his best shot."

"Hamblin. Jarvis. Hold him down."

Alex knew it was useless, foolish, to resist, but he lashed out with his feet as Hamblin and Jarvis reached for him. Jarvis grunted with pain as Alex's foot caught him in the groin.

331

Jarvis stumbled backward and Hamblin and Barrett surged forward, their weight bearing him down, holding him immobile while Barrett drew enough blood to fill a small vial.

"Hamblin, take this to the lab. Jarvis, go call our man in Hollywood and tell him I'll have the results on this batch in a few hours. Tell him if he's still interested, the price just went up five thousand dollars."

"Right, boss."

"It's all a matter of money now, isn't it?" Alex said. Sitting up, he braced his back against the wall and stared at Barrett.

"You don't have enough blood to heal the whole world," Barrett replied. "Research costs money. Selling your blood is going to pay for it."

"Right."

"You doubt me?"

"I think you're lying to yourself. This isn't about helping mankind anymore. It's about you."

"That's not true!"

"Isn't it?" Alex asked contemptuously. "What kind of man keeps another chained to a bed while he steals his blood?"

"But you're not a man," Barrett retorted with a smirk. "You're an alien who's about to do mankind a tremendous favor."

"And if you get rich in the bargain, so much the better."

Barrett shrugged. "I'll be most generous with the vaccine once the formula is established and I've made the medical journals," he said. He smiled as he imagined the accolades he would garner from his colleagues, the speaking engagements, the papers he would publish. In due time, when interest in the vaccine was flagging, he would donate the vaccine to some needy child, thereby reawakening interest in his work.

"You're no better than a vampire, Barrett, living off the blood of others, sucking my blood to keep your dream alive."

"Shut your mouth!"

"Why? Can't stand to hear the truth?"

A sharp rap on the door cut off Barrett's reply. A moment later, Hamblin stepped into the room. "Franklin's on the phone, Doc. He says you were supposed to meet him thirty minutes ago."

Barrett swore under his breath. "I forgot all about it. Keep an eye on him," Barrett snapped, jerking his chin in Alex's direction. "I'll be back late."

With a last baleful glance at Alex, Barrett stalked out of the room, muttering under his breath.

"My offer still stands," Alex said. "A hundred thousand to let me go."

Mitch stared at Alex, his expression thoughtful as he straddled the chair located across from the cot. He'd opened a savings account with the first check. It gave him a sense of security, knowing he had a tidy sum to fall back on if Barrett's get-rich quick scheme fell through. And now he had a chance to get another hundred thousand. . . .

He shook his head. "I can't. Barrett would—"

"I'll take care of Barrett."

"And Jarvis?"

"If I have to. Just turn me loose. Then take the cover off the skylight, prop it open, and get out of here."

"I don't know . . ."

"You seem like a pretty decent kid. How'd you

get mixed up with Barrett?"

"None of your business."

"You planning to take Kelsey's place? Do Barrett's killing for him?"

"No. He's paying me to be his bodyguard, that's all."

"That's all?"

"That's all."

"What about Jarvis?"

"He's a killer," Mitch admitted reluctantly.

"And if things go wrong, if Barrett thinks his scheme is going to fall apart, what do you think your odds of survival are?"

"What do you mean?"

"Think about it. Barrett was going to kill Kara because she knew too much. What do you think will happen to you?"

"He wouldn't do anything like that!" Mitch exclaimed.

"Are you willing to bet your life on it?"

"But he's a doctor."

"Yeah." Alex glanced pointedly at the heavy shackles that bound his wrists. "He's a real credit to his profession."

Rising to his feet, Mitch began to pace the floor, his hands flexing nervously. "Well, I admit he hasn't treated you very well, but you're . . . I mean . . ."

"You mean I'm an alien, so it doesn't matter."

A bright red flush crept up Hamblin's neck.

"I don't care what you think of me," Alex said curtly. "I just want to get the hell out of here."

Hamblin came to an abrupt halt near the foot of the bed. "How do I know you'll pay me?"

"I guess you'll just have to trust me."

"Trust you!" Hamblin ran a hand through his

hair, drummed his fingertips on the bed frame.

"The last check was good, wasn't it? Come on, we're wasting time."

"All right, all right, I'll do it. How will I get my money?"

"You know where Eagle Flats is?"

"Yeah."

"I'll meet you at the bank as soon as I can get there."

"And how will I know when that will be?"

"You just be there every night at ten until I show up."

"And what if you never show up?"

"I guess that's a risk you'll have to take."

"I want a hundred and fifty grand."

Alex nodded. He could sell the house in Moulton Bay for twice that much.

"I'll go open the skylight," Mitch said. "It might take me a while to get the key to those shackles out of Barrett's office. I'll have to pick the lock on his desk."

"Who else is in the building?"

"No one's inside. I think Jarvis is keeping watch out front."

"Hurry." Resting his head against the wall, Alex closed his eyes. For the first time in days, he felt a surge of hope.

A few minutes later, he felt a familiar coolness shimmer across his face. Opening his eyes, he gazed up at the moon. It was full and bright. Relief washed through him as he drew the silvery light deep within himself. He lay there for several minutes, taking deep breaths, feeling the lethargy drain out of his body, feeling his strength begin to return.

He closed his eyes again, letting the light penetrate into every cell, every fiber. It would take more than one night to restore his full strength, yet he already felt stronger, better, more like himself.

He estimated thirty-five minutes had passed before Hamblin returned.

Whistling softly, Mitch entered the room and closed the door behind him. He came to an abrupt halt when he saw Alex. "You're looking a lot better," he remarked, glancing up at the skylight. "How come?"

"I don't have time to explain it to you now. Did you find the key?"

Mitch nodded.

"What's wrong?"

"I'm not sure this is a good idea."

Alex swore softly. "We had a deal."

"How do I know I can trust you? How do I know you won't try to take my gun?"

"I just want out of here," Alex said. "I don't want to hurt you, or anyone else. I just want my freedom. Can you understand that?"

"Sure, but . . ."

"Dammit, kid, if I don't get out of here, I'm gonna be no better than an animal in a zoo!"

"Hey, calm down, man."

"I am calm. I'm also in a hurry, and . . ." Alex paused, his head lifting, his nostrils testing the air. Kara. She was there. "Mitch, turn me loose. Now, before it's too late."

"Your word. I want your word you won't try anything."

"I won't hurt you, Mitch. I swear it on Kara's life."

Mitch hesitated a moment more; then, reaching into his pocket, he withdrew a key and quickly unlocked the cuffs that bound Alex's hands.

Alex stood up, massaging his wrists. "Thanks, kid. I'll meet you in Eagle Flats as soon as I can. Take care of yourself."

Mitch nodded, a grin hovering over his lips as he watched Alex run, bare-ass naked, down the corridor toward the back door.

"How do you know he's in there?" Gail asked, peering around Kara. She stared at the dark building that was surrounded by a high fence. "Even if he's in there, how will we get in? How will we get him out?"

"Gail, hush!" Kara said.

"You don't know, do you?"

"No. I just know Alex is in there, and we have to get him out."

"I think we should call the police."

"No."

"There's no law against being an alien."

"Gail, for goodness sakes, you of all people should know what will happen to Alex if people find out what he is."

"Oh, yeah, I didn't think of that. Well, what are we gonna do?"

"I wish I knew. I . . . what's that?"

"What?"

"There?"

"Looks like a naked man," Gail said. She stepped around Kara to get a better look. "It *is* a naked man!"

"It's Alex," Kara said. *Here.* She called to him with her mind. *I'm here.*

Kara?

Yes. Hurry.

Can you distract the guard?

Yes. "Gail, I want you to go up to the fence and call the guard. Tell him you're lost. Ask if you can use the phone."

"Really? All right!" Hardly able to contain her excitement, Gail ran toward the fence. "Hey, in there!" she called. "Hey, mister, can you help me?"

Alex stood in the shadows, watching as the guard left his shack and ambled toward the gate in the fence.

"What are you doing out here at this time of night, girl?" the guard asked.

"I'm lost. Can I use your phone?"

"Where's your parents?"

"If I knew that, I wouldn't be lost. Please, mister, I'm scared. Can I use your phone?"

Gail clenched her hands together, her heart pounding as she saw Alex creeping up behind the guard. "Can I?" She'd never seen a naked man before and it took every ounce of concentration to keep from staring, to keep her voice even.

"Sure, kid," the guard said. He removed a ring of keys from his belt and unlocked the gate. "Come on . . ."

The air whooshed out of the guard's lungs as Alex struck the man over the head with a beer bottle he'd found lying beside the shack.

"Hi, Gail," Alex said.

"Hi. What happened to your clothes?"

"I lost them."

"You'll be lucky if you're not arrested for indecent exposure," Kara remarked, and then she hurled herself into his arms.

Alex hugged her hard. "We'd better get out of here."

Kara nodded. She wanted to hold him, to run her hands over him, to assure herself that he was all right, but it would have to wait. "Let's go."

"Here," Gail said. She handed Alex an overcoat. "I found it in the shack."

"Thanks." He slipped it on, then grabbed Kara's hand. "Let's get out of here."

"Stop!"

Alex glanced over his shoulder to see Barrett running toward them brandishing a pistol. Dammit! What was he doing back so early?

"Stop, damn you! Stop, or I'll shoot!"

Alex swore as a gunshot ripped through the night. "Run, Kara!" He shoved Gail toward the gate. "Hurry, both of you!"

"Alex—"

"I'm right behind you."

The sound of gunfire followed them as they ran out the gate and down the street.

"Where's your car?" Alex shouted to be heard above the staccato bark of gunfire coming from behind them.

"Around the corner."

They were going to make it, he thought. And then he saw Kara falter, heard her gasp of pain, and knew she'd been hit.

Without breaking stride, he scooped her up in one arm, grabbed Gail by the hand, and turned the corner.

There was only one car parked at the curb. "Kara, where are your keys?"

"Coat pocket," she rasped. "Door's . . . not locked."

Flinging the door open, he placed Kara on the seat, shoved Gail in beside her, then went around and slid behind the wheel.

He rammed the key into the ignition, gunned the motor and pulled away from the curb just as Barrett rounded the corner.

Chapter Twenty-eight

"She's bleeding!" Gail cried. "Kara's bleeding!"

"Where's she hit?"

"In the side. Do something!"

"Your scarf, Gail. Fold it into a square and press it over the wound. Kara?" He glanced over at her. "Kara!"

"I don't think she can hear you," Gail said, a distinct quaver in her voice. "She's not dead, is she?"

"No."

Alex glanced repeatedly in the rearview mirror, but as far as he could tell, they weren't being followed.

"What are we going to do?"

"I'm going home and grab some clothes," Alex replied. "We'll look after Kara's wound, and then we're going up to Eagle Flats."

"I think we should take Kara to the hospital."

"Not now."

Kara was unconscious by the time they reached the house. Alex carried her inside, switched on the hall light, and told Gail to wait in the den.

Carrying Kara up the stairs to the bedroom, Alex kicked the door closed with his heel, then lowered Kara onto the bed. Lifting her sweater, he removed Gail's blood-soaked scarf and examined the wound. It wasn't deep and didn't look serious, unless it became infected, but she had lost a lot of blood and that worried him.

He washed the wound with soap and water, then swore under his breath as he ripped a clean white sheet into strips and bandaged her side. He didn't have so much as an aspirin to give her for the pain. But that couldn't be helped now.

He dressed quickly in a pair of black Levi's and a black sweater, pulled on a pair of black cowboy boots, then went to the small desk beside the bed. Opening the top drawer, he removed the cash he kept on hand for emergencies and shoved it into his pants pocket; then, unlocking the bottom drawer, he withdrew a two-inch .38 Special which he tucked under his shirt at the small of his back. Then, lifting Kara into his arms, he carried her downstairs and went into the den to get Gail.

"Is she all right?"

"She'll be fine. Hand me my checkbook there on the desk, will you? Thanks." He slipped it into his back pocket. "Ready, Gail? Then let's go."

He stopped at an all-night drugstore. Leaving Gail in the car with Kara, he went into the store, gathering all the first-aid supplies he thought he might need. He asked the clerk where the alcohol was, and when the young man went to get it for him, Alex grabbed a couple of syringes from behind the counter and stuck them inside his jacket.

It was near dawn when Alex pulled into a motel. He went in alone to register, requesting a room toward the back.

Kara was awake when he returned to the car.

"How are you feeling?" he asked.

"Horrible. Where are we?"

"A motel about forty miles from Eagle Flats. We'll stay here today."

"Do you think it's safe?"

"No one's following us as near as I can tell."

"I'm hungry," Gail said.

"We'll send out for something as soon as I look after your sister." Opening the door, he lifted Kara into his arms.

"I can walk."

"Do you want to?"

"No." She wrapped her arms around his neck and closed her eyes. So many times, she'd been afraid she'd never see him again and now he was here, holding her, his dark eyes filled with love and concern.

"Do you guys want to be alone?"

Alex glanced at Gail, grinning when he saw the look on her face. "What do you think?"

"I think you should have got two rooms."

Alex shook his head. "We can't take a chance on leaving you alone. Here." He tossed her the room key. "How about opening the door?"

"And then get our bags," Kara added.

Gail grimaced. "Now I know why you brought me along," she muttered. "Gail, open the door. Gail, get the bags."

Alex laughed softly as he handed her the car keys.

Amanda Ashley

"I'd do it myself, but my hands are full."

"Yeah, yeah," Gail said irritably, but she was smiling as she walked toward the car.

Inside the room, Alex placed Kara on the bed. "Let's get you out of those bloody things," he said.

"Let's kiss instead."

"Kara . . ."

"Please, Alex, just one kiss?"

How could he refuse? Cupping her face in his hands, he kissed her gently. Sensations swamped him. Warm, soft lips, the scent of her skin and hair, the touch of her hands sliding up and down his back, massaging the sensitive skin of his spine. He remembered all the nights he had ached for her touch, yearned for the sound of her voice, the comfort of her smile . . .

Abruptly, he drew back, his gaze searching hers. "Kara . . ." He swallowed hard as he placed one hand over her abdomen. "Kara?"

"It's true," she said quietly. "I'm pregnant."

His first reaction was one of joy. She saw it dance in the depths of his eyes, in the smile that lit his face. And then, as quickly as it had appeared, it was gone.

"I'm happy, Alex, happy about the baby. I want you to be happy, too."

"How can I be?" He dropped to his knees beside the bed and buried his face in her lap. She was pregnant. The thing he had feared most had come to pass. He closed his eyes against the pain that slashed through his heart. What if she died? How could he live with the knowledge that loving him had killed her?

"Alex, please."

He lifted his head, his black eyes dull with pain. "We'll find a doctor."

"A doctor? For what?"

"There's still time."

She stared down at him. "You're talking about an abortion, aren't you?"

"It's the only way . . ."

"No!"

"Kara . . ."

"No, Alex. I won't even consider it."

A soft sound at the doorway drew Alexander's attention. Glancing over his shoulder, he saw Gail standing there, an overnight bag in each hand, her cheeks wet with tears.

Rising to his feet, Alex crossed the room and took the bags from her hands. "Why don't you order us some dinner?"

Gail went to sit beside her sister. "Are you all right?"

"I'm fine. Call the restaurant and order something to eat." She forced a smile as she placed her hand over her stomach. "I'm eating for two now, you know?"

Mouth set in a grim line, Alex removed Kara's sweater and set about cleaning and disinfecting the wound. When that was done, Kara went into the bathroom to wash up and change into her nightgown.

Gail sat on the edge of the other twin bed, fidgeting with a corner of the bedspread. "Why do you want Kara to get an abortion?"

"What'd you order for dinner?"

"Is it because you're from outer space?"

"Did Kara tell you that?"

345

Gail nodded. "You don't have to worry. I won't tell anyone."

Alex swore softly, then shook his head. Maybe it was better that Gail knew. It would certainly make things easier.

"It's true," Alex said, sitting down beside her. "I'm from another planet, and I'm worried that it might be dangerous for Kara to have my baby. Do you understand?"

"Of course."

The sound of the water running in the bathroom drew his gaze toward the door. Closing his eyes, he searched Kara's thoughts, needing to be certain she was all right. She was angry with him. Afraid for him, and for the child.

And then her mind closed against his, shutting him out as effectively as if she'd slammed a door between them.

Kara emerged from the bathroom a few minutes later, and Alex thought she'd never looked lovelier. Her face was flushed, her hair fell down her back, a few tendrils curling around her face.

She walked across the room slowly, carefully sat down on the bed.

Alex watched her, feeling the pain of her wound as if it were his own.

Five minutes later, there was a knock at the door.

Withdrawing his pistol and holding it out of sight behind his back, he motioned for Gail to open the door.

"I've got an order here for Mr. Jones."

Alex looked the young man over. Placing the gun on top of the dresser, he withdrew some money from his pocket. "How much?"

"Eighteen-fifty."

Alex paid him for the food, then closed and locked the door.

He stood near the window, looking out from time to time, while Gail and Kara ate breakfast.

"Alex, are you sure you don't want anything?" Kara asked.

"I'm sure." Needing some time alone, time to think, he went into the bathroom to shower. She was pregnant. The thought pounded at his brain as the water pummeled his flesh. Pregnant. Pregnant. How far along was she? A month? Two? Pregnant.

He dressed quickly, then stepped into the main room. Gail and Kara were asleep in each other's arms.

A wave of tenderness swept through Alex as he drew a blanket over the two of them. He checked the lock, slipped his gun under the pillow of the other bed, and stretched out on the mattress.

She was here.

She was pregnant.

It was his last thought before sleep claimed him.

Chapter Twenty-nine

They left the motel at dusk. Kara's wound, though sore, seemed to be healing nicely, and Alex was certain it was because he'd given her his blood. His own wounds had always healed swiftly, leaving no scar.

Kara glanced at Alex. She should have been weak, suffering from the blood she'd lost, but when Alex had checked her this morning, the gunshot wound had appeared to be no more serious than a scratch. Certainly it was far less painful than the awkward silence between her and Alex.

She glanced at him now, thinking how handsome he was, how much she loved him. But she loved his baby, too, and she wasn't going to get rid of it.

"I think we should drop Gail off at the Ralstons'," Kara said.

Alex glanced at her. It was the first time she'd

spoken directly to him since last night. "All right."

"No, Kara!" Gail leaned over the seat. "I want to stay with you."

Kara shook her head. "I don't think that's a good idea."

"Why not?"

"Because we might still be in danger from Barrett," Kara said. She turned in the seat so she could face Gail. "It'll only be for a little while, sweetie."

"But—"

"Please, Gail, don't argue with me. Not now. I'll keep in touch with you, I promise."

In a huff, Gail sank back on the seat and stared out the window. A short time later, she was asleep.

"Alex?"

"Hmmm?"

"I'm healing so fast because of you, aren't I? Because you gave me your blood?"

He nodded.

"That's twice you've saved my life."

He glanced at her briefly, then turned his attention to the road once again. He'd saved her life. Would he also be the one to take it from her?

The silence in the car lengthened, grew awkward.

Kara stared out the window, one hand resting protectively over her stomach. Alien or human, she already loved the child in her womb. She would fight Alex, Barrett, the whole world, if necessary, but no one was going to harm her child.

Feeling Alex's gaze on her face, she slowly turned to face him. When he spoke, she knew he'd been reading her mind again.

"You don't really think I'd hurt the child, do you?"

"No, not really. But I know you don't want it."

"Kara, that's not true." His hands tightened on the steering wheel. "I'd like nothing more than to have children with you. Dozens of children. But I don't want to put your life at risk." He glanced at her again. "How do you feel?"

"All right. I'm nauseous in the morning, but that's normal."

"That's all? You don't feel sick or anything?"

"No." She scooted across the seat and placed her hand on his thigh. "Couldn't we be happy about this until we have reason to worry? I've never been pregnant before. I don't want anything to spoil it."

"I'll try," Alex said. He covered her hand with his. "But I can't promise not to worry."

"I love you, Alex."

"There's a small wedding chapel in Eagle Flats," Alex said. "Will you marry me, Kara? Will you be my wife?"

"Yes, Alex, oh, yes." She leaned toward him and kissed him on the cheek. "Everything will be all right. I know it will."

With a nod, he put his arm around her shoulders and drew her close.

By the time they reached Darnell, Gail was resigned to staying with Mrs. Zimmermann, but she still wasn't happy about it.

As soon as Alex pulled into the driveway, Gail got out of the car and slammed the door, then ran into the house.

Kara squeezed Alex's hand as he helped her out of the car. "You look like you're about to be thrown to the lions," she remarked.

"I feel like it, too," Alex replied. He'd spent years avoiding people whenever possible. He wasn't looking forward to seeing Kara's grandmother again, or answering the questions that would inevitably follow.

"Well, come on," Kara said, grinning at him. "We might as well get it over with."

Lena Corley studied Alex through shrewd eyes when Kara introduced him. "You're the man from the hospital," she said. "The author."

"Yes. It's a pleasure to see you again, Mrs. Corley," Alex said.

Lena Corley slanted a glance in Kara's direction. "Have you known my granddaughter long?" Lena asked.

"A few months."

"She said you met in the hospital. You donated some blood, I believe."

Alex glanced at Kara. "I . . ."

"Mrs. Corley, would you mind setting the dining room table? The dishes are in the cabinet against the wall." Nancy smiled as she gave Alex a little push. "Alex, why don't you make yourself at home? My husband will be here soon. Kara, would you mind helping me in the kitchen?"

Smiling his gratitude, Alex escaped to the living room.

Taking Kara into the kitchen, Nancy dragged her to the table and practically pushed her into a chair. "He's gorgeous!" she exclaimed. "Where on earth did you meet him?"

"It's a long story," Kara said.

"Give me the Reader's Digest condensed version."

"You're a married woman, remember?"

"Oh, I know, and I love my husband, but good grief, girl, he's out of this world!"

Kara couldn't help it, she laughed. "You've got that right," she replied. "Listen, I met him while I was in the hospital. We became friends, that's all."

"Friends?"

Kara felt her cheeks redden. "All right, maybe we're more than friends." She hesitated a moment. "Nancy, I'm pregnant."

Nancy sat back in her chair, her expression almost comical. "Well, I guess you are more than friends. When's the baby due?"

Kara shook her head. "I'm not sure." She was carrying an alien baby. Would her term be nine months, or would the time be longer or shorter?

"How do you feel?"

"Fine, except for a little morning sickness."

"It'll pass. Have you told Alex?"

"Of course, but my grandmother doesn't know, and I'd rather not tell her just yet."

"I can keep a secret." Nancy shook her head. "Well, what a day this has been. Guess I'd better fix dinner. Jim will be home soon." She pulled some potatoes out of the fridge. "Wanna help me peel these?"

"Sure."

"Ah, listen, since your grandmother doesn't know about the baby, she probably doesn't know you and Alex are . . . I mean . . . anyway, Alex can sleep on the hide-a-bed in the den."

Kara nodded. "That will be fine."

The evening passed pleasantly. Nancy's husband and Alex seemed to hit it off and the conversation at the dinner table was relaxed and easy, as if they'd all been friends for years instead of hours. At one point, Nancy mentioned that her sister was expecting a baby, which led the women into a discussion of pregnancy and childbirth. Kara listened avidly, only then realizing how very little she actually knew about having a baby. She'd never realized babies required so many things—baby clothes, cribs, diapers, bottles, playpens, high chairs—the list seemed to go on and on.

After dinner, they watched television for a while. About nine o'clock Nana and Mrs. Zimmermann retired to their beds. Nancy and her husband said good-night an hour later.

"Gail, I think it's time we called it a night, too."

"It's only ten o'clock!"

"I know, but it won't hurt you to go to bed early for once."

"Oh, all right. Good-night, Alex."

"Good-night."

Kara kissed Alex on the cheek. "See you tomorrow."

"Sleep well."

"You, too."

Alone in the living room, Alex switched off the tv, then went out into the backyard. Head back, he stared up at the moon, basking in its cool light, sighing as he felt his body rejuvenate itself.

She was pregnant.

The very idea scared the hell out of him.

Alex? Are you awake?

Yes. Is anything wrong?

No, I'm just lonely for you.

Come to me, then.

He went back into the house; moments later, Kara was sitting beside him on the sofa. He drew her into his arms, holding her close, grateful beyond words that she was alive and well, that they were together again, as they were meant to be.

There was no need for words between them. He knew her thoughts as he knew his own. Wrapped in his arms, secure in his embrace, she quickly fell asleep.

He held her all through the night, content to hold her, to look at her, to walk in her dreams.

With the coming of dawn, he woke her with a kiss. "You'd better go back to your room," he said. "I don't want to upset your grandmother."

"Me, either. See you later."

She kissed him once, twice, and then, reluctantly, slipped out of his arms and went back to her own room.

They left for Eagle Flats at dusk. Kara hugged Nana, assuring her that she wouldn't be gone long, and then went to say good-bye to Gail, who was still sulking because she couldn't go with them.

"Remember, Gail, not a word to anyone about Alex. And please don't say anything about the baby to Nana."

"I won't," Gail said, her expression sullen. "Are you going to marry him?"

"Yes."

"When?"

"Tonight."

"I thought you wanted a big wedding in a church, with bridesmaids and flowers and stuff like that."

"We can't always have everything we want."

"Tell me about it."

"Gail, please don't make this difficult. Maybe when this mess is straightened out, we'll have that church wedding, and you can be my maid of honor."

"You're just saying that."

"Gail, have I ever lied to you?"

"No."

"And I'm not lying now. Take care of Nana for me. I'll call when I can."

"All right." With a sniff, Gail threw her arms around her sister and hugged her tight. "Be careful."

"I will."

"Good-bye, Gail," Alex said, coming up to stand beside Kara.

" 'Bye. You'd better take good care of my sister."

"I will, don't worry."

A last hug, a last wave, and they were on their way.

"How's your side?" Alex asked after a while.

"It's fine. A little sore is all." She slid across the seat and rested her head on his shoulder. "How are you?"

"I'm all right."

"You never told me how you managed to get away."

"I bribed Hamblin."

"Again? How much did it cost you this time?"

"A hundred and fifty grand."

"Do you have that much money?"

"Yeah."

"I guess I never realized there was so much money to be made from writing."

"It's been a lucrative career," Alex said, grinning. "I'm supposed to meet Hamblin at the bank at ten."

"How long are we going to stay in Eagle Flats?"

"I don't know. Not long. As soon as you feel up to it, we'll leave. Where would you like to go?"

"Go?"

"We can't stay in Moulton Bay as long as Barrett's looking for us."

Kara nodded. "He doesn't seem like the type to give up, does he?" She stared ahead at the road for a few minutes, then asked, "What about Gail, and Nana?"

"Once we're settled, you can send for them."

She nodded her agreement even though she wasn't crazy about the idea of moving. She liked it here. Her job was here . . . her job! She hadn't thought about her job in weeks. When they reached Eagle Flats, she'd have to call her boss and try to explain. Or maybe just call and quit, if they hadn't already replaced her.

With a sigh, she realized she no longer had to work. She was about to become the wife of a rich man. The thought made her smile. She could stay home, be a housewife. And a mother . . .

"Alex?"

"What?"

"How long are women pregnant on ErAdona?"

"Nine months, just like here."

Well, she mused, that was a relief. "Are you hoping for a boy or a girl?"

"It doesn't matter. So long as it's healthy. So long as you survive."

"I'd like a boy," she said. "One with black hair and dark eyes, just like you."

Just like you . . . Her words echoed in his mind. *Just like you.* Would his child have to live forever in the shadows, unable to run and play in the sun? Would they have to hide it away from the world? Would it even survive?

"Alex, you promised not to worry until there was something to worry about."

"Reading my mind, *natayah?*"

"No, just the expression on your face."

"We'll be in Eagle Flats soon. You haven't changed your mind about marrying me, have you?"

"No." She glanced at her attire, and frowned. "I would like to be married in something a little nicer than jeans and a sweater. Do you think we could go shopping tonight, and get married tomorrow?"

"If you wish." He smiled at her, his heart filled with love and tenderness. "What would you like me to wear?"

"A black suit, of course."

"And what will you wear?"

"I don't know. I always dreamed of getting married in a long white dress in a church filled with flowers."

"No doubt you always dreamed of marrying a human male, as well."

"Alex, don't!"

"You shouldn't have to settle for less than your dreams, Kara."

"You're every dream I've ever had," she said fervently. "Anyway, we can have a big wedding later, if it's all right with you."

"Whatever you wish."

"Maybe you don't want to marry me," she said. "I've been nothing but trouble since you met me."

"Kara! You're the best thing that's ever happened to me."

She smiled at him. "And I feel the same."

"Ah, Kara," he said softly. "Forgive me for being such a fool. It's just that I feel you deserve so much more than you're getting."

"Am I complaining?"

"No. But then, you never do."

"Are you happy?"

"Yes."

"Me, too. So, it's all settled. We'll shop tonight and get married tomorrow. And live happily ever after, just like Cinderella and the prince." She stared at him as a new thought crossed her mind. "Alex, we can't get married! We don't have a license."

"I know a minister who will marry us, Kara. He's a big fan of mine."

The Eagle Flats mall wasn't overly large, but it had several nice shops. Alex bought a black suit and tie, a white shirt, new shoes and socks, then sat on a hard-backed chair while Kara tried on dresses. It took her an hour to find one she liked, and then she refused to let him see it, saying it was bad luck for the groom to see the bride's dress before the wedding.

It was near midnight when they reached the cavern. They put away the groceries they'd bought just before they left town, then settled in front of the fireplace. Only then did Alex recall he was supposed to meet Hamblin at the bank. He swore under his breath.

"What's wrong?" Kara asked.

Alex shrugged. "Nothing. I was supposed to meet Hamblin at the bank at ten."

"We can do it tomorrow, can't we?"

Alex nodded. Tomorrow would have to be soon enough.

It was near dawn when they went to bed.

Kara snuggled up to Alex, her head pillowed on his shoulder.

Tomorrow night, she mused sleepily. Tomorrow night she would be Mrs. Alexander J. Claybourne.

Chapter Thirty

It was full dark when they drove down the mountain to Eagle Flats. Kara couldn't help feeling nervous. She was about to be married. To an alien. She was carrying his child. No matter that she loved him with all her heart and soul, she knew her life would be forever changed from this night on.

She turned to glance at him, only to find him watching her.

"Not getting cold feet, are you?" he asked.

"No. Are you?"

"Not a chance." Not a chance in a billion, he mused as he returned his attention to the road. He'd waited two centuries for this woman. "I just want you to be sure."

"I'm sure."

A single light glowed from within the church

when they drove up. There were no other cars in the driveway.

"Wait here," Alex said.

Getting out of the car, he walked around the building to the back door. He had called the minister and let him know they were coming. Opening the door, he stepped inside a small room located to the left of the pulpit.

Moving silently, he peered into the chapel. The minister, Keith Anderson, was sitting on the front pew, Bible in hand. There was no one else in the church.

Going out the way he came, Alex returned to the car.

Kara opened the door. "Is everything all right?"

"As far as I can tell, Keith's alone in there." He smiled at Kara and offered his hand. "Ready?"

"Ready." Picking up the package that held her dress, Kara took Alex's hand and slid out of the car.

Anderson stood up when they entered the church. He smiled at Kara. "You may change in there," he said, pointing to the room Alex had recently occupied.

"Thank you." She smiled at Alex. "I'll only be a minute."

Alex nodded, then glanced around the church again.

"We're quite alone," Anderson said. He sat down, gesturing for Alex to join him.

"I really appreciate this," Alex said, sitting down.

"Is there anything I can do to help?" the minister asked. "Anyone I can call?"

"No, thank you."

"Your fiancée looks familiar. She's not a movie star or anything, is she?"

"No."

"Her name seems familiar, too. Kara Crawford." Anderson frowned. "I know I've heard that name somewhere recently." He grinned. "She didn't win the lottery, did she?"

Alex laughed. "No, nothing like that. So, how did you like my last book?"

"Excellent, as always."

Alex shook his head.

"You always seem surprised that I enjoy your books."

"Well, it just seems odd somehow, a man of the cloth reading about vampires and werewolves."

" 'There are more things on heaven and earth'," Anderson quoted.

Alex nodded. "Indeed, there are," he mused wryly.

"It would be arrogant indeed for us to believe that we're the only beings in the entire galaxy. For all I know, there might be vampires on other planets. Who knows?"

"Who, indeed," Alex agreed, and then stood, his breath catching in his throat, as Kara stepped into the chapel.

She was beautiful, he thought, more beautiful than anything he had ever seen. She wore a simple dress made of white silk, and white heels. Her hair fell loose around her shoulders, adorned with a single white rose.

"Kara, you're lovely," he murmured as he went to stand beside her. "So lovely."

"Thank you. So are you."

Indeed, he had never looked more handsome than he did now. The black suit fit as though it had been custom-made. The color complemented his dark hair and eyes.

"Are you ready?" Anderson asked. "Since this is to be a rather unorthodox ceremony, I've dispensed with the need for witnesses, if that's all right with you?"

Alex nodded.

"Very well." He looked at Kara. "You understand that without a license, this is simply a religious ceremony?"

Kara nodded.

"Alex, if you'll take Kara's right hand in yours, we'll begin."

Turning to face Kara, Alex took her hand in his. He could feel her trembling. He gazed into her eyes and knew, without searching her mind, what she was thinking. He could feel the love radiating from her, the trust. Joy mingled with excitement. He knew what she was feeling because he was feeling the same.

"Marriage is a holy ordinance, instituted of God," the minister said. "It is not to be entered into lightly, or foolishly, or without sincere intent." He looked at Alex. "From this day forward, there is to be no other woman in your life, only Kara." His gaze shifted to Kara's face. "And for you, there is to be no other man, only Alex."

The minister paused, giving them time to ponder his words. And then he went on. "We are met here this day to join Kara Elizabeth Crawford in marriage to Alexander J. Claybourne.

"Kara, will you have this man as your lawfully wedded husband? Will you love him and honor him, sustain him in sickness and in health, and keep yourself only unto him so long as you both shall live?"

Kara met Alexander's eyes, gave his hand a squeeze, as she said, "I will."

"And you, Alexander, will you have this woman as your lawfully wedded wife? Will you love her and honor her, sustain her in sickness and in health, and keep yourself only unto her so long as you both shall live?"

Alex took a deep, calming breath, wondering if he would be able to speak. Two hundred years he had waited for this moment. "I will."

"Have you a ring?"

"Yes." Reaching into his pocket, Alex withdrew a plain gold band.

"You may place the ring on her finger."

And now it was Alex who trembled as he slid the ring onto Kara's finger.

"Repeat after me. With this ring, I thee wed."

"With this ring, I thee wed."

"And with all my worldly goods, I thee endow."

"And with all my worldly goods, I thee endow."

Anderson glanced at Kara, and she shook her head. She'd had no chance to buy Alex a ring and couldn't help wondering when he'd found the opportunity to buy one for her.

"Then, by the power vested in me, I pronounce that you are now man and wife." The minister smiled at Alex. "You may kiss the bride."

Heart pounding with happiness, Alex drew Kara into his arms. "I love you," he murmured. "I shall love you as long as I live." And then, with all the tenderness at his command, he kissed her. And kissed her. And kissed her again.

"I wish you both all the happiness in the world,"

the minister said. He shook Alex's hand, then gave Kara a kiss on the cheek. "I hope whatever trouble you two are in will be swiftly settled."

"Thank you," Kara said, blinking back her tears.

Alex nodded as he shook the minister's hand. "Thank you." Reaching into his pocket, he withdrew a hundred dollar bill and pressed it into the minister's hand.

"I can't take this," Anderson said. "It's too much."

"It isn't enough," Alex said as he wrapped his arm around Kara's shoulders. "Believe me, it isn't nearly enough."

"I shall accept it on behalf of the church," Anderson said. "And I shall remember you daily in my prayers."

After another farewell, Kara and Alex left the church. Kara couldn't stop smiling. She was Alexander's wife. Mrs. Claybourne. Happiness bubbled up inside her like champagne bubbles. Married to Alex.

He helped her into the car, then drew her into his arms and kissed her again. "I can't believe it," he whispered. "You're mine now. Truly mine."

"I've always been yours," she replied solemnly. "Even when I didn't know you, I think I was waiting for you to find me."

He kissed her again, a deep kiss filled with promise, and then he switched on the engine and drove toward the bank. It was time to meet Hamblin.

Mitch paced back and forth in front of the bank, his gaze constantly shifting up and down the street. He'd been a fool to agree to this, a fool to believe Claybourne would keep his word. The man—hell, he wasn't a man at all—had probably lit out for parts unknown.

He glanced at his watch. Five to ten. How many more nights was he going to waste his time by coming here?

A flash of headlights drew his attention. Squinting, one hand fisted around the gun inside his coat, he stepped into the shadows as the car drew up to the curb. If he ever got his hands on the money Claybourne promised him, he was going to get out of this business. It was too hard on the nerves.

He blew out a sigh of relief as Claybourne stepped out of the car. " 'Bout time you showed up."

"I said I would." Alex reached into his shirt pocket and withdrew an envelope. "I hope a check is satisfactory."

"I'd prefer cash."

"I'm sure you would, but it's difficult for me to get to the bank during working hours. Don't worry," Alex said, offering him the envelope, "this check's as good as the last one."

"It better be." Mitch took the envelope, opened it, and glanced at the check. One hundred and fifty thousand dollars. Just thinking about that much money, combined with the other hundred thousand in his savings account, made his heart race with excitement.

"You'd better get out of town," Alex suggested.

"I'm on my way," Mitch said with a grin. "Thanks for everything."

"Yes," Alex said wryly. "I hope you enjoy the Porsche."

"Been a pleasure knowing you, man."

"Profitable, anyway."

Mitch laughed. "You got that right. So long."

Alex grunted softly as he watched the kid slide into the Porsche and drive away. He'd miss the car, he mused, but what the heck, he could buy another.

And then he thought of Kara, waiting for him around the corner, and he forgot about Mitch and Barrett, forgot everything but the fact that this was his wedding night.

The drive up the mountain seemed to take forever. Kara felt a glow in her heart each time she looked at Alexander. Her husband. For better or worse . . . She felt a twinge of unease as she wondered if things would ever be better, if they would ever be free of Barrett, able to get on with their lives without always looking over their shoulders.

"Not having regrets already, are you?" Alex asked.

"Of course not." She scooted closer, pressing herself against him.

"Worrying about Barrett?"

She nodded. "I can't help it. Do you think he'll ever give up?"

"I don't know. I hope so." Bending toward her, his gaze on the road, he kissed her cheek. "I love you, *natayah*."

His words, the husky tremor in his voice, chased all thoughts of Dale Barrett from her mind. Placing her hand on Alex's knee, she ran her fingertips up and down his hard-muscled thigh. "Can't you drive a little faster?"

"Keep that up, and I'll probably run us off the road."

"Really?" She let her hand caress his inner thigh, smiled when his foot pressed down on the accelerator.

"Vixen," he growled. Wrapping his arm around her shoulders, he drew her even closer, until there was no space between them at all.

They reached the cavern a short time later. Switching off the engine, Alex alighted from the car and walked around to open the door for Kara. Taking her hand, he helped her out, then swung her into his arms and carried her to the entrance of the cave.

"We're home, Mrs. Claybourne."

"Mrs. Claybourne," she repeated. "It sounds wonderful."

He touched the rock face and the portal opened. With ease, he carried her inside, then paused in the corridor, gazing down into her eyes. "Did I tell you how beautiful you are?"

"Yes, but tell me again."

"You are beautiful, Kara Claybourne. The most beautiful woman I've ever seen."

"Thank you, Alex Claybourne."

He smiled at her as he carried her into the kitchen, where he plucked a bottle of champagne from the shelf.

"Did I tell you how much I love you?"

Kara shook her head.

"I love you," he said as he carried her down the corridor toward the bedroom. "I shall tell you that each day of our life together."

"And I shall say it back."

In the bedroom, he placed the champagne on the table, then lowered Kara slowly to the floor, delighting in the warmth of her body sliding against his own.

"I'll try to make you happy, Kara."

"You already make me happy." Gazing up at him,

a smile curving her lips, she slid his jacket off his shoulders and tossed it on a chair. "So happy." She began to unbutton his shirt, pleased that he wore nothing underneath as her fingers encountered warm male flesh. He trembled at her touch, and her smile grew wider. It gave her a feeling of power, of pleasure, to know that her touch excited him.

Tugging his shirttail from his trousers, she slipped the shirt from his shoulders and tossed it after his suit coat, then scattered kisses over his chest, laughing softly as he sucked in a deep breath.

"You're not playing fair," he said, and she felt his hands at her back, unzipping her dress, sliding it down her arms until it pooled at her feet. He removed her camisole, then cupped her breasts in his hands. "Beautiful," he murmured. "So beautiful."

And suddenly it was a contest to see who could finish undressing who first. It ended a tie, with both of them laughing breathlessly.

And then their eyes met and the laughter died in their throats.

"Kara." Whispering her name, he swept her into his arms and carried her to the bed, his lips dropping kisses on her eyelids, the tip of her nose, her cheeks, her brow.

Sweeping the covers aside with one hand, he placed her on the bed and sank down beside her, hardly able to believe that she was his now, truly his. Forever his.

"I love you, Mr. Claybourne."

"And I you."

"We'll live happily ever after, won't we? Just like in the fairy tales?"

He grinned. "Like Beauty and the Beast?"

"No. Like Snow White and the Prince."

Alex nodded. "A good comparison, for you are truly the fairest of them all."

She cupped his face in her hands and kissed him. "You are."

"No," he argued softly, his hands lightly caressing her, "you are."

She wrapped her arms around his neck and drew him down until his body covered hers. "Kiss me, my prince. Kiss me, kiss me, kiss me!"

"Your wish is my command, princess," he replied, and slanting his mouth over hers, he kissed her with all the love and passion in his soul, kissed her until her toes curled and her heart sang a new song. Kissed her so she would never doubt his love, or his devotion.

He worshipped her silently with his hands and his lips, stoking the fires of desire, until she drew him inside her, surrounding him with velvet heat. And two became one, and that one soared upward, reaching for the heavens.

Kara sobbed his name as heat flowed through her, bathing her in a warm glow, like sunshine on a summer day.

And for the first time in more than two hundred years, Alexander Claybourne welcomed the sun, felt its heat explode within him as he cried Kara's name, his body convulsing with pleasure.

Locked in each other's arms, they fell asleep. Hearts and minds melded, they slept peacefully sharing each other's dreams.

Chapter Thirty-one

They heard the news on the radio the following night. A young man, identified as Mitch Hamblin, had been found dead in an alley behind the Eagle Flats Bank. The apparent motive was listed as robbery.

Kara stared at Alex, her heart pounding. "You don't think . . . ?"

Alex nodded. "Barrett."

"How?"

"He must have followed Hamblin."

Kara sat back in her chair. It was never going to end, she thought bleakly.

Alex crossed the room and placed his hand on her shoulder. "It will end, Kara. Soon."

"What do you mean?"

"I'm going after him. Tonight."

"No!"

"We can't go on like this. I don't know about you, but I'm tired of hiding, tired of being hunted. One way or another, it ends tonight."

"How are you going to find him?"

"He must have followed Mitch hoping the kid would lead him to me. I'm guessing Barrett's still in town. And if he is, I'll find him."

"And then what?"

His silence was all the answer she needed.

"Alex, you don't have to do this. We can leave the state, change our names, relocate somewhere else."

He shook his head, and even though he didn't say anything, she knew what was in his mind. There was a child to think of now, and he wanted the trouble with Barrett over before their child was born. She knew why, knew he was afraid that Barrett would find them, that he might find a way to get hold of their child . . .

She refused to think of what that might mean. She knew what Barrett was capable of, knew the greed that drove him, the lust for fame and glory.

"I'll be back as soon as I can."

"I'm going with you."

"No."

"Yes."

"Dammit, Kara, you're pregnant!"

"So?"

He stared at her in exasperation. "I don't want to put your life, or . . . or my child's life, in danger."

"I'll feel safer with you than staying here alone."

Alex shook his head. "There's no way Barrett can get in here once the door is sealed."

"You can take me with you, or I'll walk down the damn mountain, but I'm not staying here alone."

"Stubborn," Alex muttered. "More stubborn than an ErAdonian mud-dog."

"I heard that," Kara said, "and I don't think it was a compliment."

Alex glared at her, and then he laughed. "And prettier than a Glantan wildflower, even when she's angry." Taking her by the hand, he drew her to him, enfolding her in his arms. "All right," he agreed, hating to lie to her, yet knowing it was for her own good, "you can go."

Kara smiled smugly. "I knew you'd see things my way."

"I don't think I've had my own way since I met you."

"Are you complaining, Mr. Claybourne?"

"No, ma'am. Just stating a fact."

"You can have your way next week."

"Promise?"

"Unless I change my mind. It's a woman's prerogative, you know."

He hugged her close, his lips moving in her hair as he drew in her scent. Sweet, so sweet, this beautiful, stubborn woman who was now his wife.

So sweet, he would not, could not, put her life in jeopardy.

Swinging her into his arms, he carried her into the bedroom.

"What are you doing?" Kara exclaimed.

"I'm going to make love to you."

"Now? I thought we were going after Barrett."

"All in good time."

She started to question him further, but his lips swooped down on hers, warm and hungry, driving all thought of Barrett from her mind.

He made love to her with a fierce intensity, every

touch branding her as his, every kiss filled with hope, every caress an unspoken promise for the future. His hands played over her gently, tenderly, as if she were a precious instrument, and he was the only one who could hear the music in her soul.

He called her name as his warmth spilled into her and then, holding her tightly in his arms, he whispered that he loved her, would always love her.

The sound of his voice was the last thing she heard before sleep claimed her.

Alex waited until Kara was sleeping soundly before he left the cavern. He kissed her gently, knowing there was a chance he might never see her again, knowing she would never be safe while Barrett lived.

It was after nine o'clock when he reached Eagle Flats. He drove around the bank to the alley and parked the car. He left the engine running, switched off the headlights, then stepped out of the car.

Standing in the shadows, he glanced up and down the alley. The scent of blood, too faint to be detected by mortals, stung his nostrils. Hamblin's blood. Regret and remorse rose within him. But for him, the young man would still be alive, he thought, and then shook his head. Barrett was to blame.

There was only one motel in Eagle Flats, and that was his next stop. He drove slowly through the parking lot, his nostrils flaring as he searched for Barrett's scent, his lips curling back in a feral grin as he found what he was looking for.

He pulled up in front of the motel room and honked the horn. Once. Twice. After the third blast of the horn, the door opened and Jarvis poked his head out.

Alex heard the man swear under his breath, then Jarvis slammed the door and Alex heard him yelling for Barrett.

Less than a minute later, Jarvis and Barrett burst out of the room.

With a grin, Alex drove out of the parking lot.

Kara woke with a start. "Alex?" Sitting up, she placed her hand on his side of the mattress. The sheets were still warm. "Alex?"

Jumping out of bed, she ran toward the door. It was then she saw the note tacked to the door.

"Kara, I've gone after Barrett. If I'm not back by tomorrow afternoon, the main door will open. You'll find my instructions and your cellular phone under that big rock outside the door. I love you. Alex."

She read the note a second time, and then crumpled it in her hand. She should have known he'd do something like this! Going into the living room, she looked at the clock. Ten P.M.

"I'll never forgive you for this, Alexander Claybourne," she muttered. "Never."

But even as she said the words, she knew them for a lie.

"Please, just come back to me," she whispered. "That's all I ask."

He drove fast enough to stay ahead of Barrett, but not fast enough to lose him. And all the while, he thought of Kara, and all she'd been through.

Thought of the baby she carried. Thought of Mitch Hamblin. Thought about the torture he had personally endured at Barrett's hands. The man deserved to die.

The mountain loomed ahead, dark and mysterious in the waning light of the moon.

Alex turned up the narrow road, slowing to make sure Barrett was still behind him.

When he reached the cavern, he parked the car out of sight, then took cover in the shadows.

Moments later, Barrett's car reached the top.

From his vantage point, Alex watched the two men exit the car. Both men were armed.

"Where'd he go?" Jarvis asked.

The doctor shrugged. "I don't know, but this is the end of the road. He's got to be here somewhere. You go that way, and I'll check over here."

Jarvis grunted, then started walking slowly along the ledge toward Alex's hiding place.

Alex waited until the man walked past, then he stepped out of the shadows and struck the man over the head with a tree branch. Jarvis grunted softly as he toppled forward.

Alex caught him before he hit the ground and dragged him into the brush that grew alongside the ledge, then went back to the road and picked up the man's gun. It was a snub-nosed .38.

Moving cautiously, Alex made his way toward the far end of the ledge. And Barrett.

As he drew nearer the cavern, he could hear Barrett's footsteps, and then he saw the doctor standing at the end of the ledge near the entrance to the cavern.

"Looking for me, doc?" Alex drawled.

Barrett whirled around, his gun seeking a target,

but there was nothing to see except the darkness.

"Drop your weapon," Alex said.

"No way. Where's Jarvis?"

"Taking a nap. Drop your gun, Barrett. It's over."

"I don't think so." Barrett glanced around. "So, this is where you live."

"And this is where you die, unless you drop your gun."

"You must think I'm a fool."

"That's the best thing I ever thought of you. Why'd you kill Hamblin?"

"I didn't kill anybody."

"Maybe you didn't pull the trigger, but you killed him just the same."

"You can't prove a thing," Barrett said, his voice thick with contempt. "Even if you went to the police, who'd believe you?"

"I'm not going to the police. We're going to settle this here and now."

A gunshot ripped through the night. Alex ducked as he felt the heat of the bullet near his head, swore under his breath as Barrett fired off another round, and then another.

Alex! He heard Kara's voice inside his mind, knew she was standing at the portal, beating her fists against the door.

I'm all right, natayah.

Let me out of here!

Soon . . .

Moving silently through the underbrush, he changed position. "Barrett," he called, "drop the gun."

Muttering an oath, the doctor whirled around and fired in the direction of Alex's voice. "Damn you," he cried, "show yourself!"

"I'm here," Alex called, then flung himself to the ground as two gunshots rent the stillness of the night.

"We're doing this all wrong," Barrett said placatingly. "I'm not your enemy. We should be working together." He peered into the darkness. "We could do wonderful things for humanity. Think of the lives we could save."

"The money you could make."

"I'll split it with you. Fifty-fifty."

"That's mighty damn generous of you, doc."

"All right. Sixty-forty."

"No deal."

A wordless cry of frustration rumbled in Barrett's throat as he fired into the shadows.

"That's six," Alex remarked, stepping onto the ledge.

Barrett froze, and then cursed softly. "So, what now? You gonna kill me?"

"Right the first time."

Barrett took a step backward, the blood draining from his face. "You wouldn't. You can't."

"Who's going to stop me?"

Barrett stared at him for stretched seconds; then, with a wordless sob, he whirled around and plunged into the darkness.

The scent of fear stained the clear night air. Between one breath and the next, Alex felt the thin veneer of civilization slip away, felt the ancient urge to hunt sweep over him, and with it the almost overwhelming desire to kill, to feast on the blood of the man who had caused Kara pain. Neither of them would know a moment's peace until Dale Barrett was no longer a threat.

Tossing the gun aside, Alex ran after the doctor.

He could hear Barrett moving through the underbrush, hear the harsh rasp of his breathing, feel the vibration of his footsteps as he ran through the darkness.

The scent of Barrett's fear grew stronger as Alex closed the distance between them. Age-old legends of his warrior ancestors raced through his mind, tales of ArkLa the Terrible, who had gorged himself on the blood of his enemies.

He felt a thrill of exhilaration as he realized that Barrett was running in circles. Soon he would be back at the entrance to the cavern with nowhere else to run, nowhere to hide.

And then Barrett was in front of him, his back pressed against the wall of the cavern, his eyes wide with fear as he realized he was well and truly caught.

Slowly, inexorably, Alex closed the distance between them. Barrett let out a high-pitched squeak of fear as Alex's hand closed around his throat, slowly, slowly, choking the life from his body.

Alex stared down at the man squirming in his grasp, felt the lust for blood rise up within him swift and hot and sure.

And then he heard Kara's voice penetrate the red haze that engulfed him.

Alex?

He took a deep breath. *Everything's all right, Kara. Don't worry.*

Where's Barrett?

Alex's hand closed a little tighter around Barrett's throat. *Right here.*

You haven't . . .

Not yet.

Alex, don't. Please don't.

He stared down into Barrett's face. The doctor's eyes were white with terror, his face red with the effort to draw a breath.

Alex? It isn't worth it. Please . . .

The sound of her voice, sweet and pure, stilled the rage within him. He took a deep breath and relaxed his grip on Barrett's throat. *Kara, bring me something to tie him up with.*

Why?

Just do it.

I can't. The door's locked.

It's open now.

"You're a lucky man, Barrett."

"What . . . what are you gonna do to me?" Barrett asked tremulously.

"You'll never know."

Barrett swallowed hard. "What's that supposed to mean?"

Alex grinned as he stepped forward and struck Barrett across the temple with the butt of the gun. "Enough questions, doc."

Moments later, Kara ran outside. She gasped when she saw Barrett sprawled across the ledge. "What have you done?"

"Nothing. He's unconscious, that's all. Tie his hands behind his back while I go get the other one."

"Alex . . ."

"No time for questions now, *natayah*."

She frowned at him; then, with a sigh, she knelt beside Barrett. Removing the sash from her robe, she tied his hands together.

Kara glanced at the passing countryside. "Where are we going?" She glanced into the back seat. Alex had found Barrett's black bag in the trunk and had

379

given the doctor and Jarvis injections to keep them unconscious. Now they were sleeping peacefully in the back seat. "And why are we taking Barrett's car?"

Alex ran his hand over the steering wheel. "It's a nice car, don't you think?"

Kara nodded. Barrett drove a late model Lincoln with leather upholstery and every extra one could imagine. "You haven't answered my question."

"His car has a bigger trunk than your Camry."

"Alex!"

"It'll be light before we get to Silverdale . . ."

"Silverdale!"

Alex nodded. "When the sun comes up, I'm going to climb in the trunk." He shrugged, then grinned. "No sense being cramped in the back of your Camry. Besides, we can't leave his car up on the mountain."

"Why are we going back to Silverdale, of all places?"

"You'll see."

"Alex!"

"If I tell you, it will spoil the surprise. Do you think you can find your way to the lab from here?"

"I found it before, didn't I?"

"It's going to be light soon." He pulled off the road and switched off the engine. "I'm gonna get in the trunk now. We should reach Silverdale about midnight."

"I'm not going another mile until you tell me what's going on."

"Trust me, Kara. You'll love it."

"Stubborn man! Are you sure they won't regain consciousness before we get to Silverdale?"

"I'm sure." He kissed her then, one long sweet

kiss, then got out of the car and opened the trunk.

Kara followed him. "Are you sure you'll be all right in there?"

"I'm sure." He kissed her again, quickly, then climbed inside the trunk. "Close the lid for me, will you?"

"All right," she grumbled. "But I can't promise I'll let you out again."

"You will," he said with smug male arrogance.

"Maybe, maybe not." With a shake of her head, Kara closed the lid. Maybe *she* should write a book, she mused as she slid behind the wheel and started the ignition. Only who would believe it?

At dusk, she pulled over and opened the trunk. Alex grinned up at her, then climbed out of the trunk. "Everything all right?"

"Yes, they're still out." She watched him stretch his arms and legs. "Are you okay?"

"Never better."

They reached the lab an hour after midnight. Kara shivered as she looked at the building. She had hoped never to see this place again.

She waited beside the car while Alex carried Barrett into the building, then came back for Jarvis.

"Are you sure you know what you're doing?" Kara asked as she followed Alex into the lab and shut the door.

"Yes, ma'am."

She followed him down the dimly lit corridor, watched as he placed Jarvis on a metal table. Barrett, still unconscious, was strapped to a second table. An image of herself and Alex strapped to those very same tables flashed through her mind.

"Now what?" she asked.

"A little ErAdonian magic," Alex replied.

And then, while she watched, he filled two syringes with his blood.

Slowly, incredulously, she realized what he was going to do. "Why?" she asked, watching as he prepared to give Barrett a transfusion. "Why are you giving him your blood?"

"It's part of the magic," Alex said, grinning. "Wait and see."

He refused to say more. Taking her by the hand, he led her into the corridor, backed her up against a wall, and kissed her.

"I love you," he said, nuzzling her neck. "Did you know that?"

She nodded, her mind going in circles trying to figure out what he was going to do while her body responded to his touch.

Just when she was about to pull him down on the floor, she heard a low groan.

"He's awake," Alex said, taking her by the hand. "Come on."

Barrett and Jarvis were both awake and tugging against the straps that held them.

"Turn me loose!" Barrett demanded.

"All in good time," Alex said.

"What are you going to do?" Jarvis asked, his voice ragged with fear.

"I'm going to conduct a little experiment of my own," Alex said. "Now, who wants to go first?"

Chapter Thirty-two

Kara shook Barrett's hand, nodded to Jarvis, and then followed Alex out of the lab.

When they were in the car, the laughter she'd been holding back bubbled up. She laughed until her sides ached, until there were tears in her eyes.

"That was wonderful," she said, gasping for air. "If I hadn't seen it with my own eyes, I never would have believed it."

Alex grinned at her as he pulled away from the curb. Rolling down the window, he took a deep breath. For the first time in months, he felt that everything would work out after all.

"You weren't kidding before, when you said you could make me forget you, were you?"

"No."

"A handy trick."

Alex nodded. He had given Barrett and Jarvis just

enough blood to create a mind link between them, and then he had invaded their thoughts and erased all memory of himself and Kara from their minds. It had left him feeling weak and on the brink of exhaustion, but it had been worth it.

While he rested in Barrett's office, Kara had gone through the lab to make sure Hamblin had destroyed the last blood sample Barrett had taken and anything else that related to Barrett's work, or to the two of them.

When Barrett and his henchman woke up, they wouldn't remember anything.

Kara slid a glance in Alex's direction. "You share a mind link with them now, don't you?"

Alex nodded. If he was so inclined, he would be able to communicate telepathically with Barrett and Jarvis. He doubted he would ever feel the need.

"Are they going to have increased life spans?"

Alex shrugged. "No doubt they'll enjoy remarkably good health. As for longer lives, only time will tell."

"What about me?"

"I gave you considerably more blood than I gave either of them. I would say there's a good chance you'll live a long and healthy life."

Kara stared into the distance, trying to absorb what that might mean, wondering if she'd live as long as Alex, wondering what it would be like to stay young and healthy for another hundred years.

"Kara, are you all right?"

"Yes. I was just wondering what our next move is going to be."

"We need to find a place to spend what's left of the night. Tomorrow, you can call your grandmother and Gail and tell them it's safe for them to go home. We can pick them up tomorrow night, if you want."

"Home," Kara said, caressing the word. "I can go back to my apartment." She smiled, her eyes glowing.

Alex nodded, wondering if she meant to go back to her old life now that the danger was past. Not that he could blame her. She was a vibrant young woman. Now that the danger was past, she was probably regretting her marriage to a man who lived in the shadows, who couldn't share the sunlight.

His fingers clenched around the steering wheel. If she wanted to be free of him, he would let her go, even though he knew it would kill him to do so.

It was near dawn when they found a motel. Kara waited in the car while Alex got a room.

Inside, she sat on the bed, wondering at Alex's abrupt change of mood. He'd been jubilant a short while ago; now he looked morose, as if he had just lost his best friend.

"Are you all right?" she asked.

He nodded. "Just tired. I'm going to bed."

"I'm hungry," Kara said. "I think I'll go see if I can find something to eat." She smiled at him. "I don't guess you want anything."

"No."

"I'll be right back."

He nodded, wondering if she would come back. If he hadn't been so utterly weary, he would have probed her thoughts, but he lacked the energy.

She kissed him on the cheek, grabbed the car keys from the dresser and left the room, thinking as she did so that they would have to return Barrett's car once they picked hers up from Eagle Flats.

Lying back on the bed, Alex stared at the drapes. It would be morning soon, and he'd be trapped in this room until the sun went down.

On their wedding night, he had been so certain of her love, but now the doubts of two hundred years plagued him. Why would she want to spend her life with him? He was an alien. He couldn't stay in one place more than ten or fifteen years. He'd never be able to take their child on outings to the beach or the zoo or the park or do a hundred other things that a human male could do. How long would it take before she grew tired of the way he lived, before she started wishing she had never married him at all?

With a low groan, he covered his eyes with his arm. Life would have no meaning without Kara. If she left him now, he'd have no reason to go on living.

Kara, please don't leave me . . .

She was standing at the cash register, paying for a hamburger with the works, onion rings, and a chocolate shake to go, when Alex's voice sounded in her mind. *Kara, please don't leave me. . . .* The anguish in his voice was like a knife in her heart.

Collecting her change, she hurried out to the car. Placing her order on the passenger seat, she drove back to the motel as fast as she dared. The depths of Alexander's grief brought tears to her eyes even as she wondered why he thought she was leaving him.

I'm coming, Alex. She sent the words to his mind, marveling that she was able to do so. She repeated the same three words over and over again until she reached the motel. Inside, Alex was stretched out on the bed, one arm flung over his eyes.

Dropping the sack from the hamburger stand and the car keys on the dresser, she rushed to the bed and sat beside him.

"Alex? Alex, what's wrong?"

He shook his head. "Nothing."

"Nothing! I heard your voice in my mind begging me not to leave you, and now you tell me nothing's wrong! Talk to me, Alex."

"There's no reason for you to stay with me now," he said, his voice devoid of emotion. "You can go back home and get on with your life."

"What are you talking about?"

"You said you wanted to go back home. I won't stop you."

She stared down at him, frowning as she tried to make some sense of his words. "I don't know what you're talking about. You're my home."

"Am I?"

"Alex, I love you. You believe that, don't you?"

"If you say so."

"I do say so. Please tell me what's wrong. You're scaring me."

"I just want you to be happy, Kara."

"I am happy. Happier than I've ever been in my life."

He didn't look convinced. Feeling as if she were spying, she probed his mind, and there, deep down where he tried to hide them, she found the fears that were troubling him.

"Alex, I love you just the way you are. You must believe that." She took his hand and pressed it to her belly. "I'm having your child, Alex, and it's going to be beautiful and healthy, and we're going to

387

live happily ever after, just like Cinderella."

"Kara!" Choking back a sob, he drew her into his arms. "Forgive me for being such a fool."

"I forgive you. I only meant I was happy I could go back to my apartment because it meant I could pick up my clothes and stuff. You're my home from now on, Alex, whether we're living in Moulton Bay or on top of your mountain. You believe me, don't you?"

"I believe you, Kara. I'll never doubt you again."

"See that you don't."

"Do you want to eat your hamburger now?"

Slowly, she shook her head. "I'm not hungry for food any more."

"Oh?" A smile played over his lips. "What are you hungry for?"

"What do you think?"

He grinned at her. "Me, too." He held out his arms. "Come here, Mrs. Claybourne. I think I can satisfy your appetite."

"I know you can," Kara said, slipping her arms around his neck. "But be warned, Mr. Claybourne, I get hungry often."

"I'm counting on it," Alex said, and knew he would never doubt her love for him again.

With a sigh, he enfolded Kara in his arms and knew that, at long last, he had found a home.

Epilogue

Eight years later

Kara and her brother, Steve, exchanged smiles as Gail crossed the stage to accept her diploma.

"Hard to believe she's all grown up, isn't it?" Steve remarked.

Kara nodded. It didn't seem possible her little sister was graduating from high school. In the fall, Gail was going to college to study anthropology, parapsychology, and astronomy.

Hard as it was to think of Gail as a young woman, it was even harder to believe that her brother, Steve, had finally shaken the wanderlust out of his system and settled down. He had gotten married three years ago to a lovely girl he'd met in South America, and they were expecting their first child in December.

Kara glanced down the row of seats. All the people she loved best were here tonight. There were tears in Nana's eyes as Gail accepted her diploma; Elsie Zimmermann was beaming with pride.

Looking farther down the row, she saw Alex. He was sitting in the aisle seat, looking as handsome as ever.

He met her gaze and winked at her. *I love you.*

She felt a smile tug at her lips. *And I love you.*

It still amazed her that she was married to such an incredible man. So much had happened in the last eight years. His books, now written under his own name, were consistently on the top of the *New York Times* Best Seller list. Their family was growing.

She smiled at her three children. They were all beautiful, all perfect, from their firstborn son, Alexander, now seven, to their youngest daughter, age two.

Kara rested her hand on her swollen belly. Their fourth child was due in another seven weeks. Their son was hoping for another boy to even things out.

All Alex's fears had been groundless. Alexander had been born with a minimum of pain and fuss, as had their two daughters, Lena and Katy Jay. The only hint of their alien heritage was the pale brown stripe that darkened their spines. The doctors had said it was nothing to worry about, just a peculiar sort of birthmark that would no doubt fade in time.

As for herself, she had suffered no ill effects from receiving Alexander's blood. Quite the opposite. In the last eight years, she hadn't aged at all. As for their children, they had all been blessed with remarkable good health. None of them had been sick a day in their lives. Alex had told her that Er-

Adonian children grew to maturity normally, and then the aging process slowed. It remained to be seen what long-term effect their union would have on their children.

She knew they would have to leave Moulton Bay soon, before people began to wonder why the Claybournes didn't seem to get any older. It would be hard to leave this place, but she really didn't mind. As much as she loved Alex's house, it was, after all, just a house. He was her home, her life, and she would willingly follow him across the country, or across the world.

The graduation ended and she stood up, applauding with every one else.

And then Alex was beside her, one arm sliding around her shoulders, his dark eyes warm with love as he placed a hand over her abdomen. "You feelin' okay?"

"Fine. Are you ready to go home?"

"Whenever you are."

"Just let me give Gail her present. She's going to an all-night party with Cherise and Stephanie."

Alex nodded, and then winked at her. "Steve and Maria said they'd watch the kids for us."

"Why?"

He patted her stomach gently, felt his child give a lusty kick. "I decided if I wanted to spend any time alone with you, I'd better do it soon," he said, kissing her on the cheek, "so I've planned a little party of my own. And you're the guest of honor."

"Let's go, then," Kara said, grinning up at him. "I'm starting to feel hungry."

Alex laughed softly as he bent to kiss her again. "Me, too, *natayah*," he whispered huskily. "And after I've satisfied your hunger, we'll get something to eat."

Created at the dawn of time to protect humanity, the ancient warriors have been nearly forgotten, though magic lives on in vampires, werewolves, the Celtic Sidhe, and other beings. But now one of their own has turned rogue, and the world is again in desperate need of the

IMMORTALS

CATHY McDAVID

Night HUNTER

Every twenty-five years the cycle begins anew—a legendary creature reawakens and preys upon the innocent. When she was seven, Gillian watched in horror as it killed her mother. Now the beast is back...for her.

As the chosen Hunter, Nick is the only one who can destroy the creature. Yet a gorgeous psychology professor keeps pushing her way into his investigation—and into his most intimate fantasies. For her protection, Nick's determined to stay by Gillian's side, every day and each delicious night. And meanwhile, the monster bides its time....

ISBN 10: 0-505-52722-7
ISBN 13: 978-0-505-52722-6 $6.99 US/$8.99 CAN

Blood Moon

✠ ✠ ✠

Dawn Thompson

Jon Hyde-White is changed. Soon he will cease to be an earl's second son and become a ravening monster. Already lust grows, begging him to drink blood—and the blood of his fiancée Cassandra Thorpe will be sweetest of all. Is that not why the blasphemous creature Sebastian bursts upon them from the London shadows? But Sebastian's evil task remains incomplete, and neither Jon nor Cassandra is beyond hope. One chance remains—in faraway Moldavia, in a secret brotherhood, in an ancient ritual and in the power of love.

SANDRA SCHWAB

CASTLE OF THE WOLF

Celia Fussell's father is dead, and she reduced to the status of a poor relation in the house of her brother, the new baron, and his shrewish wife. A life of misery looms ahead.

But there is hope. Deep in the Black Forest stands Celia's inheritance, The Castle of Wolfenbach. It is a fortress of solitude, of secrets, of old wounds and older mysteries. But it is hers. And only one thing stands in her way: its former master, the hermit, the enigma…the man she is obliged to marry.

CHRISTINE FEEHAN

DARK GOLD

Alexandria Houton will sacrifice anything—even her life—to protect her orphaned little brother. But when both encounter unspeakable evil in the swirling San Francisco mists, Alex can only cry to heaven for their deliverance . . .

And out of the darkness swoops Aidan Savage, a golden being more powerful, more mysterious, than any other creature of the night. But is Aidan a miracle . . . or a monster? Alex's salvation . . . or her sin? If she surrenders to Aidan's savage, unearthly seduction will Alex truly save her brother? Or sacrifice more than her life?

MARJORIE M. LIU
SOUL SONG

Against her will, Kitala Bell foresees the future. Now her own future is in peril. From the ocean's depths rises an impossible blend of fantasy and danger, a creature whose voice is seduction incarnate, whose song can manipulate lives the way that Kitala herself manipulates the strings of her violin…even to the point of breaking. He is a prince of the sea, an enigma—a captive stretched to the limit of his endurance by a woman intent on using him for the purest evil. And when survival requires he and Kitala form a closer partnership than either has ever known, the price of their bond will threaten not just their lives, but the essence of their very souls.

ISBN 10: 0-8439-5766-2
ISBN 13: 978-0-8439-5766-2 $6.99 US/$8.99 CAN

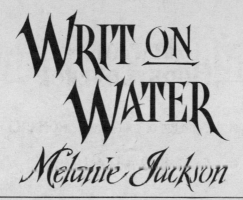

WRIT ON WATER

Melanie Jackson

Chloe is having visions, visions of her upcoming assignment to photograph tombs in Virginia. She has the Sight, just like her Gran, the witch.

But Gran hasn't taught her anything about her gift, and Chloe is at a loss. The horrible things she sees: What do they mean? Are they real? Can she stop them? She is in a new place with no allies—at least, none that she knows. MacGregor Patrick is charming, but is his kindly nature a charade? His son Rory is handsome as sin, but angelic features can hide diabolic intent. There is no one she can trust, and her enemies wish her name to be... *Writ on Water*.